Thomas Arnold, William Thomas Arnold

The Second Punic War

being chapters of the history of Rome - Edited by William T. Arnold

Thomas Arnold, William Thomas Arnold

The Second Punic War
being chapters of the history of Rome - Edited by William T. Arnold

ISBN/EAN: 9783337382681

Printed in Europe, USA, Canada, Australia, Japan

Cover: Foto ©Andreas Hilbeck / pixelio.de

More available books at **www.hansebooks.com**

THE
SECOND PUNIC WAR

BEING

CHAPTERS OF THE HISTORY OF ROME

BY THE LATE

THOMAS ARNOLD, D.D.

FORMERLY HEADMASTER OF RUGBY SCHOOL, AND REGIUS PROFESSOR OF
MODERN HISTORY IN THE UNIVERSITY OF OXFORD

EDITED BY

WILLIAM T. ARNOLD, M.A.

WITH EIGHT MAPS

LONDON

MACMILLAN AND CO.

1886

PREFACE.

THE present volume consists of Chapters XLII.-XLVII. of the third volume of Dr. Arnold's *History of Rome*. It is thus a fragment—but a particularly rounded and complete one—of a work which was itself left a fragment by Dr. Arnold's death. Dr. Arnold, as is well known, had intended to bring his history down " to the revival of the Western Empire, " in the year 800 of the Christian era, by the corona- " tion of Charlemagne at Rome," and some of the best chapters in his second volume—those in which he casts a glance over the face of that Europe which was shortly to become Roman—were due to that intention. They were meant to be preparatory to the picture he was to draw of the provinces under the Imperial rule. I have therefore felt less hesitation in isolating this fragment of a fragment than I should have felt if Dr. Arnold had been able to finish his work, if he had been able to shape the whole story into an organic unity, and if therefore such a selec-tion as I have made had necessarily borne the character of a mutilation.

There are, moreover, special reasons which justify the selection and isolation of the chapters in Dr. Arnold's history which relate to the Second Punic War. His original plan, as Dean Stanley has pointed out, was to begin his history with the Punic Wars, taking up the story at the point where Niebuhr dropped it. "As to any man being " a fit continuator of Niebuhr," he wrote to Julius Hare in 1833, "that is absurd; but I have at " least the qualification of an unbounded venera- " tion for what he has done; and as my name is " mentioned in his book, I should like to try to em- " body, in a continuation of the Roman history, the " thoughts and notions which I have learnt from " him." He changed his plan and determined to tell the history of Rome from the beginning, but wherever Niebuhr has been across the ground before him, he himself has stated in the plainest terms that he conceived his function to be that of ex- pounder and interpreter of that historian to the English reader.[1]

In September 1840 he wrote to Mr. Justice Coleridge :[2]—"I should have liked any detailed " criticism of yours upon Vol. II. of *History of* " *Rome*. I have scarcely yet been able to get any " judgments upon the first two volumes which will

---

[1] Compare *Life and Correspondence*, II. 17. *History of Rome.* II. p. v. Preface.   [2] *Life and Correspondence*, II. 196.

" help me for those to come. The second volume
" will be, I hope, the least interesting of all; for it
" has no legends, and no contemporary history.
" What I can honestly recommend to you in the
" book is its sincerity; I think that it confesses
" its own many imperfections, without attempting
" to ride grand over its subject. In the war of
" Pyrrhus I was oppressed all the time by my
" sense of Niebuhr's infinite superiority; for that
" chapter in his third volume is one of the most
" masterly pieces of history that I know—so rich
" and vigorous, as well as so intelligent. I think
" that I breathe freer in the First Punic War,
" where Niebuhr's work is scarcely more than frag-
" mentary. I hope, though, to breathe freer still
" in the Second Punic War; but there floats before
" me an image of power and beauty in history,
" which I cannot in any way realise, and which
" often tempts me to throw all that I have written
" clean into the fire."

*I hope, though, to breathe freer still in the Second
Punic War.* I take those words to be the justi-
fication both of the higher degree of interest
which English readers have always taken in
that portion of Dr. Arnold's narrative, and of my
own willingness to edit it, isolated from the
rest. The special place which this part of Dr.
Arnold's work assumes is thus indicated by Dean

Stanley:[1]—"The two earlier volumes occupy a
" place in the history of Rome, and of the ancient
" world generally, which in England had not and
" has not been otherwise filled up. Yet in the
" subjects of which they treat, his peculiar talents
" had hardly a fair field for their exercise. 'No
" man,' as he said, 'can step gracefully or boldly
" when he is groping in the dark' (*Hist. Rome*, I.
" 133), and it is with a melancholy interest that
" we read his complaint of the obscurity of the
" subject:—'I can but encourage myself, whilst
" painfully feeling my way in such thick darkness,
" with the hope of arriving at last at the light,
" and enjoying all the freshness and fulness of a
" detailed contemporary history' (*Hist. Rome*, II.
" 447). But the narrative of the Second Punic
" War, which occupies the third and posthumous
" volume, both as being comparatively unbroken
" ground, and as affording so full a scope for his
" talents in military and geographical descriptions,
" may well be taken as a measure of his historical
" powers, and has been pronounced by his editor,
" Archdeacon Hare, to be the first history which
" 'has given anything like an adequate representa-
" tion of the wonderful genius and noble character
" of Hannibal.'"

The first two volumes of the *History of Rome*

---

[1] *Life and Correspondence*, I. 170.

will long continue to be read. They abound in political generalisations[1] of a kind which does not become obsolete, and are marked by a constant endeavour to open out vistas of thought, and to lift history to the threshold, at least, of that "higher "region, whither indeed history ought for ever to "point the way, but within which she is not per-"mitted herself to enter."[2] They are animated with that sense of the greatness of the Roman fate, and of the dignity of the Roman character, which a man must have who would trace the story of those "four fatal letters that spell-bound all mankind."[3] Amiel finds the distinguishing quality of the historian in what he calls a "sympathetic and "passionate contemplation," and that quality was never wanting to Dr. Arnold when he wrote of Rome. Still it remains true that the first two volumes were written in the first blush of Niebuhr's unparalleled reputation, and that they show a dependence on that writer which was natural, perhaps inevitable, but none the less excessive. It is also, I think, the case that their literary quality is on the whole inferior to that of the third volume. Dr. Arnold's writing had always the essential qualities of simplicity and clearness, but he was diffident of his

---

[1] Compare II. 203, 269 note, 270.
[2] *History of Rome*, II. 174.
[3] Landor. The 'four fatal letters' are, of course, S P Q R.

powers, and he was also slow to conceive of the man of letters as an artist; the latter's function as an interpreter of truth seemed so much the more important to his mind. In 1821 he wrote to a friend in reference to a review which he (Dr. Arnold) had just written:[1]—" The additions which " you propose I can make readily; but as to the " general plainness of the style, I do not think I " clearly see the fault which you allude to, and " to say the truth, the plainness, *i.e.* the absence " of ornament and long words, is the result of " deliberate intention. Of course I do not mean to " justify awkwardnesses and clumsy sentences, of " which I am afraid my writings are too full, and all " of which I will do my best to alter wherever you " have marked them; but anything like puff, or " verbal ornament, I cannot bring myself to. Rich-" ness of style I admire heartily, but this I cannot " attain to for lack of power. Do consider what " you recommend is ἁπλῶς ἄριστον, but I must do " what is ἄριστον ἐμοί." Meanwhile Dr. Arnold was getting plenty of practice in writing, for between 1821 and 1827 were written the articles which were afterwards collected into a continuous history under the title of the *Later Roman Commonwealth*. At Rugby we begin to find him seriously preoccupied with the finer points of style, and I lay

---

[1] *Life and Correspondence,* I. 57.

great stress on the following passage as marking the
writer's fuller sense of his own powers, and his
greater interest in history as a fine art. In 1841
he writes in reference to the very chapters which
form this volume:[1]—"The History is intensely
" interesting, and I feel to regard it more and more
" with something of an artist's feeling as to the
" composition and arrangement of it ; points on
" which the Ancients laid great stress, and *I now*
" *think*[2] very rightly."

It is not for me, his grandson, to weigh Dr.
Arnold's History in the balance, and to attempt to
do justice to its masculine and weighty eloquence.
Even if I had the capacity, I could not claim the
necessary impartiality for the task. But I may be
permitted here to quote the generous testimony
of two contemporary historians, whose praise has
weight. In an essay on Mommsen's *History of
Rome*, Professor Freeman writes:[3]—"To this splendid
" period (the fifth and sixth centuries A.U.C.) Mommsen
" is far from doing full justice ; he understands, but
" he does not always feel ; his narrative constantly
" seems cold and tame after that of Arnold. We miss
" the brilliant picture of the great men of the fifth
" century ;[4] we miss the awful vision of Hannibal ;[5]

---

[1] *Life and Correspondence*, II. 210.   [2] The italics are mine.
[3] *Historical Essays*, second series, p. 254.
[4] Arnold, II. 272.   [5] *Ibid.* III. 70. This edition, p. 8.

" we miss the pictures of Gracchus and his en-
" franchised slaves, and of Nero's march to the
" 'fateful stream' of the Metaurus. Both tell us
" how the old Marcellus died by a snare which a
" youth might have avoided; but in how different
" a strain !"

The view of Ihne ("eines gewiss grundlichen
Kenners der römischen Geschichte"[1]) is thus expressed :[2]—"If Dr. Arnold had lived to finish his
" *History of Rome*, and to embody in successive
" editions the results of the numerous researches
" which since Niebuhr's death have thrown so much
" light on the subject, the present work would
" perhaps never have been undertaken. Arnold
" possessed in the highest degree many of the
" qualities which such a work requires. His style
" and mode of treatment have a charm that
" captivates the reader and confers interest even on
" abstruse and troublesome investigations; his writ-
" ings exhibit all the dignity of history without the
" tediousness which makes even attractive subjects
" too often repulsive; he had no need to descend
" to the level of the pamphleteer for the purpose of
" avoiding dulness. His fancy was lively; he could
" picture to himself and to his readers the most

---

[1] Professor Voigt in *Berliner Philologische Wochenschrift*, IV.
1561.

[2] In the preface to the first volume of his own masterly English
version of his *History of Rome*.

" distant situations, the motives and actions of
" men, and the outward circumstances which formed
" their background.   He entered with warmth and
" sympathy into the description of the sufferings,
" the aspirations, the struggles, triumphs, and
" failures which make up the sum total of the
" history of our race, and with his own enthusiasm
" he carried his readers with him.   At the same
" time his judgment was sound, his learning com-
" prehensive, his eye unclouded by prejudice or
" paradoxical whims.   In one respect he would, if
" he had lived longer, have removed objections
" that could justly be made.   He would have
" emancipated himself from the bondage, the willing
" bondage, to Niebuhr's convictions ; he would have
" been the interpreter of his own convictions, and not
" have continued ' jurare in verba magistri.'   But
" forty years ago the authority of Niebuhr was too
" great even for such a mind as Arnold's to resist."

Fortified by these authorities, I may briefly state
my view as being that Dr. Arnold did not fully
reveal himself as an historian till he wrote the
narrative of the Second Punic War.   His powers of
thought and expression were by that time mature,
he was no longer impeded by his loyalty to Niebuhr,
and the subject gave unusual opportunity for the
exercise of that " geographical eye " which Archdeacon Hare has rightly singled out as one of the

distinguishing traits of his historical faculty. It is therefore impossible for me to follow Archdeacon Hare, by whom the posthumous third volume was originally edited, in appending to it, "as the best substitute for what we should have had," the account of the last years of the war written by Dr. Arnold in 1823 for his life of Hannibal in the *Encyclopædia Metropolitana*. That account is of altogether different texture and value to the portrait of Hannibal which Dr. Arnold drew in the maturity of his powers, and no service is done to his memory, but the contrary, by attempting to stitch the two together. Still less, of course, have I been willing to entertain the idea of carrying on the history to the Battle of Zama in my own words. But though the present volume ends abruptly, I may point out that it nevertheless has a single theme. The theme is, in Dr. Arnold's own words,[1] "that fearful visita-" tion of Hannibal's sixteen years' invasion of Italy, " which destroyed for ever, not, indeed, the pride of " the Roman dominion, but the well-being of the " Roman people," or, to put it differently, it is the long duel between Rome and Hannibal on Italian soil,—with necessary reference to the wars in Spain and Sicily, which bore so closely on the ultimate result,—and that theme was all but worked out before the author laid down his pen.

[1] *History of Rome*, II. 540.

It remains for me to explain how I have conceived my task as editor of this portion of Dr. Arnold's History. I have had the advantage of consulting the original MS., which is in the keeping of Miss Arnold, of Fox How, and the occasional variations which may be noticed by a reader familiar with the ordinary printed text of the *History of Rome*, are due to my having restored what Dr. Arnold originally wrote in cases where Archdeacon Hare seemed to me to have taken too liberal a view of the functions of an editor.[1] The latter's corrections, however, were in the main directed to compression, by the elimination of superfluous pronouns and so forth. These are just the corrections which Dr. Arnold would have made himself, if he had lived to revise his manuscript for the press, and I have let them stand. As regards the notes, those at the bottom of the page are due to Archdeacon Hare, who, in the preface to the third volume, thus explains the nature of his work :—
" The manuscript which was put into my hands was
" singularly clear and correct: one might have thought
" at first sight that it was fit for going to the press
" immediately. But it proved that the author's

---

[1] A certain number of bad misprints—for which Dr. Arnold was in no way responsible—like "Pisa" for "Pera" (*History of Rome*, III. 151, this edition, p. 82), and "Vall' Osuira" for "Valloscura" (*History of Rome*, III. 489, this edition, p. 408), have also been set right.

" practice was not to note his references at the time
" he was composing his narrative : he used to keep
" them to be added afterwards.   Hence the only
" notes under the text which were found in the manu-
" script, are the first nine to the first chapter,[1] and
" that on the Basque numerals in p. 393.[2] I conceive
" that, after having impregnated his mind with the
" liveliest conception he could gain of the events he
" was about to record, from a comparison of the
" accounts given by the ancient writers, he was un-
" willing to interrupt the flow of the narrative by
" pausing to examine the details of the documents,
" and so reserved all specific remarks on their con-
" tents until the work was revised, after its comple-
" tion.   Owing to this cause the work became
" considerably more arduous than I had anticipated ;
" at least for one whose studies during the last
" ten years had lain in totally different regions,
" and who could only find an hour or two now
" and then, often at long intervals, to employ on
" it.   In executing it I have been much aided by
" my connection and friend, the Rev. Arthur Stanley,
" whose devoted love for his former master made
" him rejoice in doing anything for his remains,
" and is one among many like noble monuments to
" Dr. Arnold's praise.   Still, although through the

---

[1] *I.e.* Chapter XLI., which is not included in this edition.
[2] This edition, p. 307.

" chief part of the volume the only sources of infor-
" mation are the regular historians of the period,
" there are several statements for which it took me
" many hours to discover the authority ; and in some
" instances, after having abandoned the search as
" hopeless, I found the passage required in one of
" the historical fragments recently published by Mai.
" After all, I have not been able to detect what the
" author was referring to in p. 392, where mention
" is made of a story, which ' ascribed the foundation
" of Gades to Archelaus, the son of Phœnix.'[1]   The
" experience of the author's singular accuracy, which I
" have gained from the examination of his authorities,
" convinces me that he cannot have written without
" some definite ground for his assertions. Doubtless,
" too, there is some other authority than I have been
" able to find for the statement, in p. 165[2] that ' the
" older Gaulish chiefs were often averse to war, when
" the younger were in favour of it.'"

In supplying the numerous references at the
bottom of the page, Archdeacon Hare performed a
labour of love, on the execution of which it would
be churlish to be hyper-critical. A certain proportion
of them were erroneous ; these have been corrected ;
I have also added some references of my own, and in
all cases where the reference was made to obsolete

---

[1] See p. 305, note 1, of this edition.
[2] See p. 96 of this edition, note 2.

editions, have made it to the Teubner series of Greek and Latin classics, or, where the author was not represented in the Teubner series, to some recent, accessible, and authoritative edition. In cases where my notes, under the text, are of any length or importance, and are not merely additional references to classical authors, they are printed in square brackets [ ]. To the longer notes contributed by Archdeacon Hare his initials, " J. C. H.," are appended. In the notes at the end of the volume my own contributions are similarly distinguished by square brackets. In those notes my object has been in the first place to bring together any references to the point in question that may be found scattered through Dr. Arnold's writings; in the second place to give the student a full and fair synopsis of the discussion which has taken place upon it during the last forty years. I have purposely omitted all— or almost all [1]—reference to the " Quellenkritik " of the Germans, not because I regard the investigation into the possible authorities of Polybius, Livy, Plutarch, Appian, and Dio as valueless, or because I refuse to admit that there are Scipionic, Fabian, and Marcelline elements in the narrative which has

[1] I have analysed Haupt's essay on the march of Hannibal on Rome (pp. 409-412) rather more fully than I otherwise should have done, in order to give the unsophisticated English reader an opportunity of considering the kind of thing that is produced on these subjects in Germany by the yard.

been transmitted to us, but partly because the details are the essential thing in such inquiries, and it is, therefore, impossible to summarise them; partly because, though we may be sure, as Dr. Arnold was sure,[1] of the existence of elements in the narrative derived from the sometimes mendacious family-histories of the Scipios or the Marcelli, it is impossible exactly to disentangle them, and the attempt has always been to a certain extent arbitrary, where it has not been trivial and fantastic.[2] Apart from these inquiries, so far as Dr. Arnold's views on the debatable points of the Second Punic War have been supplemented or corrected, or, as is more often the case, confirmed, by Mommsen, Nissen, Neumann, and other recent writers, I believe the reader will find the notes full and, I hope, accurate.

My best thanks are due to Dr. J. S. Reid and Prof. A. S. Wilkins for several valuable references. For the index I am indebted to my wife. For the benefit of any reader who may be anxious to prosecute his study of the Second Punic War still further, I subjoin a list of the modern "literature" of the subject, from 1842 to the present time. It is as complete as I can make it——except that I only profess to give the more important treatises on the

[1] See for instance p. 414.

[2] "Der Papierkorb gentilicisher Annalenphantasien ist leider zum Überschwellen voll," says Mommsen (*Hermes*, xiii. 323).

Pass of Hannibal, and only mention an edition of
a classical author, when it has some special interest
for the purely historical student—but I shall be
grateful to any one who will point out omissions
or mistakes.

WILLIAM T. ARNOLD.

MANCHESTER, *October* 1885.

Baumgartner. — Über die Quellen des Cassius Dio für die ältere
römische Geschichte. (Laupp, Tubingen, 1880.)

Böttcher. —Kritische Untersuchungen über die Quellen des Livius
im XXI. and XXII. Buche. (V. Supplementband of the Jahrbücher für Classische Philologie. Leipsic, 1869.)

Breska, A von.—Untersuchungen über die Quellen des Polybius
im dritten Buche. (Berlin, 1880.)

Buchholtz.—Untersuchungen über die Quellen des Appian und
Dio Cassius für den zweiten Punischen Krieg. (Pyritz, 1872.)

Capes.—Livy, Books XXI. and XXII. (Macmillan, London, 1878.)

Chauvelays.—L'Art Militaire chez les Romains. (Plon, Paris,
1884.)

Desjardins.—Geographie de la Gaule Romaine. Three Vols. published. A fourth is expected. (Hachette, Paris.)

Droysen, H.—Papers on Nova Carthago and the Battle of Bæcula
in Rheinisches Museum for 1875, XXX.

Dübi.—Die Römerstrassen in den Alpen. In the Jahrbuch des
Schweizer Alpenclubs for 1884.

Egelhaaf.—Vergleichung der Berichte des Polybius and Livius
über den Italischen Krieg der Jahre 218-217. (X. Supplementband of the Jahrbücher für Classische Philologie, pp. 483-501.)

Egelhaaf.—Analekten zur Geschichte des II. Punischen Krieges.
(Sybel's Historische Zeitschrift. Neue Folge, XVII., 430 foll.)

Ellis.—Treatise on Hannibal's Passage of the Alps. (London, 1854.)

Faltin.—Zu den Berichten des Polybius und Livius über die

Schlacht am trasimenischen See. (Rheinisches Museum for 1884, XXXIX., 260-273.)

Faltin.—Der Einbruch Hannibals in Etrurien. (Hermes, XX., 71-90.)

Faltin.—Polybius oder Livius? (Berliner Philologische Wochenschrift, IV. 1017-1021, 1049-1053.)

Frantz.—Die Kriege der Scipionen in Spanien. (Ackermann, Munich, 1883.)

Freshfield.—The Pass of Hannibal. In Alpine Journal for 1883, Vol. XI. pp. 267-300.

Friedersdorff.—Livius et Polybius Scipionis rerum Scriptores. (Gottingen, 1869.)

Fröhlich.—Die Bedeutung des zweiten Punischen Krieges für die Entwickelung des Römischen Heerwesens. (Teubner, Leipsic, 1884.)

Genzken.—De rebus a P. et Cn. Corneliis Scipionibus in Hispania gestis. (Gottingen, 1879.)

Gilbert.—Rom und Karthago in ihren gegenseitigen Beziehungen. (Leipsic, 1876.)

Hagge.—Das Schlachtfeld von Cannæ. (Jahrbücher für Philologie, II. 185, foll., 1856.)

Haupt.—La Marche d'Hannibal contre Rome en 211. Published in the Mélanges d'érudition classique dédiés à la Memoire de Charles Graux, pp. 23-34. (Thorin, Paris, 1884.)

Haupt.—Jahresbericht über Dio Cassius in Philologus, XL.

Hennebert.—Histoire d'Hannibal. Two Vols. published. (Imprimerie Nationale, 1870 and 1878.)

Hesselbarth.—De Pugna Cannensi. (Hofer, Gottingen, 1874.)

Heynacher.—Die Stellung des Silius Italicus unter den Quellen zum zweiten Punischen Kriege. (Nordhausen, 1877.)

Höfler.—An essay on the Battle of Lake Thrasymene in the Sitzungsberichte der K. Akademie der Wissenschaften. (Vienna, 1870.)

Keller.—De Juba Appiani Cassiique Dionis auctore. (Marburg, 1872.)

Keller.—Zu den Quellen des Hannibalischen Krieges. In Rheinisches Museum for 1874, Vol. XXIX., pp. 88-96.

Keller.—Der Zweite Punische Krieg und seine Quellen. (Elwert, Marburg, 1875.)

Law.—Criticism of Ellis's Theory as to Hannibal's march. (London, 1855.)

Linke.—Die Controverse über Hannibal's Alpenübergang. (Breslau 1873.)

Luterbacher.—De fontibus librorum XXI. et XXII. T. Livii (Strasburg, 1875.)

Macaulay.—Livy, Books XXIII. and XXIV. (Macmillan, London, 1885.)

Magdeburg.—De Polybii re geographica. (Halle, 1873.)

Maissiat.—Annibal en Gaule. (Paris, 1874.)

Michael.—De ratione qua Livius opere Polybiano usus sit. (Bonn, 1867.)

Mommsen.—Zama. In Hermes for 1885, Vol. XX. pp. 144-156.

Müller, A.—De auctoribus rerum a M. Claudio Marcello in Sicilia gestarum dissertatio. (Halle, 1882.)

Müller, E.—Noch einmal die Schlacht an der Trebia. (Conitz, 1876.)

Müller, H.—Die Schlacht an der Trebia. (Charlottenburg, 1867.)

Neumann.—Das Zeitalter der Punischen Kriege, aus seinem Nachlasse herausgegeben und ergänzt von Gustav Faltin. (Koebner, Breslau, 1883.)

Nissen.—Die Schlacht am Trasimenus. In Rheinisches Museum for 1867. Vol. XXII., pp. 565-586.

Nissen.—De pace a. 201 ante Chr. Carthaginiensibus data. (Marburg, 1870.)

Nissen.—Die Œkonomie der Geschichte des Polybius. In Rheinisches Museum for 1871. Vol. XXVI. pp. 241-282.

Nissen.—Das Geschichtswerk des Titus Livius. In Rheinisches Museum for 1872. Vol. XXVII. pp. 539-561.

Nissen.—Italische Landeskunde. Vol. I., Land und Leute. (Weidmann, Berlin, 1883.)

Nitzsch.—Die römische Annalistik. (Borntraeger, Berlin, 1873.)

Perrin.—Marche d'Annibal des Pyrénées au Po. (Paris, 1883.)

Peter, C.—Über die Quellen des XXI. und XXII. Buches des Livius. (Halle, 1863.)

Peter, C.—Die Ersten Jahre des zweiten Punischen Krieges, pp. 19-54 of that writer's Studien zur Römischen Geschichte.— Ein Beitrag zur Kritik von Th. Mommsen's Römischer Geschichte. (Halle, 1863.)

Peter, C.—Zur Kritik der Quellen der älteren römischen Geschichte (Halle, 1879.)

Peter, H.—Die Quellen Plutarchs in den Biographieen der Römer. (Halle, 1865.)

Peter, H.—Veterum Historicorum Romanorum Relliquiæ. (Teubner, Leipsic, 1870.)

Posner.—Quibus auctoribus in bello Hannibalico enarrando usus sit Dio Cassius. (Bonn, 1874.)

Rauchenstein.—Hannibals Alpenübergang. (Aarau, 1864.)

Schemann.—De legionum per alterum bellum Punicum historia. (Bonn, 1875.)

Schillbach.—De Cannis et pugna Cannensi. (Neuruppin, 1860.)

Schiller.—Über den Stand der Frage, welchen Alpenpass Hannibal benutzt hat. In Berliner Philologische Wochenschrift for 1884, Vol. IV., 705-709, 737-740, 769-773.

Schmidt.—De Polybii Geographia. (Berlin, 1875.)

Seeck.—Über den Winter 218-217. In Hermes, VIII., 155 foll.

Sieglin.—Die Chronologie der Belagerung von Sagunt. (Leipsic, 1878.)

Sieglin.—Zwei Doubletten in Livius. In Rheinisches Museum, XXXVIII., 348-369.

Sieglin.—Der Durchzug Hannibals durch die Po Sümpfe. In Rheinisches Museum, XXXIX., 162-164.

Smith, Bosworth.—Carthage and the Carthaginians. (Longmans, London, 1878.)

Soltau.—De fontibus Plutarchi in secundo bello Punico. (Bonn, 1870.)

Stürenburg.—De Romanorum cladibus Trasumenna et Cannensi. (Edelmann, Leipsic, 1883.)

Susemihl.—Kritische Skizzen zur Vorgeschichte des zweiten Punischen Krieges. (Greifswald, 1853.)

Tartara.—Dalla battaglia della Trebbia a quella del Trasimeno. (Turin, 1882.)

Tell.—Die Schlacht bei Cannæ. In Philologus for 1856, Vol. XI., 148 foll.

Vincke, L. von.—Der zweite Punische Krieg und der Kriegsplan der Carthager. (Besser, Berlin, 1841.)

Voigt.—Die Schlacht am Trasumenus. In Philologische Wochenschrift for 1883, III. 1580-1598.

Voigt.—Hannibal's Zug nach Campanien. In Berliner Philologische Wochenschrift for 1884, IV. 1561-1566, 1593-1600, 1625-1629.

Vollmer.—Unde belli Punici secundi scriptores sua hauserint. (Gottingen, 1872.)

Weissenborn.—Livy, with German notes. Ten Vols. (Weidmann, Berlin, 1853-1878.)

Wölfflin.—Cœlius Antipater und Antiochus von Syrakus. (Winterthur, 1872.)

Wölfflin.—Titi Livii liber xxii. (Teubner, Leipsic, 1875.)

Zielinski.—Die letzten Jahre des zweiten Punischen Krieges. (Teubner, Leipsic, 1880.)

CONTENTS.

CHAPTER I.

CHAPTER II.

CHAPTER III.

CHAPTER IV.

CHAPTER V.

LIST OF MAPS.

THE SECOND PUNIC WAR.

CHAPTER I.

Hannibal—March of Hannibal from Spain to Italy—Passage of the
Alps—Battles of the Trebia, and of Thrasymenus—Q. Fabius
Maximus Dictator—Battle of Cannæ—A.U.C. 535 to 538.

TWICE in history has there been witnessed the
struggle of the highest individual genius against
the resources and institutions of a great nation ; and
in both cases the nation has been victorious.   For
seventeen years Hannibal strove against Rome ; for
sixteen years Napoleon Buonaparte strove against
England : the efforts of the first ended in Zama ;
those of the second in Waterloo.

True it is, as Polybius has said, that Hannibal
was supported by the zealous exertions of Carthage ;[1]
and the strength of the opposition to his policy
has been very possibly exaggerated by the Roman
writers.   But the zeal of his country in the contest,
as Polybius himself remarks in another place,[2] was
itself the work of his family. (Never did great men
more show themselves the living spirit of a nation
than Hamilcar and Hasdrubal and Hannibal, during a period of nearly fifty years, approved them-

A.U.C. 535.
A.C. 219.
Second
Punic war.

Greatness
of Hanni-
bal.

---

[1] Polybius, III. 10.   [2] IX. 22.

B

A.U.C. 535.
A.C. 219.

selves to be to Carthage. It is not then merely through our ignorance of the internal state of Carthage that Hannibal stands so prominent in all our conceptions of the second Punic war : he was really its moving and directing power ; and the energy of his country was but a light reflected from his own. History therefore gathers itself into his single person : in that vast tempest, which from north and south, from the west and the east, broke upon Italy, we see nothing but Hannibal.

Greatness of Rome. The success of Rome has been for the good of mankind.

But if Hannibal's genius may be likened to the Homeric god, who in his hatred of the Trojans rises from the deep to rally the fainting Greeks, and to lead them against the enemy ; so the calm courage with which Hector met his more than human adversary in his country's cause, is no unworthy image of the unyielding magnanimity displayed by the aristocracy of Rome. As Hannibal utterly eclipses Carthage, so on the contrary Fabius, Marcellus, Claudius Nero, even Scipio himself, are as nothing when compared to the spirit and wisdom and power of Rome. The senate which voted its thanks to its political enemy Varro, after his disastrous defeat, 'because he had not despaired of the Commonwealth,' and which disdained either to solicit, or to reprove, or to threaten, or in any way to notice the twelve colonies which had refused their accustomed supplies of men for the army, is far more to be honoured than the conqueror of Zama. This we should the more carefully bear in mind because our tendency is to admire individual greatness far more than national ; and as no single Roman will bear comparison with Hannibal, we are apt to murmur at the event of the contest, and to A.U.C. 535.
A.C. 219. think that the victory was awarded to the least worthy of the combatants. On the contrary, never was the wisdom of God's providence more manifest than in the issue of the struggle between Rome and Carthage. It was clearly for the good of mankind that Hannibal should be conquered: his triumph would have stopped the progress of the world. For great men can only act permanently by forming great nations; and no one man, even though it were Hannibal himself, can in one generation effect such a work. But where the nation has been merely enkindled for a while by a great man's spirit, the light passes away with him who communicated it; and the nation, when he is gone, is like a dead body, to which magic power had for a moment given an unnatural life: when the charm has ceased, the body lies cold and stiff as before. He who grieves over the battle of Zama should carry on his thoughts to a period thirty years later, when Hannibal must, in the course of nature, have been dead, and consider how that isolated Phœnician city of Carthage was fitted to receive and to consolidate the civilisation of Greece, or by its laws and institutions to bind together barbarians of every race and language into an organised empire, and prepare them for becoming, when that empire was dissolved, the free members of the commonwealth of Christian Europe.

Hannibal was twenty-six years of age when he Hannibal
takes Sa-
guntum. was appointed commander-in-chief of the Carthaginian armies in Spain, upon the sudden death of Hasdrubal. Two years, we have seen, had been

A.U.C. 535.
A.C. 219.
employed in expeditions against the native Spaniards; the third year was devoted to the siege of Saguntum. Hannibal's pretext for attacking it was, that the Saguntines had oppressed one of the Spanish tribes in alliance with Carthage;[1] but no caution in the Saguntine government could have avoided a quarrel. which their enemy was determined to provoke. Saguntum, although not a city of native Spaniards. resisted as obstinately as if the very air of Spain had breathed into foreign settlers on its soil the spirit so often, in so many different ages, displayed by the Spanish people. Saguntum was defended like Numantia and Gerona: for eight months the siege lasted; and when all hope was gone, several of the chiefs kindled a fire in the market-place, and after having thrown into it their most precious effects. leapt into it themselves and perished. Still the spoil found in the place was very considerable: there was a large treasure of money, which Hannibal kept for his war expenses; there were numerous captives, whom he distributed amongst his soldiers as their share of the plunder; and there was much costly furniture from the public and private buildings, which he sent home to decorate the temples and palaces of Carthage.[2]

Ambassadors sent to Carthage, who declare war.
It must have been towards the close of the year, but apparently before the consuls were returned from Illyria, that the news of the fall of Saguntum reached Rome. Immediately ambassadors were sent to Carthage; M. Fabius Buteo, who had been consul seven-and-twenty years before, C. Licinius

---

[1] Polybius, III. 15. Appian Hispan. XI.
[2] Livy, XXI. 14. Polybius. III. 17.

Varus, and Q. Bæbius Tamphilus.   Their orders were simply to demand that Hannibal and his principal officers should be given up for their attack upon the allies of Rome in breach of the treaty, and, if this were refused, to declare war.[1]   The Carthaginians tried to discuss the previous question, whether the attack on Saguntum was a breach of the treaty; but to this the Romans would not listen.   At length M. Fabius gathered up his toga, as if he was wrapping up something in it, and holding it out thus folded together, he said, 'Behold, here are peace and war; which shall I give you?' The Carthaginian suffete or judge answered, 'Be it whichever thou wilt.'   Hereupon Fabius shook out the folds of his toga, saying, 'Then here we give you war;' to which several members of the council shouted in answer, 'With all our hearts we welcome it.'   Thus the Roman ambassadors left Carthage, and returned forthwith to Rome.

But before the result of this embassy could be known in Spain, Hannibal had been making preparations for his intended expedition, in a manner which showed, not only that he was sure of the support of his government, but that he was able to dispose at his pleasure of all the military resources of Carthage. At his suggestion fresh troops from Africa were sent over to Spain to secure it during his absence, and to be commanded by his own brother, Hasdrubal; and their place was to be supplied by other troops raised in Spain;[2] so that Africa was to be defended by Spaniards, and Spain by Africans, the soldiers of

[1] Polybius, III. 20.   Zonaras, VIII. 22.
[2] Polybius, III. 33.   Livy, XXI. 21.

 each nation, when quartered amongst foreigners, being cut off from all temptation or opportunity to revolt. So completely was he allowed to direct every military measure, that he is said to have sent Spanish and Numidian troops to garrison Carthage itself; in other words, this was a part of his general plan, and was adopted accordingly by the government. Meanwhile he had sent ambassadors into Gaul, and even across the Alps, to the Gauls who had so lately been at war with the Romans, both to obtain information as to the country through which his march lay, and to secure the assistance and guidance of the Gauls in his passage of the Alps, and their co-operation in arms when he should arrive in Italy. His Spanish troops he had dismissed to their several homes at the end of the last campaign, that they might carry their spoils with them, and tell of their exploits to their countrymen, and enjoy, during the winter, that almost listless ease which is the barbarian's relief from war and plunder. At length he received the news of the Roman embassy to Carthage, and the actual declaration of war; his officers also had returned from Cisalpine Gaul. 'The natural difficulties of the passage of the Alps were great,' they said, 'but by no means insuperable; while the disposition of the Gauls was most friendly, and they were eagerly expecting his arrival.'[1] Then Hannibal called his soldiers together, and told them openly that he was going to lead them into Italy. 'The Romans,' he said, 'have demanded that I and my principal officers should be delivered up to them as male-

[1] Polybius, III. 34.

factors.   Soldiers, will you suffer such an indignity ? A.U.C. 536
The Gauls are holding out their arms to us, invit- A.C. 218.
ing us to come to them, and to assist them in
revenging their manifold injuries.   And the country
which we shall invade, so rich in corn and wine
and oil, so full of flocks and herds, so covered with
flourishing cities, will be the richest prize that could
be offered by the gods to reward your valour.'   One
common shout from the soldiers assured him of their
readiness to follow him.   He thanked them, fixed
the day on which they were to be ready to march,
and then dismissed them.

In this interval, and now on the very eve of com- Hannibal's
mencing his appointed work, to which for eighteen sacrifice.
years he had been solemnly devoted, and to which
he had so long been looking forward with almost
sickening hope, he left the headquarters of his army
to visit Gades, and there, in the temple of the
supreme god of Tyre and all the colonies of Tyre,
to offer his prayers and vows for the success of his
enterprise.[1]   He was attended only by those immediately attached to his person ; and amongst
these was a Sicilian Greek, Silenus, who followed
him throughout his Italian expedition, and lived at
his table.   When the sacrifice was over, Hannibal
returned to his army at New Carthage ; and everything being ready, and the season sufficiently advanced, for it was now late in May, he set out on
his march for the Iberus.

And here the fulness of his mind, and his strong His vision.
sense of being the devoted instrument of his country's
gods to destroy their enemies, haunted him by night

<hr>

[1] Livy, XXI. 21. Compare Polybius, XXXIV. 9.

A.U.C. 536.
A.C. 218.
as they possessed him by day. In his sleep, so he told Silenus, he fancied that the supreme god of his fathers had called him into the presence of all the gods of Carthage, who were sitting on their thrones in council. There he received a solemn charge to invade Italy; and one of the heavenly council went with him, and with his army, to guide him on his way. He went on, and his divine guide commanded him, 'See that thou look not behind thee.' But after a while, impatient of the restraint, he turned to look back, and there he beheld a huge and monstrous form, thick set all over with serpents; whereever it moved, orchards and woods and houses fell crashing before it. He asked of his guide in wonder what was that monster form. The god answered, 'Thou seest the desolation of Italy; go on thy way, straight forwards, and cast no look behind.'[1] Thus, with no divided heart, and with an entire resignation of all personal and domestic enjoyments for ever, Hannibal went forth, at the age of twenty-seven,[2] to do the work of his country's gods, and to redeem his early vow.

Miscalculations of the Romans. The consuls of Rome came into office at this period on the 15th of March: it was possible therefore for a consular army to arrive on the scene of action in time to dispute with Hannibal not only the passage of the Rhone but that of the Pyrenees. But the Romans exaggerated the difficulties of his march, and seem to have expected that the resistance of the Spanish tribes between the Iberus

---

[1] Cicero de Div. I. 24. Livy, XXI. 22. Valerius Maximus, I. 7. 1. Externa. Zonaras, VIII. 22.

[2] Nepos, Hannibal, c. 3.

and the Pyrenees, and of the Gauls between the Pyrenees and the Rhone, would so delay him that he would not reach the Rhone till the very end of the season. They therefore made their preparations leisurely.

Of the consuls for this year, the year of Rome 536, and 218 before the Christian era, was one P. Cornelius Scipio, the son of L. Scipio, who had been consul in the sixth year of the first Punic war, and the grandson of L. Scipio Barbatus, whose services in the third Samnite war are recorded in his famous epitaph. The other was Ti. Sempronius Longus, probably, but not certainly, the son of that C. Sempronius Blæsus, who had been consul in the year 501. The consuls' provinces were to be Spain and Sicily; Scipio, with two Roman legions, and 15,600 of the Italian allies and with a fleet of 60 quinqueremes, was to command in Spain; Sempronius, with a somewhat larger army, and a fleet of 160 quinqueremes, was to cross over to Lilybæum, and from thence, if circumstances favoured, to make a descent on Africa. A third army, consisting also of two Roman legions and 11,000 of the allies, was stationed in Cisalpine Gaul under the prætor, L. Manlius Vulso.[1] The Romans suspected that the Gauls would rise in arms ere long, and they hastened to send out the colonists of two colonies, which had been resolved on before, but not actually founded, to occupy the important stations of Placentia and Cremona on the opposite banks of the Po. The colonists sent to each of these places were no fewer than 6000; and they received notice to be at their colonies in

___

[1] Polybius, III. 40, 41.

 thirty days.   Three commissioners, one of them, C. Lutatius Catulus, being of consular rank, were sent out as usual to superintend the allotment of lands to the settlers ; and these 12,000 men, together with the prætor's army, were supposed to be capable of keeping the Gauls quiet.[1]

Revolt of the Gauls.   It is a curious fact that the danger on the side of Spain was considered to be so much the least urgent that Scipio's army was raised the last, after those of his colleague and of the prætor, L. Manlius.[2] Indeed Scipio was still at Rome, when tidings came that the Boians and Insubrians had revolted, had dispersed the new settlers of Placentia and Cremona. and driven them to take refuge at Mutina, had treacherously seized the three commissioners at a conference, and had defeated the prætor L. Manlius, and obliged him also to take shelter in one of the towns of Cisalpine Gaul, where they were blockading him.[3]   One of Scipio's legions, with 5000 of the allies, was immediately sent off into Gaul under another prætor, C. Atilius Serranus ; and Scipio waited till his own army should again be completed by new levies.   Thus he cannot have left Rome till late in the summer ; and when he arrived with his fleet and army at the mouth of the eastern branch of the Rhone, he found that Hannibal had crossed the Pyrenees ; but he still hoped to impede his passage of the river.

Hannibal conquers the north of Spain.   Hannibal meanwhile, having set out from New Carthage with an army of 90,000 foot, and 12,000 horse, crossed the Iberus ;[4] and from thenceforward

[1] Polybius, III. 40.   [2] Livy, XXI. 26.
[3] Polybius. III. 40.   [4] Polybius, III. 35.   Livy. XXI. 23.

the hostile operations of his march began. He might probably have marched through the country between the Iberus and the Pyrenees, had that been his sole object, as easily as he made his way from the Pyrenees to the Rhone; a few presents and civilities would easily have induced the Spanish chiefs to allow him a free passage. But some of the tribes northward of the Iberus were friendly to Rome: on the coast were the Greek cities of Rhoda and Emporiæ, Massaliot colonies, and thus attached to the Romans as the old allies of their mother city: if this part of Spain were left unconquered the Romans would immediately make use of it as the base of their operations, and proceed from thence to attack the whole Carthaginian dominion. Accordingly Hannibal employed his army in subduing the whole country, which he effected with no great loss of time, but at a heavy expense of men, as he was obliged to carry the enemy's strongholds by assault, rather than incur the delay of besieging them. He left Hanno with 11,000 men to retain possession of the newly-conquered country; and he further diminished his army by sending home as many more of his Spanish soldiers, probably those who had most distinguished themselves, as an earnest to the rest, that they too, if they did their duty well, might expect a similar release, and might look forward to return ere long to their homes full of spoil and of glory. These detachments, together with the heavy loss sustained in the field, reduced the force with which Hannibal entered Gaul to no more than 50,000 foot and 9000 horse.[1]

[1] Polybius, III. 35.

A.U.C. 536.
A.C. 218.
He marches
to the
Rhone.

From the Pyrenees to the Rhone his progress was easy. Here he had no wish to make regular conquests; and presents to the chiefs mostly succeeded in conciliating their friendship, so that he was allowed to pass freely. But on the left bank of the Rhone the influence of the Massaliots with the Gaulish tribes had disposed them to resist the invader; and the passage of the Rhone was not to be effected without a contest.

Scipio's
move-
ments.

Scipio by this time had landed his army near the eastern mouth of the Rhone; and his information of Hannibal's movements was vague and imperfect. His men had suffered from sea-sickness on their voyage from Pisa to the Rhone; and he wished to give them a short time to recover their strength and spirits, before he led them against the enemy. He still felt confident that Hannibal's advance from the Pyrenees must be slow, as he supposed that he would be obliged to fight his way; so that he never doubted that he should have ample time to oppose his passage of the Rhone. Meanwhile he sent out 300 horse, with some Gauls, who were in the service of the Massaliots, ordering them to ascend the left bank of the Rhone, and discover, if possible, the situation of the enemy. He seems to have been unwilling to place the river on his rear, and therefore never to have thought of conducting his operations on the right bank, or even of sending out reconnoitring parties in this direction.[1]

Hannibal's
prepara-
tions for
passing the
Rhone.

The resolution which Scipio formed a few days afterwards, of sending his army to Spain when he himself returned to Italy, was deserving of such

[1] Polybius. III. 41.   Livy. XXI. 26.

high praise that we must hesitate to accuse him of A.U.C. 536. over caution or needless delay at this critical A.C. 218. moment. Yet he was sitting idle at the mouth of the Rhone while the Gauls were vainly endeavouring to oppose Hannibal's passage of the river. We must understand that Hannibal kept his army as far away from the sea as possible, in order to conceal his movements from the Romans; therefore he came upon the Rhone, not on the line of the later Roman road from Spain to Italy, which crossed the river at Tarasco, between Avignon and Arles, but at a point much higher up, above its confluence with the Durance, and nearly half-way, if we can trust Polybius' reckoning, from the sea to its confluence with the Isere.[1] Here he obtained from the natives on the right bank, by paying a fixed price, all their boats and vessels of every description, with which they were accustomed to traffic down the river: they allowed him also to cut timber for the construction of others; and thus in two days he was provided with the means of transporting his army. But finding that the Gauls were assembled on the eastern bank to oppose his passage, he sent off a detachment of his army by night with native guides, to ascend the right bank, for about two-and-twenty miles, and there to cross as they could, where there was no enemy to stop them. The woods which then lined the river supplied this detachment with the means of constructing barks and rafts enough for the passage; they took advantage of one of the many islands in this part of the Rhone to cross where the stream was divided; and thus they all

<hr>

[1] Polybius, III. 42, 49.

A.U.C. 536.
A.C. 218.

reached the left bank in safety. There they took up a strong position, probably one of those strange masses of rock which rise here and there with steep cliffy sides, like islands out of the vast plain, and rested for four-and-twenty hours after their exertions in the march and the passage of the river.

The army crosses the river.

Hannibal allowed eight-and-forty hours to pass from the time when the detachment left his camp; and then on the morning of the fifth day after his arrival on the Rhone he made his preparations for the passage of his main army. The mighty stream of the river, fed by the snows of the high Alps, is swelled rather than diminished by the heats of summer, so that, although the season was that when the southern rivers are generally at their lowest, it was rolling the vast mass of its waters along with a startling fulness and rapidity. The heaviest vessels were therefore placed on the left, highest up the stream, to form something of a breakwater for the smaller craft crossing below. The small boats held the flower of the light-armed foot, while the cavalry were in the larger vessels; most of the horses being towed astern swimming, and a single soldier holding three or four together by their bridles. Everything was ready, and the Gauls on the opposite side had poured out of their camp, and lined the bank in scattered groups at the most accessible points, thinking that their task of stopping the enemy's landing would be easily accomplished. At length Hannibal's eye observed a column of smoke rising on the further shore, above or on the right of the barbarians. This was the concerted signal which assured him of the arrival of his detachment, and he instantly ordered his men to embark and to push across with all possible speed. They pulled vigorously against the rapid stream, cheering each other to the work, while behind them were their friends, cheering them also from the bank; and before them were the Gauls singing their war songs, and calling them to come on with tones and gestures of defiance. But on a sudden a mass of fire was seen on the rear of the barbarians; the Gauls on the bank looked behind, and began to turn away from the river; and presently the bright arms and white linen coats of the African and Spanish soldiers appeared above the bank, breaking in upon the disorderly line of the Gauls. Hannibal himself, who was with the party crossing the river, leaped on shore amongst the first, and forming his men as fast as they landed, led them instantly to the charge. But the Gauls, confused and bewildered, made little resistance. They fled in utter rout, whilst Hannibal, not losing a moment, sent back his vessels and boats for a fresh detachment of his army; and before night his whole force, with the exception of his elephants, was safely established on the eastern side of the Rhone.[1]

As the river was no longer between him and the enemy, Hannibal early on the next morning sent out a party of Numidian cavalry to discover the position and numbers of Scipio's forces, and then called his army together, to see and hear the communications of some chiefs of the Cisalpine Gauls, who were just arrived from the other side of the Alps. Their words were explained to the Africans and Spaniards in the army by interpreters; but the

A.U.C.536.
A.C. 218.

Arrival of emissaries from the Cisalpine Gauls.

---

[1] Polybius, III. 42, 43.

 very sight of the chiefs was itself an encouragement, for it told the soldiers that the communication with Cisalpine Gaul was not impracticable, and that the Gauls had undertaken so long a journey for the purpose of obtaining the aid of the Carthaginian army against their old enemies the Romans. Besides, the interpreters explained to the soldiers that the chiefs undertook to guide them into Italy by a short and safe route, on which they would be able to find provisions, and spoke strongly of the great extent and richness of Italy when they did arrive there, and how zealously the Gauls would aid them. Hannibal then came forward himself and addressed his army : their work, he said, was more than half accomplished by the passage of the Rhone ; their own eyes and ears had witnessed the zeal of their Gaulish allies in their cause ; for the rest, their business was to do their duty, and obey his orders implicitly, leaving everything else to him. The cheers and shouts of the soldiers again satisfied him how fully he might depend upon them ; and he then addressed his prayers and vows to the gods of Carthage, imploring them to watch over the army, and to prosper its work to the end, as they had prospered its beginning. The soldiers were now dismissed, with orders to prepare for their march on the morrow.[1]

Scipio sends his army to Spain, and returns to Italy.

Scarcely was the assembly broken up when some of the Numidians, who had been sent out in the morning, were seen riding for their lives to the camp, manifestly in flight from a victorious enemy. Not half of the original party returned, for they had

[1] Polybius, III. 44.

fallen in with Scipio's detachment of Roman and A.U.C. 536.
Gaulish horse, and after an obstinate conflict had A.C. 218.
been completely beaten. Presently after the Roman
horsemen appeared in pursuit ; but when they
observed the Carthaginian camp they wheeled about
and rode off to carry back word to their general.
Then at last Scipio put his army in motion, and
ascended the left bank of the river to find and
engage the enemy.[1] But when he arrived at the
spot where his cavalry had seen the Carthaginian
camp he found it deserted, and was told that Hannibal had been gone three days, having marched
northwards, ascending the left bank of the river.
To follow him seemed desperate ; it was plunging
into a country wholly unknown to the Romans,
where they had neither allies nor guides, nor resources of any kind, and where the natives, over
and above the common jealousy felt by all barbarians
toward a foreign army, were likely, as Gauls, to regard the Romans with peculiar hostility. But if
Hannibal could not be followed now he might easily
be met on his first arrival in Italy ; from the mouth
of the Rhone to Pisa was the chord of a circle, while
Hannibal was going to make a long circuit ; and
the Romans had an army already in Cisalpine Gaul,
while the enemy would reach the scene of action
exhausted with the fatigues and privations of his
march across the Alps. Accordingly Scipio descended the Rhone again, embarked his army, and
sent it on to Spain under the command of his
brother Cnæus Scipio as his lieutenant ; while he
himself, in his own ship, sailed for Pisa, and im-

[1] Polybius, III. 45.

A.U.C. 536.
A.C. 218. mediately crossed the Apennines to take the command of the forces of the two prætors, Manlius and Atilius, who, as we have seen, had an army of about 25,000 men, over and above the colonists of Placentia and Cremona, still disposable in Cisalpine Gaul.[1]

Wisdom of this resolution. This resolution of Scipio to send his own army on to Spain, and to meet Hannibal with the army of the two prætors, appears to show that he possessed the highest qualities of a general, which involve the wisdom of a statesman no less than of a soldier. As a mere military question his calculation, though baffled by the event, was sound; but if we view it in a higher light, the importance to the Romans of retaining their hold on Spain would have justified a far greater hazard, for if the Carthaginians were suffered to consolidate their dominion in Spain, and to avail themselves of its immense resources, not in money only, but in men, the hardiest and steadiest of barbarians, and, under the training of such generals as Hannibal and his brother, equal to the best soldiers in the world, the Romans would hardly have been able to maintain the contest. Had not P. Scipio then despatched his army to Spain at this critical moment, instead of carrying it home to Italy, his son in all human probability would never have won the battle of Zama.

The elephants are carried over the Rhone. Meanwhile Hannibal, on the day after the skirmish with Scipio's horse, had sent forward his infantry, keeping the cavalry to cover his operations, as he still expected the Romans to pursue him, while he himself waited to superintend the passage of the

[1] Polybius, III. 49.

elephants. These were thirty-seven in number, and their dread of the water made their transport a very difficult operation. It was effected by fastening to the bank large rafts of 200 feet in length, covered carefully with earth; to the end of these smaller rafts were attached, covered with earth in the same manner, and with towing lines extended to a number of the largest barks, which were to tow them over the stream. The elephants, two females leading the way, were brought upon the rafts by their drivers without difficulty; and as soon as they came upon the smaller rafts these were cut loose at once from the larger, and towed out into the middle of the river. Some of the elephants in their terror leaped overboard, and drowned their drivers; but they themselves, it is said, held their huge trunks above water and struggled to the shore, so that the whole thirty-seven were landed in safety.[1] Then Hannibal called in his cavalry, and, covering his march with them and with the elephants, set forward up the left bank of the Rhone to overtake the infantry.

In four days they reached the spot where the Isere,[2] coming down from the main Alps, brings to the Rhone a stream hardly less full or mighty than his own. In the plains above the confluence two Gaulish brothers were contending which should be chief of their tribe; and the elder called in the stranger general to support his cause. Hannibal readily complied, established him firmly on the throne, and received important aid from him in return. He supplied the Carthaginian army plentifully with provisions, furnished them with new

A.U.C. 536.
A.C. 218.

Hannibal's
march
through
Gaul.

[1] Polybius, III. 46. Livy, XXI. 28.   [2] Polybius, III. 49.

A.U.C. 536.
A.C. 218.

arms, gave them new clothing, especially shoes, which were found very useful in the subsequent march, and accompanied them to the first entrance on the mountain country, to secure them from attacks on the part of his countrymen.

Difficulty of determining his line of march. The attentive reader, who is acquainted with the geography of the Alps and their neighbourhood, will perceive that this account of Hannibal's march is vague. It does not appear whether the Carthaginians ascended the left bank of the Isere, or the right bank; or whether they continued to ascend the Rhone for a time, and leaving it only so far as to avoid the great angle which it makes at Lyons, rejoined it again just before they entered the mountain country, a little to the left of the present road from Lyons to Chambery. But these uncertainties cannot now be removed, because Polybius neither possessed a sufficient knowledge of the bearings of the country, nor sufficient liveliness as a painter, to describe the line of the march so as to be clearly recognised. I believe, however, that Hannibal crossed the Isere, and continued to ascend the Rhone; and that afterwards, striking off to the right across the plains of Dauphiné, he reached what Polybius calls the first ascent of the Alps, at the northern extremity of that ridge of limestone mountains, which, rising abruptly from the plain to the height of 4000 or 5000 feet, and filling up the whole space between the Rhone at Belley and the Isere below Grenoble, first introduces the traveller coming from Lyons to the remarkable features of Alpine scenery.[1]

[1] See Note A.

At the end of the lowland country the Gaulish chief, who had accompanied Hannibal thus far, took leave of him : his influence probably did not extend to the Alpine valleys ; and the mountaineers, far from respecting his safe conduct, might be in the habit of making plundering inroads on his own territory. Here then Hannibal was left to himself; and he found that the natives were prepared to beset his passage. They occupied all such points as commanded the road ; which, as usual, was a sort of terrace cut in the mountain side, overhanging the valley whereby it penetrated to the central ridge. But as the mountain line is here of no great breadth, the natives guarded the defile only by day and withdrew when night came on to their own homes, in a town or village among the mountains, and lying in the valley behind them.[1] Hannibal having learned this from some of his Gaulish guides whom he sent among them, encamped in their sight just below the entrance of the defile ; and as soon as it was dusk, he set out with a detachment of light troops, made his way through the pass, and occupied the positions which the barbarians, after their usual practice, had abandoned at the approach of night.

Day dawned ; the main army broke up from its camp, and began to enter the defile ; while the natives finding their positions occupied by the enemy, at first looked on quietly, and offered no disturbance to the march. But when they saw the long narrow line of the Carthaginian army winding its way along the steep mountain side, and the cavalry and baggage cattle struggling at every step with the

<hr>

[1] Polybius, III. 50.

A.U.C. 536.
A.C. 218.
difficulties of the road, the temptation to plunder was too strong to be resisted ; and from many points of the mountain above the road they rushed down upon the Carthaginians. The confusion was terrible ; for the road or track was so narrow that the least crowd or disorder pushed the heavily-loaded baggage cattle down the steep below; and the horses, wounded by the barbarians' missiles, and plunging about wildly in their pain and terror, increased the mischief. At last Hannibal was obliged to charge down from his position, which commanded the whole scene of confusion, and to drive the barbarians off. This he effected : yet the conflict of so many men on the narrow road made the disorder worse for a time ; and he unavoidably occasioned the destruction of many of his own men.[1]   At last, the barbarians being quite beaten off, the army wound its way out of the defile in safety, and rested in the wide and rich valley which extends from the lake of Bourget, with scarcely a perceptible change of level, to the Isere at Montmeillan. Hannibal meanwhile attacked and stormed the town, which was the barbarians' principal stronghold ; and here he not only recovered a great many of his own men, horses, and baggage cattle, but also found a large supply of corn and cattle belonging to the barbarians, which he immediately made use of for the consumption of his soldiers.

Difficulties of the march.
In the plain which he had now reached he halted for a whole day, and then, resuming his march, proceeded for three days up the valley of the Isere on the right bank, without encountering any difficulty.

[1] Polybius, III. 51.

Then the natives met him with branches of trees in their hands, and wreaths on their heads, in token of peace: they spoke fairly, offered hostages, and wished, they said, neither to do the Carthaginians any injury, nor to receive any from them. Hannibal mistrusted them, yet did not wish to offend them; he accepted their terms, received their hostages, and obtained large supplies of cattle; and their whole behaviour seemed so trustworthy that at last he accepted their guidance, it is said, through a difficult part of the country, which he was now approaching.[1] For all the Alpine valleys become narrower, as they draw nearer to the central chain; and the mountains often come so close to the stream that the roads in old times were often obliged to leave the valley and ascend the hills by any accessible point, to descend again when the gorge became wider, and follow the stream as before. If this is not done, and the track is carried nearer the river, it passes often through defiles of the most formidable character, being no more than a narrow ledge above a furious torrent, with cliffs rising above it absolutely precipitous, and coming down on the other side of the torrent abruptly to the water, leaving no passage by which man or even goat could make its way.

It appears that the barbarians persuaded Hannibal to pass through one of these defiles, instead of going round it; and while his army was involved in it they suddenly, and without provocation, as we are told, attacked him. Making their way along the mountain sides above the defile, they rolled down masses of rock on the Carthaginians below, or

A.U.C. 536.
A.C. 218.

Attacks of the mountaineers.

[1] Polybius, III. 52.

even threw stones upon them from their hands, stones and rocks being equally fatal against an enemy so entangled. It was well for Hannibal that, still doubting the barbarians' faith, he had sent forward his cavalry and baggage, and covered the march with his infantry, who thus had to sustain the brunt of the attack. Foot soldiers on such ground were able to move, where horses would be quite helpless; and thus at last Hannibal, with his infantry, forced his way to the summit of one of the bare cliffs overhanging the defile, and remained there during the night, whilst the cavalry and baggage slowly struggled out of the defile.[1] Thus again baffled, the barbarians made no more general attacks on the army; some partial annoyance was occasioned at intervals, and some baggage was carried off; but it was observed that wherever the elephants were, the line of march was secure; for the barbarians beheld those huge creatures with terror, having never had the slightest knowledge of them, and not daring to approach when they saw them.

Hannibal reaches the summit of the Alps. Without any further recorded difficulty, the army on the ninth day after they had left the plains of Dauphiné arrived at the summit of the central ridge of the Alps. Here there is always a plain of some extent, immediately overhung by the snowy summits of the high mountains, but itself in summer presenting in many parts a carpet of the freshest grass, with the chalets of the shepherds scattered over it, and gay with a thousand flowers. But far different is its aspect through the greatest part of the year: then it is one unvaried waste of snow; and the

[1] Polybius, III. 53.

little lakes, which on many of the passes enliven the summer landscape, are now frozen over, and covered with snow, so as to be no longer distinguishable. Hannibal was on the summit of the Alps about the end of October: the first winter snows had already fallen; but two hundred years before the Christian era, when all Germany was one vast forest, the climate of the Alps was far colder than at present, and the snow lay on the passes all through the year. Thus the soldiers were in dreary quarters: they remained two days on the summit, resting from their fatigues, and giving opportunity to many of the stragglers, and of the horses and cattle, to rejoin them by following their track; but they were cold and worn and disheartened; and mountains still rose before them, through which, as they knew too well, even their descent might be perilous and painful.

A.U.C. 536.
A.C. 218.

But their great general, who felt that he now stood victorious on the ramparts of Italy, and that the torrent which rolled before him was carrying its waters to the rich plains of Cisalpine Gaul, endeavoured to kindle his soldiers with his own spirit of hope. He called them together; he pointed out the valley beneath, to which the descent seemed the work of a moment: 'That valley,' he said, 'is Italy; it leads us to the country of our friends the Gauls; and yonder is our way to Rome.' His eyes were eagerly fixed on that point of the horizon; and as he gazed, the distance between seemed to vanish, till he could almost fancy that he was crossing the Tiber and assailing the Capitol.[1]

Looks down upon Italy.

[1] Polybius, III. 54.   Livy, XXI. 35.

After the two days' rest the descent began. Hannibal experienced no more open hostility from the barbarians, only some petty attempts here and there to plunder: a fact strange in itself, but doubly so, if he was really descending the valley of the Doria Baltea, through the country of the Salassians, the most untamable robbers of all the Alpine barbarians. It is possible that the influence of the Insubrians may partly have restrained the mountaineers; and partly also they may have been deterred by the ill success of all former attacks, and may by this time have regarded the strange army and its monstrous beasts with something of superstitious terror. But the natural difficulties of the ground on the descent were greater than ever. The snow so covered the track that the men often lost it, and fell down the steep below. At last they came to a place where an avalanche had carried it away altogether, for about three hundred yards, leaving the mountain side a mere wreck of scattered rocks and snow. To go round was impossible, for the depth of the snow on the heights above rendered it hopeless to scale them; nothing therefore was left but to repair the road. A summit of some extent was found, and cleared of the snow; and here the army were obliged to encamp whilst the work went on. There was no want of hands, and every man was labouring for his life; the road therefore was restored, and supported with solid substructions below; and in a single day it was made practicable for the cavalry and baggage cattle, which were immediately sent forward, and reached the lower valley in safety, where they were turned out to pasture.

A harder labour was required to make a passage for the elephants; the way for them must be wide and solid, and the work could not be accomplished in less than three days. The poor animals suffered severely in the interval from hunger, for no forage was to be found in that wilderness of snow, nor any trees whose leaves might supply the place of other herbage. At last they too were able to proceed with safety.[1] Hannibal overtook his cavalry and baggage: and in three days more the whole army had got clear of the Alpine valleys, and entered the country of their friends, the Insubrians, on the wide plain of northern Italy.[2]

Hannibal was arrived in Italy, but with a force so weakened by its losses in men and horses, and by the exhausted state of the survivors, that he might seem to have accomplished his great march in vain. According to his own statement, which there is no reason to doubt, he brought out of the Alpine valleys no more than 12,000 African and 8000 Spanish infantry, with 6000 cavalry,[3] so that his march from the Pyrenees to the plains of northern Italy must have cost him 33,000 men; an enormous loss, which proves how severely the army must have suffered from the privations of the march and the severity of the Alpine climate, for not half of these 33,000 men can have fallen in battle. With his army in this condition, some period of repose was absolutely necessary: accordingly, Hannibal remained in the country of the Insubrians till rest and a more temperate climate, and wholesome food, with which the Gauls plentifully supplied him, restored the

A.U.C. 536.
A.C. 218.

Arrival in Italy.
Losses on the march.

---

[1] Polybius, III. 54, 55.   [2] See Note B.   [3] Polybius, III. 56.

bodies and spirits of his soldiers, and made them again ready for action.[1] His first movement was against the Taurinians, a Ligurian people, who were constant enemies of the Insubrians, and therefore would not listen to Hannibal when he invited them to join his cause. He therefore attacked and stormed their principal town, put the garrison to the sword, and struck such terror into the neighbouring tribes that they submitted immediately and became his allies. This was his first accession of strength in Italy, the first fruits, as he hoped, of a long succession of defections among the allies of Rome, so that the swords of the Italians might effect for him the conquest of Italy.

Scipio marches to meet him. Meanwhile Scipio had landed at Pisa, had crossed the Apennines, and taken the command of the prætors' army, sending the prætors themselves back to Rome, had crossed the Po at Placentia, and was ascending its left bank, being anxious to advance with all possible haste, in order to hinder a general rising of the Gauls by his presence.[2] Hannibal, for the opposite reason, was equally anxious to meet him, being well aware that the Gauls were only restrained from revolting to the Carthaginians by fear, and that on his first success in the field they would hasten to join him.[3] He therefore descended the left bank of the Po, keeping the river on his right; and Scipio, having thrown a bridge over the Ticinus, had entered what are now[4] the Sardinian dominions, and was still advancing westward, with the Po on his left, although, as the river here makes

<hr>

[1] Polybius, III. 60.   [2] Polybius, III. 56.
[3] Polybius, III. 60.   [4] Written in 1841.

a bend to the southward, he was no longer in its A.U.C. 536.
A.C. 218.
immediate neighbourhood.[1]

Each general was aware that his enemy was at Engage-
ment on the
Ticinus.
hand, and both pushed forward with their cavalry
and light troops in advance of their main armies,
to reconnoitre each other's position and numbers.
Thus was brought on accidentally the first action
between Hannibal and the Romans in Italy, which,
with some exaggeration, has been called the battle of
the Ticinus.[2] The Numidians in Hannibal's army,
being now properly supported by heavy cavalry, were
able to follow their own manner of fighting, and,
falling on the flanks and rear of the Romans, who
were already engaged in front with Hannibal's
heavy horsemen, took ample vengeance for their
defeat on the Rhone. The Romans were routed,
and the consul himself was severely wounded, and
owed his life, it is said, to the courage and fidelity
of a Ligurian slave.[3] With their cavalry thus
crippled, it was impossible to act in such an open
country; the Romans therefore hastily retreated,
recrossed the Ticinus, and broke down the bridge,
yet with so much hurry and confusion, that 600
men were left on the right bank and fell into the
enemy's hands; and then, crossing the Po also,
established themselves under the walls of their colony
Placentia.

Hannibal, finding the bridge over the Ticinus Hannibal's
advance.
destroyed, reascended the left bank of the Po till he
found a convenient point to cross, and then, having
constructed a bridge with the river boats, carried

<hr>

[1] Polybius, III. 64. [2] Polybius, III. 65.
[3] Livy, XXI. 46.

A.U.C. 536.
A.C. 218. over his army in safety. Immediately, as he had expected, the Gauls on the right bank received him with open arms; and again descending the river, he arrived on the second day after his passage in sight of the Roman army, and on the following day offered them battle. But as the Romans did not move, he chose out a spot for his camp, and posted his army five or six miles from the enemy, and apparently on the east of Placentia, cutting off their direct communication with Ariminum and Rome.[1]

Campaign in Sicily. Sempronius joins Scipio. On the first news of Hannibal's arrival in Italy, the senate had sent orders to the other consul, Ti. Sempronius, to return immediately to reinforce his colleague.[2] No event of importance had marked the first summer of the war in Sicily. Hannibal's spirit so animated the Carthaginian government that they were everywhere preparing to act on the offensive; and before the arrival of Sempronius, M. Æmilius, the prætor, had already had to fight a naval action with the enemy in order to defend Lilybæum.[3] He had defeated them and prevented their landing, but the Carthaginian fleet still kept the sea; and whilst Sempronius was employing his whole force in the conquest of the island of Melita, the enemy were cruising on the northern side of Sicily, and making descents on the coast of Italy. On his return to Lilybæum, he was going in pursuit of them, when he received orders to return home and join his colleague. He accordingly left part of his fleet with the prætor in Sicily, and part he com-

---

¹ Polybius, III. 66.   ² Polybius, III. 61.
³ Livy, XXI. 49, 50.

mitted to Sex. Pomponius, his lieutenant, for the protection of the coasts of Lucania and Campania; while, from a dread of the dangers and delays of the winter navigation of the Adriatic, his army was to march from Lilybæum to Messana, and after crossing the strait to go by land through the whole length of Italy, the soldiers being bound by oath to appear on a certain day at Ariminum. They completed their long march, it is said, in forty days; and from Ariminum they hastened to the scene of action, and effected their junction with the army of Scipio.[1]

Sempronius found his colleague no longer in his original position, close by Placentia and the Po, but withdrawn to the first hills which bound the great plain on the south, and leave an interval here of about six miles between themselves and the river.[2] But Hannibal's army lying, as it seems, to the eastward, the Roman consul retreated westward, and leaving Placentia to its own resources, crossed to the left bank of the Trebia, and there lay encamped just where the stream issues from the last hills of the Apennines. It appears that the Romans had several magazines on the right bank of the Po above Placentia, on which the consul probably depended for his subsistence; and these posts, together with the presence of his army, kept the Gauls on the immediate bank of the river quiet, so that they gave Hannibal no assistance. When the Romans fell back behind the Trebia, Hannibal followed them, and encamped about five miles off from them, directly between them and Placentia.[3]

A.U.C. 536.
A.C. 218.

Position of the Roman army.

---

[1] Polybius, III. 61, 68.   Livy, XXI. 51.
[2] Polybius, III. 67.   [3] Polybius, III. 68.

A.U.C. 536.
A.C. 218.

But his powerful cavalry kept his communications open in every direction ; and the Gauls who lived out of the immediate control of the Roman army and garrisons, supplied him with provisions abundantly.

Hannibal's policy.

It is not explained by any existing writer how Sempronius was able to effect his junction with his colleague without any opposition from Hannibal. The regular road from Ariminum to Placentia passes though a country unvaried by a single hill ; and the approach of a large army should have been announced to Hannibal by his Numidian cavalry soon enough to allow him to intercept it.   But so much in war depends upon trifling accidents that it is vain to guess where we are without information. We only know that the two consular armies were united in Scipio's position on the left bank of the Trebia ; that their united forces amounted to 40,000 men ; and that Hannibal, with an army so reinforced by the Gauls since his arrival in Italy that it was little inferior to the enemy's,[1] was so far from fearing to engage either consul singly, that he wished for nothing so much as to bring on a decisive battle with the combined armies of both. Depending on the support of the Gauls for his very existence, he must not be too long a burden to them : they had hoped to be led to live on the plunder of the enemy's country, not to maintain him at the expense of their own.   In order to force the Romans to a battle, he began to attack their magazines. Clastidium, now Casteggio, a small town on the right bank of the Po, nearly opposite to the mouth

[1] Polybius, III. 72.   Livy, XXI. 53.

of the Ticinus, was betrayed into his hands by the governor; and he here found large supplies of corn.[1]

A.U.C. 536.
A.C. 218.

On the other hand, Sempronius, having no fears for the event of a battle, was longing for the glory of a triumph over such an enemy as Hannibal;[2] and, as Scipio was still disabled by his wound, he had the command of the whole Roman army. Besides, the Gauls who lived in the plain between the Trebia and Placentia, not knowing which side to espouse, had been plundered by Hannibal's cavalry, and besought the consuls to protect them. This was no time, Sempronius thought, to neglect any ally who still remained faithful to Rome: he sent out his cavalry and light troops over the Trebia to drive off the plunderers; and in such skirmishes he obtained some partial success, which made him the more disposed to risk a general battle.[3]

Sempronius commands the Roman army, and is anxious to engage.

For this, as a Roman officer, and before Hannibal's military talents were fully known, he ought not to be harshly judged; but his manner of engaging was rash, and unworthy of an able general. He allowed the attacks of Hannibal's light cavalry to tempt him to follow them to their own field of battle. Early in the morning the Numidians crossed the river, and skirmished close up to the Roman camp; the consul first sent out his cavalry, and then his light infantry to repel them,[4] and when they gave way and recrossed the river, he led his regular infantry out of his camp and gave orders for the

His rashness.

<hr>

[1] Polybius, III. 69.
[3] Polybius, III. 69.
[2] Polybius, III. 70.
[4] Polybius, III. 71, 72.

A.U.C. 536.
A.C. 218.

whole army to advance over the Trebia and attack the enemy.

Commencement of the battle on the Trebia.

It was mid-winter, and the wide pebbly bed of the Trebia, which the summer traveller may almost pass dry-shod, was now filled with a rapid stream running breast-high. In the night it had rained or snowed heavily, and the morning was raw and chilly, threatening sleet or snow.[1] Yet Sempronius led his soldiers through the river before they had eaten anything, and, wet, cold, and hungry as they were, he formed them in order of battle on the plain. Meanwhile Hannibal's men had eaten their breakfast in their tents, and had oiled their bodies, and put on their armour around their fires. Then, when the enemy had crossed the Trebia, and were advancing in the open plain, the Carthaginians marched out to meet them, and about a mile in front of their camp they formed in order of battle.- Their disposition was simple: the heavy infantry, Gauls, Spaniards, and Africans to the number of 20,000, were drawn up in a single line; the cavalry, 10,000 strong, was, with the elephants, on the two wings; the light infantry and Balearian slingers were in the front of the whole army. This was all Hannibal's visible force. But near the Trebia, and now left in their rear by the advancing Roman legions, were lying close hid in the deep and overgrown bed of a small watercourse, 2000 picked soldiers, horse and foot, commanded by Hannibal's younger brother Mago, whom he had posted there during the night, and whose ambush the Romans passed with no suspicion. Arrived on the field of

[1] Polybius, III. 72.

battle the legions were formed in their usual order, A.U.C. 536.
with the allied infantry on the wings, and their A.C. 218.
weak cavalry of 4000 men, ill able to contend with
the numerous horsemen of Hannibal, were on the
flanks of the whole line.[1]

The Roman velites, or light infantry, who had *Defeat of the Roman light infantry and cavalry.*
been in action since daybreak, and had already shot
away half their darts and arrows, were soon driven
back upon the hastati and principes, and passed
through the intervals of the maniples to the rear.
With no less ease were the cavalry beaten on both
wings by Hannibal's horse and elephants.   But
when the heavy infantry, superior in numbers and
better armed both for offence and defence, closed
with the enemy, the confidence of Sempronius
seemed to be justified : and the Romans, numbed
and exhausted as they were, yet by their excellence
in all soldierly qualities, maintained the fight with
equal advantage.[2]

On a sudden a loud alarm was heard ; and Mago, *Rout of the whole army.*
with his chosen band, broke out from his ambush,
and assaulted them furiously in the rear.   Meantime both wings of the Roman infantry were broken
down by the elephants, and overwhelmed by the
missiles of the light infantry, till they were utterly
routed and fled towards the Trebia.   The legions
in the centre, finding themselves assailed on the
rear, pushed desperately forwards, forced their way
through the enemy's line, and marched off the field
straight to Placentia.   Many of the routed cavalry
made off in the same direction, and so escaped.
But those who fled towards the river were slaughtered

[1] See Note C.   [2] Polybius, III. 73.

 unceasingly by the conquerors till they reached it, and the loss here was enormous. The Carthaginians, however, stopped their pursuit on the brink of the Trebia : the cold was piercing, and to the elephants so intolerable that they almost all perished; even of the men and horses many were lost, so that the wreck of the Roman army reached their camp in safety; and when night came on Scipio again led them across the river, and passing unnoticed by the camp of the enemy, took refuge with his colleague within the walls of Placentia.[1]

Hannibal winters in Gaul.

So ended Hannibal's first campaign in Italy. The Romans, after their defeat, despaired of maintaining their ground on the Po; and the two consular armies retreated in opposite directions, Scipio's upon Ariminum, and that of Sempronius across the Apennines into Etruria. Hannibal remained master of Cisalpine Gaul; but the season did not allow him to besiege Placentia and Cremona; and the temper of the Gauls rendered it evident that he must not make their country the seat of war in another campaign. Already they bore the burden of supporting his army so impatiently, that he made an attempt, in the dead of the winter, to cross the Apennines into Etruria, and was only driven back by the extreme severity of the weather, the wind sweeping with such fury over the ridges and through the passes of the mountains that neither men nor beasts could stand against it.[2] He was forced, therefore, to winter in Gaul; but the innate fickleness and treachery of the people led him to suspect that attempts would be made against his life, and

[1] Polybius, III. 74.   [2] Livy. XXI. 58.

that a Gaulish assassin might hope to purchase for- A.U.C. 537.
A.C. 217.
giveness from the Romans for his country's revolt
by destroying the general who had seduced them.
He therefore put on a variety of disguises to baffle
such designs; he wore false hair, appearing sometimes as a man of mature years, and sometimes with
the grey hairs of old age;[1] and if he had that taste
for humour which great men are seldom without,
and which some anecdotes of him imply, he must
have been often amused by the mistakes thus
occasioned, and have derived entertainment from
that which policy or necessity had dictated.

We should be glad to catch a distinct view of Flaminius
the state of Rome when the news first arrived of consul, and
the battle of the Trebia. Since the disaster of takes the
command.
Caudium, more than a hundred years before, there
had been known no defeat of two consular armies
united, and the surprise and vexation must have
been great. Sempronius, it is said, returned to
Rome to hold the comitia; and the people resolved
to elect as consul a man who, however unwelcome
to the aristocracy, had already distinguished himself
by brilliant victories in the very country which was
now the seat of war. They accordingly chose C.
Flaminius for the second time consul; and with
him was elected Cn. Servilius Geminus, a man of
an old patrician family, and personally attached to
the aristocratical party, but unknown to us before
his present consulship. Flaminius' election was
most unpalatable to the aristocracy; and as numerous prodigies were reported, and the Sibylline books
consulted, and it was certain that various rites would

---

[1] Polybius, III. 78.

 be ordered to propitiate the favour of the gods,[1] he had some reason to suspect that his election would again be declared null and void, and he himself be thus deprived of his command. He was anxious, therefore, to leave Rome as soon as possible. As his colleague was detained by the religious ceremonies, and by the care of superintending the new levies, Flaminius, it is said, left the city before the 15th of March, when his consulship was to begin, and actually entered upon his office at Ariminum, whither he had gone to superintend the formation of magazines, and to examine the state of the army.[2] But the aristocracy thought it was no time to press party animosities. They made no attempt to disturb Flaminius' election; and he appears to have had his province assigned him without opposition, and to have been appointed to command Sempronius' army in Etruria, while Servilius succeeded Scipio at Ariminum. The levies of soldiers went on vigorously: two legions were employed in Spain; one was sent to Sicily, another to Sardinia, and another to Tarentum; and four legions, more or less thinned by the defeat at the Trebia, still formed the nucleus of two armies in Ariminum and in Etruria. It appears that four new legions were levied, with an unusually large proportion of soldiers from the Italian allies and the Latin name, and these being divided between the two consuls, the armies opposed to Hannibal on either line by which he might advance, must have been in point of numbers exceedingly formidable. Servilius, as we have seen, had his headquarters at Ariminum; and Scipio,

<hr>

[1] Livy, XXI. 62.   [2] Livy, XXI. 63.

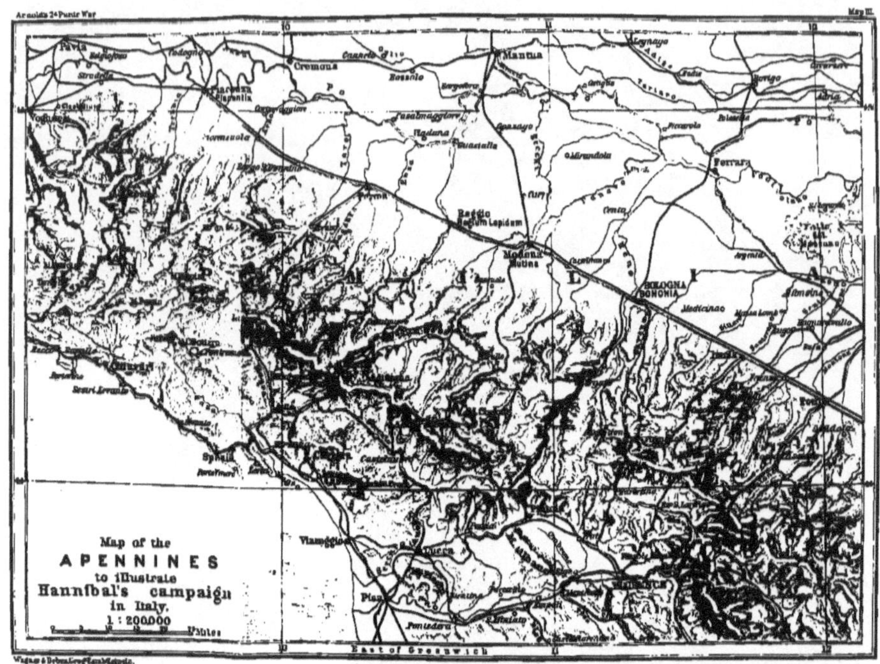

Arnold's 2d Punic War
Map II.
Pavia
Belgiojoso
Stradella
Todogno
Cremona
Mantua
Reynago
Adige
Fidus
Rovigo
Guarari
Po
Bassano
Placentia
Sorgostra
Genghe
Tartaro
Adria
Vogheria
Casteggio
Carpardagine
Fiorenzuola
Vasalmaggiore
Ngdana
Correggio
Mirandola
Picarolo
Po
Ferrara
Fermuola
Borgo S. Donnino
Parma
Carpi
Reggio
Regium Lepidum
Modena
Mutina
Cento
Castelfranco
BOLOGNA
BONONIA
Medicinao
Imola
Faenza
Genua
Nervi
Rapallo
Sestri Levante
Spezia
Porto Venere
Viareggio
Lucca
Pisa
Pontedera
East of Greenwich
London, Macmillan & Co.
Map of the
A P E N N I N E S
to illustrate
Hannibal's campaign
in Italy.
1 : 2000000
Miles

whom he superseded, sailed as proconsul into Spain to take the command of his original army there. Flaminius succeeded to Sempronius in Etruria, and lay encamped, it is said, in the neighbourhood of Arretium.[1]

A.U.C. 537.
A.C. 217.

Thus the main Roman armies lay nearly in the same positions which they had held eight years before to oppose the expected invasion of the Gauls. But as the Gauls then broke into Etruria unperceived by either Roman army, so the Romans were again surprised by Hannibal on a line where they had not expected him. He crossed the Apennines, not by the ordinary road to Lucca, descending the valley of the Macra, but, as it appears, by a straighter line down the valley of the Auser or Serchio; and leaving Lucca on his right, he proceeded to struggle through the low and flooded country which lay between the right bank of the Arno and the Apennines below Florence, and of which the marsh or lake of Fucecchio still remains a specimen. Here again the sufferings of the army were extreme; but they were rewarded when they reached the firm ground below Fæsulæ, and were let loose upon the plunder of the rich valley of the upper Arno.[2]

Hannibal
enters
Etruria.

Flaminius lay quiet at Arretium, and did not attemp to give battle, but sent messengers to his colleague to inform him of the enemy's appearance in Etruria. Hannibal was now on the south of the Apennines, and in the heart of Italy, but the experience of the Samnites and of Pyrrhus had shown that the Etruscans were scarcely more to be relied on than the Gauls; and it was in the south, in

Advances
toward
Perugia.

---

[1] Livy, XXII. 2.   [2] Polybius, III. 78, 79. See Note D.

A.U.C. 537.
A.C. 217.

Samnium and Lucania and Apulia, that the only materials existed for organising a new Italian war against Rome. Accordingly Hannibal advanced rapidly into Etruria, and finding that Flaminius still did not move, passed by Arretium, leaving the Roman army in his rear, and marching, as it seemed, to gain the great plain of central Italy, which reaches from Perusia to Spoletum, and was traversed by the great road from Ariminum to Rome.

Flaminius follows him.

The consul Flaminius now at last broke up from his position and followed the enemy. Hannibal laid waste the country on every side with fire and sword to provoke the Romans to a hasty battle, and leaving Cortona on his left untouched on its mountain seat, he approached the lake of Thrasymenus, and followed the road along its north-eastern shore till it ascended the hills which divide the lake from the basin of the Tiber.[1] Flaminius was fully convinced that Hannibal's object was not to fight a battle, but to lay waste the richest part of Italy. Had he wished to engage, why had he not attacked him when he lay at Arretium, and while his colleague was far away at Ariminum? With this impression he pressed on his rear closely, never dreaming that the lion would turn from the pursuit of his defenceless prey to spring on the shepherds who were dogging his steps behind.

Difficulty of marking out the field of battle.

The modern road along the lake, after passing the village of Passignano, runs for some way close to the water's edge on the right, hemmed in on the left by a line of cliffs, which make it an absolute

[1] Polybius, III. 82. Livy, XXII. 3.

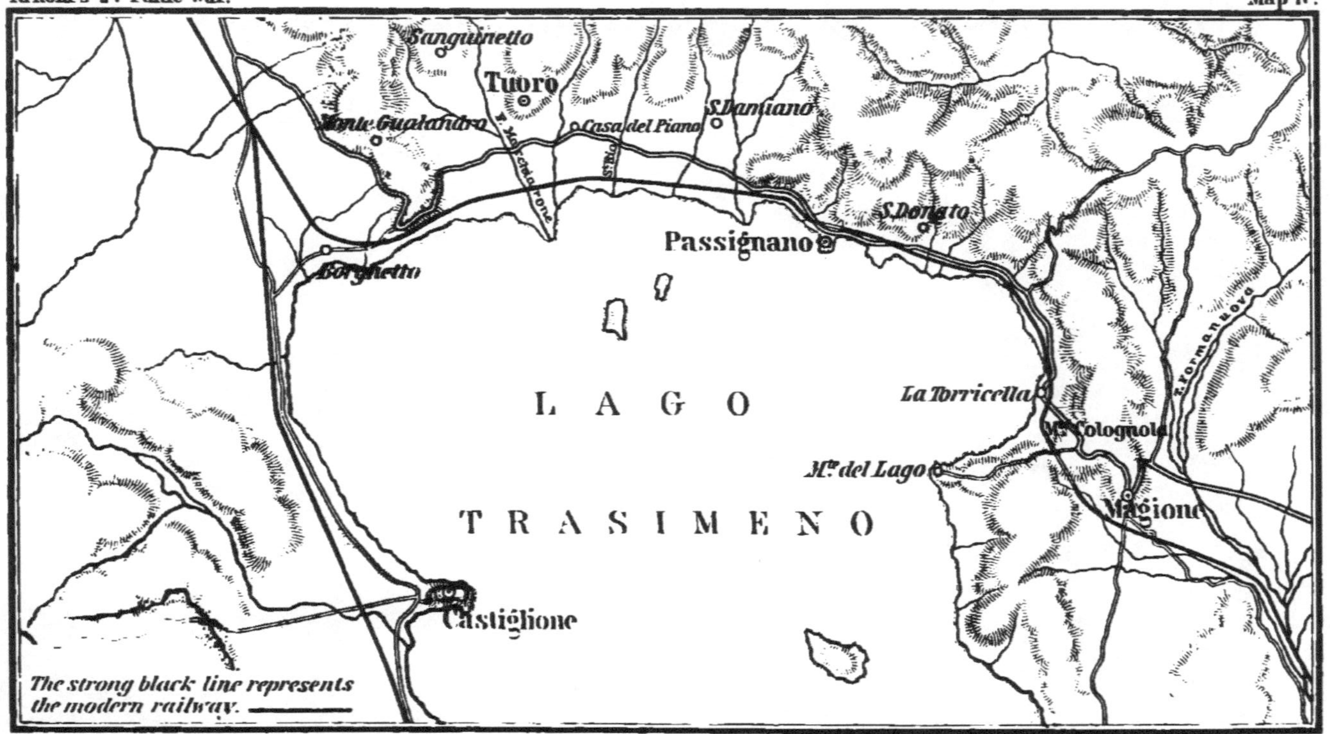

Arnold's 2nd Punic War.
Map IV.
Sanguinetto
Tuoro
Monte Gualandra
Casa del Piano
S. Damiano
F. Macerone
S. Donato
Passignano
Borghetto
LAGO
La Torricella
Mte Cologuola
Mte del Lago
TRASIMENO
Magione
T. Forman nova
Castiglione
The strong black line represents
the modern railway.
Wagner & Debes' Geogl. Estabt. Leipsic.
1:160.000
0   1   2   3   4   Miles.
Battle of Lake Thrasymene: see note E.
London, Macmillan & Co.

defile.   Then it turns from the lake and ascends the A.U.C. 537.
hills ; yet, although they form something of a curve, A.C. 217.
there is nothing to deserve the name of a valley,
and the road, after leaving the lake, begins to ascend
almost immediately, so that there is a very short
distance during which the hills on the right and
left command it.   The ground therefore does not
well correspond with the description of Polybius,
who states that the valley in which the Romans
were caught was not the narrow interval between
the hills and the lake, but a valley beyond this
defile, and running down to the lake, so that the
Romans when engaged in it had the water not on
their right flank, but on their rear.[1]   Livy's account
is different, and represents the Romans as caught in
the defile beyond Passignano, between the cliff and
the lake.   It is possible that, if the exact line of
the ancient road could be discovered, it might assist
in solving the difficulty : in the meantime the
battle of Thrasymenus must be one of the many
events in ancient military history where the accounts
of historians, differing either with each other or
with the actual appearances of the ground, are to us
inexplicable.[2]

The consul had encamped in the evening on the Flaminius
side of the lake just within the present Roman advances to attack
frontier, and on the Tuscan side of Passignano ; he Hannibal.
had made a forced march, and had arrived at his
position so late that he could not examine the
ground before him.[3]   Early the next morning he
set forward again ; the morning mist hung thickly
over the lake and the low grounds, leaving the

---

[1] III. 83.   [2] See Note E.   [3] Polybius, III. 83, 84.

A.U.C. 537.
A.C. 217.

heights, as is often the case, quite clear. Flaminius, anxious to overtake his enemy, rejoiced in the friendly veil which thus concealed his advance, and hoped to fall upon Hannibal's army while it was still in marching order and its columns encumbered with the plunder of the valley of the Arno. He passed through the defile of Passignano and found no enemy; this confirmed him in his belief that Hannibal did not mean to fight. Already the Numidian cavalry were on the edge of the basin of the Tiber; unless he could overtake them speedily they would have reached the plain, and Africans, Spaniards, and Gauls would be rioting in the devastation of the garden of Italy. So the consul rejoiced as the heads of his columns emerged from the defile, and turning to the left began to ascend the hills where he hoped at least to find the rearguard of the enemy.

Destruction of the main body of the Romans.

At this moment the stillness of the mist was broken by barbarian war-cries on every side, and both flanks of the Roman column were assailed at once. Their right was overwhelmed by a storm of javelins and arrows shot as if from the midst of darkness, and striking into the soldier's unguarded side where he had no shield to cover him; while ponderous stones, against which no shield or helmet could avail, came crashing down upon their heads. On the left were heard the trampling of horse, and the well-known war-cries of the Gauls; and presently Hannibal's dreaded cavalry emerged from the mist, and were in an instant in the midst of their ranks; and the huge forms of the Gauls and their vast broad-swords broke in upon them at the same

moment. The head of the Roman column, which A.U.C. 537.
was already ascending to the higher ground, found A.C. 217.
its advance also barred; for here was the enemy
whom they had so longed to overtake; here were
some of the Spanish and African foot of Hannibal's
army drawn up to wait their assault. The Romans
instantly attacked these troops and cut their way
through; these must be the covering parties, they
thought, of Hannibal's main battle; and, eager to
bring the contest to a decisive issue, they pushed
forward up the heights not doubting that on the
summit they should find the whole force of the
enemy. And now they were on the top of the
ridge, and to their astonishment no enemy was
there; but the mist drew up, and as they looked
behind they saw too plainly where Hannibal was:
the whole valley was one scene of carnage, while on
the sides of the hills above were the masses of the
Spanish and African foot witnessing the destruction
of the Roman army which had scarcely cost them a
single stroke.

The advanced troops of the Roman column had Of the rear-guard.
thus escaped the slaughter; but being too few to
retrieve the day, they continued their advance, which
was now become a flight, and took refuge in one of
the neighbouring villages. Meantime, while the
centre of the army was cut to pieces in the valley,
the rear was still winding through the defile beyond between the cliffs and the lake; but they too
were attacked from the heights above by the Gauls,
and forced in confusion into the water. Some of
the soldiers in desperation struck out into the deep
water swimming, and weighed down by their armour

presently sank ; others ran in as far as was within their depth, and there stood helplessly till the enemy's cavalry dashed in after them. Then they lifted up their hands and cried for quarter ; but on this day of sacrifice the gods of Carthage were not to be defrauded of a single victim ; and the horsemen pitilessly fulfilled Hannibal's vow.

Death of Flaminius.

Thus, with the exception of the advanced troops of the Roman column, who were about 6000 men, the rest of the army was utterly destroyed. The consul himself had not seen the wreck consummated. On finding himself surrounded he had vainly endeavoured to form his men amidst the confusion and to offer some regular resistance. When this was hopeless he continued to do his duty as a brave soldier, till one of the Gaulish horsemen, who is said to have known him by sight from his former consulship, rode up and ran him through the body with his lance, crying out, ' So perish the man who slaughtered our brethren, and robbed us of the lands of our fathers.'[1] In these last words we probably rather read the unquenchable hatred of the Roman aristocracy to the author of an agrarian law than the genuine language of the Gaul. Flaminius died bravely, sword in hand, having committed no greater military error than many an impetuous soldier, whose death in his country's cause has been felt to throw a veil over his rashness, and whose memory is pitied and honoured. The party feelings which have so coloured the language of the ancient writers respecting him need not be shared by a modern historian: Flaminius was indeed an unequal antagonist to

[1] Livy, XXII. 6.

Hannibal, but in his previous life, as consul and as
censor, he had served his country well; and if the
defile of Thrasymenus witnessed his rashness, it also
contains his honourable grave.

The battle must have been ended before noon;
and Hannibal's indefatigable cavalry, after having
destroyed the centre and rear of the Roman army,
hastened to pursue the troops who had broken off
from the front, and had for the present escaped the
general overthrow.   They were supported by the
light-armed foot and the Spaniards, and finding the
Romans in the village to which they had retreated,
proceeded to invest it on every side.   The Romans,
cut off from all relief and with no provisions, surrendered to Maharbal, who commanded the party
sent against them.   They were brought to Hannibal; with the other prisoners taken in the battle,
the whole number amounted to 15,000.   The
general addressed them by an interpreter; he told
the soldiers who had surrendered to Maharbal that
their lives, if he pleased, were still forfeited, for
Maharbal had no authority to grant terms without
his consent.   Then he proceeded, with the vehemence often displayed by Napoleon in similar circumstances, to inveigh against the Roman government and people, and concluded by giving all his
Roman prisoners to the custody of the several
divisions of his army.   Then he turned to the
Italian allies: they were not his enemies, he said;
on the contrary, he had invaded Italy to aid them
in casting off the yoke of Rome; he should still
deal with them as he had treated his Italian
prisoners taken at the Trebia; they were free from

A.U.C. 537.
A.C. 217.

Capture of
the ad-
vanced
guard.
Conduct of
Hannibal
to the pri-
soners.

A.U.C. 537.
A.C. 217.

that moment, and without ransom.[1] This being done, he halted for a short time to rest his army, and buried with great solemnity thirty of the most distinguished of those who had fallen on his own side in the battle. His whole loss had amounted only to 1500 men, of whom the greater part were Gauls. It is said also that he caused careful search, but in vain, to be made for the body of the consul Flaminius, being anxious to give him honourable burial.[2] So he acted afterwards to L. Æmilius and to Marcellus; and these humanities are worthy of notice, as if he had wished to show that, though his vow bound him to unrelenting enmity towards the Romans while living, it was a pleasure to him to feel that he might honour them when dead.

He ravages Umbria.

The army of Hannibal now broke up from the scene of its victory, and leaving Perusia unassailed, crossed the infant stream of the Tiber, and entered upon the plains of Umbria. Here Maharbal, with the cavalry and light troops, obtained another victory over a party of some 1000 men, commanded by C. Centenius, and killed, took prisoners, or dispersed the whole body.[3] Then that rich plain, extending from the Tiber under Perusia to Spoletum at the foot of the Monte Somma, was laid waste by the Carthaginians without mercy. The white oxen of the Clitumnus, so often offered in sacrifice to the gods of Rome by her triumphant generals, were now the spoil of the enemy, and were slaughtered on the altars of the gods of Carthage, amidst prayers for

[1] Polybius, III. 85.
[2] Livy, XXII. 7. Compare Valerius Maximus, V. 1. Ext. 6.
[3] Polybius, III. 86.

the destruction of Rome. The left bank of the A.U.C. 537.
Tiber again heard the Gaulish war-cry; and the A.C. 217.
terrified inhabitants fled to the mountains or into
the fortified cities from this unwonted storm of
barbarian invasion. The figures and arms of the
Gauls, however formidable, might be familiar to
many of the Umbrians; but they gazed in wonder
on the slingers from the Balearian islands, on the
hardy Spanish foot, conspicuous by their white linen
coats bordered with scarlet;[1] on the regular African
infantry, who had not yet exchanged their long
lances and small shields for the long shield and
stabbing sword of the Roman soldier; on the heavy
cavalry, so numerous, and mounted on horses so
superior to those of Italy; above all, on the bands
of wild Numidians, who rode without saddle or
bridle, as if the rider and his horse were one
creature, and who scoured over the country with a
speed and impetuosity defying escape or resistance.
Amidst such a scene the colonists of Spoletum deserved well of their country for shutting their
gates boldly and not yielding to the general panic;
and when the Numidian horsemen reined up their
horses, and turned away from its well-manned walls,
the colonists, with an excusable boasting, might
claim the glory of having repulsed Hannibal.[2]

But Hannibal's way lay not over the Monte He marches
Somma, although its steep pass, rising immediately into Apulia.
behind Spoletum, was the last natural obstacle between him and Rome. Beyond that pass the country
was full, not of Roman colonies merely, but of Roman

---

[1] Polybius, III. 114. Livy, XXII. 46.
[2] Livy, XXII. 9.

citizens : he would soon have entered on the territory of the thirty-five Roman tribes, where every man whom he would have met was his enemy. His eyes were fixed elsewhere ; the south was entirely open to him ; the way to Apulia and Samnium was cleared of every impediment. He crossed the Apennines in the direction of Ancona, and invaded Picenum ; he then followed the coast of the Adriatic, through the country of the Marrucinians and Frentanians, till he arrived in the northern part of Apulia, in the country called by the Greeks Daunia.[1] He advanced slowly and leisurely, encamping after short marches, and spreading devastation far and wide ; the plunder of slaves, cattle, corn, wine, oil, and valuable property of every description, was almost more than the army could carry or drive along. The soldiers, who after their exhausting march from Spain over the Alps had ever since been in active service, or in wretched quarters, and who from cold and the want of oil for anointing the skin had suffered severely from scorbutic disorders, were now revelling in plenty in a land of corn and olives and vines, where all good things were in such abundance that the very horses of the army, so said report, were bathed in old wines to improve their condition.[2] Meanwhile, wherever the army passed, all Roman or Latins, of an age to bear arms, were by Hannibal's express orders put to the sword.[3] Many an occupier of domain land, many a farmer of the taxes, or of those multiplied branches of revenue which the Roman government possessed all

<hr>

[1] Polybius, III. 86. Livy, XXII. 9.
[2] Polybius, III. 87, 88.   [3] Polybius, III. 86.

over Italy, collectors of customs and port duties, surveyors and farmers of the forests, farmers of the mountain pastures, farmers of the salt on the sea coast, and of the mines in the mountains, were cut off by the vengeance of the Carthaginians; and Rome, having lost thousands of her poorer citizens in battle, and now losing hundreds of the richer classes in this exterminating march, lay bleeding at every pore.

But her spirit was invincible. When the tidings of the disaster of Thrasymenus reached the city the people crowded to the Forum, and called upon the magistrates to tell them the whole truth.[1] The prætor peregrinus, M. Pomponius Matho, ascended the rostra, and said to the assembled multitude, 'We have been beaten in a great battle; our army is destroyed; and C. Flaminius, the consul, is killed.' Our colder temperaments scarcely enable us to conceive the effect of such tidings on the lively feelings of the people of the south, or to image to ourselves the cries, the tears, the hands uplifted in prayer, or clenched in rage, the confused sound of ten thousand voices, giving utterance with breathless rapidity to their feelings of eager interest, of terror, of grief, or of fury. All the northern gates of the city were beset with crowds of wives and mothers, imploring every fresh fugitive from the fatal field for some tidings of those most dear to them. The prætors, M. Æmilius and M. Pomponius, kept the senate sitting for several days, from sunrise to sunset, without adjournment, in earnest consultation on the alarming state of their country.

A.U.C. 537. A.C. 217.

State of Rome on hearing the news of the battle.

---

[1] Polybius, III. 85. Livy, XXII. 7.

A.U.C. 537.
A.C. 217.
Fabius
Maximus is
appointed
dictator.

Peace was not thought of for a moment, nor was it proposed to withdraw a single soldier from Spain, or Sicily, or Sardinia; but it was resolved that a dictator ought to be appointed to secure unity of command. There had been no dictatorship for actual service since that of A. Atilius Calatinus, two-and-thirty years before, in the disastrous consulship of P. Claudius Pulcher and L. Junius Pullus. But it is probable that some jealousy was entertained of the senate's choice if, in the absence of the consul Cn. Servilius, the appointment, according to ancient usage, had rested with them; nor was it thought safe to leave the dictator to nominate his master of the horse. Hence an unusual course was adopted; the centuries in their comitia elected both the one and the other, choosing one from each of the two parties in the state; the dictator, Q. Fabius Maximus, from one of the noblest, but at the same time the most moderate families of the aristocracy, and himself a man of a nature no less gentle than wise; the master of the horse, M. Minucius Rufus, as representing the popular party.[1]

Measures
to propi-
tiate the
gods.

Religion in the mind of Q. Fabius was not a mere instrument for party purposes: although he may have had little belief in its truth, he was convinced of its excellence, and that a reverence for the gods was an essential element in the character of a nation, without which it must assuredly degenerate. Therefore, on the very day that he entered on his office, he summoned the senate, and, dwelling on the importance of propitiating the gods, moved that the Sibylline books should forthwith be consulted.[2] They

---

[1] Polybius, III. 87. Livy, XXII. 8.   [2] Livy, XXII. 9.

directed, among other things, that the Roman people A.U.C. 537.
A.C. 217. should vow to the gods what was called 'a holy spring'—that is to say, that every animal fit for sacrifice born in the spring of that year, between the first day of March and the thirtieth of April, and reared on any mountain or plain or river bank or upland pasture throughout Italy, should be offered to Jupiter.[1] Extraordinary games were also vowed to be celebrated in the Circus Maximus; prayers were put up at all the temples; new temples were vowed to be built; and for three days those solemn sacrifices were performed, in which the images of the gods were taken down from their temples and laid on couches richly covered, with tables full of meat and wine set before them, in the sight of all the people, as if the gods could not but bless the city where they had deigned to receive hospitality.

Then the dictator turned his attention to the state of the war. A long campaign was in prospect, for it was still so early in the season that the prætors had not yet gone out to their provinces, and Hannibal was already in the heart of Italy. All measures were taken for the defence of the country; even the wall and towers of Rome were ordered to be made good against an attack. Bridges were to be broken down, the inhabitants of open towns were to withdraw into places of security, and in the expected line of Hannibal's march the country was to be laid waste before him, the corn destroyed, and the houses burnt.[2] This would probably be done effectually in the Roman territory, but the allies were not likely to make such extreme sacrifices, and this of itself

Plan of Fabius for the campaign.

---

[1] Livy, XXII. 10.   [2] Livy, XXII. 11.

A.U.C. 537.
A.C. 217.
was a reason why Hannibal did not advance directly upon Rome.

Roman levies. More than 30,000 men, in killed and prisoners, had been lost to the Romans in the late battle. The consul, Cn. Servilius, commanded above 30,000 in Cisalpine Gaul, and he was now retreating in all haste, after having heard of the total defeat of his colleague. Two new legions were raised, besides a large force out of the city tribes, which was employed partly for the defence of Rome itself, and partly, as it consisted largely of the poorer citizens, for the service of the fleet. This last indeed was become a matter of urgent necessity, for the Carthaginian fleet was already on the Italian coast, and had taken a whole convoy of corn-ships off Cosa, in Etruria, carrying supplies to the army in Spain, while the Roman ships, both in Sicily and at Ostia, had not yet been launched after the winter.[1] Now all the ships at Ostia and in the Tiber were sent to sea in haste, and the consul, Cn. Servilius, commanded them, whilst the dictator and master of the horse, having added the two newly raised legions to the consul's army, proceeded through Campania and Samnium into Apulia, and, with an army greatly superior in numbers, encamped at a distance of about five or six miles from Hannibal.[2]

Hannibal ravages Samnium and enters Campania. Besides the advantage of numbers the Romans had that of being regularly and abundantly supplied with provisions. They had no occasion to scatter their forces in order to obtain subsistence; but keeping their army together, and exposing no weak point to fortune, they followed Hannibal at a certain distance,

[1] Livy, XXII. 11.   [2] Polybius, III. 88.

54'

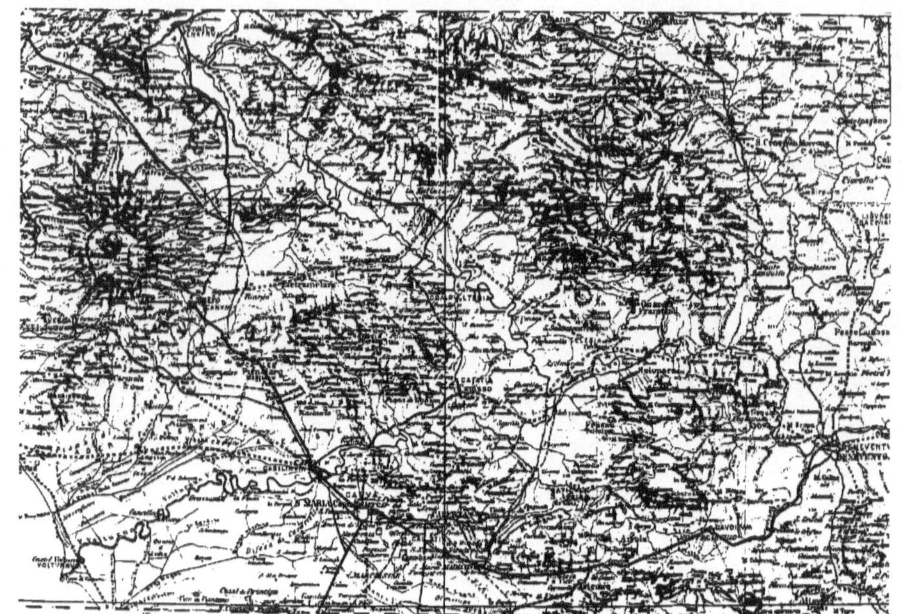

watched their opportunity to cut off his detached A.U.C. 537.
parties, and above all, by remaining in the field with A.C. 217.
so imposing an army, overawed the allies, and checked
their disposition to revolt.[1]   Thus Hannibal, finding
that the Apulians did not join him, recrossed the
Apennines, and moved through the country of the
Hirpinians into that of the Caudinian Samnites.
But Beneventum, once a great Samnite city, was
now a Latin colony, and its gates were close shut
against the invader.   Hannibal laid waste its territory with fire and sword, then moved onwards under
the south side of the Matese, and took possession of
Telesia, the native city of C. Pontius, but now a
decayed and defenceless town; thence descending
the Calor to its junction with the Vulturnus, and
ascending the Vulturnus till he found it easily fordable, he finally crossed it near Allifæ, and passing
over the hills behind Calatia, descended by Cales
into the midst of the Falernian plain, the glory of
Campania.[2]

Fabius steadily followed him, not descending into Fabius fol-
the plain, but keeping his army on the hills above lows him.
it, and watching all his movements.   Again the
Numidian cavalry were seen scouring the country on
every side, and the smoke of burning houses marked
their track.   The soldiers in the Roman army beheld the sight with the greatest impatience.   They
were burning for battle, and the master of the horse
himself shared and encouraged the general feeling.
But Fabius was firm in his resolution; he sent
parties to secure even the pass of Tarracina, lest
Hannibal should attempt to advance by the Appian

---

[1] Polybius, III. 90.   [2] Polybius, III. 90. Livy, XXII. 13.

A.U.C. 537.
A.C. 217.

road upon Rome; he garrisoned Casilinum on the enemy's rear; the Vulturnus from Casilinum to the sea barred all retreat southwards; the colony of Cales stopped the outlet from the plain by the Latin road; while from Cales to Casilinum the hills formed an unbroken barrier, steep and wooded, the few paths over which were already secured by Roman soldiers.[1] Thus Fabius thought that Hannibal was caught as in a pitfall; that his escape was cut off, while his army, having soon wasted its plunder, could not possibly winter where it was, without magazines, and without a single town in its possession. For himself, he had all the resources of Campania and Samnium on his rear, while on his right the Latin road, secured by the colonies of Cales, Casinum, and Fregellæ, kept his communications with Rome open.

Hannibal's artifice to escape the Roman army.

Hannibal on his part had no thought of wintering where he was; but he had carefully husbanded his plunder that it might supply his winter consumption, so that it was important to him to carry it off in safety. He had taken many thousand cattle, and his army besides was encumbered with its numerous prisoners, over and above the corn, wine, oil, and other articles which had been furnished by the ravage of one of the richest districts in Italy. Finding that the passes in the hills between Cales and the Vulturnus were occupied by the enemy, he began to consider how he could surprise or force his passage without abandoning any of his plunder. He first thought of his numerous prisoners, and dreading lest in a night march they should either escape or

[1] Livy, XXII. 15.

overpower their guards and join their countrymen A.U.C. 537.
in attacking him, he commanded them all, to the A.C. 217.
number it is said of 5000 men, to be put to the
sword. Then he ordered 2000 of the stoutest
oxen to be selected from the plundered cattle, and
pieces of split pine wood, or dry vine wood, to be
fastened to their horns. About two hours before
midnight the drovers began to drive them straight
to the hills, having first set on fire the bundles of
wood about their heads; while the light infantry
following them till they began to run wild, then
made their own way to the hills, scouring the points
just above the pass occupied by the enemy. Hannibal then commenced his march; his African infantry
led the way, followed by the cavalry. Then came
all the baggage, and the rear was covered by the
Spaniards and Gauls. In this order he followed
the road in the defile, by which he was to get out
into the upper valley of the Vulturnus, above Casilinum and the enemy's army.[1]

He found the way quite clear; for the Romans Its success.
who had guarded it, seeing the hills above them
illuminated on a sudden with a multitude of moving
lights, and nothing doubting that Hannibal's army
was attempting to break out over the hills in despair
of forcing the road, quitted their position in haste,
and ran towards the heights to intercept or embarrass
his retreat. Meanwhile Fabius, with his main army,
confounded at the strangeness of the sight, and
dreading lest Hannibal was tempting him to his
ruin as he had tempted Flaminius, kept close within
his camp till the morning. Day dawned only to

[1] Polybius, III. 93. Livy, XXII. 16, 17. See Note F.

show him his own troops, who had been set to occupy the defile, engaged on the hills above with Hannibal's light infantry. But presently the Spanish foot were seen scaling the heights to reinforce the enemy, and the Romans were driven down to the plain with great loss and confusion, while the Spaniards and the light troops, having thoroughly done their work, disappeared behind the hills, and followed their main army.[1] Thus completely successful, and leaving his shamed and baffled enemy behind him, Hannibal no longer thought of returning to Apulia by the most direct road, but resolved to extend his devastations still further before the season ended. He mounted the valley of the Vulturnus towards Venafrum, marched from thence into Samnium, crossed the Apennines, and descended into the rich Pelignian plain by Sulmo, which yielded him an ample harvest of plunder, and thence retracing his steps into Samnium, he finally returned to the neighbourhood of his old quarters in Apulia.

His plan for the winter.

The summer was far advanced; Hannibal had overrun the greater part of Italy: the meadows of the Clitumnus and the Vulturnus, and the forest glades of the high Apennines, had alike seen their cattle driven away by the invading army; the Falernian plain and the plain of Sulmo had alike yielded their tribute of wine and oil; but not a single city had as yet opened its gates to the conqueror, not a single state of Samnium had welcomed him as its champion, under whom it might revenge its old wrongs against Rome. Everywhere the

[1] Polybius, III. 94. Livy, XXII. 18.

aristocratical party had maintained its ascendency, A.U.C. 537.
A.C. 217.
and had repressed all mention of revolt from Rome.
Hannibal's great experiment therefore had hitherto
failed. He knew that his single army could not
conquer Italy; as easily might King William's
Dutch guards have conquered England; and six
months had brought Hannibal no fairer prospect of
aid within the country itself than the first week
after his landing in Torbay brought to King William.
But among Hannibal's greatest qualities was the
patience with which he knew how to abide his
time. If one campaign had failed of its main
object another must be tried; if the fidelity of the
Roman allies had been unshaken by the disaster of
Thrasymenus, it must be tried by a defeat yet more
fatal. Meantime he would take undisputed possession of the best winter quarters in Italy; his men
would be plentifully fed; his invaluable cavalry
would have forage in abundance, and this at no cost
to Carthage, but wholly at the expense of the enemy.
The point which he fixed upon to winter at was the
very edge of the Apulian plain, where it joins the
mountains: on one side was a boundless expanse
of corn, intermixed with open grass land, burnt up
in summer, but in winter fresh and green, whilst
on the other side were the wide pastures of the
mountain forests where his numerous cattle might
be turned out till the first snows of autumn fell.
These were as yet far distant, for the corn in the
plain, although ripe, was still standing, and the
rich harvests of Apulia were to be gathered this
year by unwonted reapers.

Descending from Samnium, Hannibal accordingly He takes
Geronium.

A.U.C. 537. A.C. 217. appeared before the little town of Geronium, which was situated somewhat more than twenty miles north-west of the Latin colony of Luceria, in the immediate neighbourhood of Larinum.[1] The town, refusing to surrender, was taken, and the inhabitants put to the sword, but the houses and walls were left standing, to serve as a great magazine for the army, and the soldiers were quartered in a regularly fortified camp without the town. Here Hannibal posted himself, and, keeping a third part of his men under arms to guard the camp and to cover his foragers, he sent out the other two-thirds to gather in all the corn of the surrounding country, or to pasture his cattle on the adjoining mountains. In this manner the storehouses of Geronium were in a short time filled with corn.

Unpopularity of Fabius. Meanwhile the public mind at Rome was strongly excited against the dictator. He seemed like a man who, having played a cautious game, at last makes a false move and is beaten. His slow, defensive system, unwelcome in itself, seemed rendered contemptible by Hannibal's triumphant escape from the Falernian plain. But here too Fabius showed a patience worthy of all honour. Vexed as he must have been at his failure in Campania, he still felt sure that his system was wise; and again he followed Hannibal into Apulia, and encamped as before on the high grounds in his neighbourhood. Certain religious offices called him at this time to Rome; but he charged Minucius to observe his system strictly, and on no account to risk a battle.[2]

---

[1] Polybius, III. 100. Livy. XXII. 23.
[2] Polybius, III. 94. Livy. XXII. 18.

The master of the horse conducted his operations wisely: he advanced his camp to a projecting ridge of hills immediately above the plain, and sending out his cavalry and light troops to cut off Hannibal's foragers, obliged the enemy to increase his covering force, and to restrict the range of his harvesting. On one occasion he cut off a great number of the foragers, and even advanced to attack Hannibal's camp, which, owing to the necessity of detaching so many men all over the country, was left with a very inferior force to defend it. The return of some of the foraging parties obliged the Romans to retreat; but Minucius was greatly elated, and sent home very encouraging reports of his success.[1]

The feeling against Fabius could no longer be restrained. Minucius had known how to manage his system more ably than he had done himself. Such merit at such a crisis deserved to be rewarded; nor was it fit that the popular party should continue to be deprived of its share in the conduct of the war. Even among his own party Fabius was not universally popular. He had magnified himself and his system somewhat offensively, and had spoken too harshly of the blunders of former generals. Thus it does not appear that the aristocracy offered any strong resistance to a bill brought forward by the tribune M. Metilius for giving the master of the horse power equal to the dictator's. The bill was strongly supported by C. Terentius Varro, who had been prætor in the preceding year, and was easily carried.[2]

---

[1] Polybius, III. 101, 102. Livy, XXII. 24.
[2] Polybius, III. 103. Livy, XXII. 25, 26.

A.U.C. 537.
A.C. 217.
He is
routed, and
Fabius
saves him.

The dictator and master of the horse now divided the army between them, and encamped apart, at more than a mile's distance from each other. Their want of co-operation was thus notorious; and Hannibal was not slow to profit by it. He succeeded in tempting Minucius to an engagement on his own ground; and having concealed about 5000 men in some ravines and hollows close by, he called them forth in the midst of the action to fall on the enemy's rear. The rout of the Trebia was well-nigh repeated; but Fabius was near enough to come up in time to the rescue; and his fresh legions checked the pursuit of the conquerors, and enabled the broken Romans to rally. Still the loss already sustained was severe; and it was manifest that Fabius had saved his colleague from total destruction. Minucius acknowledged this generously; he instantly gave up his equal and separate command, and placed himself and his army under the dictator's orders.[1] The rest of the season passed quietly; and the dictator and master of the horse resigning their offices as usual at the end of six months, the army during the winter was put under the command of the consuls; Cn. Servilius having brought home and laid up the fleet, which he had commanded during the summer, and M. Atilius Regulus having been elected to fill the place of Flaminius.

State of
feeling at
Rome.

Meanwhile the elections for the following year were approaching, and it was evident that they would be marked by severe party struggles. The mass of the Roman people were impatient of the

[1] Polybius, III. 104, 105. Livy, XXI. 28, 29. Plutarch, Fabius, 13.

continuance of the war in Italy; not only the a.u.c. 537.
a.c. 217. poorer citizens, whom it obliged to constant military service through the winter, and with no prospect of plunder, but still more perhaps the moneyed classes, whose occupation as farmers of the revenue was so greatly curtailed by Hannibal's army. Again, the occupiers of domain lands in remote parts of Italy could get no returns from their property; the wealthy graziers, who fed their cattle on the domain pastures, saw their stock carried off to furnish winter provisions for the enemy. Besides, if Hannibal were allowed to be unassailable in the field, the allies sooner or later must be expected to join him; they would not sacrifice every thing for Rome, if Rome could neither protect them nor herself. The excellence of the Roman infantry was undisputed; if with equal numbers they could not conquer Hannibal's veterans, let their numbers be increased, and they must overwhelm him. These were no doubt the feelings of many of the nobility themselves, as well as of the majority of the people, but they were embittered by party animosity; the aristocracy, it was said, seemed bent on throwing reproach on all generals of the popular party, as if none but themselves were fit to conduct the war; Minucius himself had yielded to this spirit by submitting to be commanded by Fabius when the law had made him his equal; one consul at least must be chosen, who would act firmly for himself and for the people; and such a man, to whose merits the bitter hatred of the aristocratical party bore the best testimony, was to be found in C. Terentius Varro.[1]

---

[1] Livy, XXII. 34.

Varro, his enemies said, was a butcher's son; nay, it was added that he had himself been a butcher's boy,[1] and had only been enabled by the fortune which his father had left him to throw aside his ignoble calling, and to aspire to public offices. So Cromwell was called a brewer, but Varro had been successively elected quæstor, plebeian and curule ædile, and prætor, while we are not told that he was ever tribune, and it is without example in Roman history that a mere demagogue, of no family, with no other merits, civil or military, should be raised to such nobility. Varro was eloquent, it is true, but eloquence alone would scarcely have so recommended him, and if in his prætorship, as is probable, he had been one of the two home prætors, he must have possessed a competent knowledge of law. Besides, even after his defeat at Cannæ, he was employed for several years in various important offices, civil and military, which would never have been the case had he been the mere factious braggart that historians have painted him. The aristocracy tried in vain to prevent his election; he was not only returned consul, but he was returned alone, no other candidate obtaining a sufficient number of votes to entitle him to the suffrage of a tribe.[2] Thus he held the comitia for the election of his colleague, and considering the great influence exercised by the magistrate so presiding, it is creditable to him, and to the temper of the people generally, that the other consul chosen was L. Æmilius Paullus, who was not only a known partisan of the aristocracy, but having been consul three years before,

---

[1] Valerius Maximus, III. 4, 4.　　　[2] Livy, XXII. 35.

had been brought to trial for an alleged misappro-
priation of the plunder taken in the Illyrian war,
and, although acquitted, was one of the most unpopular men in Rome. Yet he was known to be a
good soldier, and the people having obtained the
election of Varro, did not object to gratify the
aristocracy by accepting the candidate of their
choice.

No less moderate and impartial was the temper
shown in the elections of prætors. Two of the four
were decidedly of the aristocratical party, M. Marcellus and L. Postumius Albinus; the other two
were also men of consular rank, and no way known
as opponents of the nobility, P. Furius Philus and
M. Pomponius Matho. The two latter were to
have the home prætorships, Marcellus was to command the fleet, and take charge of the southern
coast of Italy, L. Postumius was to watch the
frontier of Cisalpine Gaul.

The winter and spring passed without any mili-
tary events of importance. Servilius and Regulus
retained their command as proconsuls for some time
after their successors had come into office, but
nothing beyond occasional skirmishes took place
between them and the enemy. Hannibal was at
Geronium, maintaining his army on the supplies
which he had so carefully collected in the preceding
campaign; the consuls apparently were posted a
little to the southward, receiving their supplies from
the country about Canusium, and immediately from
a large magazine, which they had established at the
small town of Cannæ, near the Aufidus.[1]

<hr>

[1] Polybius, III. 107.

Never was Hannibal's genius more displayed than during this long period of inactivity. More than half of his army consisted of Gauls, of all barbarians the most impatient and uncertain in their humour, whose fidelity, it was said, could only be secured by an ever open hand; no man was their friend any longer than he could gorge them with pay or plunder. Those of his soldiers who were not Gauls were either Spaniards or Africans; the Spaniards were the newly conquered subjects of Carthage, strangers to her race and language, and accustomed to divide their lives between actual battle and the most listless bodily indolence, so that, when one of their tribes first saw the habits of a Roman camp, and observed the centurions walking up and down before the prætorium for exercise, the Spaniards thought them mad, and ran up to guide them to their tents, thinking that he who was not fighting could do nothing but lie at his ease and enjoy himself.[1] Even the Africans were foreigners to Carthage; they were subjects harshly governed, and had been engaged within the last twenty years in a war of extermination with their masters. Yet the long inactivity of winter quarters, trying to the discipline of the best national armies, was borne patiently by Hannibal's soldiers; there was neither desertion nor mutiny amongst them; even the fickleness of the Gauls seemed spell-bound, they remained steadily in their camp in Apulia, neither going home to their own country nor over to the enemy. On the contrary, it seems that fresh bands of Gauls must have joined the Carthaginian army after the

[1] Strabo, III. 4, 16. Cas. p. 164.

battle of Thrasymenus, and the retreat of the Roman A.U.C. 538. army from Ariminum.   For the Gauls and the A.C. 216. Spaniards and the Africans were overpowered by the ascendency of Hannibal's character; under his guidance they felt themselves invincible: with such a general the yoke of Carthage might seem to the Africans and Spaniards the natural dominion of superior beings; in such a champion the Gauls beheld the appointed instrument of their country's gods to lead them once more to assault the Capitol.

Silenus, the Greek historian, was living with Silenus. Hannibal daily;[1] and though not entrusted with his military and political secrets, he must have seen and known him as a man; he must have been familiar with his habits of life, and must have heard his conversation in those unrestrained moments when the lightest words of great men display the character of their minds so strikingly.   His work is lost to us; but had it been worthy of his opportunities, anecdotes from it must have been quoted by other writers, and we should know what Hannibal was.   Then, too, the generals who were his daily companions would be something more to us than names: we should know Maharbal, the best cavalry officer of the finest cavalry service in the world; and Hasdrubal, who managed the commissariat of the army for so many years in an enemy's country; and Hannibal's young brother, Mago, so full of youthful spirit and enterprise, who commanded the ambush at the battle of the Trebia.   We might learn something too of that Hannibal, surnamed the Fighter, who was the general's counsellor,

---

[1] Nepos, Hannib. c. XIII.

F

ever prompting him, it was said, to deeds of savage cruelty,[1] but whose counsels Hannibal would not have listened to had they been merely cruel, had they not breathed a spirit of deep devotion to the cause of Carthage, and of deadly hatred to Rome, such as possessed the heart of Hannibal himself. But Silenus saw and heard without heeding or recording, and on the tent and camp of Hannibal there hangs a veil which the fancy of the poet may penetrate, but the historian turns away in deep disappointment, for to him it yields neither sight nor sound.

Spring was come, and well-nigh departing; and in the warm plains of Apulia the corn was ripening fast, while Hannibal's winter supplies were now nearly exhausted. He broke up from his camp before Geronium, descended into the Apulian plains, and whilst the Roman army was still in its winter position, he threw himself on its rear, and surprised its great magazine at Cannæ.[2] The citadel of Cannæ was a fortress of some strength; this accordingly he occupied, and placed himself, on the very eve of harvest, between the Roman army and its expected resources, while he secured to himself all the corn of southern Apulia. It was only in such low and warm situations that the corn was nearly ready; the higher country, in the immediate neighbourhood of Samnium, is cold and backward, and the Romans were under the necessity of receiving their supplies from a great distance, or else of retreating or of offering battle. Under these circumstances the proconsuls sent to Rome to ask what they were to do.

[1] Polybius, IX. 24.　　[2] Polybius, III. 107. Livy, XXII. 40, 43.

The turning point of this question lay in the disposition of the allies. We cannot doubt that Hannibal had been busy during the winter in sounding their feelings; and now it appeared that if Italy was to be ravaged by the enemy for a second summer without resistance their patience would endure no longer. The Roman government therefore resolved to risk a battle; but they sent orders to the proconsuls to wait till the consuls should join them with their newly raised army; for, a battle being resolved upon, the senate hoped to secure success by an overwhelming superiority of numbers. We do not exactly know the proportion of the new levies to the old soldiers; but when the two consuls arrived on the scene of action, and took the supreme command of the whole army, there were no fewer than eight Roman legions under their orders, with an equal force of allies; so that the army opposed to Hannibal must have amounted to 90,000 men.[1] It was evident that so great a multitude could not long be fed at a distance from its resources; and thus a speedy engagement was inevitable.

But the details of the movements by which the two armies were brought in presence of each other on the banks of the Aufidus are not easy to discover. It appears that the Romans, till the arrival of the new consuls, had not ventured to follow Hannibal closely; for, when they did follow him, it took them two days' march to arrive in his neighbourhood, where they encamped at about six miles' distance from him.[2] They found him on the left

A.U.C. 538.
A.C. 216.
The Roman
army.

Varro re-
solves to
bring on a
battle.

---

[1] Polybius, III. 107.   [2] Polybius, III. 110.

<table>
<tr><td>A.U.C. 538.
A.C. 216.</td><td>bank of the Aufidus, about eight or nine miles from the sea, and busied probably in collecting the corn from the early district on the coast, the season being about the middle of June. The country here was so level and open that the consul L. Æmilius was unwilling to approach the enemy more closely, but wished to take a position on the hilly ground farther from the sea, and to bring on the action there.[1] But Varro, impatient for battle, and having the supreme command of the whole army alternately with Æmilius every other day, decided the question irrevocably on the very next day, by interposing himself between the enemy and the sea, with his left resting on the Aufidus, and his right communicating with the town of Salapia.</td></tr>
<tr><td>Æmilius
crosses the
Aufidus.</td><td>From this position Æmilius, when he again took the command in chief, found it impossible to withdraw. But availing himself of his great superiority in numbers, he threw a part of his army across the river, and posted them in a separate camp on the right bank, to have the supplies of the country south of the Aufidus at command, and to restrain the enemy's parties who might attempt to forage in that direction. When Hannibal saw the Romans in this situation, he also advanced nearer to them, descending the left bank of the Aufidus, and encamped over against the main army of the enemy, with his right resting on the river.</td></tr>
<tr><td>Prepara-
tory man-
œuvres and
skirmishes.</td><td>The next day, which, according to the Roman calendar, was the last of the month Quinctilis, or July, the Roman reckoning being six or seven weeks in advance of the true season, Hannibal was making</td></tr>
</table>

[1] Polybius, III. 110.

his preparations for battle, and did not stir from his A.U.C. 538. A.C. 216. camp; so that Varro, whose command it was, could not bring on an action. But on the first of Sextilis, or August, Hannibal, being now quite ready, drew out his army in front of his camp and offered battle. Æmilius, however, remained quiet, resolved not to fight on such ground, and hoping that Hannibal would soon be obliged to fall back nearer the hills, when he found that he could no longer forage freely in the country near the sea.[1] Hannibal, seeing that the enemy did not move, marched back his infantry into his camp, but sent his Numidian cavalry across the river to attack the Romans on that side, as they were coming down in straggling parties to the bank to get water. For the Aufidus, though its bed is deep and wide, to hold its winter floods, is a shallow or a narrow stream in summer, with many points easily fordable, not by horse only but by infantry. The watering parties were driven in with some loss, and the Numidians followed them to the very gates of the camp, and obliged the Romans, on the right bank, to pass the summer night in the burning Apulian plain without water.

At daybreak on the next morning, the red ensign, which was the well-known signal for battle, was seen flying over Varro's headquarters;[2] and he issued orders, it being his day of command, for the main army to cross the river, and form in order of battle on the right bank. Whether he had any farther object in crossing to the right bank than to enable the soldiers on that side to get water in security we

Hannibal draws out his army.

---

[1] Polybius, III. 111. Livy, XXII. 45.
[2] Plutarch, Fabius, 15.

do not know; but Hannibal, it seems, thought that the ground on either bank suited him equally, and he too forded the stream at two separate points, and drew out his army opposite to the enemy. The strong town of Canusium was scarcely three miles off in his rear; he had left his camp on the other side of the river; if he were defeated, escape seemed hopeless. But when he saw the wide open plain around him, and looked at his numerous and irresistible cavalry, and knew that his infantry, however inferior in numbers, were far better and older soldiers than the great mass of their opponents, he felt that defeat was impossible. In this confidence his spirits were not cheerful merely, but even mirthful; he rallied one of his officers jestingly, who noticed the overwhelming numbers of the Romans; those near him laughed; and as any feeling at such a moment is contagious, the laugh was echoed by others; and the soldiers, seeing their great general in such a mood, were satisfied that he was sure of victory.[1]

Its position. The Carthaginian army faced the north, so that the early sun shone on their right flank, while the

---

[1] Plutarch, Fabius, 15. Εἰπόντος δέ τινος τῶν περὶ αὐτὸν ἀνδρὸς ἰσοτίμου, τοὔνομα Γίσκωνος, ὡς θαυμαστὸν αὐτῷ φαίνεται τὸ πλῆθος τῶν πολεμίων, συναγαγὼν τὸ πρόσωπον ὁ Ἀννίβας, 'ἕτερον,' εἶπεν, 'ὦ Γίσκων, λέληθέ σε τούτου θαυμασιώτερον.' Ἐρομένου δὲ τοῦ Γίσκωνος 'Τὸ ποῖον;' '"Οτι,' ἔφη, 'τούτων ὄντων τοσούτων, οὐδεὶς ἐν αὐτοῖς Γίσκων καλεῖται.' Γενομένου δὲ παρὰ δόξαν αὐτοῖς τοῦ σκώμματος ἐμπίπτει γέλως πᾶσι· καὶ κατέβαινον ἀπὸ τοῦ λόφου τοῖς ἀπαντῶσιν ἀεὶ τὸ πεπαιγμένον ἀπαγγέλλοντες, ὥστε διὰ πολλῶν πολὺν εἶναι τὸν γέλωτα καὶ μηδ' ἀναλαβεῖν ἑαυτοὺς δύνασθαι τοὺς περὶ τὸν Ἀννίβαν. Τοῦτο τοῖς Καρχηδονίοις ἰδοῦσι θάρρος παρέστη λογιζομένοις ἀπὸ πολλοῦ καὶ ἰσχυροῦ τοῦ καταφρονοῦντος ἐπιέναι γελᾶν οὕτω καὶ παίζειν τῷ στρατηγῷ παρὰ τὸν κίνδυνον.

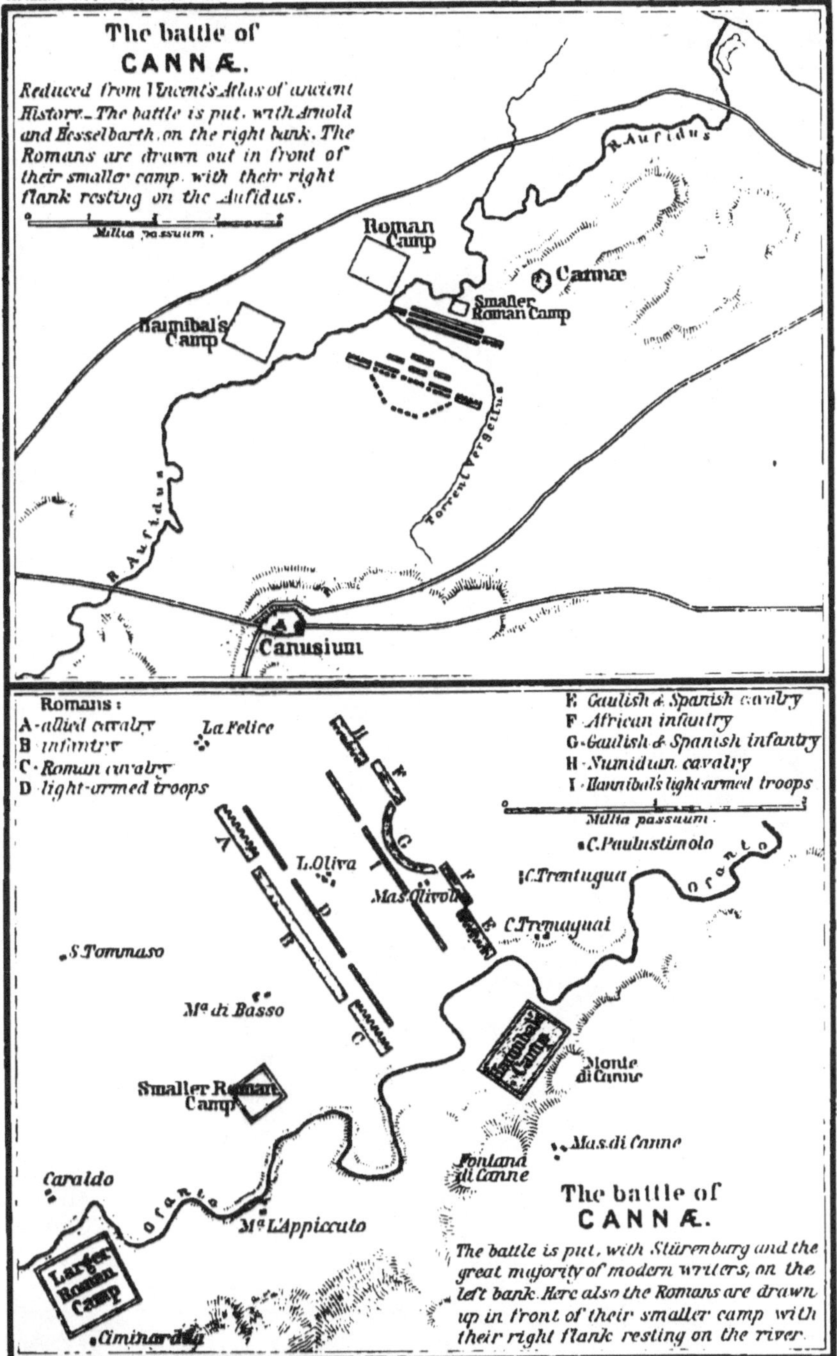

Battle of Cannæ: see note H.

London, Macmillan & Co.

wind, which blew strong from the south, but with- A.U.C. 538.
out a drop of rain, swept its clouds of dust over A.C. 216.
their backs, and carried them full into the faces of
the enemy.[1] On their left, resting on the river,
were the Spanish and Gaulish horse; next in the
line, but thrown back a little, were half of the
African infantry armed like the Romans; on their
right, somewhat in advance, were the Gauls and
Spaniards, with their companies intermixed; then
came the rest of the African foot, again thrown back
like their comrades; and on the right of the whole
line were the Numidian light horsemen.[2] The right
of the army rested, so far as appears, on nothing;
the ground was open and level; but at some distance were hills overgrown with copsewood, and
furrowed with deep ravines, in which, according to
one account of the battle, a body of horsemen and
of light infantry lay in ambush. The rest of the
light troops, and the Balearian slingers, skirmished
as usual in front of the whole line.

Meanwhile the masses of the Roman infantry That of the
were forming their line opposite. The sun on their Roman army.
left flashed obliquely on their brazen helmets, now
uncovered for battle, and lit up the waving forest
of their red and black plumes, which rose upright
from their helmets a foot and a half high.[3]

They stood brandishing their formidable pila,
covered with their long shields, and bearing on
their right thigh their peculiar and fatal weapon,
the heavy sword, fitted alike to cut and to stab.[4]

[1] Livy, XXII. 46.   Plutarch, Fabius, 16.
[2] Polybius, III. 113.   Livy, XXII. 46.
[3] Polybius, IV. 23.   [4] See Note G.

A.U.C. 538.
A.C. 216. On the right of the line were the Roman legions; on the left the infantry of the allies; while between the Roman right and the river were the Roman horsemen, all of them of wealthy or noble families; and on the left, opposed to the Numidians, were the horsemen of the Italians and of the Latin name. The velites or light infantry covered the front, and were ready to skirmish with the light troops and slingers of the enemy.

drawn up in columns. For some reason or other, which is not explained in any account of the battle, the Roman infantry were formed in columns rather than in line, the files of the maniples containing many more than their ranks.[1] This seems an extraordinary tactic to be adopted in a plain by an army inferior in cavalry, but very superior in infantry. Whether the Romans relied on the river as a protection to their right flank, and their left was covered in some manner which is not mentioned,—one account would lead us to suppose that it reached nearly to the sea,[2]—or whether the great proportion of new levies obliged the

---

[1] Polybius, III. 113. ποιῶν πολλαπλάσιον τὸ βάθος ἐν ταῖς σπείραις τοῦ μετώπου. Raleigh suggests that 'this had been found convenient against the Carthaginians in the former war. It was indeed no bad way of resistance against elephants, to make the ranks thick and short, but the files long, as also to strengthen well the rear, that it might stand fast compacted as a wall, under shelter whereof the disordered troops might rally themselves. Thus much it seems that Terentius had learned of some old soldiers; and therefore he now ordered his battles accordingly, as meaning to show more skill than was in his understanding. But the Carthaginians had here no elephants with them in the field : their advantage was in horse, against which this manner of embattailing was very unprofitable, forasmuch as their charge is better sustained in front, than upon a long flank.'

[2] Appian, Hannibal, 21. ὁι τὸ λαιὸν ἔχοντες ἐπὶ τῇ θαλάσσῃ.

Romans to adopt the system of the phalanx, and to place their raw soldiers in the rear, as incapable of fighting in the front ranks with Hannibal's veterans, —it appears at any rate that the Roman infantry, though nearly double the number of the enemy, yet formed a line of only equal length with Hannibal's. A.U.C. 538.
A.C. 216.

The skirmishing of the light-armed troops preluded as usual to the battle: the Balearian slingers slung their stones like hail into the ranks of the Roman line, and severely wounded the consul Æmilius himself. Then the Spanish and Gaulish horse charged the Romans front to front, and maintained a standing fight with them, many leaping off their horses and fighting on foot, till the Romans, outnumbered and badly armed, without cuirasses, with light and brittle spears, and with shields made only of ox-hide, were totally routed, and driven off the field.[1] Hasdrubal, who commanded the Gauls and Spaniards, followed up his work effectually; he chased the Romans along the river till he had almost destroyed them; and then, riding off to the right, he came up to aid the Numidians, who, after their manner, had been skirmishing indecisively with the cavalry of the Italian allies. These, on seeing the Gauls and Spaniards advancing, broke away and fled; the Numidians, most effective in pursuing a flying enemy, chased them with unweariable speed, and slaughtered them unsparingly; while Hasdrubal, to complete his signal services on this day, charged fiercely upon the rear of the Roman infantry. Defeat of
the Roman
cavalry:

He found its huge masses already weltering in Of the
whole
army.

[1] Polybius, III. 115, VI. 25. Livy, XXII. 47.

A.U.C. 538.
A.C. 216. helpless confusion, crowded upon one another, totally disorganised, and fighting each man as he best could, but struggling on against all hope by mere indomitable courage. For the Roman columns on the right and left, finding the Gaulish and Spanish foot advancing in a convex line or wedge, pressed forwards to assail what seemed the flanks of the enemy's column ; so that, being already drawn up with too narrow a front by their original formation, they now became compressed still more by their own movements, the right and left converging towards the centre, till the whole army became one dense column, which forced its way onwards by the weight of its charge, and drove back the Gauls and Spaniards into the rear of their own line. Meanwhile its victorious advance had carried it, like the English column at Fontenoy, into the midst of Hannibal's army ; it had passed between the African infantry on its right and left ; and now, whilst its head was struggling against the Gauls and Spaniards, its long flanks were fiercely assailed by the Africans, who, facing about to the right and left, charged it home and threw it into utter disorder. In this state, when they were forced together into one unwieldy crowd, and already falling by thousands, whilst the Gauls and Spaniards, now advancing in their turn, were barring further progress in front, and whilst the Africans were tearing their mass to pieces on both flanks, Hasdrubal with his victorious Gaulish and Spanish horsemen broke with thundering fury upon their rear. Then followed a butchery such as has no recorded equal, except the slaughter of the Persians in their camp when the Greeks

forced it after the battle of Platæa. Unable to fight A.U.C. 538. or fly, with no quarter asked or given, the Romans A.C. 216. and Italians fell before the swords of their enemies, till, when the sun set upon the field, there were left out of that vast multitude no more than 3000 men alive and unwounded; and these fled in straggling parties, under cover of the darkness, and found a refuge in the neighbouring towns.[1] The consul Æmilius, the proconsul Cn. Servilius, the late master of the horse M. Minucius, two quæstors, twenty-one military tribunes, and eighty senators, lay dead amidst the carnage; Varro with seventy horsemen had escaped from the rout of the allied cavalry on the right of the army, and made his way safely to Venusia.[2]

But the Roman loss was not yet completed. A large force had been left in the camp on the left bank of the Aufidus, to attack Hannibal's camp during the action, which it was supposed that, with his inferior numbers, he could not leave adequately guarded. But it was defended so obstinately, that the Romans were still besieging it in vain, when Hannibal, now completely victorious in the battle, crossed the river to its relief. Then the besiegers fled in their turn to their own camp, and there, cut off from all succour, they presently surrendered. A few resolute men had forced their way out of the smaller camp on the right bank, and had escaped to Canusium; the rest who were in it followed the example of their comrades on the left bank, and surrendered to the conqueror.

Less than 6000 men of Hannibal's army had

Capture of the camps.

Results of the battle.

---

[1] Polybius, III. 116. Livy, XXII. 49. [2] See Note H.

 fallen : no greater price had he paid for the total destruction of more than 80,000 of the enemy, for the capture of their two camps, for the utter annihilation, as it seemed, of all their means for offensive warfare.   It is no wonder that the spirits of the Carthaginian officers were elated by this unequalled victory.   Maharbal, seeing what his cavalry had done, said to Hannibal, 'Let me advance instantly with the horse, and do thou follow to support me ; in four days from this time thou shalt sup in the Capitol.'[1]   There are moments when rashness is wisdom ; and it may be that this was one of them.   The statue of the goddess Victory in the Capitol may well have trembled in every limb on that day, and have dropped her wings, as if for ever. But Hannibal came not; and if for one moment panic had unnerved the iron courage of the Roman aristocracy, on the next their inborn spirit revived ; and their resolute will, striving beyond its present power, created, as is the law of our nature, the power which it required.

[1] Livy, XXII. 51.

CHAPTER II.

FROM New Carthage to the plains of Cannæ, Hannibal's march resembles a mighty torrent, which,
rushing along irresistible and undivided, fixes our
attention to the one line of its course: all other
sights and sounds in the landscape are forgotten,
while we look on the rush of the vast volume of
waters, and listen to their deep and ceaseless roar.
Therefore I have not wished to draw away the
reader's attention to other objects, but to keep it
fixed upon the advance of Hannibal. But from
Cannæ onwards the character of the scene changes.
The single torrent, joined · by a hundred lesser
streams, has now swelled into a wide flood, overwhelming the whole valley; and the principal object of our interest is the one rock, now islanded
amid the waters, and on which they dash furiously
on every side, as though they must inevitably sweep
it away. But the rock stands unshaken : the waters
become feebler ; and their streams are again divided:
and the flood shrinks ; and the rock rises higher and

A.U.C. 538.
A.C. 216.

higher; and the danger is passed away. In the next part of the second Punic war, our attention will be mainly fixed on Rome, as it has hitherto been on Hannibal. But, in order to value aright the mightiness of her energy, we must consider the multitude of her enemies; how all southern Italy, led by Hannibal, struggled with her face to face; how Sicily and Macedon struck at her from behind; how Spain supplied arms to her most dangerous enemy. Yet her policy and her courage were everywhere; Sicily was struck to the earth by one blow; Macedon obliged to defend himself against his nearer enemies; the arms which Spain was offering to Hannibal were torn out of his grasp; revolted Italy was crushed to pieces; and the great enemy, after all his forces were dispersed and destroyed, was obliged, like Hector, to fight singly under his country's walls, and to fall, like Hector, with the consolation of 'having done mighty deeds, to be famed in after ages.'

The news of the defeat reaches Rome.

The Romans, knowing that their army was in presence of the enemy, and that the consuls had been ordered no longer to decline a battle, were for some days in the most intense anxiety. Every tongue was repeating some line of old prophecy, or relating some new wonder or portent; every temple was crowded with supplicants; and incense and sacrifices were offered on every altar. At last the tidings arrived of the utter destruction of both the consular armies, and of a slaughter such as Rome had never before known. Even Livy felt himself unable adequately to paint the grief and consternation of that day;[1] and the experience of the

[1] Livy, XXII. 54.

bloodiest and most embittered warfare of modern A.U.C. 538. times would not help us to conceive it worthily. A.C. 216. But one simple fact speaks eloquently; the whole number of Roman citizens able to bear arms had amounted at the last census to 270,000 ;[1] and supposing, as we fairly may, that the loss of the Romans in the late battles had been equal to that of their allies, there must have been killed or taken, within the last eighteen months, no fewer than 60,000, or more than a fifth part of the whole population of citizens above seventeen years of age. It must have been true, without exaggeration, that every house in Rome was in mourning.

The two home prætors summoned the senate to consult for the defence of the city. Fabius was no longer dictator; yet the supreme government at this moment was effectually in his hands; for the resolutions which he moved were instantly and unanimously adopted. Light horsemen were to be sent out to gather tidings of the enemy's movements; the members of the senate, acting as magistrates, were to keep order in the city, to stop all loud or public lamentations, and to take care that all intelligence was conveyed in the first instance to the prætors : above all, the city gates were to be strictly guarded, that no one might attempt to fly from Rome, but all abide the common danger together.[2] Then the forum was cleared, and the assemblies of the people suspended; for at such a moment, had any one tribune uttered the word 'peace,' the tribes would have caught it up with eagerness, and obliged the senate to negotiate.

Measures taken by the senate.

---

[1] Livy, Epit. XX.   [2] Livy, XXII. 55.

A.U.C. 538.
A.C. 216.
Arrival of
despatches
from Varro.
Thus the first moments of panic passed; and Varro's despatches arrived, informing the senate that he had rallied the wrecks of the army at Canusium, and that Hannibal was not advancing upon Rome.[1] Hope then began to revive; the meetings of the senate were resumed, and measures taken for maintaining the war.

Marcellus
is sent into
Apulia.
M. Marcellus, one of the prætors for the year, was at this moment at Ostia, preparing to sail to Sicily. It was resolved to transfer him at once to the great scene of action in Apulia; and he was ordered to give up the fleet to his colleague P. Furius Philus, and to march with the single legion which he had under his command into Apulia, there to collect the remains of Varro's army, and to fall back as he best could into Campania, while the consul returned immediately to Rome.[2]

Varro's
manly
conduct.
In the meantime the scene at Canusium was like the disorder of a ship going to pieces, when fear makes men desperate, and the instinct of self-preservation swallows up every other feeling. Some young men of the noblest families, a Metellus being at the head of them, looking upon Rome as lost, were planning to escape from the ruin, and to fly beyond sea, in the hope of entering into some foreign service. Such an example at such a moment would have led the way to a general panic: if the noblest citizens of Rome despaired of their country, what allied state, or what colony, could be expected to sacrifice themselves in defence of a hopeless cause? The consul exerted himself to the utmost to check

---

[1] Livy, XXII. 56.
[2] Livy, XXII. 57. Plutarch, Marcellus, 9.

this spirit, and, aided by some firmer spirits amongst A.U.C. 538.
the officers themselves, he succeeded in repressing A.C. 216.
it.[1]   He kept his men together, gave them over to
the prætor Marcellus on his arrival at Canusium,
and prepared instantly to obey the orders of the
senate by returning to Rome.   The fate of P.
Claudius and L. Junius in the last war might have
warned him of the dangers which threatened a defeated general; he himself was personally hateful to
the prevailing party at Rome; and·if the memory
of Flaminius was persecuted, notwithstanding his
glorious death, what could he look for, a fugitive

---

[1] The author would doubtless have explained his reasons for
ascribing the suppression of this conspiracy to leave Italy to Varro.
By Livy, XXII. 53, by Valerius Maximus, V. 6, 7, by Dion, Fragm.
57. § 28 (in the Tauchnitz edition numbered 49, in Gros's text 193)
it is attributed to Scipio.   See also Silius Italicus, X. 427, foll.
It is somewhat remarkable that Polybius makes no mention of the
fact, either in the account of the battle of Cannæ, or in the
character of Scipio, X. 2-5, where he speaks of Scipio's early
exploits [cf. Ranke. Weltgeschichte, II. 2, p. 193].   According to
Livy, with whose account Dion's concurs, the fugitives at Canusium
were headed by four tribunes, who voluntarily submitted to the
command of Scipio and Appius Claudius, two of their number ; and
Scipio, by a characteristic act of youthful heroism, stifled the plot.
Meanwhile Varro is represented to have been at Venusia.   Appian's
account too, Hannibal, 26, though differing as to the order of the
events, and plainly inaccurate,—since it makes Varro resign the
command to Scipio, instead of Marcellus, when he went to Rome,—
implies that Scipio distinguished himself at Canusium.   Dion's statement is the more trustworthy as he did not join in the cry against
Varro, but speaks with high praise of his conduct after the defeat.
'Ες δὲ τὸ Κανύσιον ἐλθὼν τά τε ἐνταῦθα κατεστήσατο, καὶ τοῖς πλησιο-
χώροις φρουρὰς ὡς ἐκ τῶν παρόντων ἔπεμψεν, προσβάλλοντάς τε τῇ πόλει
ἱππέας ἀπεκρούσατο· τότε σύνολον οὔτ' ἀθυμήσας, οὔτε καταπτήξας, ἀλλ'
ἀπ' ὀρθῆς τῆς διανοίας, ὥσπερ μηδενὸς σφίσι δεινοῦ συμβεβηκότος, πάντα
τὰ πρόσφορα τοῖς παροῦσι καὶ ἐβούλευσε καὶ ἔπραξεν. Zonaras (IX. 2,
Dind.) was so careless in abridging his author that he transfers what
Dion here says of Varro to Scipio.—J. C. H.   [See below, p. 280.]

general from that field where his colleague and all his soldiers had perished ?   Demosthenes dared not trust himself to the Athenian people after his defeat in Ætolia ; but Varro, with a manlier spirit, returned to bear the obloquy and the punishment which the popular feeling, excited by party animosity, was so likely to heap on him.   He stopped as usual without the city walls, and summoned the senate to meet him in the Campus Martius.

The senate thank him.

The senate felt his confidence in them, and answered it nobly.   All party feeling was suspended ; all popular irritation was subdued ; the butcher's son, the turbulent demagogue, the defeated general, were all forgotten ; only Varro's latest conduct was remembered, that he had resisted the panic of his officers, and, instead of seeking shelter at the court of a foreign king, had submitted himself to the judgment of his countrymen.   The senate voted him their thanks, ' because he had not despaired of the commonwealth.'[1]

A dictator appointed.

It was resolved to name a dictator ; and some writers related that the general voice of the senate and people offered the dictatorship to Varro himself, but that he positively refused to accept it.[2] This story is extremely doubtful ; but the dictator actually named was M. Junius Pera, a member of a popular family, and who had himself been consul and censor.   His master of the horse was T.

---

[1] Livy, XXII. 61.   Plutarch, Fabius, 18.   See also Florus, I. 22, 17.

[2] Valerius Maximus, III. 4. § 4 ; IV. 5. § 2.   Frontinus, IV. 5, 6 : 'Honoribus, quum ei deferrentur a populo, renuntiavit, dicens, felicioribus magistratibus reipublicæ opus esse.'

Sempronius Gracchus, the first of that noble but ill-
fated name who appears in the Roman annals.[1]

Already, before the appointment of the dictator,
the Roman government had shown that its resolution was fixed to carry on the war to the death.
Hannibal had allowed his Roman prisoners to send
ten of their number to Rome to petition that the
senate would permit the whole body to be ransomed
by their friends at the sum of three minæ, or 3000
asses, for each prisoner.   But the senate absolutely
forbade the money to be paid, neither choosing to
furnish Hannibal with so large a sum, nor to show
any compassion to men who had allowed themselves
to fall alive into the enemies' hands.[2]   The prisoners,
therefore, were left in hopeless captivity, and the
armies which the state required were to be formed
out of other materials.   The expedients adopted
showed the urgency of the danger.

When the consuls took the field at the beginning
of the campaign, two legions had been left, as usual,
to cover the capital.   These were now to be employed in active service; and with them was a
small detachment of troops, which had been drawn
from Picenum and the neighbourhood of Ariminum,
where their services were become of less importance.
The contingents from the allies were not ready, and
there was no time to wait for them.   In order,
therefore, to enable the dictator to take the field
immediately, eight thousand slaves were enlisted,
having expressed their willingness to serve, and

A.U.C. 538.
A.C. 216.

The senate
refuses to
ransom the
prisoners.

Measures
to raise
troops.

---

[1] Livy, XXII. 57.

[2] Polybius, VI. 58.   Livy, XXII. 58-61.   Appian, VII. 28.
Cicero de Off. I. 13 ; III. 32.   Aulus Gellius, VI. 18.

A.U.C. 538.
A.C. 216.
arms were provided by taking down from the temples the spoils won in former wars.[1] The dictator went still further: he offered pardon to criminals and release to debtors if they were willing to take up arms; and amongst the former class were some bands of robbers, who then, as in later times, infested the mountains, and who consented to serve the state on receiving an indemnity for their past offences.[2] With this strange force, amounting it is said to about 25,000 men, M. Junius marched into Campania, whilst a new levy of the oldest and youngest citizens supplied two new legions for the defence of the capital in the place of those which followed the dictator into the field. M. Junius fixed his head-quarters at Teanum,[3] on high ground upon the edge of the Falernian plain, with the Latin colony of Cales in his front, and communicating by the Latin road with Rome.

Position of the Roman army.

The dictator was at Teanum, and M. Marcellus with the army of Cannæ, whom we left in Apulia, is described as now lying encamped above Suessula,[4] —that is, on the right bank of the Vulturnus, on the hills which bound the Campanian plain, ten or twelve miles to the east of Capua, on the right of the Appian road as it ascends the pass of Caudium towards Beneventum. Thus we find the seat of war removed from Apulia to Campania; but the detail of the intermediate movements is lost, and we must restore the broken story as well as we can by tracing Hannibal's operations after the battle of Cannæ, which are undoubtedly the key to those of his enemies.

[1] Livy, XXII. 57.   [2] Livy, XXIII. 14.
[3] Livy, XXIII. 24.   [4] Livy, XXIII. 14.

The fidelity of the allies of Rome, which had not been shaken by the defeat of Thrasymenus, could not resist the fiery trial of Cannæ. The Apulians joined the conqueror immediately, and Arpi and Salapia opened their gates to him. Bruttium, Lucania, and Samnium were ready to follow the example,[1] and Hannibal was obliged to divide his army, and send officers into different parts of the country to receive and protect those who wished to join him, and to organise their forces for effective co-operation in the field. Meanwhile he himself remained in Apulia, not perhaps without hope that this last blow had broken the spirit as well as the power of the enemy, and that they would listen readily to proposals of peace. With this view he sent a Carthaginian officer to accompany the deputation of the Roman prisoners to Rome, and ordered him to encourage any disposition on the part of the Romans to open a negotiation.[2] When he found, therefore, on the return of the deputies, that his officer had not been allowed to enter the city, and that the Romans had refused to ransom their prisoners, his disappointment betrayed him into acts of the most inhuman cruelty. The mass of the prisoners left in his hands he sold for slaves, and so far he did not overstep the recognised laws of warfare; but many of the more distinguished among them he put to death, and those who were senators he obliged to fight as gladiators with each other in the presence of his whole army. It is added that brothers were in some instances brought out to fight

A.U.C. 538.
A.C. 216.
Revolt of the allies : conduct of Hannibal.

---

[1] Livy, XXII. 61.   Polybius III. 118.   Appian, Hannibal, 31.
[2] Livy, XXII. 58.

A.U.C. 538.
A.C. 216.

Hannibal
enters
Campania :
revolt of
Capua.

with their brothers, and sons with their fathers, but that the prisoners refused so to sin against nature, and chose rather to suffer the worst torments than to draw their swords in such horrible combats.[1] Hannibal's vow may have justified all these cruelties in his eyes, but his passions deceived him, and he was provoked to fury by the resolute spirit which ought to have excited his admiration. To admire the virtue which thwarts our dearest purposes, however natural it may seem to indifferent spectators, is one of the hardest trials of humanity.

Finding the Romans immovable, Hannibal broke up from his position in Apulia, and moved into Samnium. The popular party in Compsa opened their gates to him, and he made the place serve as a depôt for his plunder, and for the heavy baggage of his army.[2] His brother Mago was then ordered to march into Bruttium with a division of the army, and after having received the submission of

---

[1] Diodorus, XXVI. 14, 2. Appian, Hannibal, 28. Zonaras, IX. 2. Valerius Maximus, IX. 2. Ext. 2. But as even Livy does not mention these stories, though they would have afforded such a topic for his rhetoric,—nor does Polybius, either in IX. 24, when speaking of Hannibal's alleged cruelty, or in VI. 58, where he gives the account of the mission of the captives, and adds that Hannibal, when he heard that the Romans had refused to ransom them, κατεπλάγη τὸ στάσιμον καὶ τὸ μεγαλόψυχον τῶν ἀνδρῶν ἐν τοῖς διαβουλίοις,—there must doubtless be a great deal of exaggeration in them, even if they had any foundation at all. The story in Pliny, VIII. 7, that the last survivor of these gladiatorial combats had to fight against an elephant, and killed him, and was then treacherously waylaid and murdered by Hannibal's orders, was probably invented with reference to this very occasion. The remarks of Polybius should make us slow to believe the stories of Hannibal's cruelties, which so soon became a theme for the invention of poets and rhetoricians.—J. C. H. [See also Baumgartner, pp. 19, 32, 57.]　　　　　　　　　[2] Livy, XXIII. 1.

the Hirpinians on his way, to embark at one of the A.U.C. 538.
Bruttian ports, and carry the tidings of his success A.C. 216.
to Carthage.[1] ✗ Hanno, with another division, was
sent into Lucania to protect the revolt of the
Lucanians,[2] while Hannibal himself, in pursuit of a
still greater prize, descended once more into the
plains of Campania. The Pentrian Samnites, partly
restrained by the Latin colony of Æsernia, and
partly by the influence of their own countryman,
Num. Decimius of Bovianum, a zealous supporter of
the Roman alliance, remained firm in their adher-
ence to Rome: but the Hirpinians and the Caudinian Samnites all joined the Carthaginians, and
their soldiers no doubt formed part of the army with
which Hannibal invaded Campania.[3] There all was
ready for his reception. The popular party in
Capua were headed by Pacuvius Calavius, a man of
the highest nobility, and married to a daughter of
Appius Claudius, but whose ambition led him to
aspire to the sovereignty, not of his own country
only, but, through Hannibal's aid, of the whole of
Italy, Capua succeeding, as he hoped, to the supre-
macy now enjoyed by Rome. The aristocratical
party were weak and unpopular, and could offer no
opposition to him, while the people, wholly subject
to his influence, concluded a treaty with Hannibal,
and admitted the Carthaginian general and his
army into the city.[4] Thus the second city in Italy,
capable, it is said, of raising an army of 30,000 foot
and 4000 horse,[5] connected with Rome by the

---

[1] Livy, XXIII. 11.   [2] Livy, XXIII. 37.
[3] Livy, XXII. 61.   [4] Livy, XXIII. 2–4.
[5] Livy, XXIII. 5, and Weissenborn's note *in loc.*

A.U.C. 538.
A.C. 216.
closest ties, and which for nearly a century had remained true to its alliance under all dangers, threw itself into the arms of Hannibal, and took its place at the head of the new coalition of southern Italy, to try the old quarrel of the Samnite wars once again.

Marcellus encamps at Suessula. This revolt of Capua, the greatest result, short of the submission of Rome itself, which could have followed from the battle of Cannæ, drew the Roman armies towards Campania. Marcellus had probably fallen back from Canusium by the Appian road through Beneventum, moving by an interior and shorter line; whilst Hannibal advanced by Compsa upon Abellinum, descending into the plain of Campania by what is now the pass of Monteforte. Hannibal's cavalry gave him the whole command of the country, and Marcellus could do no more than watch his movements from his camp above Suessula, and wait for some opportunity of impeding his operations in detail.

How came it that Rome was not destroyed? At this point in the story of the war the question arises, How was it possible for Rome to escape destruction? Nor is this question merely prompted by the thought of Hannibal's great victories in the field, and the enormous slaughter of Roman citizens at Thrasymenus and Cannæ; it appears even more perplexing to those who have attentively studied the preceding history of Rome. A single battle, evenly contested and hardly won, had enabled Pyrrhus to advance into the heart of Latium; the Hernican cities and the impregnable Præneste had opened their gates to him. Yet Capua was then faithful to Rome, and Samnium and Lucania, exhausted by

long years of unsuccessful warfare, could have A.U.C. 538.
yielded him no such succour, as now, after fifty A.C. 216.
years of peace, they were able to afford to Hannibal.
But now, when Hannibal was received into Capua,
the state of Italy seemed to have gone backwards a
hundred years, and to have returned to what it had
been after the battle of Lautulæ in the second
Samnite war, with the immense addition of the
genius of Hannibal and the power of Carthage
thrown into the scale of the enemies of Rome.
Then, as now, Capua had revolted, and Campania,
Samnium, and Lucania were banded together against
Rome ; but this same confederacy was now supported
by all the resources of Carthage, and at its head
in the field of battle was an army of 30,000
veteran and victorious soldiers, led by one of the
greatest generals whom the world has ever seen.
How could it happen that a confederacy so formidable was only formed to be defeated ?—that the
revolt of Capua was the term of Hannibal's progress ?
—that from this day forwards his great powers
were shown rather in repelling defeat than in commanding victory ?—that, instead of besieging Rome,
he was soon employed in protecting and relieving
Capua ?—and that his protection and his succours
were alike unavailing ?

No single cause will explain a result so extra- Causes
ordinary.   Rome owed her deliverance principally which saved her.
to the strength of the aristocratical interest throughout Italy, to her numerous colonies of the Latin
name, to the scanty numbers of Hannibal's
Africans and Spaniards, and to his want of an
efficient artillery.   The material of a good artillery

must surely have existed in Capua, but there seem to have been no officers capable of directing it, and no great general's operations exhibit so striking a contrast of strength and weakness as may be seen in Hannibal's battles and sieges. And when Cannæ had taught the Romans to avoid pitched battles in the open field, the war became necessarily a series of sieges, where Hannibal's strongest arm, his cavalry, could render little service, while his infantry was in quality not more than equal to the enemy, and his artillery was decidedly inferior.[1]

Military measures in Campania. With two divisions of his army absent in Lucania and Bruttium, and while anxiously waiting for the reinforcements which Mago was to procure from Carthage, Hannibal could not undertake any great offensive operation after his arrival in Campania. He attempted only to reduce the remaining cities of the Campanian plain and sea coast, and especially to dislodge the Romans from Casilinum, which, lying within three miles of Capua, and commanding the passage of the Vulturnus, not only restrained all his movements, but was a serious annoyance to Capua, and threatened its territory with continual incursions. Atella and Calatia had revolted to him already with Capua, and he took Nuceria, Alfaterna, and Acerræ. The Greek cities on the coast, Neapolis and Cumæ, were firmly attached to Rome, and were too strong to be besieged with success, but Nola lay in the midst of the plain nearly midway between Capua and Nuceria, and the popular party there, as elsewhere, were ready to open their gates to Hannibal. He was preparing to appear before

[1] See Note I.

the town, but the aristocracy had time to apprise A.U.C. 538.
the Romans of their danger, and Marcellus, who A.C. 216.
was then at Casilinum, marched round behind the
mountains to escape the enemy's notice, and descended suddenly upon Nola from the hills which
rise directly above it. He secured the place, repressed the popular party by some bloody executions,
and when Hannibal advanced to the walls, made a
sudden sally, and repulsed him with some loss.[1]
Having done this service, and left the aristocratical
party in absolute possession of the government, he
returned again to the hills, and lay encamped on
the edge of the mountain boundary of the Campanian plain, just above the entrance of the famous
pass of Caudium. His place at Casilinum was to be
supplied by the dictator's army from Teanum; but
Hannibal watched his opportunity, and, anticipating
his enemies this time, laid regular siege to Casilinum,
which was defended by a garrison of about 1000 men.

　　This garrison had acted the very same part Conduct of
towards the citizens of Casilinum which the Cam- the garri-
panians had acted at Rhegium in the war with Casilinum.
Pyrrhus. About 500 Latins of Præneste, and 450
Etruscans of Perusia, having been levied too late to
join the consular armies when they took the field,
were marching after them into Apulia by the
Appian road, when they heard the tidings of the
defeat of Cannæ. They immediately turned about,
and fell back upon Casilinum where they established
themselves, and for their better security massacred the
Campanian inhabitants, and, abandoning the quarter
of the town which was on the left bank of the

[1] Livy, XXIII. 14-17. Plutarch, Marcellus, 11.

Vulturnus, occupied the quarter on the right bank.[1] Marcellus, when he retreated from Apulia with the wreck of Varro's army, had fixed his head-quarters for a time at Casilinum, the position being one of great importance, and there being some danger lest the garrison, while they kept off Hanni-bal, should resolve to hold the town for themselves rather than for the Romans. They were now left to themselves, and dreading Hannibal's vengeance for the massacre of the old inhabitants, they resisted his assaults desperately, and obliged him to turn the siege into a blockade. This was the last active operation of the campaign: all the armies now went into winter quarters. The dictator remained at Teanum, Marcellus lay in his mountain camp above Nola, and Hannibal's army was at Capua.[2] Being quartered in the houses of the city, instead of being encamped by themselves, their discipline, it is likely, was somewhat impaired by the various temptations thrown in their way; and as the wealth and enjoy-ments of Capua at that time were notorious, the writers who adopted the vulgar declamations against luxury pretended that Hannibal's army was ruined by the indulgences of this winter, and that Capua was the Cannæ of Carthage.[3]

Progress of the war in other quarters.
This intermission of active warfare will afford us an opportunity of noticing the progress of events elsewhere, which we have hitherto unavoidably ne-glected. From the banks of the Iberus Hannibal had made his way without interruption to Capua,

---

[1] Livy, XXIII. 17.   [2] Livy, XXIII. 18.
[3] Livy, XXIII. 45. Florus, I. 22, 21. Valerius Maximus, IX. 1. Ext. 1.

and the countries which he left behind him sink in like manner from the notice of the historian. We must now see what had happened in each of them since Hannibal's passage.

A.U.C. 538.
A.C. 216.

It has been mentioned above that P. Scipio, when he returned from the Rhone to Italy, to be ready to meet Hannibal in Cisalpine Gaul, sent his army into Spain under the command of his brother.[1] After his consulship was over, his province of Spain was still continued to him as proconsul, and he went thither accordingly to take the command. He found that his brother had already effected much; he had defeated and made prisoner the Carthaginian general Hanno, whom Hannibal had left to maintain his latest conquests in Spain, and had driven the Carthaginians beyond the Iberus.[2] His own arrival in Spain took place in the summer of the year 537, three or four months after the battle of Thrasymenus; and although little was done in the field before the end of the season, the Carthaginian governor of Saguntum was persuaded to set at liberty all the Spanish hostages left in his custody; and the Spaniard who had advised this step under the mask of goodwill to Carthage, as a means of securing the affections of the Spanish people, had no sooner received the hostages with orders to take them back to their several homes, than he delivered them up to the Romans. Thus Scipio enjoyed the whole credit of restoring them to their friends, and made the Roman name generally popular.[3] In the following year, Hasdrubal, the son of Hamilcar, having received orders to march into Italy to co-operate

Success of the Romans in Spain.

---

[1] Above, p. 16.   [2] Polybius, III. 76.   [3] Polybius, III. 98, 99.

A.U.C. 538.
A.C. 216.

with his brother, was encountered by the Romans near the Iberus and defeated,[1] so that his invasion of Italy was for the present effectually prevented.

Its great importance.

The importance of the Spanish war cannot be estimated too highly, for, by disputing the possession of Spain, the Romans deprived their enemy of his best nursery of soldiers, from which otherwise he would have been able to raise army after army for the invasion of Italy. But its importance consisted not so much in the particular events as in its being kept up at all: nor is there anything requiring explanation in the success of the Romans. Their army had originally consisted of 20,000 men, and P. Scipio had brought some reinforcements, while Hasdrubal and Hanno in their two armies had a force not much superior: hence, after the total defeat of Hanno, Hasdrubal could not meet the Romans with any chance of success. For Spanish levies were now no longer to be depended on, while the Romans were inviting the nations of Spain to leave the Carthaginians and come over to them. In this contest between the two nations, which should most influence the minds of the Spaniards, the ascendency of the Roman character was clearly shown, and the natives were drawn, as by an invincible attraction, to the worthier.

Tranquillity of Cisalpine Gaul.

While Spain was thus the scene of active warfare, Cisalpine Gaul, after Hannibal's advance into Italy, seems to have sunk back into a state of tranquillity, such as it had enjoyed in the first Punic war. It is very remarkable that the colonies of Placentia and Cremona so far in advance of

---

[1] Livy, XXIII. 27–29.

the Roman frontier, and surrounded by hostile A.U.C. 538.
tribes, were left unassailed from the time when A.C. 216.
Hannibal crossed the Apennines into Etruria.   We
are only told that L. Postumius Albinus, one of the
prætors of the year 538, was sent with an army into
Gaul, when Varro and Æmilius marched into
Apulia, with the express object of compelling the
Gauls in Hannibal's service to return to the defence
of their own country.[1]   What he did in the course
of that summer we know not: at the end of the
consular year he was still in his province, and was
elected consul for the year following, with Ti. Sempronius Gracchus.   But before his consulship began,
early in March apparently, according to the Roman
calendar, he fell into an ambuscade, while advancing
into the enemy's country, and was cut to pieces,[2]
with his whole army.   We are told that the Romans
found it utterly impossible to replace the army thus
lost, and that it was resolved for the present to leave
the Gauls to themselves.[3]   But it was not so certain
that the Gauls, if unopposed, would leave the
Romans to themselves; and we find that M. Pomponius Matho, who had been city prætor in 538,
was sent, on the expiration of his office, with proconsular power to Ariminum, and that he remained
on that frontier for two years with an army of two
legions,[4] while C. Varro with another legion was
quartered in Picenum, to support him in time of
need.[5]   Still the inaction of the Gauls is extraordinary, the more so as we find them in arms immedi-

---

[1] Polybius, III. 106.   [2] Livy, XXIII. 24. Polybius, III. 118.
[3] Livy, XXIII. 25.   [4] Livy, XXIV. 10, 44.
[5] Livy, XXIII. 32, XXIV. 44.

 ately after the end of the war with Carthage, and attacking Placentia and Cremona, which they had so long left in peace.[1] We can only suppose that the absence of a large portion of their soldiers, who were serving in Hannibal's army, crippled the power of the Gauls who were left at home, and that long experience had taught them that unless when conducted by a general of a more civilised nation they could not carry on war successfully with the Romans. The older Gaulish chiefs also were often averse to war when the younger chiefs were in favour of it;[2] and the Romans were likely to be lavish of presents at a time so critical, to confirm their friends in their peaceful sentiments, and to win over their adversaries. It seems probable that some truce was concluded which restrained either the Gauls or Romans from invading each other's territory; and the Romans were contented not to require the recall of the Gauls serving with Hannibal; some of whom, we know, continued to be with him till a much later period. The multitude of the Gauls rejoiced, perhaps, that they had won thus much from their proud enemy, and were well content that the war should be carried on far from their own frontiers, and yet that they should share in its advantages. But wiser men might regret that better use was not made of the favourable

---

[1] Livy, XXXI. 10.

[2] See, for instance, Cæsar, B. G. II. 13, 28; III. 17; VII. 4, 37, 39. [I have corrected and supplemented Archdeacon Hare's erroneous reference to Cæsar. The following may also be consulted :—Polybius, II. 21; Dio, XXXIX. 47, 48 (for the same contrast among the Germans); while Livy, XXI. 20, brings out a somewhat similar contrast between old and young among the Gauls.]

moment; that no Carthaginian officer had been left A.U.C. 538.
with them to organise their armies and conduct them A.C. 216.
into the field; that the Roman encroachments on their
soil were still maintained, and that there was no Gellius
Egnatius in northern Italy to rouse the Etruscans and
Umbrians to unite their forces with those of the Gauls
on the south of the Apennines, and, while Hannibal
lay triumphant in Capua, to revenge the defeat of Sen-
tinum by a second victory on the Alia or the Tiber.

Whatever was the cause, the inactivity of the Resources of the Romans.
Gauls, after their great victory over L. Postumius,
might strengthen the argument of those Greeks who
ascribed the conquests of the Romans to their good
fortune. It was no less timely than the peace with
Etruria, concluded at the very moment when Pyrrhus
was advancing upon Rome, or than the quiet of these
same Gauls during the first Punic war. The consequence was that the Romans had the whole force of
Etruria and Umbria disposable for the contest in
the south; and that any disposition to revolt, which
might have existed in those countries, was unable to
show itself in action. Their soldiers served as allies
in the Roman armies, and with the Sabines, Picentians, Vestinians, Frentanians, Marrucinians, Marsians, and Pelignians, together with the cities of the
Latin name, composed the Roman confederacy after
the revolt of southern Italy. That revolt made the
drain, both of men and money, press more heavily
on the states which still remained faithful; and the
friends of Rome must everywhere have had the
greatest difficulty in persuading their countrymen
not to desert a cause which seemed so ruinous.
Under such a pressure the Roman government

plainly told its officers in Sardinia and Sicily that they must provide for their armies as they best could, for that they must expect no supplies of any kind from home.[1] The proprætor of Sicily applied to the never-failing friendship of Hiero, and obtained from him, almost as the last act of his long life, money enough to pay his soldiers, and corn for six months' consumption. But the proprætor of Sardinia had no such friend to help him; and he was obliged to get both corn and money from the people of the province.[2] The money, it seems, like the benevolences of our own government in old times, was nominally a free-will offering of the loyal cities of Sardinia to the Roman people; but the Sardinians knew that it was a gift which they could not help giving; and, impatient of this addition to their former burdens, they applied to Carthage for aid, and broke out the following year into open revolt.[3]

Their financial difficulties.

It is not without reason that the Roman government had abandoned its officers in the provinces to their own resources. Their financial difficulties were enormous. Large tracts of land, arable, pasture, and forest, from which the state ordinarily derived a revenue, were in the hands of the enemy; the number of tax-payers had been greatly diminished by the slaughter of so many citizens in battle; and in many cases their widows and children would be unable to cultivate their little property, and would be altogether insolvent. If the poorer citizens were again obliged, as after the Gaulish invasion, to borrow money of the rich, discontent and misery would have been the sure consequence; and the

[1] Livy, XXIII. 21.   [2] Livy, XXIII. 21.   [3] Livy, XXIII. 32.

debtor would regard his creditor as a worse enemy than Hannibal. Accordingly three commissioners were appointed, on the proposition of the tribune Minucius, like the five commissioners of the year 403, with the express object of facilitating the circulation, and assisting the distressed tax-payer.[1] Their measures are not recorded; but we may suppose that they acted like the former commissioners, and allowed the poorer citizens to pay their taxes in kind, when they could not procure money, and did not force them to sell their property when it must have been sold at a certain loss.[2] The war must no doubt have raised the value of money, and diminished that of land; and the agricultural population, who had to pay a fixed amount of taxation in money, were thus doubly sufferers. As a mere financial operation, the commissioners' measures may not have been very profitable; but the government had the wisdom to see that everything depended on the unanimity and devotion of all classes to the cause of their country; and it was worth a great pecuniary sacrifice, even in the actual financial difficulties, to attach the people heartily to the government, and to prevent that intolerable evil of a general state of debt, which must speedily have led to a revolution, and laid Rome prostrate at the feet of Hannibal.

[1] Livy, XXIII. 21. Compare VII. 21.

[2] Salmasius (de Usuris, p. 510) conceives that the reduction of the as to an ounce, which Pliny (XXXIII. 3. (13)) says took place in the dictatorship of Fabius Maximus, was a measure of these commissioners.—J. C. H. [But there is no ground for doubting Pliny. Compare Mommsen's *Römische Münzwesen* (1860), p. 288. Mommsen, however, believes, p. 291, that the weight of the as had been steadily sinking—but without legislative authority for the change —ever since B.C. 264.]

A.U.C.538.
A.C. 216.
Events of
the naval
war.

Neither Rome nor Carthage could be said to have the undisputed mastery of the sea. Roman fleets sometimes visited the coasts of Africa; and Carthaginian fleets in the same way appeared off the coasts of Italy. Hannibal received supplies from Carthage, which were landed in the ports of Bruttium; and when the Carthaginians wished to assist the revolt of the Sardinians, the expedition which they sent, although it suffered much from bad weather, was neither delayed nor prevented by the enemy.[1] On the other hand, the Romans had gained a naval victory of some importance in Spain:[2] and their cruising squadrons in the Ionian Gulf, having the ports of Brundisium and Tarentum to run to in case of need, were of signal service, as we shall see hereafter, in intercepting the communications which the king of Macedon was trying to open with Hannibal.[3]

Reinforcements from Carthage.

Meantime the news of the battle of Cannæ had been carried to Carthage, as we have seen, by Hannibal's brother Mago, accompanied with a request for reinforcements. Nearly two years before, when he first descended from the Alps into Cisalpine Gaul, his Africans and Spaniards were reduced to no more than 20,000 foot and 6000 horse. The Gauls, who had joined him since, had indeed more than double this number at first; but three great battles, and many partial actions, besides the unavoidable losses from sickness during two years of active service, must again have greatly diminished it; and this force was now to be divided: a part of it was employed in Bruttium, a part in Lucania, leaving an inconsiderable body under Hannibal's own command.

[1] Livy, XXIII. 34.   [2] Polybius, III. 96.   [3] Livy, XXIII. 32, 34.

On the other hand, the accession of the Campanians, A.U.C. 538.
Samnites, Lucanians, and Bruttians supplied him A.C. 216.
with auxiliary troops in abundance, and of excellent
quality; so that large reinforcements from home
were not required, but only enough for the Africans
to form a substantial part of every army employed
in the field, and, above all, to maintain his superiority in cavalry.   It is said that some of the reinforcements which were voted on Mago's demand,
were afterwards diverted to other services;[1] and we
do not know what was the amount of force actually
sent over to Italy, nor when it arrived.[2]   It consisted chiefly, if not entirely, of cavalry and elephants; for all the elephants which Hannibal had
brought with him into Italy had long since perished;
and his anxiety to obtain others, troublesome and
hazardous as it must have been to transport them
from Africa by sea, speaks strongly in favour of their
use in war, which modern writers are perhaps too
much inclined to depreciate.[3]

We have no information as to the feelings enter- Feelings of
tained by Hannibal and the Campanians towards the Campa-
each other while the Carthaginians were wintering nians.
in Capua.   The treaty of alliance had provided
carefully for the independence of the Campanians,
that they might not be treated as Pyrrhus had
treated the Tarentines.   Capua was to have its

---

[1] Livy, XXIII. 13., 32.

[2] He is represented as having elephants at the siege of Casilinum.
Livy, XXIII. 18.   If this be correct, the reinforcements must
already have joined him.

[3] See the interesting dissertation on elephants by A. W. Schlegel
in his *Indische Bibliothek*, vol. i. 173, foll.   [See also Fröhlich, pp.
19–23.   See Note J.]

A.U.C. 538.
A.C. 216.
own laws and magistrates; no Campanian was to be compelled to any duty civil or military, nor to be in any way subject to the authority of the Carthaginian officers.[1] There must have been something of a Roman party opposed to the alliance with Carthage altogether, though the Roman writers mention one man only, Decius Magius, who was said to have resisted Hannibal to his face with such vehemence that Hannibal sent him prisoner to Carthage.[2] But three hundred Campanian horsemen of the richer classes, who were serving in the Roman army in Sicily when Capua revolted, went to Rome as soon as their service was over, and were there received as Roman citizens;[3] and others, though unable to resist the general voice of their countrymen, must have longed in their hearts to return to the Roman alliance. Of the leaders of the Campanian people we know little: Pacuvius Calavius, the principal author of the revolt, is never mentioned afterwards; nor do we know the fate of his son Perolla, who, in his zeal for Rome, wished to assassinate Hannibal at his own father's table, when he made his public entrance into Capua.[4] Vibius Virrius is also named as a leading partisan of the Carthaginians;[5] and, amid the pictures of the luxury and feebleness of the Campanians, their cavalry, which was formed entirely out of the wealthiest classes, is allowed to have been excellent;[6] and one brave and practised soldier, Jubellius Taurea, had acquired a high reputation amongst the

---

[1] Livy, XXIII. 7. [2] Livy, XXIII. 7. 10.
[3] Livy, XXIII. 4. 7. 31. [4] Livy, XXIII. 8, 9.
[5] Livy, XXIII. 6. [6] Frontinus, *Strateg.* IV. 7. 29.

Romans when he served with them, and had attracted A.U.C. 538.
A.C. 216. the notice and respect of Hannibal.[1]

During the interval from active warfare afforded by the winter the Romans took measures for filling up the numerous vacancies which the lapse of five years and so many disastrous battles had made in the numbers of the senate.[2] The natural course would have been to elect censors, to whom the duty of making out the roll of the senate properly belonged; but the vacancies were so many, and the censor's power in admitting new citizens and degrading old ones was so enormous, that the senate feared, it seems, to trust to the result of an ordinary election, and resolved that the censor's business should be performed by the oldest man in point of standing of all those who had already been censors, and that he should be appointed dictator for this especial duty, although there was one dictator already for the conduct of the war. The person thus selected was M. Fabius Buteo, who had been censor six-and-twenty years before, at the end of the first Punic war, and who had more recently been the chief of the embassy sent to declare war on Carthage after the destruction of Saguntum. That his appointment might want no legal formality, C. Varro, the only surviving consul, was sent for home from Apulia to nominate him, the senate intending to detain Varro in Rome till he should have presided at the comitia for the election of the next year's magistrates. The nomination as usual took place at midnight, and on the following morning M.

---

[1] Livy, XXIII. 8. 46. 47. XXVI. 15. Valerius Maximus, III. 2. Ext. 1.   [2] Livy, XXIII. 22.

Fabius appeared in the forum with his four-and-twenty lictors, and ascended the rostra to address the people. Invested with absolute power for six months, and especially charged with no less a task than the formation, at his discretion, of that great council which possessed the supreme government of the commonwealth, the noble old man neither shrunk weakly from so heavy a burden, nor ambitiously abused so vast an authority. He told the people that he would not strike off the name of a single senator from the list of the senate, and that, in filling up the vacancies, he would proceed by a defined rule; that he would first add all those who had held curule offices within the last five years without having been admitted as yet into the senate; that in the second place he would take all who within the same period had been tribunes, ædiles, or quæstors; and thirdly, all those who could show in their houses spoils won in battle from an enemy, or who had received the wreath of oak for saving the life of a citizen in battle. In this manner one hundred and seventy-seven new senators were placed on the roll, the new members thus forming a large majority of the whole number of the senate, which amounted only to three hundred. This being done forthwith, the dictator, as he stood in the rostra, resigned his office, dismissed his lictors, and went down into the forum a private man. There he purposely lingered amidst the crowd lest the people should leave their business to follow him home; but their admiration was not cooled by this delay; and when he withdrew at the usual hour the whole people attended him to

his house.[1] Such was Fabius Buteo's dictatorship, A.U.C. 539.
so wisely fulfilled, so simply and nobly resigned, A.C. 215.
that the dictatorship of Fabius Maximus himself has
earned no purer glory.

Varro, it is said, not wishing to be detained in Election of
Rome, returned to his army the next night without officers for
the year
giving the senate notice of his departure.   The 539.
dictator, M. Junius, was therefore requested to
repair to Rome to hold the comitia, and Ti.
Gracchus and M. Marcellus were to come with
him to report on the state of their several armies,
and to concert measures for the ensuing campaign.[2]
There is no doubt that the senate determined on the
persons to be proposed at the ensuing elections, and
that if any one else had come forward as a candidate the dictator who presided would have refused
to receive votes for him.   Accordingly the consuls
and prætors chosen were all men of the highest
reputation for ability and experience : the consuls
were L. Postumius, whose defeat and death in Cisalpine Gaul were not yet known at Rome, and Ti.
Gracchus, now master of the horse.   The prætors
were M. Valerius Lævinus ; Ap. Claudius Pulcher,
a grandson of the famous censor, Appius the blind ;
Q. Fulvius Flaccus, old in years but vigorous in
mind and body, who had already been censor and
twice consul ; and Q. Mucius Scævola.[3]   When the
death of L. Postumius was known his place was
finally filled by no less a person than Q. Fabius
Maximus : whilst Marcellus was still to retain his
command with proconsular power, as his activity

---

[1] Livy, XXIII. 23.   [2] Livy, XXIII. 24.
[3] Livy, XXIII. 30.

A.U.C. 539.
A.C. 215.

and energy could ill be spared at a time so critical.[1]

Distribution of provinces and troops.

The officers for the year being thus appointed, it remained to determine their several provinces, and to provide them with sufficient forces.[2] Fabius was to succeed to the army of the dictator, M. Junius, and his headquarters were advanced from Teanum to Cales, at the northern extremity of the Falernian plain, about seven English miles from Casilinum and the Vulturnus, and less than ten from Capua. The other consul, Ti. Sempronius, was to have no other Roman army than two legions of volunteer slaves, who were to be raised for the occasion ; but both he and his colleague had the usual contingent of Latin and Italian allies. Gracchus named Sinuessa, on the Appian road, at the point where the Massic hills run out with a bold headland into the sea, as the place of meeting for his soldiers, and his business was to protect the towns on the coast, which were still faithful to Rome, such as Cumæ and Neapolis. Marcellus was to command two new Roman legions, and to lie as before in his camp above Nola ; while his old army was sent into Sicily to relieve the legions there, and enable them to return to Italy, where they formed a fourth army under the command of M. Valerius Lævinus, the prætor peregrinus, in Apulia. The small force which Varro had commanded in Apulia was ordered to Tarentum to add to the strength of that important place ; while Varro himself was sent with proconsular power into Picenum to raise soldiers, and to watch the road along the Adriatic by which the Gauls might have sent

[1] Livy, XXIII. 31.　　　[2] Livy, XXIII. 31, 32.

reinforcements to Hannibal.   Q. Fulvius Flaccus, the prætor urbanus, remained at Rome to conduct the government, and had no other military command than that of a small fleet for the defence of the coast on both sides of the Tiber.   Of the other two prætors, Ap. Claudius was to command in Sicily, and Q. Mucius in Sardinia; and P. Scipio, as proconsul, still commanded his old army of two legions in Spain.   On the whole, including the volunteer slaves, there appeared to have been fourteen Roman legions in active service at the beginning of the year 539, without reckoning the soldiers who served in the fleets; and, of these fourteen legions, nine were employed in Italy.   If we suppose that the Latin and Italian allies bore their usual proportion to the number of Roman soldiers in each army, we shall have a total of 140,000 men, thus divided—20,000 in Spain, and the same number in Sicily; 10,000 in Sardinia;   20,000 under each of the consuls; 20,000 with Marcellus;   20,000 under Lævinus in Apulia; and 10,000 in Tarentum.

A.V.C. 539.
A.C. 215.

Seventy thousand men were thus in arms, besides the seamen, out of a population of citizens which, at the last census before the war, had amounted only to 270,213,[1] and which had since been thinned by so many disastrous battles.   Nor was the drain on the finances of Rome less extraordinary.   The legions in the provinces had indeed been left to their own resources as to money; but the nine legions serving in Italy must have been paid regularly, for war could not there be made to support war, and if the Romans had been left to live at free quarters

Extraordi-
nary exer-
tions of the
Romans,
military
and finan-
cial.

---

[1] Livy, Epit. XX.

upon their Italian allies, they would have driven them to join Hannibal in mere self-defence. Yet the legions in Italy cost the government in pay, food, and clothing, at the rate of 541,800 denarii a month, and, as they were kept on service throughout the year, the annual expense was 6,501,600 denarii, or in Greek money, reckoning the denarius as equal to the drachma, 1083 Euboic talents. To meet these enormous demands on the treasury the government resorted to the simple expedient of doubling the year's taxes, and calling at once for the payment of one half of this amount, leaving the other to be paid at the end of the year.[1] It was a struggle for life and death, and the people were in a mood to refuse no sacrifices, however costly; but the war must have cut off so many sources of wealth, and agriculture itself must have so suffered from the calling away of so many hands from the cultivation of the land, that we wonder how the money could be found, and how many of the poorer citizens' families could be provided with daily bread.

Other military means of the Romans.

In addition to the five regular armies which the Romans brought into the field in Italy, an irregular warfare was also going on, we know not to what extent, and bands of peasants and slaves were armed in many parts of the country to act against the revolted Italians, and to ravage their territory. For instance, a great tract of forest in Bruttium, as we have seen, was the domain of the Roman people; this would be farmed like all the other revenues, and the publicani who farmed it, or the wealthy citizens who turned out cattle to pasture in it, would

____
[1] Livy. XXIII. 31.

have large bodies of slaves employed as shepherds, A.U.C. 539.
herdsmen, and woodmen, who, when the Bruttian A.C. 215.
towns on the coast revolted, would at once form a
guerilla force capable of doing them great mischief.
And lastly, besides all these forces, regular and
irregular, the Romans still held most of the principal
towns in the south of Italy, because they had long
since converted them into Latin colonies.   Brundisium on the Ionian Sea, Pæstum on the coast of
Lucania, Luceria, Venusia, and Beneventum in the
interior, were all so many strong fortresses, garrisoned
by soldiers of the Latin name, in the very heart of
the revolted districts;[1] whilst the Greek cities of
Cumæ and Neapolis in Campania, and Rhegium on
the straits of Messina, were held for Rome by their
own citizens with a devotion no way inferior to that
of the Latin colonies themselves.[2]

Against this mass of enemies, the moment that *Hannibal's*
they had learnt to use their strength, Hannibal, even *resources.*
within six months after the battle of Cannæ, was
already contending at a disadvantage.   We have
seen that he had detached two officers with two
divisions of his army, one into Lucania, the other
into Bruttium, to encourage the revolt of those
countries, and then to organise their resources in
men and money for the advancement of the common
cause.   Most of the Bruttians took up arms immediately as Hannibal's allies, and put themselves
under the command of his officer Himilco; but
Petelia, one of their cities, was, for some reason
or other, inflexible in its devotion to Rome, and

---

[1] Livy, XXVII. 10.   [2] Livy, XXIII. 1. 36, 37.   XXIV. 1.
[Cf. Neumann, Das Zeitalter der Punischen Kriege, p. 375.]

 endured a siege of eleven months, suffering all extremities of famine before it surrendered.[1]   Thus Himilco must have been still engaged in besieging it long after the campaign was opened in the neighbourhood of Capua.   The Samnites also had taken up arms, and apparently were attached to Hannibal's own army ; the return of their whole population of the military age, made ten years before, during the Gaulish invasion, had stated it at 70,000 foot and 7000 horse ;[2] but the Pentrians, the most powerful tribe of their nation, were still faithful to Rome ; and the Samnites, like the Romans themselves, had been thinned by the slaughter of Thrasymenus and Cannæ, which they had shared as their allies.   It is vexatious that we have no statement of the amount of Hannibal's old army, any more than of the allies who joined him at any period of the war later than the battle of Cannæ.   His reinforcements from home, as we have seen, were very trifling ; while his two divisions in Lucania and Bruttium, and the garrisons which he had been obliged to leave in some of the revolted towns, as, for example, at Arpi in Apulia,[3] must have considerably lessened the force under his own personal command.   Yet, with the accession of the Samnites and Campanians, it was probably much stronger than any one of the Roman armies opposed to him ; quite as strong indeed in all likelihood as was consistent with the possibility of feeding it.

Fall of
Casilinum.
    Before the winter was over Casilinum fell.   The garrison had made a valiant defence, and yielded at

----

[1] Polybius, VII. 1. Livy, XXIII. 20. 30. Appian, Hannibal, 29. Valerius Maximus, VI. 6. Ext. 2.
[2] Polybius, II. 24. 10.   [3] Livy. XXIV. 46, 47. Appian, VII. 31.

last to famine; they were allowed to ransom them- A.U.C. 539.
selves by paying each man seven ounces of gold A.C. 215.
for his life and liberty. The plunder which they
had won from the old inhabitants enabled them to
discharge this large sum, and they were then allowed
to march out unhurt and retire to Cumæ. Casilinum
again became a Campanian town, but its important
position, at once covering Capua and securing a
passage over the Vulturnus, induced Hannibal to
garrison it with 700 soldiers of his own army.[1]

The season for active operations was now arrived. Hannibal
The three Roman armies of Fabius, Gracchus, and encamps on
Marcellus, had taken up their positions round Cam- Mount
pania; and Hannibal marched out of Capua and Tifata.
encamped his army on the mountain above it, on Rome de-
that same Tifata where the Samnites had so often serted by
taken post in old times when they were preparing her allies.
to invade the Campanian plain.[2] Tifata did not
then exhibit that bare and parched appearance which
it has now; the soil, which has accumulated in the
plain below so as to have risen several feet above its
ancient level, has been washed down in the course
of centuries, and, after the destruction of its protecting woods, from the neighbouring mountains; and
Tifata in Hannibal's time furnished grass in abundance for his cattle in its numerous glades, and
offered cool and healthy summer quarters for his
men.[3] There he lay waiting for some opportunity
of striking a blow against his enemies around him,
and eagerly watching the progress of his intrigues
with the Tarentines and his negotiations with the
king of Macedon. A party at Tarentum began to

[1] Livy, XXIII. 19, 20. [2] Livy, XXIII. 36. VII. 29. [3] See Note K.

 open a correspondence with him immediately after the battle of Cannæ,[1] and since he had been in Campania he had received an embassy from Philip, king of Macedon, and had concluded an alliance, offensive and defensive, with the ambassadors, who acted with full powers in their master's name.[2] Such were his prospects on one side, while, if he looked westward and south-west, he saw Sardinia in open revolt against Rome;[3] and in Sicily the death of Hiero at the age of ninety, and the succession of his grandson Hieronymus, an ambitious and inexperienced youth, were detaching Syracuse also from the Roman alliance. Hannibal had already received an embassy from Hieronymus, to which he had replied by sending a Carthaginian officer of his own name to Sicily, and two Syracusan brothers, Hippocrates and Epicydes, who had long served with him in Italy and in Spain, being in fact Carthaginians by their mother's side, and having become naturalised at Carthage, since Agathocles had banished their grandfather, and their father had married and settled in his place of exile.[4] Thus the effect of the battle of Cannæ seemed to be shaking the whole fabric of the Roman dominion: their provinces were revolting; their firmest allies were deserting them; while the king of Macedon himself, the successor of Alexander, was throwing the weight of his power and of all his acquired and inherited glory into the scale of their enemies. Seeing the

[1] Livy, XXII. 61. Appian, Hannibal, 32.
[2] Livy, XXIII. 33. Zonaras, IX. 4.
[3] Livy, XXIII. 32, 34.
[4] Livy, XXIV. 4. 6. Polybius, VII. 2.

fruit of his work thus fast ripening, Hannibal sat A.U.C. 539.
quietly on the summit of Tifata, to break forth like A.C. 215.
the lightning flash when the storm should be fully
gathered.

Thus the summer of 539 was like a breathing Measures
time, in which both parties were looking at each of Fabius
other and considering each other's resources, while Hannibal's
they were recovering strength after their past efforts supplies.
and preparing for a renewal of the struggle.   Fabius,
with the authority of the senate, issued an order
calling on the inhabitants of all the country, which
either actually was, or was likely to become, the
seat of war, to clear their corn off the ground and
carry it into the fortified cities before the first. of
June, threatening to lay waste the land, sell the
slaves, and burn the farm-buildings of any one who
should disobey the order.[1]   In the utter confusion
of the Roman calendar at this period it is difficult
to know whether, in any given year, it was in
advance of the true time or behind it; so that we
can scarcely tell whether the corn was only to be
got in when ripe without needless delay, or whether
it was to be cut when green, lest Hannibal should
use it as forage for his cavalry.   But at any rate
Fabius was now repeating the system which he had
laid down in his dictatorship, and hoped by wasting
the country to oblige Hannibal to retreat, for his
means of transport were not sufficient for him to
feed his army from a distance : hence, when the
resources in his immediate neighbourhood were
exhausted, he was obliged to move elsewhere.

Meanwhile Gracchus had crossed the Vulturnus

---

[1] Livy, XXIII. 32.

A.U.C. 539.
A.C. 215.
Massacre of 2000 Capuans at a festival by Gracchus.

near its mouth, and was now at Liternum busily employed in exercising and training his heterogeneous army. The several Campanian cities were accustomed to hold a joint festival every year at a place called Hamæ, only three miles from Cumæ.[1] These festivals were seasons of general truce, so that the citizens even of hostile nations met at them safely: the government of Capua announced to the Cumæans that their chief magistrate and all their senators would appear at Hamæ as usual on the day of the solemnity, and they invited the senate of Cumæ to meet them. At the same time they said that an armed force would be present to repel any interruption from the Romans. The Cumæans informed Gracchus of this, and he attacked the Capuans in the night, when they were in such perfect security that they had not even fortified a camp but were sleeping in the open country, and massacred about 2000 of them, among whom was Marius Alfius, the supreme magistrate of Capua. The Romans charge the Capuans with having meditated treachery against the Cumæans, and say that they were caught in their own snare ; but this could only be a suspicion, while the overt acts of violence were their own. Hannibal no sooner heard of this disaster than he descended from Tifata, and hastened to Hamæ, in the hope of provoking the enemy to battle in the confidence of their late success. But Gracchus was too wary to be so tempted, and had retreated in good time to Cumæ, where he lay safe within the walls of the town.[2] It is said that Hannibal, having supplied himself with all things necessary for a siege, attacked

---

[1] Livy, XXIII. 35.   [2] Livy, XXIII. 36.

the place in form and was repulsed with loss, so A.U.C. 539.
that he returned defeated to his camp at Tifata.   A A.C. 215.
consular army defending the walls of a fortified
town was not indeed likely to be beaten in an
assault, and neither could a maritime town, with the
sea open, be easily starved; nor could Hannibal
linger before it safely, as Fabius, with a second consular army, was preparing to cross the Vulturnus.

Casilinum being held by the enemy, Fabius was Strength of
obliged to cross at a higher point behind the mount- the Roman
ains, nearly opposite to Allifæ; and he then de- armies.
scended the left bank to the confluence of the Calor
with the Vulturnus, crossed the Calor, and passing
between Taburnus and the mountains above Caserta
and Maddaloni, stormed the town of Saticula, and
joined Marcellus in his camp above Suessula.[1]   He
was again anxious for Nola, where the popular party
were said to be still plotting the surrender of the
town to Hannibal: to stop this mischief he sent
Marcellus with his whole army to garrison Nola,
while he himself took his place in the camp above
Suessula.   Gracchus on his side advanced from
Cumæ towards Capua; so that three Roman armies,
amounting in all to above 60,000 men, were on
the left bank of the Vulturnus together; and all,
so far as appears, in free communication with each
other.   They availed themselves of their numbers
and of their position to send plundering parties out
on their rear to overrun the lands of the revolted
Samnites and Hirpinians; and as the best troops of
both these nations were with Hannibal on Tifata,
no force was left at home sufficient to check the

[1] Livy, XXIII. 39.

A.U.C. 539.
A.C. 215.

enemy's incursions. Accordingly the complaints of the sufferers were loud, and a deputation was sent to Hannibal, imploring him to protect his allies.[1]

Hannibal receives his reinforcements.

Already Hannibal felt that the Roman generals understood their business, and had learnt to use their numbers wisely. On ground where his cavalry could act he would not have feared to engage their three armies together; but when they were amongst mountains, or behind walls, his cavalry were useless, and he could not venture to attack them: besides, he did not wish to expose the territory of Capua to their ravages; and therefore he did not choose lightly to move from Tifata. But the prayers of the Samnites were urgent; his partisans in Nola might require his aid, or might be able to admit him into the town; and his expected reinforcement of cavalry and elephants from Carthage had landed safely in Bruttium, and was on its way to join him, which the position of Fabius and Marcellus might render difficult, if he made no movement to favour it. He therefore left Tifata, advanced upon Nola, and timed his operations so well that his reinforcements arrived at the moment when he was before Nola; and neither Fabius nor Marcellus attempted to prevent their junction.[2]

Advantages gained by Marcellus. Hannibal marches into Apulia.

Thus encouraged, and perhaps not aware of the strength of the garrison, Hannibal not only overran the territory of Nola, but surrounded the town with his soldiers, in the hope of taking it by escalade. Marcellus was alike watchful and bold; he threw open the gates and made a sudden sally, by which he drove back the enemy within their camp; and

---

[1] Livy, XXIII. 41, 42.   [2] Livy, XXIII. 43.

this success, together with his frank and popular _{A.U.C. 539.} bearing, won him, it is said, the affections of all _{A.C. 215.} parties at Nola, and put a stop to all intrigues within the walls.[1]   A more important consequence of this action was the desertion of above 1200 men, Spanish foot and Numidian horse, from Hannibal's army to the Romans:[2] as we do not find that their example was followed by others, it is probable that they were not Hannibal's old soldiers, but some of the troops which had just joined him, and which could not as yet have felt the spell of his personal ascendency.   Still their treason naturally made him uneasy, and would for the moment excite a general suspicion in the army: the summer too was drawing to a close; and wishing to relieve Capua from the burden of feeding his troops, he marched away into Apulia, and fixed his quarters for the winter near Arpi.   Gracchus, with one consular army. followed him; while Fabius, after having ravaged the country round Capua, and carried off the green corn, as soon as it was high enough out of the ground, to his camp above Suessula, to furnish winter food for his cavalry, quartered his own army there for the winter, and ordered Marcellus to retain a sufficient force to secure Nola, and to send the rest of his men home to be disbanded.[3]

Thus the campaign was ended, and Hannibal had not marked it with a victory.   The Romans had employed their forces so wisely that they had forced him to remain mostly on the defensive; and his two offensive operations, against Cumæ and against

Complete success of the Romans in Sardinia.

---

[1] Livy, XXIII. 44–46.   [2] Livy, XXIII. 46.
[3] Livy, XXIII. 46. 48.

Nola, had both been baffled. In Sardinia their success had been brilliant and decisive. Mucius the prætor fell ill soon after he arrived in the island; upon which the senate ordered Q. Fabius, the city prætor, to raise a new legion, and to send it over into Sardinia, under any officer whom he might think proper to appoint. He chose a man in age, rank, and character most resembling himself, T. Manlius Torquatus, who in his first consulship, twenty years before, had fought against the Sardinians, and obtained a triumph over them. Manlius's second command in the island was no less brilliant than his first: he totally defeated the united forces of the Sardinians and Carthaginians, took their principal generals prisoners, reduced the revolted towns to obedience, levied heavy contributions of corn and money as a punishment of their rebellion, and then embarked with the troops which he had brought out with him, only leaving the usual force of a single legion in the island, and returned to Rome to report the complete submission of Sardinia. The money of his contributions was paid over to the quæstors, for the payment of the armies; the corn was given to the ædiles to supply the markets of Rome.[1]

Capture of the Macedonian ambassadors. Expedition to Greece.

Fortune in another quarter served the Romans no less effectually. The Macedonian ambassadors, after having concluded their treaty with Hannibal at Tifata, made their way back into Bruttium in safety, and embarked to return to Greece. But their ship was taken off the Calabrian coast by the Roman squadron on that station; and the ambas-

[1] Livy, XXIII. 34. 41.

sadors with all their papers were sent prisoners to A.U.C. 539.
A.C. 215.
Rome.[1]   A vessel which had been of their company
escaped the Romans, and informed the king what
had happened.   He was obliged therefore to send
a second embassy to Hannibal, as the former treaty
had never reached him; and although this second
mission went and returned safely, yet the loss of
time was irreparable, and nothing could be done till
another year.[2]   Meanwhile the Romans, thus timely
made aware of the king's intention, resolved to find
such employment for him at home as should prevent
his invading Italy.   M. Valerius Lævinus was to
take the command of the fleet at Tarentum and
Brundisium, and to cross the Ionian Gulf, in order
to rouse the Ætolians, and the barbarian chiefs
whose tribes bordered on Philip's western frontier,
and, with such other allies as could be engaged
in the cause, to form a Greek coalition against
Macedon.[3]

These events, and the continued successes of their Measures of
army in Spain, revived the spirits of the Romans, the Romans
and encouraged them to make still greater sacrifices, money: a
in the hope that they would not be made in vain. loan.
The distress of the treasury was at its height: P.
Scipio, in announcing his victories, reported that his
soldiers and seamen were in a state of utter destitution; that they had no pay, corn, or clothing; and
that the two latter articles must at any rate be
supplied from Rome.[4]   His demands were acknowledged to be reasonable; but the republic had lost

---

[1] Livy, XXIII. 38.   [2] Livy, XXIII. 39.
[3] Livy, XXIII. 38. 48.   XXIV. 10.   Zonaras, IX. 4.
[4] Livy, XXIII. 48.

so large a portion of her foreign revenue that her chief resource now lay in the taxation of her own people: this had been doubled in the present year, yet was found inadequate, and to increase it, or even to continue it at its present amount, was altogether impossible. Accordingly, the city prætor, Q. Fulvius, addressed the people from the rostra, explained the distress of the government to them, and appealed to the patriotism of the monied class to assist their country with a loan. Fabius did not mean to hold out an opportunity to the public creditor of investing his money to advantage, subject only to the risk of a national bankruptcy; on this Roman loan no interest was to be paid; the creditors were simply assured that as soon as the treasury was solvent their demands should be discharged before all others; in the meantime their money was totally lost to them.

But, on the other hand, opportunities of investing money profitably must have been greatly diminished by the war; to lend it to the government was not, therefore, so great a sacrifice. Still, a public spirit was shown in the ready answer to the prætor's appeal, such as merchants have often honourably displayed in seasons of public danger; mixed up, however—for when are human motives altogether pure?—with a considerable regard to personal advantage. Three companies were formed, each, as it seems, composed of eighteen members and a president, or chairman; and these were to supply the corn and clothing which the armies might require. But in return they demanded an exemption from military service whilst they were thus serving the state with their money; and they also

required the government to undertake the whole A.U.C. 539.
A.C. 215.
sea risk, whether from storms, or from the enemy;
whatever articles were thus lost were to be the loss
of the nation, and not of the companies.[1] It will
be seen hereafter how some of the contractors abused
this equitable condition, and wilfully destroyed cargoes of small value, in order to recover the insur-
ance upon them from the government. That a
citizen should enrich himself by frauds practised
on his country in such a season of distress and
danger is sufficiently monstrous; but the spirit of
what is so emphatically called jobbing is inveterate
in human nature; and we cannot wonder at its
existence among Roman citizens while Rome was
struggling for life or death, when it has been known
to find its way into the prison of Christian martyrs.[2]

Yet neither the ordinary taxation, nor the loan in Property
addition to it, were sufficient for the vast expenditure tax.
of the war. The hostility of Macedon had made it
necessary to raise an additional fleet, for the coasts
of Italy must be protected, and Hannibal's free communications with Africa must be restrained; and
now another fleet was required by the threatening
aspect of affairs in Sicily. Accordingly a graduated
property tax for the occasion was imposed on all
citizens whose property amounted to or exceeded
100,000 asses; that is, they were required to furnish
a certain number of their slaves as seamen, to arm
and equip them, and to provide them with dressed

---

[1] Livy, XXIII. 49, XXV. 3.

[2] See Cyprian, Epp. XV. and XXVII. ed. Hartel (Vienna Corpus
Scriptorum Ecclesiasticorum Latinorum). [Cyprian's Epistles are
referred to in Dr. Arnold's *Life and Correspondence*, II. 193, 237.]

provisions for thirty days, and with pay, in some cases for six months, in others for a whole year.[1] The senators, who were rated higher than all other citizens, were obliged in this manner each to provide eight sea-men, with pay for the longer term of the whole year.

Whilst the commonwealth was making these extraordinary efforts, it was of the last importance that they should not be wasted by incompetent leaders, either at home or abroad. Gracchus was watching Hannibal in Apulia ; so that Fabius went to Rome to hold the comitia. It was not by accident, doubtless, that he had previously sent home to fix the day of the meeting, or that his own arrival was so nicely timed that he reached Rome when the tribes were actually met in the Campus Martius ; thus, without entering the city, he passed along under the walls, and took his place as presiding magistrate at the comitia,[2] while his lictors still bore the naked axe in the midst of their fasces, the well-known sign of that absolute power which the consul enjoyed everywhere out of Rome. Fabius, in concert, no doubt, with Q. Fulvius and T. Manlius, and other leading senators, had already determined who were to be consuls ; when the first century, in the free exercise of its choice, gave its vote in favour of T. Otacilius and M. Æmilius Regillus, he at once stopped the election, and told the people that this was no time to choose ordinary consuls, that they were electing generals to oppose Hannibal, and should fix upon those men under whom they would most gladly risk their sons' lives and their own, if

[1] Livy, XXIV. 11 ; comp. XXVI. 36. XXXIV. 6.
[2] Livy, XXIV. 7.

they stood at that moment on the eve of battle. A.U.C. 540.
'Wherefore, crier,' he concluded, 'call back the A.C. 214.
century to give its votes over again.'[1]

Otacilius, who was present, although he had Fabius and
married Fabius's niece, protested loudly against this Marcellus
interference with the votes of the people, and charged are elected
Fabius with trying to procure his own re-election. consuls.
The old man had always been so famous for the
gentleness of his nature that he was commonly
known by the name of 'the Lamb';[2] but now he
acted with the decision of Q. Fulvius or T. Manlius;
he peremptorily ordered Otacilius to be silent, and
bade him remember that his lictors carried the
naked axe; the century was called back, and now
gave its voice for Fabius and Marcellus. All the
centuries of all the tribes unanimously confirmed
this choice.[3] Q. Fulvius was also re-elected prætor;
and the senate by a special vote continued him in
the prætorship of the city, an office which put him
at the head of the home government. The election
of the other three prætors, it seems, was left free;
so the people, as they could not have Otacilius for
their consul, gave him one of the remaining prætorships, and bestowed the other two on Q. Fabius, the

[1] Livy, XXIV. 8.

[2] Ovicula: see Aurelius Victor de Vir. Illustr. c. 43. Plutarch,
Fabius, c. 1. Ὁ δὲ Ὀουικούλας σημαίνει μὲν τὸ προβάτιον· ἐτέθη δὲ
πρὸς τὴν πρᾳότητα καὶ βαρύτητα τοῦ ἤθους ἔτι παιδὸς ὄντος. Τὸ γρὰ
ἡσύχιον αὐτοῦ καὶ σιωπηλὸν καὶ μετὰ πολλῆς εὐλαβείας τῶν παιδικῶν
ἁπτόμενον ἡδονῶν, βραδέως δὲ καὶ διαπόνως δεχόμενον τὰς μαθήσεις,
εὔκολον δὲ πρὸς τοὺς συνήθεις καὶ κατήκοον ἀβελτηρίας τινὸς καὶ
νωθρότητος ὑπόνοιαν εἶχε παρὰ τοῖς ἐκτός· ὀλίγοι δ' ἦσαν οἱ τὸ
δυσκίνητον ὑπὸ βάθους καὶ τὸ μεγαλόψυχον καὶ λεοντῶδες ἐν τῇ φύσει
καθορῶντες αὐτοῦ.

[3] Livy, XXIV. 9.

consul's son, who was then curule ædile, and on P. Cornelius Lentulus.

Great as the exertions of the commonwealth had been in the preceding year, they were still greater this year. . Ten legions were to be employed in different parts of Italy, besides the reserve army of the two city legions, which was to protect the capital. Two legions were to hold Sardinia, where the sparks of revolt were probably not altogether extinguished; two were sent to Sicily with a prospect of no inactive service; and two were stationed in Cisalpine Gaul, there being some likelihood, we must suppose, that the Gauls would soon require a force in their neighbourhood; or possibly the colonies of Placentia and Cremona were thought insecure if they were left to their own resources, insulated as they were in the midst of the enemy's country. Finally, the Scipios still commanded their two legions in Spain; and the naval service in Sicily and on the coast of Calabria required no fewer than a hundred and fifty ships of war.[1]

The Italian armies were disposed as follows :— Cales, and the camp above Suessula and Nola, were again to be the headquarters of the two consuls, each of whom was to command a regular consular army of two legions. Gracchus, with proconsular power, was to keep his own two legions, and was at present wintering near Hannibal in the north of Apulia. Q. Fabius, one of the new prætors, was to be ready to enter Apulia with an army of equal strength, so soon as Gracchus should be called into Lucania and Samnium, to take part in the active

---

[1] Livy, XXIV. 11.

operations of the campaign. C. Varro, with his single legion, was still to hold Picenum; and M. Lævinus, also with proconsular power, was to remain at Brundisium with another single legion.[1] The two city legions served as a sort of depôt to recruit the armies in the field in case of need; and there was a large armed population, serving as garrisons in the Latin colonies and in other important posts in various parts of the country, the amount of which it is not possible to estimate. Nor can we calculate the numbers of the guerilla bands which were on foot in Lucania, Bruttium, and possibly in Samnium, and which hindered Hannibal from having the whole resources of those countries at his disposal. The Roman party was nowhere probably altogether extinct; wealthy Lucanians, who were attached to Rome, would muster their slaves and peasantry, and, either by themselves, or getting some Roman officer to lead them, would ravage the lands of the Carthaginian party, and carry on a continued harassing warfare against the towns or districts which had joined Hannibal. Thus the whole south of Italy was one wide flood of war, the waters everywhere dashing and eddying, and running in cross currents innumerable; while the regular armies, like the channels of the rivers, held on their way, distinguishable amidst the chaos by their greater rapidity and power.

Hannibal watched this mass of war with the closest attention. To make head against it directly being impossible, his business was to mark his opportunities, to strike wherever there was an open-

A.U.C. 540.
A.C. 214.

Hannibal marches into Campania.

----

[1] Livy, XXIV. 12. 10.

ing; and, being sure that the enemy would not dare to attack him on his own ground, he might maintain his army in Italy for an indefinite time, while Carthage, availing herself of the distraction of her enemy's power, renewed her efforts to conquer Spain and recover Sicily. He hoped ere long to win Tarentum, and, if left to his own choice, he would probably have moved thither at once when he broke up from his winter quarters; but the weakness or fears of the Campanians hung with encumbering weight upon him, and an earnest request was sent to him from Capua, calling on him to hasten to its defence lest the two consular armies should besiege it.[1] Accordingly he broke up from his winter quarters at Arpi, and marched once more into Campania, where he established his army as before on the summit of Tifata.

Fabius collects the Roman armies around Hannibal.

The perpetual carelessness and omissions in Livy's narrative, drawn as it is from various sources, with no pains to make one part correspond with another, render it a work of extreme difficulty to present an account of these operations which shall be at once minute and intelligible. We also miss that notice of chronological details which is essential to the history of a complicated campaign. Even the year in which important events happened is sometimes doubtful; yet we want, not to fix the year only, but the month, that we may arrange each action in its proper order. When Hannibal set out on his march into Campania, Fabius was still at Rome; but the two new legions which were to form his army were already assembled at Cales, and Fabius, on

---

[1] Livy, XXIV. 12.

hearing of Hannibal's approach, set out instantly to take the command. His old army, which had wintered in the camp above Suessula, had apparently been transferred to his colleague Marcellus, and a considerable force had been left at the close of the last campaign to garrison Nola. Fabius, however, wished to have three Roman armies co-operating with each other, as had been the case the year before; and he sent orders to Gracchus to move forwards from Apulia and to occupy Beneventum; while his son, Q. Fabius, the prætor, with a fourth army, was to supply the place of Gracchus at Luceria.[1] It seemed as if Hannibal, having once entered Campania, was to be hemmed in on every side and not permitted to escape: but these movements of the Roman armies induced him to call Hanno to his aid, the officer who commanded in Lucania and Bruttium, and who, with a small force of Numidian cavalry, had an auxiliary army under his orders, consisting chiefly of Italian allies. Hanno advanced accordingly in the direction of Beneventum, to watch the army of Gracchus, and, if an opportunity offered, to bring it to action.[2]

Meanwhile Hannibal, having left some of his best troops to maintain his camp at Tifata, and probably to protect the immediate neighbourhood of Capua, descended into the plain towards the coast, partly in the hope of surprising a fortified post which the Romans had lately established at Puteoli, and partly to ravage the territory of Cumæ and Neapolis. But the avowed object of his expedition was to offer sacrifice to the powers of the

A.U.C. 540.
A.C. 214.

Hannibal offers sacrifice at the lake Avernus.

---

[1] Livy, XXIV. 12.   [2] Livy, XXIV. 14.

A.U.C. 540.
A.C. 214.
unseen world on the banks of the dreaded lake of Avernus.[1] That crater of an old volcano, where the very soil still seemed to breathe out fire, while the unbroken rim of its basin was covered with the uncleared masses of the native woods, was the subject of a thousand mysterious stories, and was regarded as one of those spots where the lower world approached most nearly to the light of day, and where offerings paid to the gods of the dead were most surely acceptable. Such worship was a main part of the national religion of the Carthaginians, and Hannibal, whose latest act before he set out on his great expedition had been a journey to Gades to sacrifice to the god of his fathers, the Hercules of Tyre, visited the lake of Avernus, it is probable, quite as much in sincere devotion as in order to mask his design of attacking Puteoli. Whilst he was engaged in his sacrifice five noble citizens of Tarentum came to him, entreating him to lead his army into their country, and engaging that the city should be surrendered as soon as his standard should be visible from the walls. He listened to their invitation gladly : they offered him one of the richest cities in Italy with an excellent harbour, equally convenient for his own communication with Carthage, and for the reception of the fleet of his Macedonian allies, whom he was constantly expecting to welcome in Italy. He promised that he would soon be at Tarentum, and the Tarentines returned home to prepare their plans against his arrival.[2]

He marches against Tarentum,   With this prospect before him it is not likely that he would engage in any serious enterprise in

<hr>

[1] Livy, XXIV. 12, 13.   [2] Livy, XXIV. 13.

Campania.   Finding that he could not surprise A.U.C. 540.
Puteoli, he ravaged the lands of the Cumæans and A.C. 214.
Neapolitans. According to the ever-suspicious stories
of the exploits of Marcellus, he made a third attempt
upon Nola, and was a third time repulsed, Marcellus
having called down the army from the camp above
Suessula to assist him in defending the town. Then,
says the writer whom Livy copied, despairing of
taking a place which he had so often attacked in
vain, he marched off at once towards Tarentum.[1]
The truth probably is that, finding a complete consular army in Nola, and having left his light cavalry
and some of the flower of his infantry in the camp
on Tifata, he had no thought of attacking the town,
but returned to Tifata to take the troops from thence;
and having done this, and stayed long enough in
Campania for the Capuans to get in their harvest
safely, he set off on his march for Tarentum. None
of the Roman armies attempted to stop him, or so
much as ventured to follow him. Fabius and Marcellus took advantage of his absence to besiege
Casilinum with their united forces;[2] Gracchus kept
wisely out of his reach, whilst he swept on like a
fiery flood, laying waste all before him, from Tifata
to the shores of the Ionian Sea.[3] He certainly did
not burn or plunder the lands of his own allies, either
in Samnium or Lucania, but his march lay near the
Latin colony of Venusia, and the Lucanians and
Samnites in his army would carefully point out
those districts which belonged to their countrymen
of the Roman party ; above all, those ample tracts

[1] Livy, XXIV. 17.   [2] Livy, XXIV. 19.
[3] Livy, XXIV. 20.

which the Romans had wrested from their fathers, and which were now farmed by the Roman publicani, or occupied by Roman citizens. Over all these, no doubt, the African and Numidian horse poured far and wide, and the fire and sword did their work.

but fails.
Yet, after all, Hannibal missed his prey. Three days before he reached Tarentum a Roman officer arrived in the city, whom M. Valerius Lœvinus had sent in haste from Brundisium to provide for its defence.[1] There was probably a small Roman garrison in the citadel to support him in case of need; but the aristocratical party in Tarentum itself, as elsewhere, was attached to Rome, and with their aid Livius, the officer whom Lœvinus had sent, effectually repressed the opposite party, embodied the population of the town, and made them keep guard on the walls, and selecting a certain number of persons, whose fidelity he most suspected, sent them off as hostages to Rome. When the Carthaginian army therefore appeared before the walls no movement was made in their favour, and, after waiting a few days in vain, Hannibal was obliged to retreat. His disappointment, however, did not make him lose his temper; he spared the Tarentine territory, no less when leaving it than when he first entered it, in the hope of winning the city; a moderation which doubtless produced its effect, and confirmed the Tarentines in the belief that his professions of friendship had been made in honesty. But he carried off all the corn which he could find in the neighbourhood of Metapontum and Heraclea, and then returned to Apulia, and fixed his quarters for the winter at Salapia.

[1] Livy, XXIV. 20.

His cavalry overran all the forest country above A.U.C. 540. Brundisium, and drove off such numbers of horses A.C. 214. which were kept there to pasture, that he was enabled to have 4000 broken in for the service of his army.[1]

Meanwhile the Roman consuls in Campania were availing themselves of his absence to press the siege of Casilinum. The place was so close to Capua that it was feared the Capuans would attempt to relieve it; Marcellus therefore, with a second consular army, advanced from Nola to cover the siege. The defence was very obstinate, for there were 700 of Hannibal's soldiers in the place and 2000 Capuans, and Fabius, it is said, was disposed to raise the siege; but his colleague reminded him of the loss of reputation if so small a town were allowed to baffle two consular armies, and the siege was continued. At last the Capuans offered to Fabius to surrender the town on condition of being allowed to retire to Capua, and it appears that he accepted the terms, and that the garrison had begun to march out when Marcellus broke in upon them, seized the open gate from which they were issuing, cut them down right and left, and forced his way into the city. Fabius, it is said, was able to keep his faith to no more than 50 of the garrison, who had reached his quarters before Marcellus arrived, and whom he sent unharmed to Capua. The rest of the Capuans and of Hannibal's soldiers were sent prisoners to Rome, and the inhabitants were divided amongst the neighbouring cities, to be kept in custody till the senate should determine their fate.[2]

The Romans take Casilinum.

---

[1] Livy, XXIV. 20.   [2] Livy, XXIV. 19.

A.U.C. 540.
A.C. 214.
Fabius
ravages
Samnium.

After this scandalous act of treachery Marcellus returned to Nola, and there remained inactive, being confined, it was said, by illness,[1] till the senate, before the end of the summer, sent him over to Sicily to meet the danger that was gathering there. Fabius advanced into Samnium, combining his operations, it seems, with his son, who commanded a prætorian army in Apulia, and with Gracchus, who was in Lucania, and whose army formed the link between the prætor in Apulia and his father in Samnium. These three armies were so formidable that Hanno, the Carthaginian commander in Lucania, could not maintain his ground, but fell back towards Bruttium, leaving his allies to their own inadequate means of defence. Accordingly the Romans ravaged the country far and wide, and took so many towns, that they boasted of having killed or captured 25,000 of the enemy.[2] After these expeditions Fabius, it seems, led back his army to winter quarters in the camp above Suessula; Gracchus remained in Lucania, and Fabius the prætor wintered at Luceria.

Gracchus
defeats
Hanno, and
enfran-
chises the
slaves in
his army.

I have endeavoured to follow the operations of main armies on both sides throughout the campaign, without noticing those of Gracchus and Hanno in Lucania. But the most important action of the year, if we believe the Roman accounts, was the victory obtained by Gracchus near Beneventum, when he moved thither out of Apulia to co-operate with the consuls in Campania, and Hanno was ordered by Hannibal to march to the same point out of Lucania. Hanno, it is said, had about 17,000 foot, mostly Bruttians and Lucanians, and 1200 Numi-

[1] Livy, XXIV. 20.   [2] Livy, XXIV. 20.

dian and Moorish horse; and Gracchus, encounter- A.U.C. 540.
ing him near Beneventum, defeated him with the A.C. 214.
loss of almost all his infantry; he himself and his
cavalry being the only part of the army that escaped.[1]
The numbers, as usual, are probably exaggerated
immensely; but there is no reason to doubt that
Gracchus gained an important victory; and it was
rendered famous by his giving liberty to the volunteer slaves, by whose valour it had been mainly won.
Some of these had behaved ill in the action, and
were afraid that they should be punished rather
than rewarded; but Gracchus first set them all free
without distinction, and then, sending for those who
had misbehaved, made them severally swear that
they would eat and drink standing, so long as their
military service should last, by way of penance for
their fault. Such a sentence, so different from the
usual merciless severity of the Roman discipline,
added to the general joy of the army; the soldiers
marched back to Beneventum in triumph; and the
people poured out to meet them, and entreated
Gracchus that they might invite them all to a public
entertainment. Tables were set out in the streets;
and the freed slaves attracted every one's notice by
their white caps, the well-known sign of their enfran-
chisement, and by the strange sight of those who, in
fulfilment of their penance, ate standing, and waited
upon their worthier comrades. The whole scene
delighted the generous and kindly nature of Gracchus:
to set free the slave and to relieve the poor appear
to have been hereditary virtues in his family: to
him, no less than to his unfortunate descendants,

---

[1] Livy, XXIV. 14–16.

A.U.C. 540.
A.C. 214.

beneficence seemed the highest glory.   He caused a picture to be painted, not of his victory over Hanno, but of the feasting of the enfranchised slaves in the streets of Beneventum, and placed it in the Temple of Liberty in the Aventine, which his father had built and dedicated.[1]

Hanno retrieves his loss.

The battle of Beneventum obliged Hanno to fall back into Lucania, and perhaps as far as the confines of Bruttium.   But he soon recruited his army, the Lucanians and Bruttians, as well as the Picentines, who lived on the shores of the Gulf of Salerno, being very zealous in the cause ; and ere long he revenged his defeat by a signal victory over an army of Lucanians of the Roman party whom Gracchus had enlisted to act as an irregular force against their countrymen of the opposite faction.   Still Hanno was not tempted to risk another battle with a Roman consular army ; and when Gracchus advanced from Beneventum into Lucania, he retired again into Bruttium.[2]

Comitia for new officers.

There seems to have been no further dispute with regard to the appointment of consuls.   Fabius and the leading members of the senate appear to have nominated such men as they thought most equal to the emergency ; and no other candidates came forward.   Fabius again held the comitia ; and his son, Q. Fabius, who was prætor at the time, was elected consul together with Gracchus.   The prætors were entirely changed.   Q. Fulvius was succeeded in the city prætorship by M. Atilius Regulus, who had just resigned the censorship, and who had already been twice consul : the other three prætors were M.

<hr>

[1] Livy, XXIV. 16.   [2] Livy, XXIV. 20.

Æmilius Lepidus, Cn. Fulvius Centumalus, and P. A.U.C. 541.
A.C. 213. Sempronius Tuditanus. The two former were men of noble families : Sempronius appears to have owed his appointment to his resolute conduct at Cannæ, when he cut his way from the camp through the surrounding enemies, and escaped in safety to Canusium.[1]

Thus another year passed over; and, although the state of affairs was still dark, the tide seemed to be on the turn. Hannibal had gained no new victory ; Tarentum had been saved from his hands ; and Casilinum had been wrested from him. Public spirit was rising daily; and fresh instances of the patriotic devotion which possessed all classes of the commonwealth were continually occurring. The owners of the slaves whom Gracchus had enfranchised refused to receive any price for them: the wealthy citizens who served in the cavalry determined not to take their pay; and their example was followed by the centurions of the legions. Trust moneys belonging to minors, or to widows and unmarried women, were deposited in the treasury ; and whatever sums the trustees had occasion to draw for, were paid by the quæstor in bills on the banking commissioners, or triumviri mensarii : it is probable that these bills were actually a paper currency, and that they circulated as money, on the security of the public faith. In the same way we must suppose that the government contracts were also paid in paper ; for the censors, we are told, found the treasury unable to supply the usual sums for public works and entertainments ; there was no

Public spirit shown by the Romans.

---

[1] Livy, XXIV. 43.

A.U.C. 541.
A.C. 213.

money to repair or keep up the temples, or to provide horses for the games of the circus. Upon this the persons who were in the habit of contracting for these purposes came forward in a body to the censors, and begged them to make their contracts as usual, promising not to demand payment before the end of the war. This must mean, I conceive, that they were to be paid in orders upon the treasury, which orders were to be converted into cash when the present difficulties of the government should be at an end.[1]

Severe measures of the censors.

While such was the spirit of the people, any severity exercised by the government towards the timid or the unpatriotic was sure to be generally acceptable. The censors, M. Atilius Regulus and P. Furius Philus, summoned all those persons, most of them members of noble, and all of wealthy families, who had proposed to fly from Italy after the battle of Cannæ. L. Metellus, who was said to have been the first author of that proposal, was at this time quæstor; but he and all who were concerned in it were degraded from the equestrian order, and removed from their respective tribes. Two thousand citizens of lower rank were also removed from their tribes, and deprived of their political franchise, for having evaded military service during the last four years; and the senate inflicted an additional punishment by ordering that they should serve as foot soldiers in Sicily, along with the remains of the army of Cannæ, and should continue to serve so long as the enemy was in Italy.[2] The case of Metellus seems to have been considered a

<hr>

[1] Livy, XXIV. 18.   [2] Livy, XXIV. 18.

hard one: in spite of the censors' sentence he was elected one of the tribunes in the following year. A.U.C. 541. A.C. 213. He then impeached the censors before the people; but the other nine tribunes interposed, and would not allow the trial to proceed.[1] If Metellus had been wronged, the people had made up for it by electing him tribune; but it was thought a dangerous precedent to subject the censors to a trial for the exercise of their undoubted prerogative, when there was no reason to suspect the honesty of their motives.

The forces to be employed in Italy in the approaching campaign were to consist of nine legions, three fewer than in the year before. The consuls were each to have their two legions; Gracchus in Lucania and Fabius in Apulia. M. Æmilius was to command two legions also in Apulia, having his headquarters at Luceria; Cn. Fulvius with two more was to occupy the camp above Suessula, and Varro was to remain with his one legion in Picenum. Two consular armies of two legions each were required in Sicily; one commanded by Marcellus as proconsul, the other by P. Lentulus as proprætor; two legions were employed in Cisalpine Gaul under P. Sempronius, and two in Sardinia under their old commander, Q. Mucius. M. Valerius Lævinus retained his single legion and his fleet to act against Philip on the eastern side of the Ionian Sea, and P. Scipio and his brother were still continued in their command in Spain.[2]

Distribution of the Roman armies.

Hannibal passed the winter at Salapia, where, the Romans said, was a lady whom he loved, and who

Opening of the campaign.

---

[1] Livy, XXIV. 43.   [2] Livy, XXIV. 44.

became famous from her influence over him.[1] Whether his passion for her made him careless of everything else, or whether he was really taken by surprise, we know not; but the neighbouring town of Arpi was attacked by the consul Fabius and given up to him by the inhabitants, and some Spaniards, who formed part of the garrison, entered into the Roman service.[2] Gracchus obtained some slight successes in Lucania, and some of the Bruttian towns returned to their old alliance with Rome; but a Roman contractor, T. Pomponius Veientanus, who had been empowered by the government to raise soldiers in Bruttium and to employ them in plundering the enemy's lands, was rash enough to venture a regular action with Hanno, in which he was defeated and made prisoner.[3] This disaster checked the reaction in Bruttium for the present.

Hannibal lingers near Tarentum.

Meanwhile Hannibal's eyes were still fixed upon Tarentum, and thither he marched again as soon as he took the field, leaving Fabius behind him in Apulia. He passed the whole summer in the neighbourhood of Tarentum, and reduced several small towns in the surrounding country; but his friends in Tarentum made no movement, for they dared not compromise the safety of their countrymen and relations who had been carried off as hostages to Rome. Accordingly the season wore away unmarked by any memorable action. Hannibal still lingered in the country of the Sallentines, unwilling to give

[1] Appian, Hannibal, 43. Pliny, III. 11. See Lucian, Dial. Mortuor. XII., where Alexander is made to reproach Hannibal for such weaknesses.

[2] Livy, XXIV. 46, 47.   [3] Livy, XXV. 1.

up all hope of winning the prize he had so long A.U.C. 541.
sought, and, to lull the suspicions of the Romans, A.C. 213.
he gave out that he was confined to his camp by
illness, and that this had prevented his army from
returning to its usual winter quarters in Apulia.[1]

Matters were in this state when tidings arrived Conspiracy to betray it to Hannibal.
at Tarentum that the hostages, for whose safety
their friends had been so anxious, had been all
cruelly put to death at Rome for having attempted
to escape from their captivity.[2]   Released in so
shocking a manner from their former hesitation, and
burning to revenge the blood of their friends, Hannibal's partizans delayed no longer.   They communicated secretly with him, arranged the details of their
attempt, and signed a treaty of alliance, by which
he bound himself to respect the independence and
liberty of the Tarentines, and only stipulated for the
plunder of such houses as were occupied by Roman
citizens.[3]   Two young men, Philemenus and Nicon,
were the leaders of the enterprise.   Philemenus,
under pretence of hunting, had persuaded the officer
at one of the gates to allow him to pass in and out
of the town by night without interruption.   He was
known to be devoted to his sport; he scarcely ever
returned without having caught or killed some game
or other, and, by liberally giving away what he had
caught, he won the favour and confidence not only
of the officer of the gate but also of the Roman
governor himself, M. Livius Macatus, a relation of
M. Livius Salinator, who afterwards defeated Hasdrubal, but a man too indolent and fond of good cheer

---

[1] Polybius, VIII. 28. Livy, XXV. 8.   [2] Livy, XXV. 7.
[3] Polybius, VIII. 26, 27. Livy, XXV. 8.

A.U.C. 541.
A.C. 213.
to be the governor of a town threatened by Hannibal. So little did Livius suspect any danger that, on the very day which the conspirators had fixed for their attempt, and when Hannibal with 10,000 men was advancing upon the town, he had invited a large party to meet him at the temple of the Muses, near the market-place, and was engaged from an early hour in festivity.[1]

Situation of Tarentum favourable to the conspirators.

The city of Tarentum formed a triangle, two sides of which were washed by the water; the outer or western side by the Mediterranean; the inner or north-eastern side by that remarkable land-locked basin, now called the Little Sea, which has a mouth narrower than the entrance into the Norwegian Fiords, but runs deep into the land, and spreads out into a wide surface of the calmest water, scarcely ruffled by the hardest gales. Exactly at the mouth of this basin was a little rocky knoll, forming the apex of the triangle of the city and occupied by the citadel; the city itself stood on low and mostly level ground, and its south-eastern wall, the base of the triangle, stretched across from the Little Sea to the Mediterranean.[2] Thus the citadel commanded the entrance into the basin, which was the port of the Tarentines, and it was garrisoned by the Romans, although many of the officers and soldiers were allowed to lodge in the city. All attempts upon the town by land must be made then against the south-eastern side, which was separated from the citadel by the whole length of the city; and there was another circumstance which was likely to favour

---

[1] Polybius, VIII. 28, 29. Livy, XXV. 8, 9.
[2] Strabo, VI., 3, Cas. p. 278.

a surprise, for the Tarentines, following the direction of an oracle, as they said, buried their dead within the city walls, and the street of the tombs was interposed between the gates and the inhabited parts of the town.[1] This the conspirators turned to their own purposes; in this lonely quarter two of their number, Nicon and Tragiscus, were waiting for Hannibal's arrival without the gates. As soon as they perceived the signal which was to announce his presence, they, with a party of their friends, were to surprise the gates from within, and put the guards to the sword, while others had been left in the city to keep watch near the Museum, and prevent any communication from being conveyed to the Roman governor.[2]

The evening wore away; the governor's party broke up, and his friends attended him to his house. On their way home they met some of the conspirators, who, to lull all suspicion, began to jest with them, as though themselves going home from a revel, and joining the party amidst riotous shouts and loud laughter, accompanied the governor to his own door. He went to rest in joyous and careless mood; his friends were all gone to their quarters; the noise of revellers returning from their festivities died away through the city, and when midnight was come the conspirators alone were abroad. They now divided into three parties : one was posted near the governor's house, a second secured the approaches to the market-place, and the third hastened to the quarter of the tombs to watch for Hannibal's signal.[3]

[1] Polybius, VIII. 30. [2] Polybius, VIII. 29, 30. Livy. XXV. 9.
[3] Polybius, VIII. 29.

A.U.C. 541.
A.C. 213.
Hannibal
enters one
of the gates.

They did not watch long in vain; a fire in a particular spot without the walls assured them that Hannibal was at hand. They lit a fire in answer; and presently, as had been agreed upon, the fire without the walls disappeared. Then the conspirators rushed to the gate of the city, surprised it with ease, put the guards to the sword, and began to hew asunder the bar by which the gates were fastened. No sooner was it forced, and the gates opened, than Hannibal's soldiers were seen ready to enter; so exactly had the time of the operation been calculated. The cavalry were left without the walls as a reserve; but the infantry, marching in regular column, advanced through the quarter of the tombs to the inhabited part of the city.[1]

Another is
opened to
him by
Phile-
menus.

Meantime Philemenus with 1000 Africans had been sent to secure another gate by stratagem. The guards were accustomed to let him in at all hours, whenever he returned from his hunting expeditions; and now, when they heard his usual whistle, one of them went to the gate to admit him. Philemenus called to the guard from without to open the wicket quickly; for that he and his friends had killed a huge wild boar, and could scarcely bear the weight any longer. The guard, accustomed to have a share in the spoil, opened the wicket; and Philemenus, and three other conspirators, disguised as countrymen, stepped in, carrying the boar between them. They instantly killed the poor guard, as he was admiring and feeling their prize; and then let in about 30 Africans, who were following close behind. With

---

[1] Polybius, VIII. 30, 31.

this force they mastered the gate-house and towers, A.U.C. 541.
killed all the guards, and hewed asunder the bars A.C. 213.
of the main gates to admit the whole column of
Africans, who marched in on this side also in
regular order, and advanced towards the market-
place.[1]

No sooner had both Hannibal's columns reached Slaughter
their destination, and as it seems without exciting of the
any general alarm, than he detached three bodies of Roman
Gaulish soldiers to occupy the principal streets which troops.
led to the market-place. The officers in command
of these troops had orders to kill every Roman who
fell in their way; but some of the Tarentine conspirators were sent with each party to warn their
countrymen to go home and remain quiet, assuring
them that no mischief was intended to them. The
toils being thus spread, the prey was now to be
enticed into them. Philemenus and his friends had
provided some Roman trumpets; and these were
loudly blown, sounding the well-known call to arms
to the Roman soldier. Roused at this summons,
the Romans quartered about the town armed themselves in haste, and poured into the streets to make
their way to the citadel. But they fell in scattered
parties into the midst of Hannibal's Gauls, and were
cut down one after another. The governor alone
had been more fortunate: the alarm had reached
him in time, and being in no condition to offer any
resistance,—for he felt, says Polybius, that the
fumes of wine were still overpowering him,—he
hastened to the harbour, and getting on board a
boat, was carried safely to the citadel.[2]

[1] Polybius, VIII. 31.   [2] Polybius, VIII. 32. Livy, XXV. 10.

A.U.C. 541.
A.C. 213.
Hannibal
addresses
the Taren-
tines, and
promises to
protect
them.

Day at last dawned, but did not quite clear up the mystery of the night's alarm to the mass of the inhabitants of Tarentum. They were safe in their houses, unmassacred, unplundered; the only blast of war had been blown by a Roman trumpet; yet Roman soldiers were lying dead in the streets, and Gauls were spoiling their bodies. Suspense at length was ended by the voice of the public crier summoning the citizens of Tarentum, in Hannibal's name, to appear without their arms in the market-place, and by repeated shouts of 'Liberty! Liberty!' uttered by some of their own countrymen, who ran round the town calling the Carthaginians their deliverers. The firm partisans of Rome made haste to escape into the citadel, while the multitude crowded to the market-place. They found it regularly occupied by Carthaginian troops; and the great general, of whom they had heard so much, was preparing to address them. He spoke to them, in Greek apparently, declaring, as usual, that he was come to free the inhabitants of Italy from the dominion of Rome. 'The Tarentines therefore had nothing to fear; they should go home, and write each over his door *a Tarentine's house;* those words would be a sufficient security; no door so marked should be violated. But the mark must not be set falsely upon any Roman's quarters; a Tarentine guilty of such treason would be put to death as an enemy, for all Roman property was the lawful prize of the soldiers.' Accordingly all houses where Romans had been quartered were given up to be plundered, and the Carthaginian soldiers gained a harvest, says Polybius, which fully answered their hopes. This can only be explained by supposing .that the Romans were quartered generally in the houses of the wealthier Tarentines, who were attached to the Roman alliance, and that the plunder was not the scanty baggage of the legionary soldiers, but the costly furniture of the richest citizens in the greatest city of southern Italy.[1]

Thus Tarentum was won; but the citadel on its rocky knoll was still held by the Romans, and its position at once threatened the town, and shut up the Tarentine fleet useless in the harbour. Hannibal proceeded to sink a ditch, and throw up a wall along the side of the town towards the citadel, in order to repress the sallies of the garrison. While engaged in these works he purposely tempted the Romans to a sally, and having lured them on to some distance from their cover, turned fiercely upon them, and drove them back with such slaughter, that their effective strength was greatly reduced. He then hoped to take the citadel; but the garrison was reinforced by sea from Metapontum, the Romans withdrawing their troops from thence for this more important service; and a successful night-sally destroyed the besiegers' works, and obliged them to trust to a blockade. But as this was hopeless while the Romans were masters of the sea, Hannibal instructed the Tarentines to drag their ships overland, through the streets of the city, from the harbour to the outer sea, and this being effected without difficulty, as the ground was quite level, the Tarentine fleet became at once effective, and the sea communications of the enemy were cut off.

A.U.C. 541.
A.C. 213.

He drags the Taren-tine fleet through the town, and returns into Apulia.

[1] Polybius, VIII. 33. Livy, XXV. 10.

A.U.C. 541.
A.C. 213.

Having thus, as he hoped, enabled the Tarentines to deal by themselves with the Roman garrison, he left a small force in the town, and returned with the mass of his troops to his winter quarters in the country of the Sallentines, or on the edge of Apulia.[1]

What were the Romans doing?

It will be observed that the only events recorded of this year, 541, are the reduction of Arpi by Fabius, the unimportant operations of Gracchus in Lucania, and Hannibal's surprise of Tarentum; which last action, however, did not happen till the end of the campaign, about the middle of the winter. According to Livy, Hannibal had passed the whole summer near Tarentum; he must therefore have been some months in that neighbourhood; and what was going on elsewhere the while?   Gracchus, we are told, was engaged in Lucania; but where was the consul Fabius, with his father? and what was done by the four Roman legions, Fabius's consular army, and the prætorian army of M. Æmilius, which were both stationed in Apulia?   Allowing that Cn. Fulvius with his two legions in the camp above Suessula was busied in watching the Campanians, yet Fabius and Æmilius had nearly 40,000 men at their disposal; and yet Capua was not besieged; nor was Hannibal impeded in his attempts upon Tarentum.   Is it to be conceived that so large a portion of the power of Rome, directed by old Fabius himself, can have been totally wasted during a whole summer, useless alike for attack or defence?

Chronological difficulties.

The answer to this question depends upon another point, which is itself not easy to fix: the true date,

---

[1] Polybius, VIII. 34–36. Livy, XXV. 11.

namely, of the surprise of Tarentum.   Livy tells us A.U c. 541.
A.C. 213.
that it was placed by different writers in different
years; and he himself prefers the later date,[1] yet
does not give it correctly.   For as Tarentum was
surprised in the winter, the doubt must have been
whether to fix it towards the end of the consulship
of Fabius and Gracchus, or of Fulvius and Appius
Claudius: it could never have been placed so early
as the consulship of Fabius and Marcellus.   Livy
describes it after he has mentioned the coming into
office of Fulvius and Claudius, as if it belonged to
their year; yet he places it before the opening of
the campaign, which implies that it must have
occurred in the preceding winter, whilst Fabius and
Gracchus were still in office.   Polybius evidently
gave the later date, that is, the year of Fulvius and
Appius, but the end of it: according to him it
followed the death of Gracchus, and the various
events of the summer of 542.   And there are some
strong reasons for believing this to be the more
probable position.   If this were so, we must suppose
that the summer of 541 was passed without any
important action, because Hannibal, after the loss
of Arpi, continued to watch the two Roman armies
in Apulia; and that either the fear of losing
Tarentum, or the hope of recovering Salapia and
other Apulian towns, detained Fabius in the south-
east, and delayed the siege of Capua.

In the meantime men's minds at Rome were Disorders
at Rome.
restless and uneasy; and the government had enough
to do to prevent their running wild in one direction

---

[1] Livy, XXV. 11.   [Cf. Nissen in Rheinisches Museum, XXVI.
254, 257, note 2.]

A.U.C. 541.
A.C. 213.

or another.   The city had suffered from a fire, which lasted a whole day and two nights, and destroyed all the buildings along the river, with many of those on the slope of the Capitoline Hill, and between it and the Palatine.[1]   The distress thus caused would be great; and the suspicions of treason and incendiarism, the constant attendants of great fires in large cities, would be sure to embitter the actual suffering.   At such a time every one would crave to know what the future had in store for him; and whoever professed to be acquainted with the secrets of fate found many to believe him.   Faith in the gods of Rome was beginning to be shaken : if they could not or would not save, other powers might be more propitious; and sacrifices and prayers to strange gods were offered in the Forum and Capitol; while prophets, deceiving or deceived, were gathering crowds in every street, making a profit of their neighbours' curiosity and credulity.[2]   Nor were these vagabond prophets the only men who preyed upon the public distress : the wealthy merchants who had come forward with patriotic zeal to supply the armies when the treasury was unable to bear the burden, were now found to be seeking their own base gain out of their pretended liberality.   M. Postumius of Pyrgi was charged by public rumour with the grossest frauds; he had demanded to be reimbursed for the loss of stores furnished by him at sea, when no such loss had occurred; he had loaded old rotten vessels with cargoes of trifling value; the sailors had purposely sunk the ships, and had escaped in their boats; and then Postumius

[1] Livy, XXIV. 47.   [2] Livy, XXV. 1. 12.

magnified the value of the cargo, and prayed to be indemnified for the loss.[1] Even the virtue of Roman matrons could not stand the contagion of this evil time: more than one case of shame was brought by the ædiles before the judgment of the people.[2] Man's spirit failed with woman's modesty: the citizens of the military age were slow to enlist; and many from the country tribes would not come to Rome when the consuls summoned them.[3] All this unsoundness at home may have had its effect on the operations of the war, and tended to make Fabius more than usually cautious, as another defeat at such a moment might have extinguished the Roman name.

Against this weight of evils the senate bore up vigorously. The superstitions of the people, their worship of strange gods, and their shrinking from military service, required to be noticed without delay. The city prætor, M. Atilius, issued an edict forbidding all public sacrifices to strange gods, or with any strange rites. All books of prophecies, all formularies of prayer or of sacrifice, were to be brought to him before the first of April; that is, before he went out of office.[4] The great ceremonies of the national religion were celebrated with more than usual magnificence; the great games of the circus were kept up for an additional day; two days were added to the celebration of the games of the commons; and they were farther marked by a public entertainment given in the precincts of the temple of Jupiter on the Capitol to all the poorer

A.U.C. 541.
A.C. 213.

Vigorous measures of the senate.

---

¹ Livy, XXV. 3, 4.   ² Livy XXV. 2.
³ Livy, XXV. 5.   ⁴ Livy, XXV. 1.

A.U.C. 542.
A.C. 212.

citizens.[1] A great military effort was to be made in the ensuing campaign; old Q. Fulvius Flaccus, one of the ablest as well as hardest men in Rome, was chosen consul for the third time, and Appius Claudius was elected at his colleague.[2] The armies, notwithstanding the difficulty of enlisting soldiers, were to be augmented: two extraordinary commissions of three members each were appointed, one to visit all the country tribes within fifty miles of Rome, and the other such as were more remote. Every free-born citizen was to be passed in review; and boys under seventeen were to be enlisted, if they seemed strong enough to bear arms; but their years of service were to count from their enlistment; and if they were called out before the military age began, they might claim their discharge before it ended.[3]

Punish-
ment of
Postumius.

While dealing thus strictly with the disorders and want of zeal of the multitude, the senate, it might have been supposed, would not spare the fraud of the contractor Postumius. But with that neglect of equal justice which is the habitual sin of an aristocracy, they punished the poor, but were afraid to attack the wealthy; and, although the city prætor had made an official representation of the tricks practised by Postumius, no steps were taken against him. Amongst the new tribunes, however, were two of the noble house of the Carvilii, who, indignant at the impunity of so great an offender, resolved to bring him to trial. They at first demanded no other penalty than that a fine of

---

[1] Livy, XXV. 2.   [2] Livy, XXV. 3.

[3] Livy, XXV. 5.

200,000 asses should be imposed on him; but when the trial came on, a large party of the monied men broke up the assembly by creating a riot, and no sentence was passed. This presumption, however, overshot its mark; the consuls took up the matter and laid it before the senate; the senate resolved that the peace of the commonwealth had been violently outraged, and the tribunes now proceeded against Postumius and the principal authors of the disturbance capitally. Bail was demanded of them, but they deserted their bail and went into exile, upon which the people, on the motion of the tribunes, ordered that their property should be sold, and themselves outlawed.[1] Thus the balance of justice was struck, and this doubtless contributed to conciliate the poorer citizens, and to make them more ready to bear their part in the war.

It was resolved that Capua should be besieged without delay. In the preceding year 112 noble Capuans had left the city, and come over to the Romans, stipulating for nothing but their lives and properties.[2] This shows that the aristocratical party in Capua could not be depended on; if the city were hard pressed, they would not be ready to make any extraordinary sacrifices in its behalf. Hannibal was far away in the farthest corner of Italy; and as long as the citadel of Tarentum held out he would be unwilling to move towards Campania. Even if he should move, four armies were ready to oppose him; those of the two consuls, of the consul's brother, Cn. Fulvius, who was prætor in Apulia, and of another prætor, C. Claudius Nero, who commanded

A.U.C. 542.
A.C. 212.

Resolution to besiege Capua.

---

[1] Livy, XXV. 4.   [2] Livy, XXIV. 47.

A.U.C. 542
A.C. 212.

two legions in the camp above Suessula. Besides this mass of forces, Ti. Gracchus, the consul of the preceding year, still retained his army as proconsul in Lucania, and might be supposed capable of keeping Hanno and the army of Bruttium in check.

The Campanians apply to Hannibal for aid.

It was late in the spring before the consuls took the field. One of them succeeded to the army of the late consul Fabius; the other took the two legions with which Cn. Fulvius Centumalus had held the camp above Suessula.[1] These armies marching, the one from Apulia, the other from Campania, met at Bovianum; there, at the back of the Matese, in the country of the Pentrian Samnites, the faithful allies of Rome, the consuls were making preparations for the siege of Capua, and perhaps were at the same time watching the state of affairs in the south, and the movements of Hannibal. The Campanians suspected that mischief was coming upon them, and sent a deputation to Hannibal, praying him to aid them. If they were to stand a siege, it was important that the city should be well supplied with provisions; and their own harvest had been so insufficient, owing to the devastation caused by the war, that they had scarcely enough for their present consumption. Hannibal would therefore be pleased to order that supplies should be sent to them from the country of his Samnite and Lucanian allies, before their communications were cut off by the presence of the Roman armies.[2]

He sends Hanno to relieve them, who fails through

Hannibal was still near Tarentum, whether hoping to win the town or the citadel the doubtful chronology of this period will not allow us to decide.

---

[1] Livy, XXV. 3.　　　　[2] Livy, XXV. 13.

He ordered Hanno, with the army of Bruttium, A.U.C. 542.
to move forward into Samnium—a most delicate A.C. 212.
operation, if the two consuls were with their armies
at Bovianum, and Gracchus in Lucania itself, in the
very line of Hanno's march, and if C. Nero with two
legions more was lying in the camp above Suessula.
But the army from Suessula had been given to one
of the consuls; and the legions which were to take
its place were to be marched from the coast of
Picenum, and perhaps had hardly reached their
destination.   The Lucanians themselves seem to
have found sufficient employment for Gracchus; and
Hanno moved with a rapidity which friends and
enemies were alike unprepared for.   He arrived
safely in the neighbourhood of Beneventum, encamped his army in a strong position about three
miles from the town, and despatched word to the
Capuans that they should instantly send off every
carriage and beast of burden in their city to carry
home the corn which he was going to provide for
them.   The towns of the Caudine Samnites emptied
their magazines for the purpose, and forwarded all
their corn to Hanno's camp.   Thus far all prospered;
but the negligence of the Capuans ruined everything; they had not carriages enough ready, and
Hanno was obliged to wait in his perilous situation,
where every hour's delay was exposing him to
destruction.[1]   Beneventum was a Latin colony, in
other words, a strong Roman garrison, watching all
his proceedings; from thence information was sent
to the consuls at Bovianum, and Fulvius with his
army instantly set out, and entered Beneventum by

____

[1] Livy, XXV. 13.

night.   There he found that the Capuans with their means of transport were at length arrived; that all disposable hands had been pressed into the service; that Hanno's camp was crowded with cattle and carriages, and a mixed multitude of unarmed men, and even of women and children, and that a vigorous blow might win it with all its spoil: the more so as the indefatigable general was absent, scouring the country for additional supplies of corn.   Fulvius sallied from Beneventum a little before daybreak, and led his soldiers to assault Hanno's position.   Under all disadvantages of surprise and disorder, the Carthaginians resisted so vigorously, that Fulvius was on the point of calling off his men, when a brave Pelignian officer threw the standard of his cohort over the enemy's wall, and desperately climbed the rampart and scaled the wall to recover it.   His cohort rushed after him, and a Roman centurion then set the same example, which was followed with equal alacrity.   Then the Romans broke into the camp on every side, even the wounded men struggling on with the mass, that they might die within the enemy's ramparts.   The slaughter was great, and the prisoners many; but, above all, the whole of the corn which Hanno had collected for the relief of Capua was lost, and the object of his expedition totally frustrated.   He himself, hearing of the wreck of his army, retreated with all speed into Bruttium.[1]

The Capuans again apply for aid.

Again the Capuans sent to Hannibal, requesting him to aid them ere it was too late.   Their negligence had just cost him an army, and had frustrated all his pains for their relief, but, with unmoved

---

[1] Livy, XXV. 14.   Valerius Maximus, III. 2. 20.

temper, he assured them that he would not forget them, and sent back 2000 of his invincible cavalry with the deputation, to protect their lands from the enemy's ravages. It was important to him not to leave the south of Italy till the very last moment; for since he had taken Tarentum, the neighbouring Greek cities of Metapontum, Heraclea, and Thurii had joined him, and, as he had before won Croton and Locri, he was now master of the whole coast from the Straits of Messana to the mouth of the Adriatic, with the exception of Rhegium and the citadel of Tarentum. Into the latter the Romans had lately thrown supplies of provisions; and the garrison was so strong that Hannibal was unwilling to march into Campania while such a powerful force of the enemy was left behind in so favourable a position.[1]

A.U.C. 542.
A.C. 212.

The consuls, meanwhile, not content with their own two armies and with the two legions expected, if not yet arrived in the camp above Suessula, sent to Gracchus in Lucania, desiring him to bring up his cavalry and light troops to Beneventum, to strengthen them in that kind of force in which they fully felt their inferiority. But before he could leave his own province he was drawn into an ambuscade, by the treachery of a Lucanian in the Roman interest, and perished.[2] His quæstor, Cn. Cornelius, marched with his cavalry towards Beneventum, according to the consul's orders, but the infantry, consisting of the slaves whom he had enfranchised, thought that their service was ended by the death of their deliverer, and immediately

Death of
Gracchus :
Centenius
raises an
army in
Lucania.

[1] Livy, XXV. 15.
[2] Livy, XXV. 16. Appian, Hannibal, 35.

A.U.C. 542.
A.C. 212.

dispersed to their homes.[1] Thus Lucania was left without either a Roman army or general; but M. Centenius, an old centurion, distinguished for his strength and courage, undertook the command there, if the senate would entrust him with a force equal to a single legion. Perhaps, like T. Pomponius Veientanus, he was connected with some of the contractors and monied men, and owed his appointment as much to their interest as to his own reputation. But he was a brave and popular soldier, and so many volunteers joined him on his march, hoping to be enriched by the plunder of Lucania, that he arrived there with a force, it is said, amounting to near 16,000 men. His confidence and that of his followers was doomed to be woefully disappointed.[2]

The Romans are repulsed by a sally from Capua.

The consuls knew that Hannibal was far away, and they did not know that any of his cavalry were in Capua. They issued boldly therefore from the Caudine Forks on the great Campanian plain, and scattered their forces far and wide to destroy the still green corn. To their astonishment the gates of Capua were thrown open, and with the Campanian infantry they recognised the dreaded cavalry of Hannibal. In a moment their foragers were driven in, and as they hastily formed their legions in order of battle to cover them, the horsemen broke upon them like a whirlwind, and drove them with great loss and confusion to their camp.[3] This sharp lesson taught them caution; but their numbers were overwhelming, and their two armies, encamped before Capua, cut off the communications of the city, and had the harvest of the whole country in their power.

---

[1] Livy, XXV. 20.   [2] Livy, XXV. 19.   [3] Livy, XXV. 18.

But ere many days had elapsed, an unwelcome A.U.C. 542. sight was seen on the summit of Tifata; Hannibal A.C. 212. was there once more with his army. He descended Hannibal returns to Tifata. into Capua, two days afterwards he marched out to battle; again his invincible Numidians struck terror into the Roman line, when the sudden arrival of Cn. Cornelius with the cavalry of Gracchus' army broke off the action; and neither side, it is said, knowing what this new force might be, both as if by common consent retreated.[1] How Hannibal so out-stripped Cornelius as to arrive from Tarentum on the scene of action two or three days before him, who was coming from Lucania, we are not told, and can only conjecture. But the arrival of this rein-forcement, though it had saved the consuls from defeat, did not embolden them to hold their ground: they left their camps as soon as night came on, Fulvius fell down upon the coast near Cumæ, Appius Claudius retreated in the direction of Lucania.

Few passages in history can offer a parallel to He enters Capua. Hannibal's campaigns; but this confident gathering of the enemies' overwhelming numbers round the city of his nearest allies, his sudden march, the un-looked-for appearance of his dreaded veterans, and the instant scattering of the besieging armies before him remind us of the deliverance of Dresden in 1813, when Napoleon broke in upon the Allies' con-fident expectations of victory, and drove them away in signal defeat. And like the Allies in that great campaign, the Roman generals knew their own strength, and though yielding to the shock of their adversary's surpassing energy and genius, they did

---

[1] Livy, XXV. 19.

A.U.C. 542.
A.C. 212.

not allow themselves to be scared from their purpose, but began again steadily to draw the toils, which he had once broken through. Great was the joy in Capua when the people rose in the morning and saw the Roman camps abandoned; there needs no witness to tell us with what sincere and deep admiration they followed and gazed on their deliverer, how confident they felt that with him for a shield no harm could reach them. But almost within sight and hearing of their joy the stern old Fulvius was crouching as it were in his thicket, watching the moment for a second spring upon his prey; and when Hannibal left that rejoicing and admiring multitude to follow the traces of Appius, he passed through the gates of Capua to enter them again no more.

On his return into Lucania he destroys the army of Centenius;

Appius retreated in the direction of Lucania: this is all that is reported of his march, and then, after a while, having led his enemy in the direction which suited his purposes, he turned off by another road and made his way back to Campania.[1] With such a total absence of details, it is impossible to fix the line of this march exactly. It was easy for Appius to take the round of the Matese; retiring first by the great road to Beneventum, then turning to his left and regaining his old quarters at Bovianum, from whence, the instant that Hannibal ceased to follow him, he would move along under the north side of the Matese to Æsernia, and descend again upon Campania by the valley of the Vulturnus. Hannibal's pursuit was necessarily stopped as soon as Appius moved northwards from Beneventum; he

[1] Livy, XXV. 19.

could not support his army in the country of the A.U.C. 542.
Pentrian Samnites, where everything was hostile to A.C. 212.
him, nor did he like to abandon his line of direct
communication with southern Italy.   He had gained
a respite for Capua, and had left an auxiliary force
to aid in its defence; meanwhile other objects must
not be neglected, and the fall of the citadel of Tarentum might of itself prevent or raise the siege of
Capua.   So he turned off from following Appius,
and was marching back to the south when he was
told that a Roman army was attempting to bar his
passage in Lucania.   This was the motley multitude
commanded by Centenius, which had succeeded, as
we have seen, to the army of Gracchus.   With what
mad hope, or under what false impression, Centenius
could have been tempted to rush upon certain
destruction we know not, but in the number no less
than the quality of his troops he must have been
far inferior to his adversary.   His men fought
bravely, and he did a centurion's duty well, however
he may have failed as a general; but he was killed,
and nearly 15,000 men are said to have perished with
him.[1]

Thus Lucania was cleared of the Romans; and and that of Cn. Fulvius in Apulia.
as the firmest partisan of the Roman interest among
the Lucanians had been the very man who had
betrayed Gracchus to his fate, it is likely that the
Carthaginian party was triumphant through the
whole country.   Only one Roman army was left in
the south of Italy, the two legions commanded by
Cn. Fulvius Flaccus, the consul's brother, in Apulia.
But Cn. Fulvius had nothing of his brother's ability;

---

[1] Livy, XXV. 19.

he was a man grown old in profligacy, and the discipline of his army was said to be in the worst condition. Hannibal, hoping to complete his work, moved at once into Apulia, and found Fulvius in the neighbourhood of Herdonea. The Roman general met him in the open field without hesitation, and was presently defeated; he himself escaped from the action; but Hannibal had occupied the principal roads in the rear of the enemy with his cavalry, and the greatest part of the Roman army was cut to pieces.[1]

What were the results of these victories?

We naturally ask what result followed from these two surprising victories, and to this question we find no recorded answer. Hannibal, we are told, returned to Tarentum; but finding that the citadel still held out, and could neither be forced nor surprised, and that provisions were still introduced by sea, a naval blockade in ancient warfare being always inefficient, he marched off towards Brundisium, on some prospect that the town would be betrayed into his hands. This hope also failed him; and he remained inactive in Apulia, or in the country of the Sallentines, during the rest of the year. Meantime the consuls received orders from the senate to collect the wrecks of the two beaten armies, and to search for the soldiers of Gracchus' army, who had dispersed, as we have seen, after his death. The city prætor, P. Cornelius, carried on the same search nearer Rome, and these duties, says Livy, were all performed most carefully and vigorously.[2] This is all the information which exists for us in the remains of the ancient writers, but assuredly this is no military history of a campaign.

[1] Livy, XXV. 20, 21.   [2] Livy, XXV. 22.

It is always to be understood that Hannibal could not remain long in an enemy's country, from the difficulty of feeding his men, especially his cavalry. But the country round Capua was not all hostile; Atella and Calatia, in the plain of Campania itself, were still his allies, so were many of the Caudine Samnites, from whose cities Hanno had collected the corn early in this year for the relief of Capua. Again, we can conceive how the number of the Roman armies sometimes oppressed him; how he dared not stay long in one quarter, lest a greater evil should befall him in another. But at this moment three great disasters, the dispersion of the army of Gracchus, and the destruction of those of Centenius and Fulvius, had cleared the south of Italy of the Romans; and his friends in Apulia, in Lucania, at Tarentum, and in Bruttium, could have nothing to fear had he left them for the time to their own resources. Why, after defeating Fulvius, did he not retrace his steps towards Campania, hold the field with the aid of his Campanian and Samnite allies till the end of the military season, and then winter close at hand, on the shores of the Gulf of Salerno, in the country of his allies, so as to make it impossible for the Romans either to undertake or to maintain the siege of Capua?

That his not doing this was not his own fault, his extraordinary ability and energy may sufficiently assure us. But where the hindrance was we cannot certainly discover. His army must have been worn by its long and rapid march to and from Campania, and by two battles fought with so short an interval. His wounded must have been numerous:

nor can we tell how such hard service in the heat of summer may have tried the health of his soldiers. His horses too must have needed rest; and to overstrain the main arm of his strength would have been fatal. Perhaps too, great as was Hannibal's ascendency over his army, there was a point beyond which it could not be tried with safety. Long marches and hard-fought battles gave the soldier, especially the Gaul and the Spaniard, what in his eyes was a rightful claim to a season of rest and enjoyment: the men might have murmured had they not been permitted to taste some reward of their victories. Besides all these reasons, the necessity of a second march into Campania may not have seemed urgent; the extent of Capua was great; if the Roman consuls did encamp before it, still the city was in no immediate danger; after the winter another advance would again enable him to throw supplies into the town, and to drive off the Roman armies. So Capua was left for the present to its own resources, and Hannibal passed the autumn and winter in Apulia.

The Romans surround Capua with a double wall.

Immediately the Roman armies closed again upon their prey. Three grand magazines of corn were established, to feed the besieging army during the winter, one at Casilinum within three miles of Capua; another at a fort built for the purpose at the mouth of the Vulturnus; and a third at Puteoli. Into these two last magazines the corn was conveyed by sea from Ostia, whither it had already been collected from Sardinia and Etruria.[1] Then the consuls summoned C. Nero from his camp above

---

[1] Livy, XXV. 22.

Suessula; and the three armies began the great A.U.C. 542.
A.C. 212. work of surrounding Capua with double continuous lines, strong enough to repel the besieged on the one side, and Hannibal on the other, when he should again appear in Campania.   The inner line was carried round the city, at a distance of about a quarter of a mile from the walls; the outer line was concentric with it; and the space between the two served for the cantonments and magazines of the besiegers.   The lines, says Appian,[1] looked like a great city, inclosing a smaller city in the middle; like the famous lines of the Peloponnesians before Platæa.   What time was employed in completing them we know not: they were interrupted by continual sallies of the besieged; and Jubellius Taurea and the Capuan cavalry were generally too strong for the Roman horsemen.[2]   But their infantry could do nothing against the legions; the besieging army must have amounted nearly to 60,000 men; and slowly but surely the imprisoning walls were raised, and their circle completed, shutting out the last gleams of light from the eyes of the devoted city.

Before the works were closed all round, the consuls, according to the senate's directions, signified to them by the city prætor, announced to the Capuans that whoever chose to come out of the city with his family and property before the ides of March might do so with safety, and should be untouched in body or goods.[3]   It would seem then that the works were not completed till late in the winter; for we cannot suppose that the term of

Their offer to allow any of the citizens to come out safely is rejected.

---

[1] Hannibal 37.

[2] Appian, Hannibal, 37.   Livy, XXVI. 4.   [3] Livy, XXV. 22.

A.U.C. 543.
A.C. 211.

grace would have been prolonged to a remote day, especially as the ides of March were the beginning of the new consular year; and it could not be known long beforehand whether the present consuls would be continued in their command or no. The offer was received by the besieged, it is said, with open scorn; their provisions were as yet abundant, their cavalry excellent; their hope of aid from Hannibal, as soon as the campaign should open, was confident. But Fulvius waited his time; nor was his thirst for Capuan blood to be disappointed by his removal from the siege at the end of the year: it would seem as if the new consuls were men of no great consideration, appointed probably for that very reason, that their claims might not interfere with those of their predecessors. One of them, P. Sulpicius Galba, had filled no curule office previously; the other, Cn. Fulvius Centumalus, had been prætor two years before, but was not distinguished by any remarkable action. The siege of Capua was still to be conducted by Appius Claudius and Fulvius, and they were ordered not to retire from their positions till they should have taken the city.[1]

State of
Capua.

What was the state of affairs in Capua meantime, we know not. The Roman stories are little to be credited, which represent all the richer and nobler citizens as abandoning the government, and leaving the office of chief magistrate, Meddix Tuticus, to be filled by one Seppius Lesius, a man of obscure condition, who offered himself as a candidate.[2] Neither

---

[1] Livy, XXVI. 1. Frontinus, Strat. III. 18. 3.
[2] Livy, XXVI. 6. [For the title of Meddix Tuticus, see the references given in Revue Archeologique, V. 390 (1885)].

Vibius Virrius nor Jubellius Taurea wanted resolu- A.U.C. 543.
A.C. 211.
tion to abide by their country to the last; and it is
expressly said that, down to the latest period of the
siege, there was no Roman party in Capua; no
voice was heard to speak of peace or surrender; no
citizen had embraced the consul's offers of mercy.[1]
Even when they had failed to prevent the completion
of the Roman lines, they continued to make frequent
sallies; and the pro-consuls could only withstand
their cavalry by mixing light-armed foot soldiers
amongst the Roman horsemen, and thus strengthening that weakest arm in the Roman service.[2] Still,
as the blockade was now fully established, famine
must be felt sooner or later; accordingly a Numidian
was sent to implore Hannibal's aid, and succeeded in
getting through the Roman lines, and carrying his
message safely to Bruttium.[3]

Hannibal listened to the prayer, and leaving his Hannibal
comes to its
relief.
heavy baggage, and the mass of his army behind,
set out with his cavalry and light infantry, and with
33 elephants.[4] Whether his Samnite and Lucanian
allies joined him on the march, is not stated; if
they did not, and if secrecy and expedition were
deemed of more importance than an addition of
force, the troops which he led with him must have
been more like a single corps than a complete army.
Avoiding Beneventum he descended the valley of
the Calor towards the Vulturnus, stormed a Roman
post, which had been built apparently to cut off the
communications of the besieged with the upper
valley of the Vulturnus, and encamped immediately

---

[1] Livy, XXVI. 12.   [2] Frontinus, Strat. IV. 7. 29.
[3] Livy. XXVI. 4.   [4] Livy, XXVI. 5.

behind the ridge of Tifata. From thence he descended once more into the plain of Capua, displayed his cavalry before the Roman lines in the hope of tempting them out to battle, and finding that this did not succeed, commenced a general assault upon their works.

Hannibal attacks the Roman lines ineffectually, and resolves to march against Rome.

Unprovided with any artillery, his best hope was that the Romans might be allured to make some rash sally: his cavalry advanced by squadrons up to the edge of the trench, and discharged showers of missiles into the lines; while his infantry assailed the rampart, and tried to force their way through the palisade which surmounted it. From within the lines were attacked by the Campanians and Hannibal's auxiliary garrison; but the Romans were numerous enough to defend both fronts of their works; they held their ground steadily, neither yielding nor rashly pursuing; and Hannibal, finding his utmost efforts vain, drew off his army.[1] Some resolution must be taken promptly; his cavalry could not be fed where he was, for the Romans had previously destroyed or carried away everything that might serve for forage; nor could he venture to wait till the new consuls should have raised their legions, and be ready to march from Rome and threaten his rear. One only hope remained; one attempt might yet be made, which should either raise the siege of Capua or accomplish a still greater object: Hannibal resolved to march upon Rome.

He sets out suddenly by night.

A Numidian was again found, who undertook to pass over to the Roman lines as a deserter, and from thence to make his escape into Capua, bearing

[1] Polybius, IX. 3. Livy, XXVI. 5.

a letter from Hannibal, which explained his purpose, A.U.C.543.
and conjured the Capuans patiently to abide the A.C. 211.
issue of his attempt for a little while.[1]　When this
letter reached Capua Hannibal was already gone;
his camp-fires had been seen burning as usual all
night in his accustomed position on Tifata; but he
had begun his march the preceding evening, immediately after dark, while the Romans still thought that
his army was hanging over their heads, and were
looking for a second assault.[2]

His army disappeared from the eyes of the Difficulty
Romans behind Tifata; and they knew not whither of making
he was gone.　Even so is it with us at this day; of march.
we lose him from Tifata; we find him before Rome;
but we know nothing of his course between.　Con-
flicting and contradictory accounts have made the
truth undiscoverable: what regions of Italy beheld
with fear or hope the march of the great general
and his famous soldiers, it is impossible from our
existing records to determine.　Whether he followed
the track of Pyrrhus, and spread havoc through the
lands of the numerous colonies on the Latin road,
Cales, Casinum, Interamna, and Fregellæ;[3] or whether,
to baffle the enemy's pursuit, and avoid the delay of
crossing the Vulturnus, he plunged northwards into
the heart of Samnium,[4] astonished the Latin colonists
of Æsernia with his unlooked-for passage, crossed the
central Apennines into the country of the Pelignians,
and then, turning suddenly to his left, broke down
into the land of the Marsians, passing along the
glassy waters of Fucinus, and under the ancient

---

[1] Polybius, IX. 5.　Livy, XXVI. 7.　　[2] Polybius, IX. 5.
[3] Livy, XXVI. 9.　　　　　　　　　[4] Polybius, IX. 5.

A.U.C. 543.
A.C. 211.

walls of Alba, and scaring the upland glades and quiet streams of the aboriginal Sabines with the wild array of his Numidian horsemen; we cannot with any confidence decide. Yet the agreement of all the stories as to the latter part of his march seems to point out the line of its beginning. All accounts say that descending nearly by the old route of the Gauls, he kept the Tiber on his right, and the Anio on his left; and that, finally, he crossed the Anio, and encamped at a distance of less than four miles from the walls of Rome.[1]

Terror in Rome: fortitude of the senate. Before the sweeping pursuit of his Numidians, crowds of fugitives were seen flying towards the city, while the smoke of burning houses arose far and wide into the sky. Within the walls the confusion and terror were at their height: he was come at last, this Hannibal, whom they had so long dreaded; he had at length dared what even the slaughter of Cannæ had not emboldened him to venture; some victory greater even than Cannæ must have given him this confidence; the three armies before Capua must be utterly destroyed; last year he had destroyed or dispersed three other armies, and had gained possession of the entire south of Italy, and now he had stormed the lines before Capua, had cut to pieces the whole remaining force of the Roman people, and was come to Rome to finish his work. So the wives and mothers of Rome lamented, as they hurried to the temples; and there, prostrate before the gods, and sweeping the sacred pavement with their unbound hair in the

[1] Polybius, IX. 5 fin. Livy, XXVI. 9. Appian, Hannibal, 38. See Note L.

agony of their fear, they remained pouring forth their prayers for deliverance. Their sons and husbands hastened to man the walls and the citadel, and to secure the most important points without the city; whilst the senate, as calm as their fathers of old, whom the Gauls massacred when sitting at their own doors, but with the energy of manly resolution, rather than the resignation of despair, met in the forum, and there remained assembled, to direct every magistrate on the instant, how he might best fulfil his duty.[1]

But God's care watched over the safety of a people whom He had chosen to work out the purposes of His providence: Rome was not to perish. Two city legions were to be raised, as usual, at the beginning of the year, and it so happened that the citizens from the country tribes were to meet at Rome on this very day for the enlistment for one of these legions, while the soldiers of the other, which had been enrolled a short time before, were to appear at Rome on this same day in arms, having been allowed, as the custom was, to return home for a few days after their enlistment, to prepare for active service. Thus it happened that 10,000 men were brought together at the very moment when they were most needed, and were ready to repel any assault upon the walls.[2] The allies, it seems, were not ordinarily called out to serve with the two city legions, but on this occasion it is mentioned that the Latin colony of Alba, having seen Hannibal pass by their walls, and guessing the object of his march, sent its whole force to assist in the

A.U.C. 543.
A.C. 211.

Rome is preserved from an assault.

<hr>

[1] Polybius. IX. 6. Livy, XXVI. 9. [2] Polybius, IX. 6.

A.U.C. 543.
A.C. 211.

defence of Rome, a zeal which the Greek writers compared to that of Platæa, whose citizens fought alone by the side of the Athenians on the day of Marathon.[1]

Hannibal ravages the country round.

To assault the walls of Rome was now hopeless, but the open country was at Hannibal's mercy, a country which had seen no enemy for near a hundred and fifty years, cultivated and inhabited in the full security of peace. Far and wide it was overrun by Hannibal's soldiers, and the army appears to have moved about, encamping in one place after another, and sweeping cattle and prisoners and plunder of every sort, beyond numbering, within the enclosure of its camp.[2]

He rides up to the walls of Rome.

It was probably in the course of these excursions that Hannibal, at the head of a large body of cavalry, came close up to the Colline gate, rode along leisurely under the walls to see all he could of the city, and is said to have cast his javelin into it as in defiance.[3] From farthest Spain he had come into Italy, he had wasted the whole country of the Romans and their allies with fire and sword for more than six years, had slain more of their citizens than were now alive to bear arms against him, and at last he was shutting them up within their city, and riding freely under their walls, while none dared meet him in the field. If anything of disappointment depressed his mind at that instant; if he felt that Rome's strength was not broken, nor the spirit of her people quelled, that his own fortune was wavering, and that his last effort had been

[1] Appian, Hannibal, 39.   [2] Polybius, IX. 6.
[3] Livy, XXVI. 10. Pliny, XXXIV. 6. (15.)

made, and made in vain; yet thinking where he
was, and of the shame and loss which his presence
was causing to his enemies, he must have wished
that his father could have lived to see that day,
and must have thanked the gods of his country
that they had enabled him so fully to perform his vow.

For some time, we know not how long, this devastation of the Roman territory lasted without
opposition.   Meanwhile the siege of Capua was not
raised; and Fabius, in earnestly dissuading such a
confession of fear, showed that he could be firm no
less than cautious, when boldness was the highest
prudence.   But Fulvius, with a small portion of the
besieging army, was recalled to Rome; Fabius had
ever acted with him, and was glad to have the aid
of his courage and ability; and when he arrived,
and by a vote of the senate was united with the
consuls in the command, the Roman forces were led
out of the city, and encamped, according to Fabius'
old policy, within ten stadia of the enemy, to check
his free license of plunder.[1]   At the same time,
parties acting on the rear of Hannibal's army had
broken down the bridges over the Anio, his line of
retreat, like his advance, being on the right bank
of that river, and not by the Latin road.

Hannibal had purposely waited to allow time for
his movement to produce its intended effect in the
raising of the siege of Capua.   That time, according
to his calculations, was now come; the news of his
arrival before Rome must have reached the Roman
lines before Capua; and the armies from that
quarter, hastening by the Latin road to the defence

[1] Livy, XXVI. 8–10. Polybius, IX. 7. Appian, Hannibal, 40.

of their city, must have left the communication with Capua free.   The presence of Fulvius with his army in Latium, which Hannibal would instantly discover by the thrice-repeated sounding of the watch, as Hasdrubal found out Nero's arrival in the camp of Livius near Sena, would confirm him in his expectation that the other proconsul was on his march with the mass of the army; and he accordingly commenced his retreat by the Tiburtine road, that he might not encounter Appius in front, while the consuls and Fabius were pressing on his rear.

The Romans follow him at a distance.

Accordingly, as the bridges were destroyed, he proceeded to effect his passage through the river, and carried over his army under the protection of his cavalry, although the Romans attacked him during the passage, and cut off a large part of the plunder which he had collected from the neighbourhood of Rome.[1]   He then continued his retreat, and the Romans followed him, but at a careful distance, and keeping steadily on the higher grounds, to be safe from the assaults of his dreaded cavalry.[2]

He marches down into Bruttium.

In this manner Hannibal marched with the greatest rapidity for five days, which, if he was moving by the Valerian road, must have brought him at least as far as the country of the Marsians, and the shores of the lake Fucinus.[3]   From thence he would again have crossed by the Forca Carrosa to the plain of the Pelignians, and so retraced his steps through Samnium towards Capua.   But at this point he received intelligence that the Roman armies were still in their lines, that his march

---

[1] Polybius, IX. 7.
[2] Appian, Hannibal, 40.   Polybius. IX. 7.   [3] Polybius, IX. 7.

upon Rome had therefore failed, and that his com- A.U.C. 543.
munications with Capua were as hopeless as ever. A.C. 211.
Instantly he changed all his plans, and feeling
obliged to abandon Capua, the importance of his
operations in the south rose upon him in proportion.
Hitherto he had not thought fit to delay his march
for the sake of attacking the army which was pursuing him; but now he resolved to rid himself of
this enemy; so he turned fiercely upon them, and
assaulted their camp in the night.   The Romans,
surprised and confounded, were driven from it with
considerable loss, and took refuge in a strong
position in the mountains.   Hannibal then resumed
his march, but, instead of turning short to his right
towards Campania, descended towards the Adriatic
and the plains of Apulia, and from thence returned
to what was now the stronghold of his power in
Italy, the country of the Bruttians.[1]

The citadel of Tarentum still held out against He misses taking Rhegium.
him, but Rhegium, confident in its remoteness, had
never yet seen his cavalry in its territory, and was
now less likely than ever to dread his presence, as
he had so lately been heard of in the heart of Italy,
and under the walls of Rome.   With a rapid
march therefore he hastened to surprise Rhegium.
Tidings of his coming reached the city just in time
for the Rhegians to shut their gates against him,
but half their people were in the country, in the full
security of peace, and these all fell into his power.[2]
We know not whether he treated them kindly, as
hoping through their means to win Rhegium, as he
had won Tarentum. or whether disappointment was

[1] Polybius, IX. 7. Appian, Hannibal, 41–43.   [2] Polybius, IX. 7.

now stronger than hope, and, despairing of drawing the allies of Rome to his side, he was now as inveterate against them as against the Romans. He retired from his fruitless attempt to win Rhegium only to receive the tidings of the loss of Capua.

The Romans had patiently waited their time, and were now to reap their reward. The consuls were both to command in Apulia with two consular armies; one of them therefore must have returned to Rome to raise the two additional legions which were required. Fulvius hastened back to the lines before Capua. His prey was now in his power; the straitness of the blockade could no longer be endured, and aid from Hannibal was not to be hoped. It is said that mercy was still promised to any Capuan who should come over to the Romans before a certain day, but that none availed themselves of the offer, feeling, says Livy, that their offence was beyond forgiveness.[1] This can only mean that they believed the Romans to be as faithless as they were cruel, and felt sure that every promise of mercy would be evaded or openly broken. One last attempt was made to summon Hannibal again to their aid, but the Numidians employed on the service were detected this time in the Roman lines, and were sent back torn with stripes, and with their hands cut off, into the city.[2]

No Capuan writer has survived to record the last struggle of his country; and never were any people less to be believed than the Romans, when speaking of their enemies. Yet the greatest man could not have supported the expiring weakness of an unheroic

The Romans press the siege of Capua.

The chief senators of Capua poison themselves.

---

[1] Livy, XXVI. 12.   [2] Livy, XXVI. 12.

people, and we hear of no great man in Capua. A.U.C. 543
A.C. 211.
Some of the principal men in the senate met, it is
said, at the house of one of their number, Vibius
Virrius, where a magnificent banquet had been prepared for them, they ate and drank, and when the
feast was over, they all swallowed poison. Then,
having done with pleasure and with life, they took a
last leave of each other, they embraced each other,
lamenting with many tears their own and their
country's calamity, and some remained to be burned
together on the same funeral pile, while others went
away to die at their own homes. All were dead
before the Romans entered the city.[1]

In the meanwhile the Capuan government, unable Surrender
of the city.
to restrain their starving people, had been obliged
to surrender to the enemy. In modern warfare
the surrender of a besieged town involves no extreme
suffering; even in civil wars, justice or vengeance
only demands a certain number of victims, and the
mass of the population scarcely feels its condition
affected. But surrender, *deditio*, according to the
Roman laws of war, placed the property, liberties,
and lives of the whole surrendered people at the
absolute disposal of the conquerors, and that not
formally, as a right, the enforcement of which were
monstrous, but as one to abate which in any instance
was an act of free mercy. In this sense Capua was
surrendered; in the morning after Vibius Virrius's
funeral banquet, the gate of Jupiter, which looked
towards the Roman headquarters, was thrown open,
and a Roman legion, with its usual force of cavalry
doubled, marched in to take possession. It was

[1] Livy, XXVI. 14.

commanded by C. Fulvius. the brother of the pro-consul, who immediately placed guards at all the gates, caused all the arms in the city to be brought to him, made prisoners of the Carthaginian garrison, and sent all the Capuan senators into the Roman camp to abide his brother's sentence.

Fulvius puts all the senators to death.

No Roman family has preserved a more uniform character of pride and cruelty through successive generations than the Claudii, but in the treatment of the Capuans Q. Fulvius was so much the principal actor that, according to some of the annals, Appius Claudius was no longer alive, having been mortally wounded some time before the end of the siege.[1] His daughter had been married to a Campanian, and the senators of Capua might perhaps seem to him worthier of regard than the Commons of Rome.   But whether Appius was living or dead, he was unable to arrest the course of his colleague's vengeance.   The Capuan senators were immediately chained as bond-slaves, were commanded to give up all their gold and silver to the quæstors, and were then sent in custody, five-and-twenty to Cales, and twenty-eight to Teanum.   Ere the next night was over, Fulvius, with 2000 chosen horsemen, left the camp, and arrived at Teanum by daybreak.   He took his seat in the forum, ordered the magistrates of Teanum to bring forth their prisoners, and saw them all scourged and beheaded in his presence. Then he rode off to Cales, and repeated the same tragedy there.[2]

Severe treatment of all the Campanians.

Atella and Calatia followed the example of Capua,

---

[1] Livy, XXVI. 16. Zonaras, IX. 6.
[2] Livy, XXVI. 15. Valerius Maximus, III. 8. 1.

and surrendered at discretion to the Romans. There, A.U.C. 543.
also, about twenty senators were executed, and about A.C. 211.
three hundred persons of noble birth, in one or other
of the three cities, were sent to Rome, and thrown
into the Mamertine prison, there to die of starvation
and misery, while others met a similar fate in the
various allied cities whither they were sent prisoners.[1]
The besieging army was then relieved from its long
services, part of it was probably sent home, or
transferred to one of the consuls to form his army
in Apulia. C. Nero, the propraetor, was sent with
about 13,000 men into Spain, where the Roman
affairs where in a most critical state,[2] while Q.
Fulvius remained still as proconsul in Capua, exercising the utmost severity of conquest over the
remnant of the unfortunate people.

A few months afterwards, on the night of the Decrees
18th of March in the following year, a fire broke about them.
out at Rome in several places at once, in the neighbourhood of the forum. The temple of Vesta and
its eternal fire, the type of the life of the commonwealth, were saved with great difficulty. This fire
was said to be the work of some noble Capuans,
whose fathers had been beheaded by Q. Fulvius;
they were accused by one of their slaves, and a
confession of the charge having been forced from
their other slaves by torture, the young men were
put to death.[3] Fulvius made this a pretence for
fresh severities against the Capuans, and no doubt
it had an influence upon the senate when the fate
of the three revolted cities of Campania was finally

---

[1] Livy, XXVI. 16.   [2] Livy, XXVI. 17.
[3] Livy, XXVI. 27.

decided.   As the Capuans had enjoyed the franchise of Roman citizens, the senate was obliged to obtain an act of the comitia empowering them to determine their future condition.   A number of decrees were passed accordingly, as after the great Latin war, distinguishing the punishment of different classes, and even of different individuals.   All who had been senators, or held any office, were reduced to utter beggary, their lands being forfeited to Rome, together with the whole Campanian territory, and their personal property of every kind being ordered to be sold.   Some were sold, besides, for slaves, with their wives and children; and it was especially ordered that they should be sold at Rome, lest some of their countrymen or neighbours should purchase them for the purpose of restoring their liberty.   All who had been in Capua during the siege were transported beyond the Tiber, and forbidden to possess lands or houses above a certain measure, or out of certain specified districts : those who had not been in Capua, or in any other revolted city, during the war, were only transported beyond the Liris ; while those who had gone over to the Romans before Hannibal entered Capua were removed no further than across the Vulturnus.   In their exiled state, however, they were still to be personally free, but were incapable of enjoying either the Roman franchise or the Latin.[1]   The city of Capua, bereaved of all its citizens, was left to be inhabited by that mixed multitude of resident foreigners, freedmen, and half-citizens, who, as shopkeepers and mechanics, had always formed a large part of the

[1] Livy, XXVI. 33, 34.

population ; but all political organisation was strictly A.U.C. 543.
denied to them, and they were placed under the A.C. 211.
government of a præfect sent thither every year
from Rome.[1] The Campanian plain, the glory of
Italy, and all the domain lands which Capua had
won in former wars, when she was the ally of Rome,
as her share of the spoils of Samnium, were forfeited
to the Roman people. In the domain lands some
colonies were planted soon after the war,[2] but the
Campanian plain was held in occupation by a
number of Roman citizens, and the vectigal or rent
which they paid to the state was for a hundred and
fifty years an important part of the Roman revenue.[3]
Only two individuals were found deserving of favour,
it is said, among the whole Capuan people ; these
were two women, one of whom had daily sacrificed
in secret during the siege for the success of the
Romans, and the other had secretly fed some Roman
prisoners. These had their property restored to
them by a special decree of the senate, and they
were desired to go to Rome and to petition the
senate, if they thought proper, for some additional
reward.[4]

I have given the settlement of Campania and the Fulvius is
fate of the Capuans in detail, because it seems taken refused a triumph.
from authentic sources, and is characteristic of the
stern determination with which the Roman government went through its work. It is no less characteristic that when Q. Fulvius applied for a triumph,
after his most important and splendid success, the
senate refused to grant it, because he had only

<hr>

[1] Livy, XXVI. 16.   [2] Livy, XXXIV. 45.
[3] Cicero, De Leg. Agrar. II. 29.   [4] Livy, XXVI. 33, 34.

recovered what had belonged to Rome before; and the mere retrieving of losses, and restoring the dominion of the commonwealth to its former extent, was no subject of extraordinary exultation.[1]

Importance of the taking of Capua.

But, although not rewarded by a triumph, the conquest of Capua was one of the most important services ever rendered by a Roman general to his country. It did not merely deprive Hannibal of the greatest fruit of his greatest victory, and thus seem to undo the work of Cannæ, but its effect was felt far and wide, encouraging the allies of Rome, and striking terror into her enemies; tempting the cities which had revolted to return without delay to their allegiance, and filling Hannibal with suspicions of those who were still true to him, as if they only waited to purchase their pardon by some act of treachery towards his garrisons. By the recovery of Capua his great experiment seemed decided against him. It appeared impossible under any circumstances to rally such a coalition of the Italian states against the Roman power in Italy, as might be able to overthrow it. We almost ask with what reasonable hopes could Hannibal from this time forward continue the war? or why did he not change the seat of it from Southern Italy to Etruria and Cisalpine Gaul?

Hannibal's favourable prospects.

But with whatever feelings of disappointment and grief he may have heard of the fall of Capua, of the ruin of his allies, and the bloody death of so many of the Capuan senators, and of the brave Jubellius Taurea whom he had personally known and honoured, yet the last campaign was not without

---

[1] Valerius Maximus, II. 8. 4.

many solid grounds of encouragement. Never had A.U.C. 543. A.C. 211. the invincible force of his army been more fully proved. He had overrun half Italy, had crossed and recrossed the passes of the Apennines, had plunged into the midst of the Roman allies, and had laid waste the territory of Rome with fire and sword. Yet no superiority of numbers, no advantage of ground, no knowledge of the country, had ever emboldened the Romans to meet him in the field, or even to beset his road, or to obstruct and harass his march. Once only, when he was thought to be retreating, had they ventured to follow him at a cautious distance, but he had turned upon them in his strength, and the two consuls, and Q. Fulvius with them, were driven before him as fugitives to the mountains, their camp stormed, and their legions scattered. It was plain, then, that he might hold his ground in Italy as long as he pleased, supporting his army at its cost, and draining the resources of Rome and her allies year after year, till in mere exhaustion the Roman commons would probably join the Latin colonies and the allies in forcing the senate to make peace.

At this very moment Etruria was restless, and required an army of two legions to keep it quiet;[1] the Roman commons, in addition to their heavy taxation and military service, had seen their lands laid waste, and yet were called upon to bear fresh burdens; and there was a spirit of discontent working in the Latin colonies, which a little more provocation might excite to open revolt. Spain besides seemed at last to be freed from the enemy;

Unfavourable circumstances of the Romans in Italy and in Spain.

---

[1] Livy, XXVI. 1. 28; XXVII. 7. Comp. XXVII. 21, 22. 24.

 and the recent defeats and deaths of the two Scipios there held out the hope to Hannibal that now at length his brother Hasdrubal, having nothing to detain him in Spain, might lead a second Carthaginian army into Italy, and establish himself in Etruria, depriving Rome of the resources of the Etruscan and Umbrian states, as she had already lost those of half Samnium, of Lucania, Bruttium, and Apulia. Then, assailed at once by two sons of Hamilcar on the north and the south, the Roman power, which one of them singly had so staggered, must, by the joint efforts of both, be beaten to the ground and destroyed. With such hopes, and with no unreasonable confidence, Hannibal consoled himself for the loss of Capua, and allowed his army, after its severe marching, to rest for the remainder of the year in Apulia.[1] And now, as we have brought the war in Italy to this point, it is time to look abroad, and to observe the course of this mighty contest in Spain, in Greece, and in Sicily.

[1] Compare Livy, XXVI. 37.

CHAPTER III.

WARS must of necessity form a large part of all
history ; but in most wars the detail of military
operations is without interest for posterity, and
should only be given by contemporary writers.   It
was right for Thucydides to relate every little expedition of the Peloponnesian war at length, but
modern writers do wrong in following his example,
for the details of petty warfare are unworthy to
survive their own generation.   And there are also
wars conducted on a great scale, and very important
in their consequences, the particulars of which may
safely be forgotten.   For military events should only
be related circumstantially to after-ages, when they
either contain a great lesson in the art of war, or
are so striking in their incidents as to acquire the
interest of a romance, and thus retain their hold on
the imaginations and moral feelings of all ages and
countries.   Hannibal's campaigns in Italy have this
double claim on our notice : they are a most valuable
study for the soldier, whilst for readers in general
they are a varied and eventful story, rich in char-

acters, scenes, and actions. But the war in Spain, although most important in its results, and still more the feeble bickerings rather than wars of the decayed states of Greece, may and ought to be related summarily. A closer attention must be given to the war in Sicily: there again the military and the general interest of the story are great; we have the ancient art of defence exhibited in its highest perfection, we have the immortal names of Syracuse and Archimedes.

Campaign of 541 in Spain.

There is another reason, however, why we should not give a minute account of the Spanish war, and that is because we really know nothing about it.[1] The Roman annalists, whom Livy has copied here, seem to have outdone their usual exaggerations in describing the exploits of the two Scipios: and what is the truth concealed beneath this mass of fiction we are wholly unable to discover. Spain, we know, has in later wars been overrun victoriously and lost again in a single summer; and no one can say how far the Scipios may at times have penetrated into the heart of the country, but it is certain that in the first years of their command they made no lasting impression south of the Iberus. Still their maintaining their ground at all in Spain was of signal service to Rome. The Carthaginians, on the other hand, knew the importance of expelling them; but it appears that, in the year 541, they became engaged in a war with Syphax, one of the kings or chiefs of the Numidians; and a war in Africa was always so alarming to them that they recalled Hasdrubal, Hannibal's brother, from Spain, with a part of their

[1] See Note M.

forces employed in that country, and thus took off A.U.C. 542.
the pressure from the Romans at a most critical A.C. 212.
moment.[1] The Scipios availed themselves of this
relief ably, and now they seem to have advanced
into the heart of Spain with effect, to have drawn
over many of the Spanish tribes to the Roman
alliance, and thus to have obtained large recruits
for their own army, which received but slight reinforcements from Rome. It is said that 20,000
Celtiberians were raised to serve under the Scipios,
and that at the same time 300 noble Spaniards
were sent into Italy to detach their countrymen
there from Hannibal's service.[2] Cn. Scipio, we are
told, was greatly loved and reverenced by the
Spaniards,[3] and his influence probably attracted the
Celtiberians to the Roman armies; but we know
not where he found money to pay them, as the
Roman treasury was in no condition to supply him,
and he was obliged to make war support war.
However, careful economy of the plunder which he
may have won from some of the allies of Carthage,
assisted perhaps by loans from some of the Spanish
chiefs attached to himself and to Rome, had enabled
him to raise a large army ; so that, when Hasdrubal
returned from Africa, apparently late in 542,
although there were two other Carthaginian generals
in Spain,[4] each commanding a separate army, yet the
Roman generals thought themselves strong enough
to act on the offensive ; and they concerted a grand

---

[1] Appian, Hispan. 15. Livy, XXIV. 48

[2] Livy, XXV. 32 ; XXIV. 49.

[3] Livy, XXV. 36. Appian, Hispan. 15.

[4] Livy, XXV. 32. Appian, Hispan. 16.

plan for the campaign of 543, by which they hoped to destroy all the armies opposed to them, and to drive the Carthaginians out of Spain. With this confidence they divided their forces, and having crossed the Iberus, marched each in pursuit of a separate enemy. Cn. Scipio was to attack Hasdrubal, while his brother was to fall on the other two Carthaginian generals, Hasdrubal the son of Giscon and Mago.[1]

Campaign of 543 : defeat and death of the Scipios.

They had wintered, it seems, in the country of their new auxiliaries, or, according to one account, even farther to the south, in the valley of the Bætis or Guadalquiver.[2] But it is as impossible to disentangle the geography of this war as its history. The Carthaginian generals owed their triumph—and more than this we cannot ascertain—to the ascendency of Hasdrubal's name and personal character; for the Celtiberians, when brought into his neighbourhood, were unable to resist his influence, and abruptly left the Roman camp, and returned home.[3] Thus abandoned, and at a great distance from all their resources, the two Roman generals were successively attacked by the Carthaginians, defeated and killed.[4] Of the wreck of their armies some fled to the towns of their Spanish allies for refuge, and were in some instances slain by them, or betrayed to the Carthaginians; a remnant, which had either been left behind the Iberus before the opening of the campaign, or had effected its retreat thither, was still held together by Scipio's lieutenant, T. Fonteius, and by L. Marcius.[5]

<hr>

[1] Livy, XXV. 32.   [2] Appian, Hispan. 16.
[3] Livy, XXV. 33.   [4] Livy, XXV. 34–36. Appian, Hispan. 16.
[5] Livy, XXV. 36–39.

Marcius was only a simple Roman knight, that is, A.U.C. 543.
A.C. 211. a man of good fortune, who therefore served not in the infantry of the legions, but in the cavalry; he had a natural genius for war, and was called irregularly, it seems, by the common voice of the soldiers to take the command; and we need not doubt that, by some timely advantages gained over some of the enemy's parties, he raised the spirits of the men, and preserved the Roman cause in Spain from utter extinction. But the extravagant fables of his victories over the victorious Carthaginians, and of his storming their camps, show too clearly out of what wretched materials the Roman history has to be written.[1]

If the defeat of the Scipios took place, as seems probable, early in the year 543, that is, a few weeks before the fall of Capua, we may again admire the wonderful disposal of events by which the ruin of the Roman cause in Spain was delayed till their affairs in Italy had passed over their crisis, and were beginning to mend. The Scipios' army was replaced by that of C. Nero, which the fall of Capua set at liberty;[2] a year earlier this resource would not have been available. Still the Carthaginians immediately recovered all the states south of the Ebro, which had before revolted; and the Romans were confined to a narrow strip of coast between

The Ro-
mans are
driven to
the foot of
the Pyre-
nees.

---

[1] Livy, XXV. 39. According to one account, 37,000 men were slain on the Carthaginian side. Valerius Antias returned 17,000 killed, and 4330 prisoners. Appian (Hispan. 17) substitutes Marcellus by mistake for Marcius, but says he did nothing brilliant, so that the Carthaginian power increased, and spread almost over the whole of Spain.

[2] Livy, XXVI. 17.

A.U.C. 543.
A.C. 211. the Iberus and the Pyrenees,[1] from which the over-whelming force of their enemies was likely ere long to drive them.   And so it would, had not the external weakness of the Roman cause been now upheld for the first time by individual genius, so that a defeated and dispirited army became, in the hands of the young P. Scipio, the instrument by which all Spain was conquered.

Strange in-efficiency of Macedon,   Seventy years before this period a Greek army under Pyrrhus had shaken the whole power of Rome; yet the kingdom of Pyrrhus was little more than a dependency of Macedon, and Pyrrhus had struggled against the arms of the Macedonian kings vigorously, but without success.   Now a young, warlike, and popular king was seated on the throne of Macedon;[2] he had just concluded a war victori-ously with the only state in Greece which seemed capable of resisting his power.   What Pyrrhus had almost done alone, would surely be easy for Philip to accomplish, with Hannibal and his invincible army to aid him; and what could Rome have done if to the irresistible African cavalry there had been joined a body of heavy-armed Macedonians, and a force of artillery and engineers such as Greek science alone could furnish?   The strangest and most un-accountable blank in history is the early period of the Macedonian war, before the Ætolians became the allies of Rome, and a coalition was formed against Philip in Greece itself.   Philip's treaty with

---

[1] Appian, Hispan. 17.

[2] Philip was not more than seventeen years old in the archonship of Ariston, A.U.C. 534. Polybius, IV. 5. For his popular and warlike character, see Polybius, IV. 77. 82.

Hannibal was concluded in the year 539, or early enough, at any rate, to allow of his commencing operations in the year 540.[1] The Ætolians concluded their treaty with Rome in 543, after the fall of Capua.[2] More than three precious years seem to have been utterly wasted; and during all this time M. Valerius Lævinus, commanding at Brundisium with a single legion and a small fleet, was allowed to paralyse the whole power of Macedon.[3]

The cause of this is to be found in that selfish attention to separate objects which has so often been the ruin of coalitions. Philip's object, or, rather, that of Demetrius of Pharos, whose influence appears plainly in all this war with Rome, was to undo the work of the late Roman victories in Illyria, and to wrest the western coast of Epirus from their dominion. In his treaty with Hannibal, Philip had especially stipulated that the Romans should not be allowed to retain their control over Corcyra, Apollonia, Epidamnus, Pharus, Dimalla or Dimalus, the country of the Parthinians, and Atintania;[4] places which in the Illyrian wars had either submitted to, or been conquered by, the Romans. Philip does not appear to have understood that all these were to be reconquered most surely in Italy; that it was easier to crush Lævinus at Brundisium than to repel him from Epirus; more prudent to march against him at the head of the Greeks of Italy than to let him come to the aid of the Greeks on the coast of Illyria. Thus he trifled away his strength in petty

arising from Philip's selfishness.

---

[1] Livy, XXIII. 33. 39. Above, p. 112.   [2] Livy, XXVI. 24.
[3] Livy, XXIV. 10. 44 : XXV. 3 ; XXVI. 24.
[4] Polybius, VII. 9.

enterprises, and those not always successful, till the Romans found the time come to carry on the war against him in earnest; and they were not apt either to neglect their opportunities or to misuse them.

He wastes his time on petty objects.

Philip was personally brave, and could on occasion show no common activity and energy. But he had not that steadiness of purpose, without which energy in political affairs is worthless. Thus he was lightly deterred from an enterprise by dangers which he was not afraid of, but rather did not care to encounter. The naval power of Greece had long since sunk to nothing; Philip had no regular navy, and the small vessels which he could collect were no match for the Roman quinqueremes, so that a descent upon Italy appeared hazardous, while various schemes opened upon him nearer home, which his own temper, or the interests of his advisers, led him to prefer. Hence he effected but little during three years. He neither took Epidamnus, nor Apollonia, nor Corcyra; but he won Lissus, and the strong fortress which served as its citadel;[1] and he seems also to have conquered Dimalus or Dimallus, and to have enlarged his dominion more or less nominally with the countries of the Parthinians and Atintanians, of which the sovereignty had belonged to the Romans.[2] From all this Hannibal derived no benefit, and Rome sustained no serious injury.

Hiero's faithful friendship to the Romans: his death;

In the year of Rome 491, in the second year of the first Punic war, Hiero, king of Syracuse, had

[1] Polybius, VIII. 15, 16.

[2] In Livy, XXIX. 12, we find these attacked by the Romans, as being subject to Macedon.

made peace with the Romans, and had become their A.U.C. 539.
A.C. 215.
ally. Forty-seven years had passed away since, when the tidings of the battle of Cannæ arrived at Syracuse, and seemed to announce that a great part of Sicily was again to change its masters, and to be subjected once more to the Carthaginian dominion. But Hiero, although about ninety years of age, did not waver. Far from courting the friendship of Carthage, he increased his exertions in behalf of Rome; he supplied the Roman army in Sicily with money and corn at a time when all supplies from home had failed,[1] and about a year afterwards, when a fleet was prepared to meet the hostile designs of Philip of Macedon, Hiero again sent 50,000 medimni of wheat and barley to provision it.[2] This must nearly have been his last public act. Towards the close of the year 539, after a life of ninety years, and a reign of fifty-four, but still retaining all his faculties, sound in mind and vigorous in body, Hiero died.[3]

He had enjoyed and deserved the constant affection of his people, and had seen his kingdom flourishing more and more under his government. preceded by that of his son Gelon. One only thing had marred the completeness of his fortune: his son Gelon had died before him, with whom he had lived in the most perfect harmony, and who had ever rendered him the most devoted and loving obedience.[4] He had still two daughters, Damarata and Heraclea, who were married to two eminent Syracusans, Andranodorus and Zoippus;

---

[1] Livy, XXIII. 22. See above, p. 98.
[2] Livy, XXIII. 38. [3] Polybius, VII. 8.
[4] Polybius, VII. 8.

and he had one grandson, a boy of about fifteen, the son of Gelon, Hieronymus.[1]

He is suc-
ceeded by
his grand-
son Hier-
onymus:
his char-
acter.

It is the most difficult problem in a hereditary monarchy, how to educate the heir to the throne, when the circumstances of his condition, so much more powerful than any instruction, are apt to train him for evil far more surely than the lessons of the wisest teachers can train him for good. In the ancient world, moreover, there was no fear of God to sober the mind which was raised above all fear or respect for man; and if the philosophers spoke of the superiority of virtue and wisdom over all the gifts of fortune, their own example, when they were seen to sue for the king's favour, and to dread his anger, no less than ordinary men, made their doctrines regarded either as folly or hypocrisy. Hieronymus at fifteen became king of Syracuse; a child in understanding, but with passions pre-cociously vigorous because he had such large means of indulging them; insolent, licentious, and cruel, yet withal so thoughtless and so mere a slave of every impulse, that he was sure to be the instru-ment of his own ruin.

He joins the
Carthagin-
ians,

We have already noticed his early communication with Hannibal, and the arrival of Hippocrates and Epicydes at Syracuse, Syracusans by extraction, but born at Carthage, and by education and franchise Carthaginians, whom Hannibal had sent to Hierony-mus to confirm him in his alienation from Rome.[2] They won the youth's ear by telling him of Han-nibal's marches and victories; for in those days

---

[1] Livy, XXIV. 4.

[2] Polybius, VII. 2. Livy, XXIV. 6. See above, p. 112.

events that were two or three years old were still A.U.C. 539.
news to foreigners; common fame had reported the A.C. 215.
general facts, but the details could only be gathered
accidentally; and Hieronymus listened eagerly to
Hippocrates and Epicydes, when they told him
stories of their crossing the Rhone, of their passage
of the Alps and Apennines, of the slaughter of the
Romans at Thrasymenus, and of their late unequalled
victory at Cannæ, of all which they had themselves
been eye-witnesses.[1]   And when they saw Hieronymus possessed with a vague longing that he too
might achieve such great deeds, they asked him
who had such claims as he to be king of all Sicily.
His mother was the daughter of Pyrrhus; his father
was Hiero's son; with this double title to the love
and homage of all Sicilians, he should not be contented to divide the island either with Rome or
Carthage: by his timely aid to Hannibal he might
secure it wholly to himself.   The youth accordingly
insisted that the sovereignty of all Sicily should
be ceded to him as the price of his alliance with
Carthage; and the Carthaginians were well content
to humour him, knowing that, if they could drive
the Romans out of the island, they had little to fear
from the claims of Hieronymus.[2]

Appius Claudius, the Roman prætor in Sicily, and deserts
aware of what was going on, sent some of his officers the Ro-
to Syracuse to warn the king not to break off his
grandfather's long friendship with Rome, but to renew
the old alliance in his own name.[3]   Hieronymus
called his council together, and Hippocrates and

<hr>

[1] Polybius, VII. 4.   [2] Polybius, VII. 4. Livy, XXIV. 6.
[3] Polybius, VII. 5. Livy, XXIV. 6.

Epicydes were present.   His native subjects, afraid to oppose his known feelings, said nothing; but three of his council, who came from old Greece, conjured him not to abandon his alliance with Rome.   Andranodorus alone, his uncle and guardian, urged him to seize the moment, and become sovereign of all Sicily.   He listened, and then, turning to Hippocrates and Epicydes, asked them, 'And what think you?'   'We think,' they answered, 'with Andranodorus.'   'Then,' said he, 'the question is decided; we will no longer be dependent on Rome.' He then called in the Roman ambassadors, and told them that 'he was willing to renew his grandfather's league with Rome, if they would repay him all the money and corn with which Hiero had at various times supplied them; if they would restore the costly presents which he had given them, especially the golden statue of Victory, which he had sent to them only three years since, after their defeat at Thrasymenus; and finally, if they would share the island with him equally, ceding all to the east of the river Himera.'[1]   The Romans considered this answer as a mockery, and went away without thinking it worthy of a serious reply.   Accordingly from this moment Hieronymus conceived himself to be at war with Rome: he began to raise and arm soldiers, and to form magazines; and the Carthaginians, according to their treaty with him, prepared to send over a fleet and army to Sicily.

He is murdered by conspiracy.   Meanwhile his desertion of the Roman alliance was most unwelcome to a strong party in Syracuse. A conspiracy had already been formed against his

---

[1] Polybius, VII. 5. See Livy, XXII. 37.

life, which was ascribed, whether truly or not, to A.U.C. 539.
the intrigues of this party;[1] and now that he had A.C. 215.
actually joined the Carthaginians, they became more
bitter against him; and a second conspiracy was
formed with better success. He had taken the field
to attack the cities in the Roman part of the island.
Hippocrates and Epicydes were already in the
enemy's country; and the king, with the main
body of his army, was on his march to support
them, and had just entered the town of Leontini.[2]
The road, which was also the principal street of
the city, lay through a narrow gorge, with abrupt
cliffs on either side; and the houses ran along in a
row, nestling under the western cliff, and facing
towards the small river Lissus, which flowed through
the gorge between the town and the eastern cliff.[3]
An empty house in this street had been occupied by
the conspirators: when the king came opposite to
it, one of their number, who was one of the king's
guards, and close to his person, stopped just behind
him, as if something had caught his foot; and
whilst he seemed trying to get it free, he checked the
advance of the following multitude, and left the
king to go on a few steps unattended. At that
moment the conspirators rushed out of the house
and murdered him. So sudden was the act
that his guards could not save him: seeing him
dead, they were seized with a panic, and dispersed.
The murderers hastened, some into the market-
place of Leontini, to raise the cry of liberty there,
and others to Syracuse, to anticipate the king's

---

[1] Polybius, VII. 2.   Livy, XXIV. 5.   [2] Livy, XXIV. 7.
[3] Polybius, VII. 6.

A.U.C. 539.
A.C. 215.

Insurrection at Syracuse.

Murder of Andranodorus and Themistus,

friends, and secure the city for themselves and the Romans.[1]

Their tidings, however, had flown before them; and Andranodorus, the king's uncle, had already secured the island of Ortygia, the oldest part of Syracuse, in which was the citadel, and where Hiero and Hieronymus had resided.[2] The assassins arrived just at nightfall, displaying the bloody robe of Hieronymus, and the diadem which they had torn from his head, and calling the people to rise in the name of liberty. Their call was obeyed: all the city, except the island, was presently in their power; and in the island itself a strong building, which was used as a great corn magazine for the supply of the whole city, was no sooner seized by those whom Andranodorus had sent to occupy it, than they offered to deliver it up to the opposite party.[3]

The general feeling being thus manifested, Andranodorus yielded to it. He surrendered the keys of the citadel and of the treasury; and in return he and Themistus, who had married a sister of Hieronymus, were elected among the captains-general of the commonwealth, to whom, according to the old Syracusan constitution, the executive government was to be committed. But their colleagues were mostly chosen from the assassins of Hieronymus; and between such opposites there could be no real union. Suspicions and informations of plots were not long wanting. An actor told the majority of the captains-general that Andranodorus and Themistus were conspiring to massacre them and the other

---

[1] Livy, XXIV. 7.   [2] Livy, XXIV. 21.
[3] Livy, XXIV. 21, 22.

leaders of their party, and to re-establish the A.U.C. 539.
A.C. 215.
tyranny: the charge was made out to the satisfac-
tion of those who were so well disposed to believe
it: they stationed soldiers at the doors of the
council chamber, and as soon as Andranodorus and
Themistus entered, the soldiers rushed in and
murdered them.[1] The members of the council
decided that they were rightfully slain, but the
multitude were inclined to believe them less guilty
than their murderers, and beset the council, calling
for vengeance. They were persuaded, however, to
hear what the perpetrators of the deed could say in
its defence; and Sopater, one of the captains-general,
who was concerned both in the recent murder and
in that of Hieronymus, arose to justify himself and
his party. The tyrannies in the ancient world were
so hateful that they were put by common feeling
out of the pale of ordinary law: when Sopater
accused Andranodorus and Themistus of having been
the real authors of all the outrages committed by
the boy Hieronymus; when he inveighed against
their treacherous submission to their country's laws,
and against their ingratitude in plotting the deaths
of those who had so nobly forgiven all their past
offences; and when he said, finally, that they had
been instigated to all these crimes by their wives,
that Hiero's daughter and granddaughter could not
condescend to live in a private station, there arose a
cry from some, probably of their own tutored partisans,
which the whole multitude, in fear or in passion,
immediately echoed, 'Death to the whole race of the
tyrants; not one of them shall be suffered to live.'[2]

[1] Livy, XXIV. 23, 24.   [2] Livy, XXIV. 25.

A.U.C. 539.
A.C. 215.
and of all
the de-
scendants
of Hiero.

They who had purposely roused the multitude to fury were instantly ready to secure it for their own bloody ends. The captains-general proposed a decree for the execution of every person of the race of the tyrants; and the instant it was passed, they sent parties of soldiers to carry it into effect. Thus the wives of Andranodorus and Themistus were butchered; but there was another daughter of Hiero, the wife of Zoippus, who was so far from sharing in the tyranny of Hieronymus that, when sent by him as his ambassador to Egypt, he had chosen to live there in exile. His innocent wife, with her two young maiden daughters, were included in the general proscription. They took refuge at the altar of their household gods, but in vain: the mother was dragged from her sanctuary and murdered; the daughters fled wildly into the outer court of the palace, in the hope of escaping into the street, and appealing to the humanity of the passers-by; but they were pursued and cut down by repeated wounds. Ere the deed was done, a messenger came to say that the people had revoked their sentence; which seems to show that the captains-general had taken advantage of some expressions of violence, and had done in the people's name what the people had never in earnest agreed to. At any rate, their rage was now loud against their bloody government; and they insisted on having a free election of captains-general to supply the places of Andranodorus and Themistus; a demand which implies that some preceding resolutions or votes of the popular assembly had been passed under undue influence.[1]

[1] Livy, XXIV. 26.

The party which favoured the Roman alliance had done all that wickedness could to make themselves odious.   The reaction against them was natural; yet the same foreign policy which these butchers supported had been steadily pursued by the wise and moderate Hiero.   Every party in that corrupt city of Syracuse wore an aspect of evil: the partisans of Carthage were in nothing better than those of Rome.   When Hieronymus had been murdered, Hippocrates and Epicydes were at the moment deserted by their soldiers, and returned to Syracuse as private individuals.   There they applied to the government for an escort to convey them back to Hannibal in safety; but the escort was not provided immediately; and in the interval they perceived that they could serve Hannibal better by remaining in Sicily.   They found many amongst the mercenary soldiers of the late king, and amongst the poorer citizens, who readily listened to them, when they accused the captains-general of selling the independence of Syracuse to Rome: and their party was so strengthened by the atrocities of the government that, when the election was held to choose two new captains-general in the place of Andranodorus and Themistus, Hippocrates and Epicydes were nominated and triumphantly elected.[1]   Again therefore the government was divided within itself; and Hippocrates and Epicydes had been taught by the former conduct of their colleagues that one party or the other must perish.

The Roman party had immediately suspended hostilities with Rome, obtained a truce from Appius

A.U.C. 539.
A.C. 215.
The Cartha-
ginian
party
rallies.

The Ro-
man fleet
sails to the ·

---

[1] Livy, XXIV. 23, 27.

A.U.C. 539.
A.C. 215.
mouth of
the har-
bour.

Claudius renewable every ten days, and sent ambassadors to him to solicit the revival of Hiero's treaty. A Roman fleet of 100 ships was lying off the coast a little to the north of Syracuse, which the Romans on the first suspicion of the defection of Hieronymus, had manned by the most extraordinary exertions, and sent to Sicily. On the other hand, Himilco, with a small Carthaginian fleet, was at Pachynus, Rome and Carthage each anxiously watching the course of events in Syracuse, and each being ready to support its party there. Matters were nicely balanced; and the Roman fleet, in the hope of turning the scale, sailed to Syracuse, and stationed itself at the mouth of the great harbour.[1]

The Roman party becomes the more powerful.

Strengthened by this powerful aid, the Roman party triumphed, even moderate men not wishing to provoke an enemy who was already at their gates. The old league with Rome was renewed, with the stipulation that whatever cities in Sicily had been subject to King Hiero should now in like manner be under the dominion of the Syracusan people. It appears that, since the murder of Hieronymus, his kingdom had gone to pieces, many of the towns, and Leontini in particular, asserting their independence. These were, like Syracuse, in a state of hostility against Rome, owing to Hieronymus's revolt; but they had no intention of submitting again to the Syracusan dominion. Still, when the Romans threatened them, they sent to Syracuse for aid, and as the Syracusan treaty with Rome was not yet ratified or made public, the government could not decline their request. Hippocrates accordingly was

[1] Livy, XXIV. 27.

sent to Leontini, with a small army, consisting A.U.C. 539.
chiefly of deserters from the Roman fleet; for, in A.C. 215.
the exigency of the time, the fleet had been manned
by slaves furnished by private families in a certain proportion, according to their census; and the men thus
provided, being mostly unused to the sea, and forced
into the service, deserted in unusually large numbers,
insomuch that there were 2000 of them in the party
which Hippocrates led to the defence of Leontini.[1]

This auxiliary force did good service, and Appius Marcellus
Claudius, who commanded the Roman army, was arrives in Sicily:
obliged to stand on the defensive.   Meanwhile M.
Marcellus had arrived in Sicily, having been sent
over thither, as we have seen, after the close of the
campaign in Italy, to take the supreme command.
As the negotiations with Syracuse were now concluded, Marcellus required that Hippocrates should
be recalled from Leontini, and that both he and
Epicydes should be banished from Sicily.   Epicydes
upon this, feeling that his personal safety was risked
by remaining longer at Syracuse, went also to
Leontini, and both he and his brother inveighed
loudly against the Roman party who were in possession of the government; they had betrayed their
country to Rome, and were endeavouring, with the
help of the Romans, to enslave the other cities of
Sicily, and to subject them to their own dominion.
Accordingly, when some officers arrived from Syracuse requiring the Leontines to submit, and announcing to Hippocrates and Epicydes their sentence
of expulsion from Sicily, they were answered that
the Leontines would not acknowledge the Syracusan

[1] Livy, XXIV. 27, 29, 30.

A.U.C. 539.
A.C. 215.

government, nor were they bound by its treaties. This answer being reported to Syracuse, the leaders of the Roman party called upon Marcellus to fulfil his agreement with them, and to reduce Leontini to submission.[1] That city was now the refuge and centre of the popular party in Sicily, as Samos had been in Greece, when the 400 usurped the government of Athens, and Hippocrates and Epicydes looked upon their army as the true representative of the Syracusan people, just as Thrasybulus and Thrasyllus, and the Athenian fleet at Samos, regarded themselves, during the tyranny of the aristocratical party at home, as the true people of Athens.

Marcellus takes Leontini : his cruelties there

But, as we have noticed more than once before, nothing could less resemble the slowness and feebleness of Sparta than the tremendous energy of Rome. The prætor's army in Sicily at the beginning of the year consisted of two legions, and it is probable that Marcellus had brought one at least of the two legions which had formed his consular army. With this powerful force Marcellus instantly attacked Leontini, and stormed it, and in addition to the usual carnage on the sack of a town, he scourged and in cold blood beheaded 2000 of the Roman deserters, whom he found bearing arms in the army of Hippocrates ; Hippocrates and his brother escaping only with a handful of men, and taking refuge in the neighbouring town of Herbessus.[2]

excite general indignation.

For nearly thirty years war had been altogether unknown in Sicily; fifty years had passed since a hostile army had made war in the territory of Syracuse. All men therefore were struck with

---

[1] Livy, XXIV. 29.   [2] Livy, XXIV. 30.

horror at the fate of Leontini: if Ætna had rolled A.U.C. 539.
down his lava flood upon the town its destruction A.C. 215.
would scarcely have been more sudden and terrible.
But with horror indignation was largely mingled:
the bloodiness of the Romans in the sack of towns
went far beyond the ordinary practice of the Greeks;
the Syracusan government had betrayed their
countrymen of Leontini to barbarians more cruel
than the Mamertines.

The tidings spread far and wide, and met a Syra- The Syracusan army, which two of the captains-general, Sosis cusan army
refuses to
and Dinomenes, both of them assassins of Hierony- march,
mus, and devoted to the cause of Rome, were leading
out to co-operate with Marcellus. The soldiers, full
of grief and fury, refused to advance a step farther:
their blood, they said, would be sold to the Romans,
like that of their brethren at Leontini. The generals
were obliged to lead them back to Megara, within a
few miles of Syracuse, then hearing that Hippocrates
and Epicydes were at Herbessus, and dreading their
influence at a moment like this, they led their troops
to attack the town where they had taken refuge.[1]

Hippocrates and his brother threw open the gates and to act
of Herbessus, and came out to meet them. At against
Hippo-
the head of the Syracusan army marched 600 crates and
Cretans, old soldiers in Hiero's service, whom he Epicydes.
had sent over into Italy to act as light troops in
the Roman army against Hannibal's barbarians, but
who had been taken prisoners at Thrasymenus, and
with the other allies or auxiliaries of Rome had been
sent home by Hannibal unhurt. They now saw
Hippocrates and Epicydes coming towards them

[1] Livy, XXIV. 30.

with no hostile array, but holding out branches of olive tufted here and there with wool, the well-known signs of a suppliant. They heard them praying to be saved from the treachery of the Syracusan generals, who were pledged to deliver up all foreign soldiers serving in Sicily to the vengeance of the Romans. The Cretans felt that the cause of Hippocrates and Epicydes was their own, and swore to protect them. In vain did Sosis and Dinomenes ride forward to the head of the column, and trying what could be done by authority, order the instant arrest of the two suppliants. They were driven off with threats; the feeling began to spread through the army; and the Syracusan generals had no resource but to march back to Megara, leaving the Cretan auxiliaries, it seems, with Hippocrates and Epicydes in a state of open revolt.[1]

Triumph of the popular party in Syracuse.
Meantime the Cretans sent out parties to beset the roads leading to Leontini; and a letter was intercepted, addressed by the Syracusan generals to Marcellus, congratulating him on his exploit at Leontini, and urging him to complete his work by the extermination of every foreign soldier in the service of Syracuse. Hippocrates took care that the purport of this letter should be quickly made known to the army at Megara, and he followed closely with the Cretans to watch the result. The army broke out into mutiny; Sosis and Dinomenes, protesting in vain that the letter was a mere forgery of the enemy, were obliged to escape for their lives to Syracuse: even the Syracusan soldiers were accused of sharing in their generals' treason, and were for a

[1] Livy, XXIV. 30, 31.

time in great danger from the fury of the foreigners, their comrades.   But Hippocrates and Epicydes prevented this mischief, and being received as leaders by the whole army set out forthwith for Syracuse. They sent a soldier before them, most probably a native Syracusan, who had escaped from the sack of Leontini, and could tell his countrymen as an eye-witness what acts of bloodshed, outrage, and rapine the Romans had committed there.   Even in moderate men, who for Hiero's sake were well inclined to Rome, the horrors of Leontini overpowered all other thoughts and feelings : within Syracuse and without all followed one common impulse.   When Hippocrates and Epicydes arrived at the gates the citizens threw them open ; the captains-general in vain endeavoured to close them ; they fled to Achradina, the lower part of the city, with such of the Syracusan soldiers as still adhered to them, whilst the stream of the hostile army burst down the slope of Epipolæ, and, swelled by all the popular party, the foreign soldiers, and the old guards of Hiero and Hieronymus came sweeping after them with irresistible might. Achradina was carried in an instant; some of the captains-general were massacred ; Sosis escaped to add the betrayal of his country hereafter to his multiplied crimes.   The confusion raged wild and wide ; slaves were set free ; prisoners were let loose; and amidst the horrors of a violent revolution, under whatever name effected, the popular party, the party friendly to Carthage, and adverse to aristocracy and to Rome, obtained the sovereignty of Syracuse.[1]

Sosis, now in his turn a fugitive, escaped to Leon-

A.U.C 539.
A.C. 215.

Marcellus
besieges
Syracuse,

---

[1] Livy, XXIV. 31. 32.

A.U.C. 541.
A.C. 213. tini, and told Marcellus of the violence done to the friends of Rome. The fiery old man, as vehement at sixty against his country's enemies as when he slew the Gaulish king in single combat in his first consulship, immediately moved his army upon Syracuse. He encamped by the temple of Olympian Jupiter, on the right bank of the Anapus, where two solitary pillars still remain, and serve as a sea-mark to guide ships into the great harbour. Appius Claudius with the fleet beset the city by sea, and Marcellus did not doubt that in the wide extent of the Syracusan walls some unguarded spot would be found, and that the punishment of Leontini would soon be effaced by a more memorable example of vengeance.[1]

by land and by sea ;

Thus was commenced the last siege of Syracuse—a siege not inferior in interest to the two others which it had already undergone, from the Athenians and from the Carthaginians. It should be remembered that the city walls now embraced the whole surface of Epipolæ, terminating, like the lines of Genoa, in an angle formed by the converging sides of the hill, or inclined table-land, at the point where it becomes no more than a narrow ridge, stretching inland, and connecting itself with the hills of the interior. The Romans made their land attack on the south front of the walls, while their fleet, unable, as it seems, to enter the great harbour, carried on its assaults against the sea-wall of Achradina.

is baffled by Archimedes.

The land attack was committed to Appius Claudius, while Marcellus in person conducted the operations of the fleet. The Roman army is spoken of as large, but no details of its force are given: it

[1] Livy, XXIV. 33.

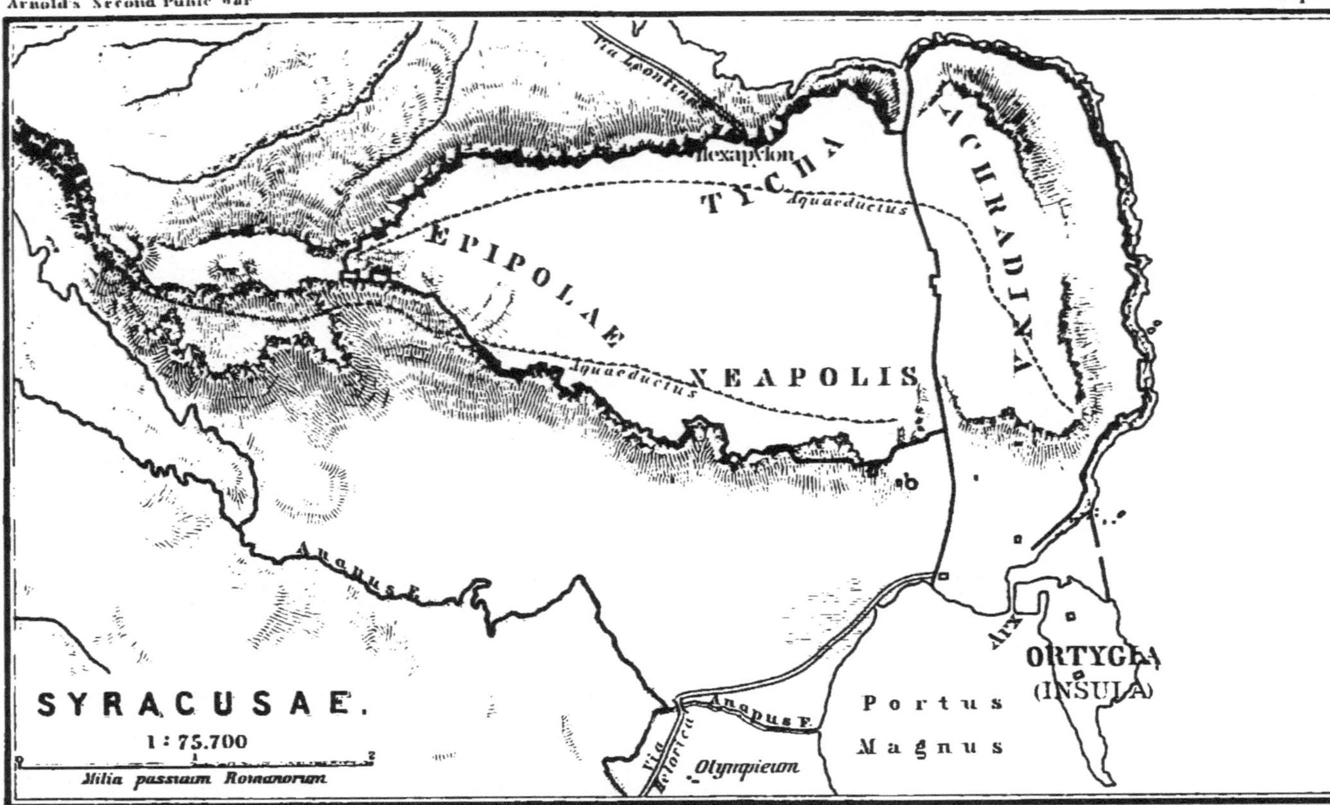

Arnold's Second Punic War
Map VII
Via Leontina
Hexapylon
TYCHA
Aquaeductus
ACHRADINA
EPIPOLAE
Aquaeductus
Aquaeductus
NEAPOLIS
b
Anapus F.
SYRACUSAE.
1:75.700
Milia passuum Romanorum
Via Helorica
Anapus F.
Olympieion
Arx
Portus
Magnus
ORTYGIA
(INSULA)
Wagner & Debes Geogl. Establ. Leipsic.
Macmillan & Co. London.

cannot have been less than 20,000 men, and A.U.C. 541. was probably more numerous. No force in Sicily, A.C. 213. whether of Syracusans or Carthaginians, could have resisted it in the field; and it had lately stormed the walls of Leontini as easily, to use the Homeric comparison, as a child tramples out the towers and castles which he has scratched upon the sand of the sea-shore. But at Syracuse it was checked by an artillery such as the Romans had never encountered before, and which, had Hannibal possessed it, would long since have enabled him to bring the war to a triumphant issue. An old man of seventy-four. a relation and friend of King Hiero, long known as one of the ablest astronomers and mathematicians of his age, now proved that his science was no less practical than deep; and amid all the crimes and violence of contending factions, he alone won the pure glory of defending his country successfully against a foreign enemy. This old man was Archimedes.[1]

Many years before, at Hiero's request, he had His extra-ordinary engines to contrived the engines which were now used so effectively.[2] Marcellus brought up his ships against defend the city. the sea-wall of Achradina, and endeavoured by a constant discharge of stones and arrows to clear the walls of their defenders, so that his men might apply their ladders and mount to the assault. These ladders rested on two ships, lashed together broadside to broadside, and worked as one by their outside oars; and when the two ships were brought close up under the wall, one end of the ladder was raised by ropes passing through blocks affixed to the two

[1] Livy, XXIV. 34. Polybius, VIII. 5.   [2] Plutarch. Marcellus, 14.

mast-heads of the two vessels, and was then let go till it rested on the top of the wall. But Archimedes had supplied the ramparts with an artillery so powerful that it overwhelmed the Romans before they could get within the range which their missiles could reach; and when they came closer they found that all the lower part of the wall was loopholed, and their men were struck down with fatal aim by an enemy whom they could not see, and who shot his arrows in perfect security. If they still persevered and attempted to fix their ladders, on a sudden they saw long poles thrust out from the top of the wall like the arms of a giant, and enormous stones or huge masses of lead were dropped from these upon them, by which their ladders were crushed to pieces and their ships were almost sunk. At other times machines like cranes, or such as are used at the turnpikes in Germany, and in the market-gardens round London to draw water, were thrust out over the wall, and the end of the lever, with an iron grapple affixed to it, was lowered upon the Roman ships. As soon as the grapple had taken hold, the other end of the lever was lowered by heavy weights and the ship raised out of the water till it was made almost to stand upon its stern; then the grapple was suddenly let go, and the ship dropped into the sea with a violence which either upset it or filled it with water. With equal power was the assault on the land side repelled; and the Roman soldiers, bold as they were, were so daunted by these strange and irresistible devices that if they saw so much as a rope or a stick hanging or projecting from the wall they would turn about and run away, crying 'that Archimedes was going to set one of his engines at work against them.' Their attempts indeed were a mere amusement to the enemy, till Marcellus in despair put a stop to his attacks; and it was resolved merely to blockade the town, and to wait for the effect of famine upon the crowded population within.[1]

A.U.C. 541.
A.C. 213.

Thus far, keeping our eyes fixed upon Syracuse only, we can give a clear and probable account of the course of events. But when we would extend our view farther, and connect the war in Sicily with that in Italy, and give the relative dates of the actions performed in the several countries involved in this great contest, we see the wretched character of our materials, and must acknowledge that, in order to give a comprehensive picture of the whole war, we have to supply, by inference or conjecture, what no actual testimony has recorded. We do not know for certain when Marcellus came into Sicily, when he began the siege of Syracuse, or how long the blockade was continued. We read of Roman and Carthaginian fleets appearing and disappearing at different times in the Sicilian seas; but of the naval operations on either side we can give no connected report. Other difficulties present themselves, of no great importance, but perplexing because they shake our confidence in the narrative which contains them. So easy is it to transcribe the ancient writers; so hard to restore the reality of those events, of which they themselves had no clear conception.

Difficulties in the history of the Sicilian war.

---

[1] Polybius, VIII. 6–9. Livy, XXIV. 34. Plutarch, Marcellus, 15–17.

Chronology
of the war.The first attacks on Syracuse are certainly mis-placed by Livy, when he classes them among the events of the year 540.[1]   The Sicilian war belongs to the year following, to the consulship of Q. Fabius the dictator's son, and of Ti. Gracchus.   Even when this is set right, it is difficult to reconcile Polybius's statement,[2] 'that the blockade of Syracuse lasted eight months,' with the account which places the capture of the city in the autumn of 542. Instead of eight months, the blockade would seem to have lasted for more than twelve; nor is there any other solution of this difficulty than to suppose that the blockade was not persevered in to the end, and was in fact given up as useless, as the assaults had been before.   I notice these points, because the narrative which follows is uncertain and unsatis-factory, and no care can make it otherwise.

A.U.C. 541.
A.C. 213.
Sicily be-
comes the
main seat
of war.The year 541 saw the whole stress of the war directed upon Sicily.   Little or nothing, if we can trust our accounts, was done in Italy; there was a pause also in the operations in Spain; but through-out Sicily the contest was raging furiously.   Four Roman officers were employed there; P. Cornelius Lentulus held the old Roman province, that is, the western part of the island, and his headquarters were at Lilybæum; T. Otacilius had the command of the fleet;[3] Appius Claudius and Marcellus carried on the war in the kingdom of Syracuse; the latter certainly as proconsul; the former as proprætor, or possibly only as the lieutenant, legatus, of the pro-consul.   Marcellus, however, as proconsul, must

[1] Livy, XXIV. 33.   [2] Polybius, VIII. 9. [Cf. Neumann, 412, note 1.]
[3] Livy, XXIV. 10.

have had the supreme command over the island, A.U.C. 541. A.C. 213.
and all its resources must have been at his disposal';
so that the fleet which he conducted in person at
the siege of Syracuse, was probably a part of that
committed to T. Otacilius, Otacilius himself either
serving under the proconsul, or possibly remaining
still at Lilybæum. It is remarkable that, although
he is said to have had the command of the fleet
continued to him for five successive years,[1] yet his
name never occurs as taking an active part in the
siege of Syracuse, and how he employed himself we
know not. Nor is it less singular that he should
have retained his naval command year after year,
though he was so meanly esteemed by the most
influential men in Rome that his election to the
consulship was twice stopped in the most decided
manner, first by Q. Fabius in 540, and again by T.
Manlius Torquatus in 544.[2] But the clue to this,
as to other things which belong to the living knowledge of these times, is altogether lost.

While the whole of Sicily was become the scene Wise con-
of war, an army of nine or ten thousand old soldiers duct of the
was purposely kept inactive by the Roman govern- senate to-
ment, and was not even allowed to take part in any wards the
active operations. These were the remains of the fugitives from
army of Cannæ, and a number of citizens who had Cannæ.
evaded their military service : as we have seen
they had been all sent to Sicily in disgrace, not to
be recalled till the end of the war.[3] Now, however,
that there was active service required in Sicily itself.

---

[1] Livy, XXIII. 32 ; XXIV. 10. 44 ; XXV. 3 ; XXVI. 1.
[2] Livy, XXIV. 9 ; XXVI. 22.
[3] Livy, XXIII. 25. See above, p. 136.

these condemned soldiers petitioned Marcellus that they might be employed in the field, and have some opportunity of retrieving their character. This petition was presented to him at the end of the first year's campaign in Sicily,. and was referred by him to the senate. The answer was remarkable: 'The senate could see no reason for entrusting the service of the commonwealth to men who had abandoned their comrades at Cannæ, while they were fighting to the death; but if M. Claudius thought differently, he might use his discretion, provided always that none of these soldiers should receive any honorary exemption or reward, however they might distinguish themselves, nor be allowed to return to Italy till the enemy had quitted it.'[1] Here was shown the consummate policy of the Roman government, in holding out so high a standard of military duty, while, without appearing to yield to circumstances, they took care not to push their severity so far as to hurt themselves. Occasions might arise when the services of these disgraced soldiers could not be dispensed with; in such a case Marcellus might employ them. Yet even then their penalty was not wholly remitted; it was grace enough to let them serve their country at all; nothing that they could do was more than their bounden duty of gratitude for the mercy shown them; they could not deserve exemption or reward. It was the glory and the happiness of Rome that her soldiers could bear such severity. Sicily was full of mercenary troops whose swords were hired by foreigners to fight their battles; and if these

[1] Livy, XXV. 5-7.

disgraced Romans had chosen to offer their services A.U.C. 541.
A.C. 213. to Carthage, they might have enjoyed wealth and honours, with full vengeance on their unforgiving country. Greek soldiers at this time would have done so; the proudest of the nobility of France in the sixteenth century did not scruple to revenge his private wrongs by treason. But these 10,000 Romans, although their case was not only hard, but grievously unjust, inasmuch as their rich and noble countrymen, who had escaped like them from Cannæ, had received no punishment, still bowed with entire submission to their country's severity, and felt that nothing could tempt them to forfeit the privilege of being Romans.

We must not suppose, however, that these men were useless, even while they were kept at a distance from the actual field of war. As soon as Syracuse became the enemy of Rome, it was certain that the Carthaginians would renew the struggle of the first Punic war for the dominion of Sicily; and the Roman province, from its neighbourhood to Carthage, was especially exposed to invasion. Lilybæum therefore and Drepanum, Eryx and Panormus, required strong garrisons for their security; and the soldiers of Cannæ, by forming these garrisons, set other troops at liberty who must otherwise have been withdrawn from active warfare. As it was these towns were never attacked, and the keys of Sicily, Lilybæum at one end of the island, and Messana at the other, remained throughout in the hands of the Romans.

Yet the example of Syracuse produced a very general effect. The cities which had belonged to

Hiero's kingdom mostly followed it, unless where the Romans secured them in time with sufficient garrisions. Himilco, the Carthaginian commander, who had been sent over to Pachynus with a small fleet to watch the course of events, sailed back to Carthage, as soon as the Carthaginian party had gained possession of Syracuse, and urged the government to increase its armaments in Sicily.[1] Hannibal wrote from Italy to the same effect; for Sicily had been his father's battle-field for five years, he had clung to it till the last moment, and his son was no less sensible of its importance. Accordingly Himilco was supplied with an army, notwithstanding the pressure of the Numidian war in Africa; and landing on the south coast of Sicily he presently reduced Heraclea, Minoa, and Agrigentum, and encouraged many of the smaller towns in the interior of the island to declare for Carthage. Hippocrates broke out of Syracuse and joined him. Marcellus, who had left his camp to quell the growing spirit of revolt amongst the Sicilian cities, was obliged to fall back again; and the enemy, pursuing him closely, encamped on the banks of the Anapus. Meanwhile a Carthaginian fleet ran over to Syracuse, and entered the great harbour, its object being apparently to provision the place and thus render the Roman blockade nugatory.[2]

Difficulties of the Romans.

It was clear that Marcellus could not make head against a Carthaginian army supported by Syracuse and half the other cities of Sicily. The fleet also was unequal to the service required of it; many ships had probably been destroyed by Archimedes; Lilybæum

<hr>

[1] Livy, XXIV. 35.   [2] Livy, XXIV. 35, 36.

could not be left unguarded, and some ships were A.U.C. 541. necessarily kept there; and in the general revolt A.C. 213. of the Sicilian cities, the Roman army could not always depend on being supplied by land, and would require corn to be brought sometimes from a distance by sea. Besides, the reinforcements which Marcellus so needed must be sent in ships and embarked at Ostia; for Hannibal's army cut off all communication by the usual line, through Lucania to Rhegium, and over the strait to Messana. Thirty ships therefore had to sail back to Rome, to take on board a legion and transport it to Panormus, from whence, by a circuitous route along the south coast of the island, the fleet accompanying it all the way, it reached Marcellus' headquarters safely. And now the Romans again had the superiority by sea; but by land Himilco was still master of the field, and the Roman garrison at Murgantia, a little to the north of Syracuse, was betrayed by the inhabitants into his hands.[1]

This example was no doubt likely to be followed, and should have increased the vigilance of the Roman garrisons. But it was laid hold of by L. Pinarius, the governor of Enna, as a pretence for repeating the crime of the Campanians at Rhegium, and of the Prænestines more recently at Casilinum. Standing in the centre of Sicily on the top of a high mountain platform, and fenced by precipitous cliffs on almost every side, Enna was a stronghold nearly impregnable, except by treachery from within; and whatever became of the Roman cause in Sicily, the holders of Enna might hope to retain it as the

Massacre of the inhabitants of Enna.

---

[1] Livy XXIV. 36.

Mamertines had kept Messana. Accordingly Pinarius having previously prepared his soldiers for what was to be done, on a signal given ordered them to fall upon the people of Enna when assembled in the theatre, and massacred them without distinction. The plunder of the town Pinarius and his soldiers kept to themselves, with the consent of Marcellus, who allowed the necessity of the times to be an apology for the deed.[1]

Revolt of the Sicilians': Marcellus winters before Syracuse.

The Romans alleged that the people of Enna were only caught in their own snare; that they had invited Hippocrates and Himilco to attack the city, and had vainly tried to persuade Pinarius to give them the keys of the gates, that they might admit the enemy to destroy the garrison. But the Sicilians saw that, if the people of Enna had meditated treachery, the Romans had practised it; a whole people had been butchered, their city plundered, and their wives and children made slaves, when they were peaceably met in the theatre in their regular assembly; and this new outrage, added to the sack of Leontini, led to an almost general revolt. Marcellus, having collected some corn from the rich plains of Leontini, carried it to the camp before Syracuse, and made his dispositions for his winter quarters. Appius Claudius went home to stand for the consulship, and was succeeded in his command by T. Quinctius Crispinus, a brave soldier, who was afterwards Marcellus's colleague as consul, and received his death-wound by his side, when Marcellus was killed by Hannibal's ambush. Crispinus lay encamped near the sea, not far from the temple of

---

[1] Livy, XXIV. 37–39.

Olympian Jupiter, and also commanded the naval A.U.C. 541.
force employed in the siege; while Marcellus, with A.C. 213.
the other part of the army, chose a position on the
northern side of Syracuse, between the city and the
peninsula of Thapsus, apparently for the purpose of
keeping up his communications with Leontini.[1] As to
the blockade of Syracuse, it was in fact virtually raised;
all the southern roads were left open, and as a large
part of the Roman fleet was again called away either
to Lilybæum or elsewhere, supplies of all sorts were
freely introduced into the town by sea from Carthage.

The events of the winter were not encouraging to
the Romans. Hannibal had taken Tarentum; and
the Tarentine fleet was employed in besieging the
Roman garrison, which still held the citadel. Thus
the Roman naval force was still further divided, as
it was necessary to convey supplies by sea to the
garrison; so that, when spring returned, Marcellus
was at a loss what to attempt, and had almost resolved to break up from Syracuse altogether, and to
carry the war to the other end of Sicily. But Sosis
and other Syracusans of the Roman party were
intriguing actively with their countrymen within the
city; and although one conspiracy, in which eighty
persons were concerned, was detected by Epicydes,
and the conspirators all put to death, yet the hopes
they had held out of obtaining easy terms from the
Romans were not forgotten; and the lawlessness of
the Roman deserters, and of the other foreign soldiers,
made many of the Syracusans long for a return of
the happy times under Hiero, when Rome and
Syracuse were friends.[2]

Intrigues of the Roman party in Syracuse.

[1] Livy, XXIV. 39.   [2] Livy, XXV. 23, 28.

A.U.C. 542.
A.C. 212.
The Syra-
cusans send
to solicit
aid from
Macedon.

Thus the spring wore away, and the summer had come, and had reached its prime, and yet the war in Sicily seemed to slumber ; for the greater part of the cities which had revolted to Carthage were undisturbed by the Romans, yet the Carthaginians were not strong enough to assail the heart of the Roman province, and to besiege Drepanum or Lilybæum.   In this state of things the Syracusans turned their eyes to Greece, and thought that the king of Macedon, who was the open enemy of Rome, and the covenanted ally of Carthage, might serve his own cause no less than theirs by leaving his ignoble warfare on the coast of Epirus and crossing the Ionian Sea to deliver Syracuse.   Damippus, a Lacedæmonian, and one of the counsellors of Hieronymus and of Hiero, was accordingly chosen as ambassador, and put to sea on his mission to solicit the aid of King Philip.[1]

The Ro-
mans pre-
pare to
scale the
walls at the
festival of
Diana.

Again the fortune of Rome interposed to delay the interference of Macedon in the contest.   The ship which was conveying Damippus was taken by the Romans on the voyage.   The Syracusans valued him highly, and opened a negotiation with Marcellus to ransom him.   The conferences were held between Syracuse and the Roman camp ; and a Roman soldier, it is said, was struck with the lowness of the wall in one particular place, and having counted the rows of stones, and so computed the whole height, reported to Marcellus that it might be scaled with ladders of ordinary length.   Marcellus listened to the suggestion ; but the low point was for that very reason more carefully guarded, because it

---

[1] Livy, XXV. 23.

seemed to invite attack; he therefore thought the attempt too hazardous, unless occasion should favour it.[1] But the great festival of Diana was at hand, a three days' solemnity, celebrated with all honours to the guardian goddess of Syracuse. It was a season of universal feasting; and wine was distributed largely among the multitude, that the neighbourhood of the Roman army might not seem to have banished all mirth and enjoyment. One vast revel prevailed through the city; Marcellus, informed of all this by deserters, got his ladders ready; and soon after dark two cohorts were marched in silence and in a long thin column to the foot of the wall, preceded by the soldiers of one maniple, who carried the ladders, and were to lead the way to the assault.

The spot selected for this attempt was in the wall which ran along the northern edge of Epipolæ, where the ground was steep, and where apparently there was no gate or regular approach to the city. But the vast lines of Syracuse enclosed a wide space of uninhabited ground; the new quarters of Tyche and Neapolis, which had been added to the original town since the great Athenian siege, were still far from reaching to the top of the hill; and what was called the quarter of Epipolæ only occupied a small part of the sloping ground known in earlier times by that name. Thus, when the Romans scaled the northern line, they found that all was quiet and lonely; nor was there any one to spread the alarm except the soldiers who garrisoned the several towers of the wall itself. These, however, heavy with wine,

A.U.C. 542.
A.C. 212.

They gain possession of Tyche and Neapolis;

---

[1] Livy, XXV. 23. Plutarch, Marcellus, 18. Polybius, VIII. 37.

A.U.C. 542.
A.C. 212.

and dreaming of no danger, were presently surprised and killed; and the assailants, thus clearing their way as they went, swept the whole line of the wall on their right, following it up the slope of the hill towards the angle formed at the summit by the meeting of the northern line with the southern. Here was the regular entrance into Syracuse from the land side; and this point, being the key of the whole fortified enclosure, was secured by the strong work called Hexapylon, or the Six Gates—probably from the number of barriers which must be passed before the lines could be fully entered. To this point the storming party made their way in the darkness, not blindly, however, nor uncertainly, for a Syracusan was guiding them,—that very Sosis[1] who had been one of the assassins of Hieronymus, and one of the murderers of Hiero's daughters, and who, when he was one of the captains-general of Syracuse, must have become acquainted with all the secrets of the fortifications. Sosis led the two Roman cohorts towards Hexapylon: from that commanding height a fire signal was thrown up, to announce the success of their attempt, and the loud and sudden blast of the Roman trumpets from the top of the walls called the Romans to come to the support of their friends, and told the bewildered Syracusans that the key of their lines was in the hands of the enemy.[2]

and take the Hexapylon.

Ladders were now set, and the wall was scaled in all directions, for the main gates of Hexapylon could not be forced till the next morning; and the only passage immediately opened was a small side

[1] Livy, XXVI. 21.   [2] Livy, XXV. 24.   Plutarch, Marcellus, 18.

gate at no great distance from them. But when
daylight came Hexapylon was entirely taken, and
the main entrance to the city was cleared, so that
Marcellus marched in with his whole army, and took
possession of the summit of the slope of Epipolæ.

From that high ground he saw Syracuse at his
feet, and, he doubted not, in his power. Two
quarters of the city, the New Town as it was called
and Tyche, were open to his first advance; their
only fortification being the general enclosure of the
lines, which he had already carried. Below, just
overhanging the sea, or floating on its waters, lay
Achradina and the island of Ortygia, fenced by their
own separate walls, which, till the time of the first
Dionysius, had been the limit of Syracuse, the walls
which the great Athenian armament had besieged
in vain. Nearer on the right, and running so deeply
into the land that it seemed almost to reach the
foot of the heights on which he stood, lay the still
basin of the great harbour, its broad surface half
hidden by the hulls of a hundred Carthaginian
ships; while further on the right was the camp of
his lieutenant T. Crispinus, crowning the rising
ground beyond the Anapus, close by the temple of
Olympian Jupiter. So striking was the view on
every side, and so surpassing was the glory of his
conquest, that Marcellus, old as he was, was quite
overcome by it; unable to contain the feelings of
that moment, he burst into tears.[1]

A deputation from the inhabitants of Tyche and
Neapolis approached him, bearing the ensigns of
suppliants, and imploring him to save them from fire

A.U.C. 542.
A.C. 212.

Marcellus,
looking
down on
Syracuse,
sheds tears.

His troops
plunder the
captured
parts of the
city.

____

[1] Livy. XXV. 24.

and massacre.   He granted their prayer, but at the price of every article of their property, which was to be given up to the Roman soldiers as plunder. At a regular signal the army was let loose upon the houses of Tyche and Neapolis, with no other restriction than that of offering no personal violence. How far such a command would be heeded in such a season of license we can only conjecture.   The Roman writers extol the humanity of Marcellus, but the Syracusans regarded him as a merciless spoiler, who had wished to take the town by assault rather than by a voluntary surrender, that he might have a pretence for seizing its plunder.[1]   Such a prize, indeed, had never before been won by a Roman army ; even the wealth of Tarentum was not to be compared with that of Syracuse.   But as yet the appetites of the Roman soldiers were fleshed rather than satisfied ; less than half of Syracuse was in their power ; and a fresh siege was necessary to win the spoil of Achradina and Ortygia.   Still, what they had already gained gave Marcellus large means of corruption ; the fort of Euryalus, on the summit of Epipolæ, near Hexapylon, which might have caused him serious annoyance on his rear while engaged in attacking Achradina, was surrendered to him by its governor, Philodemus, an Argive ; and the Romans set eagerly to work to complete their conquest.   Having formed three camps before Achradina, they hoped soon to starve the remaining quarters of the city into a surrender.[2]

The Carthaginian army, at-

Epicydes meanwhile showed a courage and activity worthy of one who had learned war under Hannibal.

---

[1] Livy, XXVI. 30.   [2] Livy, XXV. 25, 26.

A squadron of the Carthaginian fleet put to sea one A.U.C. 542. stormy night, when the Roman blockading ships A.C. 212. were driven off from the mouth of the harbour, and tempting to relieve ran across to Carthage to request fresh succours. Syracuse, is destroyed These were prepared with the greatest expedition ; by a fever. while Hippocrates and Himilco, with their combined Carthaginian and Sicilian armies, came from the western end of the island to attack the Roman army on the land side. They encamped on the shore of the harbour, between the mouth of the Anapus and the city, and assaulted the camp of Crispinus, while Epicydes sallied from Achradina to attack Marcellus. But Roman soldiers fighting behind fortifications were invincible ; their lines at Capua in the following year repelled Hannibal himself ; and now their positions before Syracuse were maintained with equal success against Hippocrates and Epicydes. Still the Carthaginian army remained in its camp on the shore of the harbour, partly in the hope of striking some blow against the enemy, but more to overawe the remains of the Roman party in Syracuse, which the distress of the siege, and the calamities of Neapolis and Tyche, must have rendered numerous and active. Meanwhile the summer advanced ; the weather became hotter and hotter ; and the usual malaria fevers began to prevail in both armies, and also in Syracuse. But the air here, as at Rome, is much more unhealthy without the city than within ; above all, the marshy ground by the Anapus, where the Carthaginian army lay, was almost pestilential ; and the ordinary summer fevers in this situation soon assumed a character of extreme malignity. The Sicilians

A.U.C. 542.
A.C. 212.
immediately moved their quarters, and withdrew into the neighbouring cities ; but the Carthaginians remained on the ground, till their whole army was effectually destroyed. Hippocrates and Himilco both perished with their soldiers.[1]

Their fleet fails in a like attempt.

The Romans suffered less ; for Marcellus had quartered his men in the houses of Neapolis and Tyche ; and the high buildings and narrow streets of the ancient towns kept off the sun, and allowed both the sick and the healthy to breathe and move in a cooler atmosphere. Still the deaths were numerous ; and as the terror of Archimedes and his artillery restrained the Romans from any attempts to batter or scale the walls, they had nothing to trust to save famine or treason. But Bomilcar was on his way from Carthage with 130 ships of war, and a convoy of 700 storeships, laden with supplies of every description ; he had reached the Sicilian coast near Agrigentum, when prevailing easterly winds checked his farther advance, and he could not reach Pachynus. Alarmed at this most unseasonable delay, and fearing lest the fleet should return to Africa in despair, Epicydes himself left Syracuse, and went to meet it, and to hasten its advance. The storeships, which were worked by sails, were obliged to remain at Heraclea ; but Epicydes prevailed on Bomilcar to bring on his ships of war to Pachynus, where the Roman fleet, though inferior in numbers, was waiting to intercept his progress. The east winds at length abated, and Bomilcar stood out to sea to double Pachynus. But when the Roman fleet advanced against him, he suddenly

[1] Livy, XXV. 26.

changed his plans, it is said; and having despatched orders to the storeships at Heraclea to return immediately to Africa, he himself, instead of engaging the Romans, or making for Syracuse, passed along the eastern coast of Sicily without stopping, and continued his course till he reached Tarentum.[1]

Here again the story in its present state greatly needs explanation. It is true that Hannibal was very anxious at this time to reduce the citadel of Tarentum; and he probably required a fleet to co-operate with him, in order to cut off the garrison's supplies by sea. But Bomilcar had been sent out especially to throw succours into Syracuse; and we cannot conceive his abandoning this object on a sudden without any intelligible reason. The probability is that the easterly winds still kept the storeships at Heraclea; and if they could not reach Syracuse, nothing was to be gained by a naval battle. And then, as the service at Tarentum was urgent, he thought it best to go thither, and to send back the convoy to Africa, rather than wait inactive on the Sicilian coast, till the wind became favourable. After all, Syracuse did not fall for want of provisions: the havoc caused by sickness, both in the city and in the Carthaginian camp on the Anapus, must have greatly reduced the number of consumers, and made the actual supply available for a longer period. It seems to have been a worse mischief than the conduct of Bomilcar; and Epicydes himself, as if despairing of fortune, withdrew to Agrigentum instead of returning to Syracuse, for from the moment of his departure the city seems

A.U.C. 542.
A.C. 212.

Epicydes
quits the
city, which
becomes a
prey to
anarchy.

---

[1] Livy, XXV. 27.

A.U.C. 542.
A.C. 212.

to have been abandoned to anarchy. At first the remains of the Sicilian army, which now occupied two towns in the interior, not far from Syracuse, began to negotiate with Marcellus, and persuaded the Syracusans to rise on the generals left in command by Epicydes, and to put them to death. New captains-general were then appointed, probably of the Roman party; and they began to treat with Marcellus for the surrender of Syracuse, and for the general settlement of the war in Sicily.[1]

Insurrection of the mercenaries in the city;

Marcellus listened to them readily; but his army was longing for the plunder of Achradina and Ortygia; and he knew not how to disappoint them: for we may be sure that no pay was issued at this period to any Roman army serving out of Italy; in the provinces war was by fair means or foul to support war. Meanwhile the miserable state of affairs in Syracuse was furthering the wish of the Roman soldiers. A besieged city, with no efficient government, and full of foreign mercenaries, whom there was no native force to restrain, was like a wreck in mutiny; utter weakness and furious convulsions were met in the same body. The Roman deserters first excited the tumult, and persuaded all the foreign soldiers to join them; a new outbreak of violence followed; the Syracusan captains-general were massacred in their turn: and the foreign soldiers were again triumphant. Three officers, each with a district of his own, were appointed to command in Achradina, and three more in Ortygia.[2]

who betray it to the Romans.

The foreign soldiers now held the fate of Syracuse in their hands; and they began to consider that

[1] Livy, XXV. 28.   [2] Livy, XXV. 29.

they might make their terms with the Romans, A.U c.542.
although the Roman deserters could not.   Their A.C. 212.
blood was not called for by the inflexible law of
military discipline; by a timely treachery they
might earn not impunity merely, but reward.   So
thought Mericus, a Spaniard, who had the charge
of a part of the sea-wall of Achradina.   Accordingly
he made his bargain with Marcellus, and admitted
a party of Roman soldiers by night at one of the
gates which opened towards the harbour.   As soon
as morning dawned Marcellus made a general
assault on the land front of Achradina; the garrison
of Ortygia hastened to join in the defence; and the
Romans then sent boats full of men round into
the great harbour, and, effecting a landing under
the walls, carried the island with little difficulty.
Meanwhile Mericus had openly joined the Roman
party, whom he had admitted into Achradina; and
Marcellus, having his prey in his power, called off
his soldiers from the assault, lest the royal treasures,
which were kept in Ortygia, should be plundered in
the general sack of the town.[1]

In the respite thus gained the Roman deserters *Syracuse is*
found an opportunity to escape out of Syracuse. *taken and plundered;*
Whether they forced their way out, or whether the *Archi-*
soldiers, hungry for plunder, and not wishing to *medes is slain.*
encounter the resistance of desperate men, obliged
Marcellus to connive at their escape, we know not;
but with them all wish or power to hold out longer
vanished from Syracuse; and a deputation from
Achradina came once more to Marcellus, praying
for nothing beyond the lives and personal freedom

[1] Livy, XXV. 30.

A.U.C. 542.
A.C. 212.

of the citizens and their families. This, it seems, was granted; but as soon as Marcellus had sent his quæstor to secure the royal treasures in Ortygia, the soldiers were let loose upon the city to plunder it at their discretion. They did not merely plunder however: blood was shed unsparingly, partly by the mere violence of the soldiers, partly by the axes of the lictors, as the punishment of rebellion against the majesty of Rome. Amidst the horrors of the sack of the city Archimedes was slain.[1] The stories of his death vary; and which, if any of them is the true one, we cannot determine. But Marcellus, who made it his glory to carry all the finest works of art from the temples of Syracuse to Rome,[2] would no doubt have been glad to have seen Archimedes walking amongst the prisoners at his triumph. He is said to have shown kindness to the relations of Archimedes for his sake;[3] and if this be true, he earned a glory which few Romans ever deserved, that of honouring merit in an enemy.

Miserable condition of the Syracusans.

Old as Archimedes was, the Roman soldier's sword dealt kindly with him, in cutting short his scanty term of remaining life, and saving him from beholding the misery of his country. It was a wretched sight to see the condition of Syracuse, when the sack was over, and what was called a state of peace and safety had returned. Every house was laid bare, every temple stript; and the

[1] Livy, XXV. 31. Plutarch, Marcellus, 19. Valerius Maximus, VIII. 7. 7. Diodorus, XXVI. Fragm. 18.

[2] Livy, XXV. 40. Polybius, IX. 10. Cicero, in Verrem, IV. 54.

[3] Livy, XXV. 31. Plutarch, Marcellus, 19.

empty pedestals showed how sweeping the spoiler's A.U.C. 542. work had been.　The Syracusans beheld their A.C. 212. captive gods carried to the Roman quarters, or put on shipboard to be conveyed to Rome; the care with which they were handled, lest the conqueror's triumph should lose its most precious ornaments, only adding to the grief and indignation of the conquered.　Those fathers and mothers, who were so happy as to gather all their children safe around them when the plunder was over, had escaped the sword indeed; and they and their sons and daughters were not yet sold as slaves; but their only choice was still between slavery or death.　They had lost everything.　What food was still remaining in the besieged city the sack had either carried off or destroyed; and, if food had been at hand, they had no money to buy it.　And this came upon them after a heavy visitation of sickness: when the body, reduced by that weakening malaria fever, needed all tender care and comfort to restore it, instead of being harassed by alarm and anxiety, and exposed to destitution and starvation.　Many therefore sold themselves to the Roman soldiers to escape dying by hunger; and the family circle, which the sack of the city had spared, was again broken up for ever.[1]　Those who, being unmarried and childless, had given no hostages to fortune, and who might yet hope to live in personal freedom, were only the more able to feel the ruin and degradation of their country.　Syracuse, who had led captive the hosts of Athens, and seen the invading armies of Carthage melt away by disease under her walls, till scarce

---

[1] Diodorus, XXVI. Fragm. 20.

A.U.C. 542.
A.C. 212.

any remained to fly,—Syracuse, where Dionysius had reigned, which Timoleon had freed, which Hiero had cherished and sheltered under his long paternal rule,—was now become subject to barbarians, whom she had helped in their utmost need, and who were repaying the unshaken friendship of Hiero with the plunder of his city and the subjugation of his people. If there was a yet keener pang to be felt by every noble Syracusan, it was to behold their countrymen, who had fought in the Roman army, returning in triumph, establishing themselves in the empty houses of the slaughtered defenders of their country, and insulting the general misery by displaying the rewards of their treason. Among these was Sosis, assassin, murderer, and traitor, who was looking forward to the triumph of Marcellus, as one to whom the shame of his country was his glory, and her ruin the making of his fortune.[1]

Cruelty of Marcellus.

Syracuse had fallen ; and the cities in the eastern part of Sicily had no other hope now than to obtain pardon, if it might be, from Rome, by immediate submission. But it was too late : they were treated as conquered enemies ;[2] that is to say, Marcellus put to death those of their citizens who were most obnoxious, and imposed such forfeitures of land on the cities, and such terms of submission for the time to come, as he judged expedient. It became the fashion afterwards to extol his humanity, and even his refinement,[3] because he showed his taste for the works of Greek art by carrying the statues of the

---

[1] Livy, XXVI. 21.   [2] Livy, XXV. 40.
[3] Cicero, in Verrem, IV. 52–59.

Syracusan temples to Rome. But his admiration A.U.C. 542.
of Greek art did not make him treat the Greeks A.C. 212.
themselves with less severity; and the Sicilians
taxed him with perfidy as well as cruelty, and
regarded him as the merciless oppressor of their
country.[1]

Meantime Hannibal's comprehensive view had Hannibal
not lost sight of Sicily. When he heard of the sends Mu-
havoc caused by the epidemic sickness, and of the tines to
death of Hippocrates, he sent over another of his Sicily; his
officers to share with Epicydes, and with the successes.
general who came from Carthage, in the command
of the war. This was Mutines, or Myttonus, a
half-caste Carthaginian, excluded on that account
from civil honours;[2] but Hannibal's camp recognised
no such distinctions; and brave and able men,
whatever was their race or condition, were sure to
be employed and rewarded there. Mutines proved
the unerring judgment of Hannibal in his choice of
officers. His arrival in Sicily was equivalent to
an army: being put at the head of the Numidian
cavalry then serving under Epicydes and Hanno, he
overran the whole island, encouraging the allies of
Carthage, harassing those of Rome, and defying
pursuit or resistance by the rapidity and skill of
his movements. He renewed the system of warfare
which Hamilcar had maintained so long in the last
war; and having the strong place of Agrigentum to
retire to in case of need, he perplexed the Roman
generals not a little. Marcellus was obliged to take
the field, and march from Syracuse westward as far

---

[1] Livy, XXVI. 29–32. Plutarch, Marcellus, 23.
[2] Livy, XXV. 40. Polybius, IX. 22.

A.U.C. 543.
A.C. 211.
as the Himera, where the enemy's army lay encamped. But he met with a rough reception; the Numidian cavalry crossed the river, and came swarming round his camp, insulting and annoying his soldiers on guard, and confining his whole army to their intrenchments; and when on the next day, impatient of this annoyance, he offered battle in the field, Mutines and his Numidians broke in upon his lines with such fury that he was fain to retreat with all speed and seek the shelter of his camp again. It appears that other arms were then tried with better success: the Numidians were tampered with; their irregular habits and impatient tempers made them at all times difficult to manage; and a party of them having left the Carthaginian camp in disgust, Mutines went after them to pacify and win them back to their duty, earnestly conjuring Hanno and Epicydes not to venture a battle till he should return. But Hanno was jealous of Hannibal's officers; and holding his own commission directly from the government of Carthage, he could not bear to be restrained by a half-caste soldier, sent to Sicily from Hannibal's camp, by the mere authority of the general. His rank probably gave him a casting vote, when only one other commander was present, so that Epicydes in vain protested against his imprudence.[1] A battle was ventured; and not only was the genius of Mutines wanting, but the Numidians whom he had left with Hanno, thinking their commander insulted, would take no active part in the action, and Hanno was defeated with loss.

[1] Livy, XXV. 40.

Marcellus, rejoiced at having thus retrieved his honour, had no mind to risk another encounter with Mutines; he forthwith retreated to Syracuse,[1] and as the term of his command was now expired, his thoughts were all turned to Rome, and to his expected triumph. He left Sicily after the fall of Capua, towards the end of the summer 543, and about a year after the conquest of Syracuse, but he was not allowed to carry his army home with him, and M. Cornelius Cethegus, one of the prætors, who succeeded him in his command, found that his province was far from being in a state of peace. The Carthaginians had reinforced their army, Mutines with his Numidians was scouring the whole country, the soldiers were discontented because they had not been permitted to return home, and the Sicilians were driven desperate by the oppressions which Marcellus had commanded or winked at, and were ready to break out in revolt again.[2]

A.U.C. 543.
A.C. 211.
Marcellus returns to Rome.

In fact it appears that in the year 544, nearly two years after the fall of Syracuse, there were as many as sixty-six towns in Sicily in a state of revolt from Rome, and in alliance with Carthage.[3] So greatly had Mutines restored the Carthaginian cause, that it was thought necessary to send one of the consuls over with a consular army, to bring the war to an end. Accordingly M. Valerius Lævinus, who had been employed for the last three or four years on the coast of Epirus, conducting the war against Philip, and who was chosen consul with Marcellus in the year 544, carried over a regular consular

Lævinus is sent to Sicily.

---

[1] Livy, XXV. 41.   [2] Livy, XXVI. 21.
[3] Livy, XXVI. 40.

 army into Sicily; while L. Cincius, one of the new prætors, and probably the same man who is known as one of the earliest Roman historians, took the command of the old province, and of the soldiers of Cannæ who were still quartered there.[1] The army with which Marcellus had won Syracuse was now at last disbanded, and the men were allowed to return home with as much of their plunder as they had not spent or wasted, but four legions were even now employed in Sicily, besides a fleet of 100 ships; and yet Mutines and his Numidians were overrunning all parts of the island; and the end of the war seemed as distant as ever.

Mutines is insulted by Hanno, and betrays Agrigentum to the Romans. Lævinus advanced towards Agrigentum, with small hope, however, of taking the place, for Mutines sallied whenever he would, and carried back his plunder in safety whenever he would, whilst the neighbourhood of Carthage made relief by sea always within calculation, whatever naval force the Romans might employ in the blockade. In this state of things, Lævinus, to his astonishment, received a secret communication from Mutines, offering to put Agrigentum into his power. The half-caste African, the officer of Hannibal, the sole stay of the Carthaginian cause in Sicily, was on all these accounts odious to Hanno, and it is likely that Mutines did not bear his glory meekly, and that he expressed the scorn which Hannibal's soldier was likely to feel for the pride and incapacity of the general sent out by the government at home, and probably by the party opposed to Hannibal, and afraid of his glory. But whatever was the secret of the quarrel, its effects

[1] Livy, XXVI. 28.

were public enough, for Hanno ventured to deprive A.U.C. 544. Mutines of his command. The Numidians, however, A.C. 210. would obey no other leader, while him they would obey in everything; and at his bidding they rose in open mutiny, took possession of one of the gates of the town, and let in the Romans. Hanno and Epicydes had just time to fly to the harbour, to hasten on board a ship, and escape to Carthage; but their soldiers, surprised and panic-struck, were cut to pieces with little resistance, and Lævinus won Agrigentum. He treated it more severely than Marcellus had dealt with Syracuse; after executing the principal citizens, he sold all the rest for slaves, and sent the money which he received for them to Rome.[1]

This blow was decisive. Twenty other towns, Lævinus accomplishes the which still held with the Carthaginians, were pre- plishes the sently betrayed to the Romans, either by their conquest of garrisons, or by some of their own citizens; six Sicily, were stormed by the Roman army, and the remainder, to the number of forty, then submitted at discretion. The consul dealt out his rewards to the traitors who had betrayed their country, and his lictors scourged and beheaded the brave men who had persevered the longest in their resistance: thus at last he was able to report to the senate that the war in Sicily was at an end.

Four thousand adventurers of all descriptions, and reduces who in the troubled state of Sicily had taken posses- it to entire submis- sion of the town of Agathyrna on the north coast sion. of the island, and were maintaining themselves there by robbery, Lævinus carried over into Italy at the

---

[1] Livy, XXVI. 40.

close of the year, and landed them at Rhegium, to be employed in a plundering warfare in Bruttium. Having thus cleared the island of all open disturbers of its peace, he obliged the Sicilians, says Livy, to turn their attention to agriculture, that its fruitful soil might grow corn to supply the wants of Italy and of Rome.[1] And he assured the senate, at the end of the year, that the work was thoroughly done; that not a single Carthaginian was left in Sicily; that the towns were re-peopled by the return of their peaceable inhabitants, and the land was again cultivated; that he had laid the foundation of a state of things equally happy for the Sicilians and for Rome.[2]

Deplorable condition of Sicily.

So Lævinus said, and so he probably believed. But with the return of peace to the island, there came a host of Italian and Roman speculators, who, in the general distress of the Sicilians, bought up large tracts of land at a low price, or became the occupiers of estates which had belonged to Sicilians of the Carthaginian party, and had been forfeited to Rome after the execution or flight of their owners. The Sicilians of the Roman party followed the example, and became rich out of the distress of their countrymen. Slaves were to be had cheap, and corn was likely to find a sure market, whilst Italy was suffering from the ravages of war. Accordingly Sicily was crowded with slaves, employed to grow corn for the great landed proprietors, whether Sicilian or Italian, and so ill-fed by their masters that they soon began to provide for themselves by robbery. The poorer Sicilians were the sufferers from this evil,

---

[1] Livy, XXVI. 40.   [2] Livy, XXVII. 5.

and as the masters were well content that their slaves should be maintained at the expense of others, they were at no pains to restrain their outrages. Thus, although nominally at peace, though full of wealthy proprietors, and though exporting corn largely every year, yet Sicily was teeming with evils, which, seventy or eighty years after, broke out in the horrible atrocities of the Servile War.[1]

A.U.C. 544.
A.C. 210.

[1] Diodorus, XXXIV. Fragm. 2.   Florus, II. 7.

CHAPTER IV.

State of Italy—Distress of the people—Twelve colonies refuse to
support the war—Eighteen colonies offer all their resources to
the Romans—Events of the war—Death of Marcellus—Fabius
recovers Tarentum — March of Hasdrubal into Italy — He
reaches the coast of the Adriatic—Great march of C. Nero from
Apulia to oppose him—Battle of the Metaurus, and death of
Hasdrubal.—A.U.C. 543 to A.U.C. 547.

A.U.C. 543.
A.C. 211.
Intermis-
sion of hos-
tilities after
the taking
of Capua.

IN following the war in Sicily to its conclusion, we
have a little anticipated the course of our narrative,
for we have been speaking of the consulship of M.
Lævinus, whilst our account of the war in Italy has
not advanced beyond the middle of the preceding
year. The latter part of the year 543 was marked,
however, by no military actions of consequence; so
great an event as the fall of Capua having, as was
natural, produced a pause, during which both parties
had to shape their future plans according to the
altered state of their affairs and of their prospects.

Hannibal
abandons
the west of
Italy.

Hannibal on his side had retired, as we have seen,
into Apulia, after his unsuccessful attempt upon
Rhegium, and there allowed his soldiers to enjoy an
interval of rest. The terrible example of Capua
shook the resolution of his Italian allies, and made
them consider whether a timely submission to Rome
might not be their wisest policy; nay, it became a
question whether their pardon might not be secured

by betraying Hannibal's garrisons, and returning to their duty not empty-handed. Hannibal therefore neither dared to risk his soldiers by dispersing them about in small and distant towns, nor could he undertake, even if he kept his army together, to cover the wide extent of country which had revolted to him at different periods of the war. His men would be worn out by a succession of flying marches; and, after all, the Roman armies were so numerous that he would always be in danger of arriving too late at the point attacked. Accordingly he found it necessary to abandon many places altogether, and from some he obliged the inhabitants to migrate, and made them remove within the limits which he still hoped to protect. In this manner, it is probable, the western side of Italy, from the edge of Campania to Bruttium, was at once left to its fate, including what had been the territory of the Capuans on the shores of the Gulf of Salernum, the country of the Picentians, and Lucania, while Apulia and Bruttium were carefully defended. But in evacuating the towns which they could not keep, and still more in the compelled migrations of the inhabitants, Hannibal's soldiers committed many excesses, property was plundered, and blood was shed; and thus the minds of the Italians were still more generally alienated.[1]

We have seen that immediately after the fall of Capua C. Nero, with a part of the troops which had been employed on the blockade, had been sent off to Spain.[2] Q. Fulvius remained at Capua with another part, amounting to a complete consular army,[3] and

A.U.C. 543.
A.C. 211.

Movements of the Roman armies.

---

[1] Livy, XXVI. 38.   [2] Livy, XXVI. 17 ; above p. 177.
[3] Livy, XXVI. 28.

A.U.C. 543.
A.C. 211.
some were probably sent home. The two consuls marched into Apulia, which was to be their province,[1] but no active operations took place during the remainder of the season, and at the end of the year P. Sulpicius was ordered to pass over into Epirus, and succeed M. Lævinus in the command of the war against Philip. The home administration was left in the hands of C. Calpurnius Piso, the city prætor.

Marcellus is unable to obtain a triumph: his splendid ovation. About the time that the two consuls took the command in Apulia, M. Cornelius Cethegus, who had obtained that province as praetor at the beginning of the year, was sent over to Sicily to command the army there, Marcellus having just left the island to return to Rome. Marcellus was anxious to obtain a triumph for his conquest of Syracuse, but the war in Sicily was still raging, and Mutines was in full activity. The senate therefore would not grant a triumph for an imperfect victory, but allowed Marcellus the honour of the smaller triumph or ovation. He was highly dissatisfied at this, and consoled himself by going up in triumphal procession to the temple of Jupiter on the highest summit of the Alban hills, and offering sacrifice there, a ceremony which by virtue of his imperium he could lawfully perform; he might go in procession where he pleased, and sacrifice where he pleased, except within the limits of Rome itself. On the day after his triumph on the hill of Alba he entered Rome with the ceremony of an ovation, walking on foot according to the rule, instead of being drawn in a chariot in kingly state as in the proper triumph. But the show was unusually splendid, for a great

[1] Livy, XXVI. 22.

picture of Syracuse with all its fortifications was
displayed, and with it some of the very artillery
which Archimedes had made so famous in his
defence of them ; besides an unwonted display of
the works of art of a more peaceful kind, the spoils
of Hiero's palace and of the temples in his city,
silver and bronze figures, embroidered carpets and
coverings of couches, and, above all, some of the
finest pictures and statues.   Men also observed the
traitor Sosis walking in the procession with a
coronet of gold on his head, as a benefactor of the
Roman people ; he was further to be rewarded with
the Roman franchise, with a house at his own choice
out of those belonging to the Syracusans who had
remained true to their country, and with five hundred
jugera of land, which had either been theirs or part
of the royal domain.[1]

At the end of the year Cn. Fulvius was summoned
to Rome from Apulia to preside at the consular
comitia.   On the day of the election the first
century of the Veturian tribe, which had obtained
the first voice by lot, gave its votes in favour of T.
Manlius Torquatus and T. Otacilius Crassus.   As
the voice of the tribe first called was generally
followed by the rest, Manlius, who was present, was
immediately greeted by the congratulations of his
friends ; but instead of accepting them he made his
way to the consul's seat, and requested him to call
back the century which had just voted, and allow
him to say a few words.   The century was summoned again, all men wondering what was about to
happen.   Manlius had been consul five-and-twenty

Comitia :
noble con-
duct of
Manlius :
Marcellus
and
Lævinus
are elected
consuls.

[1] Livy, XXVI. 21.

R

A.U.C. 544.
A.C. 210.

years before, in the memorable year when the temple of Janus was shut in token of the ratification of peace with Carthage ; twenty years had passed since he was censor, and though his vigour of body and mind was still great, he was an old man, and age had made him nearly blind. 'I am unfit to command,' he said, 'for I can only see through the eyes of others. This is no time for incompetent generals; let the century make a better choice.' But the century answered unanimously 'that they could not make a better; that they again named Manlius and Otacilius consuls.' 'Your tempers and my rule,' said the old man, 'will never suit. Give your votes over again, and remember that the Carthaginians are in Italy, and that their general is Hannibal.' A murmur of admiration burst from all around, and the voters of the century were moved. They were the younger men of their tribe, and they besought the consul to summon the century of their elders, that they might be guided by their counsel. Fulvius accordingly summoned the century of elders of the Veturian tribe, and the two centuries retired to confer on the question. The elders recommended that Fabius and Marcellus should be chosen, or, if a new consul were desirable, that they should take one of these, and with him elect M. Lævinus, who for some years past had done good service in conducting the war against King Philip. Their advice was adopted, and the century gave its votes now in favour of Marcellus and Lævinus. All the other centuries confirmed their choice ; and thus T. Otacilius was for the second time, by an extraordinary interference with the votes of the centuries,

deprived of the consulship, to which some uncom- A.U.C. 544
monly amiable qualities, or some peculiar influence, A.C. 210.
had twice, in spite of his deficient ability, recommended him.[1]

He probably never knew of this second disappointment, for scarcely was the election over when
news arrived from Sicily of his death.[2]   Cn. Fulvius
returned to his army in Apulia, and as M. Lævinus
was still absent in Epirus, Marcellus on the usual
day, the ides of March, entered upon the consulship
alone.   Q. Fulvius was still at Capua, but Q. Fabius
and T. Manlius were at Rome; and their counsels,
together with those of Marcellus, were of the greatest
influence in the senate, and probably directed the
government.

There was need of all their ability and all their Alarming
firmness, for never had the posture of affairs been posture of
more alarming.   Hannibal's unconquered and un- affairs.
conquerable army, although it had not saved Capua, Patriotic
had wasted Italy more widely than ever in the last of Lævinus:
campaign; and it had struck particularly at countries self-devo-
which had hitherto escaped its ravages, the valleys senators:
of the Sabines, and the country of the thirty-five ample fol-
tribes themselves, up to the very gates of Rome. lowed by
Many of the citizens had not only lost their standing people.
crops, but their cattle had been carried off and their
houses burnt to the ground.[3]   Actual scarcity was
added to other causes of distress, insomuch that the
modius of wheat rose to nearly three denarii, which
in a plentiful season eight years afterwards was sold
at four asses, or the fourth part of one denarius.[4]

---

[1] Livy, XXVI. 22.   [2] Livy, XXVI. 23.
[3] Livy, XXVI. 26.   [4] Polybius, IX. 45.   Livy, XXXI. 4.

The people were becoming unable to bear further burdens ; and some of the Latin colonies, which had hitherto been the firmest support of the commonwealth, were suspected to be not only unable but unwilling. It was probably to meet the urgent necessity of the case that the armies were somewhat reduced this year, four legions, it seems, being disbanded.[1] But this fruit of the fall of Capua was in part neutralised by the necessity of raising fresh seamen ; for unless the commonwealth maintained its naval superiority, Sicily would be lost, and Philip might be expected on the coasts of Italy, and the supply of corn which was looked for from Egypt in the failure of all nearer resources, would become very precarious.[2] Accordingly, a tax was imposed, requiring all persons, in proportion to the returns of their property at the last census, to provide a certain number of seamen with pay and provisions for thirty days. But our own tax of ship-money did not excite more opposition, though on different grounds. The people complained aloud ; crowds gathered in the forum, and declared that no power could force from them what they had not got ; that the consuls might sell their goods and lay hold on their persons if they chose, but they had no means of payment.[3] The consuls,—for Lævinus was by this time returned home from Macedonia,—with that dignity which the Roman government never forgot for an instant, issued an order, giving the defaulters three days to consider their determination ; thus seeming to grant as an indulgence what necessity obliged them to

---

[1] Livy, XXVI. 28.   [2] Polybius, IX. 45.
[3] Livy, XXVI. 35.

yield.   Meanwhile they summoned the senate, and A.U.C. 544.
when every one was equally convinced of the neces-   A.C. 210.
sity of procuring seamen, and the impossibility of
carrying through the tax, Lævinus, in his colleague's
name and his own, proceeded to address the senators.
He told them that, before they could call on the
people to make sacrifices, they must set the example.
' Let each senator,' he said, 'keep his gold ring, and
the rings of his wife and children ; let him keep
the golden bulla worn by his sons under age, and
one ounce of gold for ornaments for his wife, and an
ounce for each of his daughters.   All the rest of the
gold which we possess let us offer for the public
service.   Next, let all of us who have borne curule
offices reserve the silver used in the harness of our
war-horses ; and let all others, including those just
mentioned, keep one pound of silver, enough for the
plate needful in sacrifices, the small vessel to hold
the salt, and the small plate or basin for the libation;
and let us each keep five thousand asses of copper
money.   With these exceptions let us devote all our
silver and copper to our country's use, as we have
devoted all our gold.   And let us do this without
any vote of the senate, of our own free gift, as
individual senators, and carry our contributions at
once to the three commissioners for the currency.
Be sure that first the equestrian order, and then the
mass of the people, will follow our example.'   He
spoke to hearers who so thoroughly shared his spirit
that they voted their thanks to the consuls for this
suggestion.   The senate instantly broke up ; the
senators hastened home, and thence came crowding
to the forum, their slaves bearing all their stores of

copper and silver and gold, each man being anxious to have his contribution recorded first ; so that, Livy says, neither were there commissioners enough to receive all the gifts that were brought, nor clerks enough to record them.   The example, as the consuls knew, was irresistible ; the equestrian order and the commons poured in their contributions with equal zeal, and no tax could have supplied the treasury so plentifully as this free-will offering of the whole people.[1]

Value of the sacrifices.

There is no doubt that the money thus contributed was to be repaid to the contributors when the republic should see better days ; but the sacrifice consisted in this, that, while the prospect of payment was distant and uncertain, the whole profit of the money in the meantime was lost; for the Roman state creditors received no interest on their loans.   Therefore it was at their own cost mainly, and not at the cost of posterity, that the Romans maintained their great struggle ; and from our admiration of their firmness and heroic devotion to their country's cause, nothing is in this case to be abated.

Complaints of the severity of Fulvius and Marcellus.

Nor is it less striking that the senate at this very moment listened to accusations brought by vanquished enemies against their conquerors, and these conquerors men of the highest name and greatest influence in the commonwealth, Marcellus and Q. Fulvius.   When Lævinus passed through Capua on his way to Rome, he was beset by a multitude of the Capuans, who complained of the intolerable misery of their condition under the

[1] Livy, XXVI. 36.

dominion of Q. Fulvius, and besought him to take
them with him to Rome, that they might implore
the mercy of the senate.   Fulvius made them swear
that they would return to Capua within five days
after they received their answer, telling Lævinus
that he dared not let them go at liberty; for if any
Capuan escaped from the city he instantly became
a brigand, and scoured the country, burning, rob-
bing, and murdering all that fell in his way; even
at Rome, Lævinus would find the traces of Capuan
treason, for the late destructive fire in the city was
their work.   So a deputation of Campanians, thus
hardly allowed to go, followed Lævinus towards
Rome; and when he approached the city a similar
deputation of Sicilians came out to meet him, with
like complaints against Marcellus.[1]

The provinces assigned to the consuls were this
year to be the conduct of the war with Hannibal
and Sicily, and Sicily fell by lot to Marcellus.   The
Sicilians present were thrown into despair when
this was announced to them; they put on mourning and beset the senate-house weeping and bewail-
ing their hard fate, and saying that it would be
better for their island to be sunk in the sea, or
overwhelmed with the lava floods of Ætna, than
given up to the vengeance of Marcellus.   Their
feeling met with much sympathy in the senate;
and this was made so intelligible that Marcellus,
without waiting for any resolution on the subject,
came to an agreement with his colleague, and they
exchanged their provinces.[2]

This having been settled, the Sicilians were

A.U.C. 544.
A.C. 210.

The Sici-
lians en-
treat that
Marcellus
may not be
sent into
Sicily.

Their com-
plaint is

---

[1] Livy, XXVI. 27.   [2] Livy, XXVI. 29.

A.U.C. 544.
A.C. 210.
heard by
the senate :
counter-
statement
of Mar-
cellus.

admitted into the senate, and brought forward their complaint. It turned principally on the cruelty of making them responsible for the acts, first of Hieronymus, and then of a mercenary soldiery which they had no means of resisting; while the long and tried friendship of Hiero, proved by the Romans in the utmost extremity of their fortune, had been forgotten. Marcellus insisted that the deputation should remain in the senate and hear his statement —answer he would not call it, and far less defence, as if a Roman consul could plead to the accusations of a set of vanquished Greeks—but his statement of their offences, which had justly brought on all that they had suffered. He said that they had acted as enemies, had rejected his frequent offers of peace, and had resisted his attacks with all possible obstinacy, instead of doing as Sosis, whom they called a traitor, had done, and surrendering their city into his hands. He then left the senate-house, together with the Sicilians, and went to the Capitol to carry on the enlistment of the newly-raised legions.[1]

Decree of
the senate.
Marcellus
becomes
the pa-
tronus of
Syracuse.

There was a strong feeling in the senate that Syracuse had been cruelly used; and old T. Manlius expressed this as became him, especially urging the unworthy return which had been made to the country of Hiero for all his fidelity to Rome. But a sense of Marcellus's signal services, and of the urgency of the times, prevailed; and a resolution was passed confirming all that he had done, but declaring that for the time to come the senate would consult the welfare of the Syracusans, and would

---

[1] Livy, XXVI. 30, 31.

commend them especially to the care of Lævinus. A.U.C.544. A.C. 210.
A deputation of two senators was then sent to the
consul to invite him to return to the senate; the
Syracusans were called in, and the decree was read.
Then the Syracusan deputies threw themselves at
the feet of Marcellus, imploring him to forgive all
that they had said against him, to receive them
under his protection, and to become the patronus
of their city.[1] He gave them a gracious answer,
and accepted the office; and from that time forward
the Syracusans found it their best policy to extol
the clemency of Marcellus, and later writers echoed
their language; not knowing, or not remembering,
that these expressions of forced praise were their
own strongest refutation.

The Campanian deputation was heard with less
favour, but still it was heard, and the senate took
their complaint into consideration. But in this case
no mercy was shown, and it was now that those
severe decrees were passed fixing the future fate of
the Campanian people, which I have already mentioned by anticipation, at the end of the story of
the siege of Capua.[2]

Severe treatment of the Campanians.

The military history of this year is again difficult
to comprehend, owing to the omissions and inco-
herence in Livy's narrative. Two armies, as we
have seen, were employed against Hannibal, that of
Cn. Fulvius, the consul of the preceding year, in
Apulia, and that of Marcellus in Samnium. Where
Hannibal had passed the winter, or end of the preceding summer, we know not; not a word being
said of his movements after his ineffectual attempt

Opening of the campaign: the army of Fulvius is destroyed by Hannibal.

---

[1] Livy, XXVI. 32.   [2] Above, p. 177, foll. Livy, XXVI. 33.

upon Rhegium, till we hear of his march against Fulvius. We may suppose, however, that he had wintered in Apulia; and we are told that Salapia having been betrayed to the Romans, and a detachment of Numidians having been cut off in it, Hannibal again retreated into Bruttium.[1] With two armies opposed to him it was of importance not to let either of them advance to attack Tarentum and the towns on the coast, while he was engaged with the other. He was obliged therefore to abandon his garrisons in Samnium and Apulia to their own resources, and kept his army well in hand, ready to strike a blow whenever opportunity should offer. As usual he received perfect information of the enemy's proceedings through his secret emissaries, and having learned that Fulvius was in the neighbourhood of Herdonea trying to win the place, and that, relying on his distance from the Carthaginian army, he was not sufficiently on his guard, Hannibal conceived the hope of destroying this army by an unexpected attack. Again the details are given variously; but the result was that Hannibal's attempt was completely successful. The army of Fulvius was destroyed, and the proconsul killed; and Hannibal, having set fire to Herdonea, and executed those citizens who had been in correspondence with the enemy, sent away the rest of the population into Bruttium, and himself crossed the mountains into Lucania, to look after the army of Marcellus.[2]

Marcellus adopts the policy of Fabius.

Marcellus, on the news of his colleague's defeat, left Samnium, and advanced into Lucania: his object

[1] Livy, XXVII. 1.   [2] Livy, XXVII. 1.

now was to watch Hannibal closely, lest he should again resume the offensive; all attempts to recover more towns in Samnium or elsewhere must be for the time abandoned. And this service he performed with great ability and resolution, never leaving Hannibal at rest, and taking care not to fall into any ambush, but unable, notwithstanding the idle stories of his victories, to do anything more than keep his enemy in sight, as Fabius had done in his first dictatorship. Thus the rest of the season passed away unmarked by anything of importance: Marcellus wintered apparently at Venusia; Hannibal in his old quarters, in the warm plains near the sea.[1]

In spite therefore of the reduction of Capua the Roman affairs in Italy had made no progress. On the contrary another army had been totally destroyed, and the war with all its burthens seemed interminable. But in other quarters this year had been more successful: Lævinus had ended the war in Sicily, and the resources of that island were now at the disposal of the Romans, while the Carthaginian fleets had no point nearer than Carthage itself to carry on their operations, whether to the annoyance of the enemy's coasts, or the relief of their own garrisons at Tarentum, and along the southern coast of Italy. In addition to this the alliance which Lævinus had concluded with the Ætolians before he quitted Epirus had left a far easier task to his successor, P. Sulpicius, and removed all danger of Philip's co-operating with Hannibal. Meanwhile Lævinus was summoned home to hold the comitia,

A.U.C. 544
A.C. 210.

Advantages gained by the Romans out of Italy.

---

[1] Livy, XXVII. 2. 4. 12–14. 20.

A.U.C. 544.
A.C. 210. Marcellus being too busily employed with Hannibal to leave his army, and accordingly he crossed over directly from Lilybæum or Panormus to Ostia, accompanied by the African Mutines, who was now to receive the reward of his desertion, in being made by a decree of the people a citizen of Rome.[1]

Alarming news from Africa. Before his departure from Sicily Lævinus had sent the greater part of his fleet over to Africa, partly to make plundering descents on the coast, but chiefly to collect information as to the condition and plans of the enemy. Messalla, who had succeeded to T. Otacilius in the command of the fleet, accomplished this expedition in less than a fortnight; and the information which he collected was so important that, finding Lævinus was gone to Rome, he forwarded it to him without delay. Its substance bore that the Carthaginians were collecting troops with great diligence, to be sent over into Spain, and that the general report was that these soldiers were to form the army of Hasdrubal, Hannibal's brother, and were to be led by him immediately into Italy. This intelligence so alarmed the senate that they would not detain the consul to hold the comitia, but ordered him to name a dictator for that purpose, and then to return immediately to his province.[2]

A dictator appointed to hold the comitia : Fabius and Fulvius chosen consuls. With all the patriotism of the Romans it was not possible that personal ambition and jealousy should be wholly extinct among them, and the influence exercised at the present crisis by Q. Fabius, and his preference of Q. Fulvius and Marcellus to all other commanders, was no doubt regarded by some as excessive and overbearing. The magistrate who pre-

<hr>

[1] Livy, XXVII. 5.   [2] Livy, XXVII. 5.

sided at the comitia enjoyed so great a power over A.U.C. 545.
A.C. 209. the elections that the choice of the dictator on this
occasion was of some consequence, and Lævinus
intended to name the commander of his fleet, M.
Messalla, not without some view possibly to his own
re-election, if the comitia were held under the auspices
of a man not entirely devoted to Fabius and Fulvius.
But when he declared his intention to the senate, it
was objected that a person out of Italy could not be
named dictator, and the consul was ordered to take
the choice of the people, and to name whomsoever
the people should fix upon. Indignant at this interference with his rights as consul, Lævinus refused
to submit the question to the people, and forbade the
prætor, L. Manlius Acidinus, to do so. This, however, availed him nothing, for the tribunes called the
assembly, and the people resolved that the dictator
to be named should be Q. Fulvius. Lævinus probably expected this, and, as his last resource, had
left Rome secretly on the night before the decision,
that he might not be compelled to go through the
form of naming his rival dictator. Here was a new
difficulty, for the dictator could only be named by
one of the consuls, so it was necessary to apply to
Marcellus, and he nominated Q. Fulvius immediately.[1]
The old man left Capua forthwith, and proceeded to
Rome to hold the comitia, at which the century first
called gave its votes in favour of Fulvius himself and
Fabius. This no doubt had been preconcerted : but
two of the tribunes shared the feelings of Lævinus,
and objected to such a monopoly of office in the
hands of two or three men ; they also complained of

---

[1] Livy, XXVII. 5.

the precedent of allowing the magistrate presiding at the election to be himself elected. Fulvius, with no false modesty, or what in our notions would be real delicacy, maintained that the choice of the century was good, and justified by precedents, and at last the question was submitted by common consent to the senate. The senate determined that, under actual circumstances, it was important that the ablest men and most tried generals should be at the head of affairs, and they therefore approved of the election. Accordingly Fabius and Fulvius were once more appointed consuls, the former for the fifth time, the latter for the fourth.[1]

Plan for the campaign.

Thus was the great object gained of employing the three most tried generals of the republic, Fabius, Fulvius, and Marcellus, against Hannibal in the approaching campaign. Each was to command a full consular army, Marcellus retaining that which he now had, with the title of proconsul; and the plan of operations was, that, while Marcellus occupied Hannibal on the side of Apulia, a grand movement should be made against Tarentum and the other towns held by the enemy on the southern coast. Fabius was to attack Tarentum, while Fulvius was to reduce the garrisons still retained by Hannibal in Lucania,[2] and then to advance into Bruttium; and that band of adventurers from Sicily, which Lævinus had sent over to Rhegium to do some service in that quarter, was to attempt the siege of Caulon, or Caulonia. Every exertion was to be made to destroy Hannibal's power in the south, before his brother could arrive in Italy to effect a diversion in the north.[3]

[1] Livy, XXVII. 6.   [2] Livy, XXVII. 7.   [3] Livy, XXVII. 12.

Lævinus, it seems, paid the penalty of his opposi- A.U.C. 545.
tion to Fulvius's election, in being deprived of his A.C. 209.
consular army, which he was ordered to send over
to Italy to be commanded by Fulvius himself;
and he and the proprætor L. Cincius were left to
defend Sicily with the old soldiers of Cannæ, and
the remains of the defeated armies of the two Fulvii,
the prætor and the proconsul, which had been condemned to the same banishment, together with the
forces which they had themselves raised within the
island, partly native Sicilians, and partly Numidians,
who had come over to the Romans with Mutines.[1]
With these resources, and with a fleet of seventy
ships, Sicily was firmly held, and Lævinus, it is
said, was able in the course of the year to send
supplies of corn to Rome, and also to the army of
Fabius before Tarentum.[2]

But before the consuls could take the field, a Twelve of
storm burst forth more threatening than any which the Latin colonies re-
the republic had yet experienced.   The soldiers of fuse fresh
the army defeated at Herdonea, who were now to supplies.
be sent over to Sicily, were in a large proportion
Latins of the colonies, and as they were to be banished
for the whole length of the war, fresh soldiers were
to be levied to supply their place in Italy.   This
new demand was the drop which made the full cup
overflow.   The deputies of twelve of the colonies,
who were at Rome as usual to receive the consuls'
orders, when they were required to furnish fresh
soldiers, and to raise money for their payment,
replied resolutely that they had neither men nor
money remaining.[3]

[1] Livy, XXVII. 7, 8.   [2] Livy, XXVII. 8.   [3] Livy, XXVII. 9.

'The Roman people,' says Livy, 'had at this period thirty colonies;' of which number twelve thus refused to support the war any longer. The number mentioned by the historian has occasioned great perplexity, but its coincidence with the old number of the states of the Latin confederacy leaves no doubt of its genuineness, and when the maritime colonies are excepted, which stood on a different footing, as not being ordinarily bound to raise men for the regular land service, it agrees very nearly with the list which we should draw up of all the Latin colonies mentioned to have been founded before this period. But what particular causes determined the twelve recusant colonies more than the rest to resist the commands of Rome, we cannot tell. Amongst them we find the name of Alba, which two years before had shown such zeal, in hastening to the assistance of Rome unsummoned, when Hannibal threatened its very walls; we also find some of the oldest colonies, Circeii, Ardea, Cora, Nepete, and Sutrium; Cales, which had so long been an important position during the revolt of Capua, Carseoli, Suessa, Setia, Narnia, and Interamna, on the Liris. The consuls, thunderstruck at their refusal, attempted to shame them from their purpose by rebuke. 'This is not merely declining to furnish troops and money,' they said, 'it is open rebellion. Go home to your colonies; forget that so detestable a thought ever entered your heads; remind your fellow-citizens that they are not Campanians nor Tarentines, but Romans, Roman born, and sent from Rome to occupy lands conquered by Romans, to multiply the race of Rome's defenders. All duty owed by children to their parents, you owe to the senate and people of Rome.' But in vain did Fabius and Fulvius, with all the authority of their years and their great name, speak such language to the deputies. They were coldly answered 'that it was useless to consult their countrymen at home; the colonies could not alter their resolution, for they had no men nor money left.' Finding the case hopeless, the consuls summoned the senate, and reported the fatal intelligence. The courage, which had not yielded to the slaughter of Cannæ, was shaken now. 'At last,' it was said, 'the blow is struck, and Rome is lost; this example will be followed by all our colonies and allies; there is doubtless a general conspiracy amongst them to give us up bound hand and foot to Hannibal.'[1]

The consuls bade the senate take courage: the other colonies were yet true; 'even these false ones will return to their duty, if we do not condescend to entreat them, but rather rebuke them for their treason.' Everything was left to the consuls' discretion; they exerted all their influence with the deputies of the other colonies privately, and having ascertained their sentiments, they then ventured to summon them officially, and to ask, 'Whether their appointed contingents of men and money were forthcoming?' Then M. Sextilius of Fregellæ stood up and made answer in the name of the eighteen remaining colonies: 'They are forthcoming, and if more are needed, more are at your disposal. Every order, every wish of the Roman people, we will with our best efforts fulfil: to do this we have means enough, and will more than enough.' The consuls

A.U.C. 545.
A.C. 209.

Patriotic spirit of the other eighteen colonies: the senate resolves to take no notice of the twelve.

[1] Livy, XXVII. 9.

A.U.C. 545.
A.C. 209.

replied, 'Our thanks are all too little for your desert: the whole senate must thank you themselves.' They led the deputies into the senate-house, and thanks were voted to them in the warmest terms. Then the consuls were desired to lead them before the people, to remind the people of all the services which the colonies had rendered to them and to their fathers, services all surpassed by this last act of devotion. The thanks of the people were voted no less heartily than those of the senate. 'Nor shall these eighteen colonies even now,' says Livy, 'lose their just glory. They were the people of Signia, of Norba, of Saticula, of Brundisium, of Fregellæ, of Luceria, of Venusia, of Hadria, of Firmum, and of Ariminum; and from the lower sea, the people of Pontia, and of Pæstum, and of Cosa; and from the midland country, the people of Beneventum, and of Æsernia, and of Spoletum, and of Placentia, and of Cremona.' The aid of these eighteen colonies on that day saved the Roman empire. Satisfied now, and feeling their strength invincible, the senate forbade the consuls to take the slightest notice of the disobedient colonies; they were neither to send for them, nor to detain them, nor to dismiss them; they were to leave them wholly alone.[1]

Magnanimity of their conduct. Singular coincidence in the subsequent destinies of the house of Fulvius and of Fregellæ.

It is enough for the glory of any nation that its history in two successive years should record two such events as the magnanimous liberality of the senate in sacrificing their wealth to their country, and the no less magnanimous firmness and wisdom of their behaviour towards their colonies. An aristocracy endowed with such virtues deserved its

[1] Livy, XXVII. 10.

ascendency, for its inherent faults were now shown A.U.C. 545.
A.C. 209. only towards the enemies of Rome ; its nobler character alone was displayed towards her citizens. But when M. Sextilius of Fregellæ was standing before Q. Fulvius, promising to serve Rome to the death, and the old consul's stern countenance was softened into admiration and joy, and his lips, which had so remorselessly doomed the Capuan senators to a bloody death, were now uttering thanks and praises to Rome's true colonists, how would each have started, could he have looked for a moment into futurity and seen what events were to happen before a hundred years were over ! By a strange coincidence each would have seen the self-same hand red with the blood of his descendants, and extinguishing the country of the one and the family of the other. Within ninety years the Roman aristocracy were to become utterly corrupted ; and its leader, L. Opimius, as base personally as he was politically cruel, was to destroy Fregellæ, and treacherously in cold blood to slay an innocent youth, the last direct representative of the great Q. Fulvius, after he had slain M. Fulvius, the youth's father, in civil conflict within the walls of Rome.[1]   Fregellæ, to whose citizens Rome at this time owed her safety, was within ninety years to be so utterly destroyed by the Roman arms that at this day its very site is not certainly known: the most faithful of colonies has perished more entirely than the rebellious Capua.[2]

---

[1] Velleius, II. 6 ; II. 7.   Plutarch, C. Gracchus, c. xvi. Appian, B. C. I. 26.

[2] Velleius, II. 6.   Strabo, V. 6. 9, Cas. p. 233, 237.   Auctor ad Herennium, IV. 15.

A.U.C. 545.
A.C. 209.
The sacred
treasure is
brought
out.

Rome could rely on the fidelity of the majority of her colonies, but their very readiness made it desirable to spare them to the utmost. Therefore a treasure, which was reserved in the most sacred treasury for the extremest need, was now brought out, amounting, it is said, to four thousand pounds' weight of gold, and which had been accumulating during a period of about 150 years, being the produce of the tax of five per cent on the value of every emancipated slave, paid by the person who gave him his liberty. With this money the military chests of the principal armies were well replenished; and supplies of clothing were sent to the army in Spain, which P. Scipio was now commanding, and was on the point of leading to the conquest of New Carthage.[1]

Samnium
and Lu-
cania sub-
mit to the
Romans :
the Brut-
tians treat
about sub-
mission.

At length the consuls took the field. Marcellus, according to the plan agreed upon, broke up from his quarters at Venusia, and proceeded to watch and harass Hannibal; while Fabius advanced upon Tarentum, and Fulvius marched into Lucania. Caulonia at the same time was besieged by the band of adventurers from Sicily. The mass of forces thus employed was overwhelming; and Hannibal, while he clung to Apulia and to Bruttium, was unable to retain his hold on Samnium and Lucania. Those great countries, or rather the powerful party in both, which had hitherto been in revolt from Rome, now made their submission to Q. Fulvius, and delivered up such of Hannibal's soldiers as were in garrison in any of their towns. They had apparently chosen their time well; and by submitting at the beginning

---

[1] Livy, XXVII. 10.

of the campaign they obtained easy terms.   Even A.U.C. 545.
A.C. 209.
Fulvius, though not inclined to show mercy to
revolted allies, granted them a full indemnity : the
axes of his lictors were suffered this time to sleep
unstained with blood.   This politic mercy had its
effect on the Bruttians also : some of their leading
men came to the Roman camp to treat concerning
the submission of their countrymen on the terms
which had been granted to the Samnites and
Lucanians ; and the base of all Hannibal's operations, the southern coast of Italy, was in danger of
being torn away from him if he lingered any longer
in Apulia.[1]

Then his indomitable genius and energy appeared Hannibal's brilliant exploits.
once more in all its brilliancy.   He turned fiercely
upon Marcellus, engaged him twice, and so disabled Tarentum is betrayed to the Ro-mans.
him that Marcellus, with all his enterprise, was
obliged to take refuge within the walls of Venusia,
and there lay helpless during the remainder of the
campaign.[2]   Freed from this enemy Hannibal flew
into Bruttium ; the strength of Tarentum gave him
no anxiety for its immediate danger ; so he hastened
to deliver Caulonia.   The motley band who were
besieging it fled at the mere terror of his approach,
and retreated to a neighbouring hill ; thither he
pursued them, and obliged them to surrender at
discretion.[3]   He then marched back with speed to
Tarentum, hoping to crush Fabius as he had crushed
Marcellus.   He was within five miles of the city,
when he received intelligence that it was lost.   The
Bruttian commander of the garrison had betrayed

---

[1] Livy, XXVII. 15.   [2] Livy, XXVII. 12–14.
[3] Livy, XXVII. 15, 16.

it to Fabius; the Romans had entered it in arms: Carthalo, the Carthaginian commander, and Nico and Philemenus, who had opened its gates to Hannibal, had all fallen in defending it: the most important city and the best harbour in the south of Italy were in the hands of the Romans.[1]

The news of the fall of Paris, when Napoleon was hastening from Fontainebleau to deliver it, can scarcely have been a heavier disappointment to him than the news of the loss of Tarentum was to Hannibal. Yet, always master of himself, he was neither misled by passion nor by alarm: he halted and encamped on the ground, and there remained quiet for some days, to show that his confidence in himself was unshaken by the treason of his allies. Then he retreated slowly towards Metapontum, and contrived that two of the Metapontines should go to Fabius at Tarentum, offering to surrender their town and the Carthaginian garrison, if their past revolt might be forgiven. Fabius, believing the proposal to be genuine, sent back a favourable answer, and fixed the day on which he would appear before Metapontum with his army. On that day Hannibal lay in ambush close to the road leading from Tarentum, ready to spring upon his prey. But Fabius came not: his habitual caution made him suspicious of mischief; and it was announced that the omens were threatening: the haruspex, on inspecting the sacrifice, which was offered to learn the pleasure of the gods, warned the consul to beware of hidden snares, and of the arts of the enemy. The Metapontine deputies were sent back to learn the cause of

[1] Livy, XXVII. 15 16.

the delay; they were arrested, and, being threatened with the torture, disclosed the truth.[1]

A.U.C. 545.
A.C. 209.

The remaining operations of the campaign are again unknown: the Romans, however, seem to have attempted nothing further; and Hannibal kept his army in the field, marching whither he would without opposition, and again laying waste various parts of Italy with fire and sword.[2] So far as we can discover, he returned at the end of the season to his old winter quarters in Apulia.

He remains master of the field.

It is not wonderful that this result of a campaign, from which so much had been expected, should have caused great disappointment at Rome. However much men rejoiced in the recovery of Tarentum, they could not but feel that even this success was owing to treason; and that Hannibal's superiority to all who were opposed to him was more manifest than ever. This touched them in a most tender point; because it enabled him to continue his destructive ravages of Italy, and thus to keep up that distress which had long been felt so heavily. Above all, indignation was loud against Marcellus:[3] and if in his lifetime he indulged in that braggart language which his son used so largely after his death, the anger of the people against him was very reasonable. If he called his defeats victories, as his son no doubt called them afterwards, and as the falsehood through him has struck deep into Roman history, well might the people be indignant at hearing that a victorious general had shut himself up

Dissatisfaction at Rome: complaints against Marcellus, who nevertheless is elected consul.

---

[1] Livy, XXVII. 16.
[2] Livy, XXVII. 20. 'Vagante per Italiam Hannibale.'
[3] Livy, XXVII. 20. See Note N.

all the summer within the walls of Venusia, and had allowed the enemy to ravage the country at pleasure. The feeling was so strong that C. Publicius, one of the tribunes, a man of an old and respected tribunician family, brought in a bill to the people to deprive Marcellus of his command. Marcellus returned home to plead his cause, when Fulvius went home also to hold the comitia; and the people met to consider the bill in the Flaminian circus, without the walls, to enable Marcellus to be present; for his military command hindered him from entering the city. It is likely that the influence of Fulvius was exerted strongly in his behalf; and his own statement, if he told the simple truth, left no just cause of complaint against him. He had executed his part of the campaign to the best of his ability: twice had he fought with Hannibal to hinder him from marching into Bruttium; and it was not his fault, if the fate of all other Roman generals had been his also; he had but failed to do what none had done, or could do. The people felt for the mortification of a brave man, who had served them well from youth to age, and in the worst of times had never lost courage: they not only threw out the bill, but elected Marcellus once more consul, giving him, as his colleague, his old lieutenant in Sicily, T. Quintius Crispinus, who was now prætor, and during the last year had succeeded to Fulvius in the command at Capua.[1]

Julius
Cæsar
prætor.
It marks our advance in Roman history, that among the prætors of this year we find the name of Sex. Julius Cæsar; the first Cæsar who appears in the Roman Fasti.

[1] Livy, XXVII. 20, 21

For some time past the Romans seem to have mistrusted the fidelity of the Etruscans, and an army of two legions had been regularly stationed in Etruria to check any disposition to revolt. But now C. Calpurnius Piso, who commanded in Etruria, reported that the danger was becoming imminent, and he particularly named the city of Arretium as the principal seat of disaffection.[1] Why this feeling should have manifested itself at this moment, we can only conjecture. It is possible that the fame of Hasdrubal's coming may have excited the Etruscans. It is possible that Hannibal may have had some correspondence with them, and persuaded them to co-operate with his brother. But other causes may be imagined ; the continued pressure of the war upon all Italy, and the probability that the defection of the twelve colonies must have compelled the Romans to increase the burdens of their other allies. If, as Niebuhr thinks,[2] the Etruscans were not in the habit of serving with the legions in the regular infantry, their contributions in money, and in seamen for the fleets, would have been proportionably greater ; and both these would fall heavily on the great Etruscan chiefs, or Lucumones, from whose vassals the seamen would be taken, as their properties would have to furnish the money. Again, in the year 544, when corn was at so enormous a price, we read of a large quantity purchased in Etruria by the Roman government for the use of their garrison in the citadel of Tarentum.[3] This

A.U.C. 546.
A.C. 208.
Doubts
about the
fidelity of
Etruria.

---

[1] Livy, XXVII. 21.

[2] Vol. III. p. 432 of Eng. Transl., III. 376 of Isler's German edition of 1874.   [3] Livy, XXV. 15.

A.U.C. 546.
A.C. 208.

corn the allied states were bound to sell at a fixed price; so that the Etruscan landholders would consider themselves greatly injured in being forced to sell at a low price what, in the present condition of the markets, was worth four or five times as much. But whatever was the cause, Marcellus was sent into Etruria, even before he came into office as consul, to observe the state of affairs, that, if necessary, he might remove the seat of war from Apulia to Etruria. The report of his mission seemed satisfactory : and it did not appear necessary to bring his army from Apulia.[1]

Disaffection of Arretium.

Yet some time afterwards, before Marcellus left Rome to take the field, the reports of the disaffection of Arretium became more serious ; and C. Hostilius, who had succeeded Calpurnius in the command of the army stationed in Etruria, was ordered to lose no time in demanding hostages from the principal inhabitants. C. Terentius Varro was sent to receive them, to the number of 120, and to take them to Rome. Even this precaution was not thought sufficient ; and Varro was sent back to Arretium to occupy the city with one of the home legions, while Hostilius, with his regular army, was to move up and down the country, that any attempt at insurrection might be crushed in a moment.[2] It appears also that, besides the hostages, several sons of the wealthy Etruscans were taken away to serve in the cavalry of Marcellus's army, to prevent them at any rate from being dangerous at home.[3]

Disposition of the

The two consuls were to conduct the war against

---

[1] Livy, XXVII. 21.   [2] Livy, XXVII. 24.
[3] Livy, XXVII. 26.

Hannibal, whilst Q. Claudius, one of the prætors, with a third army, was to hold Tarentum, and the country of the Sallentines. Fulvius with a single legion resumed his old command at Capua. Fabius returned to Rome, and from this time forward no more commanded the armies of his country, although he still in all probability directed the measures of the government.[1]

Crispinus had left Rome before his colleague, and, with some reinforcements newly raised, proceeded to Lucania to take the command of the army which had belonged to Fulvius. His ambition was to rival the glory of Fabius, by attacking another of the Greek cities on the southern coast. He fixed upon Locri, and having sent for a powerful artillery from Sicily, with a naval force to operate against the sea front of the town, commenced the siege. Hannibal's approach, however, forced him to raise it; and as Marcellus had now arrived at Venusia, he retreated thither to co-operate with his colleague. The two armies were encamped apart, about three miles from each other: two consuls, it was thought, must at any rate be able to occupy Hannibal in Apulia, while the siege of Locri was to be carried on by the fleet and artillery from Sicily, with the aid of one of the two legions commanded by the prætor Q. Claudius at Tarentum. Such was the Roman plan of campaign for the year 546, the eleventh of this memorable war.[2]

The two armies opposed to Hannibal must have amounted at least to 40,000 men; he could not venture to risk a battle against so large a force; but

A.U.C. 545.
A.C. 208.
Roman armies.
Fabius retires from military service.

Plan of the campaign.

Hannibal destroys a legion sent to besiege Locri.

[1] Livy, XXVII. 22, 35, 40.   [2] Livy, XXVII. 25.

his eye was everywhere, and he was neither ignorant nor unobservant of what was going on in his rear, and of the intended march of the legion from Tarentum to carry on the siege of Locri by land. So confident was he in his superiority that he did not hesitate to detach a force of 3000 horse and 2000 foot from his already inferior numbers, to intercept these troops on their way ; and while the Romans marched on in confidence, supposing that Hannibal was far away in Apulia, they suddenly found their road beset, and Hannibal's dreaded cavalry broke in upon the flanks of their column. The rout was complete; in an instant the whole Roman division was destroyed or dispersed, and the fugitives, escaping over the country in all directions, fled back to Tarentum.[1] The fleet from Sicily were obliged therefore to carry on the siege of Locri as well as they could, with no other help.

Position of the two armies.
Marcellus is killed in an ambush.

This signal service rendered, Hannibal's detachment returned to his camp, bringing back their numerous prisoners. Frequent skirmishes took place between the opposed armies, and Hannibal was continually hoping for some opportunity of striking a blow. A hill covered with copsewood rose between the two armies, and had been occupied hitherto by neither party ; only Hannibal's light cavalry were used to lurk amongst the trees at its foot, to cut off any stragglers from the enemy's camp. The consuls, it seems, wished to remove their camp—for the two consular armies were now encamped together—to this hill ; or at any rate to

[1] Livy, XXVII. 26.

occupy it as an entrenched post, from which they A.U.C. 546. might command the enemy's movements. But they A.C. 208. resolved to reconnoitre the ground for themselves; and accordingly they rode forward with 200 cavalry, and a few light-armed soldiers, leaving their troops behind in the camp, with orders to be in readiness on a signal given to advance and take possession of the hill.[1] The party ascended the hill without opposition, and rode on to the side towards the enemy, to take a view of the country in that direction. Meantime the Numidians, who had always one of their number on the look-out, to give timely notice of anything that approached, as they were lurking under the hill, were warned by their scout that a party of Romans were on the heights above them. No doubt he had marked the scarlet war-cloaks of the generals, and the lictors who went before them, and told his companions of the golden prize that fortune had thrown into their hands. The Numidians stole along under the hill, screened by the trees, till they got round it, between the party on the summit and the Roman camp; then they charged up the ascent, and fell suddenly upon the astonished enemy. The whole affair was over in an instant: Marcellus was run through the body with a spear, and killed on the spot; his son and Crispinus were desperately wounded; the Etruscan horsemen, who formed the greater part of the detachment, had no inclination to fight in a service which they had been forced to enter; the Fregellans, who formed the remainder of it, were too few to do anything; all were obliged to ride for their lives,

---

[1] Livy, XXVII. 26.

and to leap their horses down the broken ground on the hill sides to escape to their camp. The legions in the camp saw the skirmish, but could not come to the rescue in time. Crispinus and the young Marcellus rode in covered with blood, and followed by the scattered survivors of the party; but Marcellus, six times consul, the bravest and stoutest of soldiers, who had dedicated the spoils of the Gaulish king, slain by his own hand, to Jupiter Feretrius in the Capitol, was lying dead on a nameless hill, and his arms and body were Hannibal's.[1]

The Numidians, hardly believing what they had done, rode back to their camp to report their extraordinary achievement. Hannibal instantly put his army in motion, and occupied the fatal hill. There he found the body of Marcellus, which he is said to have looked at for some time with deep interest, but with no word or look of exultation; then he took the ring from the finger of the dead, and ordered, as he had done before in the case of Flaminius and Gracchus, that the body should be honourably burned, and that the ashes should be sent to Marcellus's son.[2] The Romans left their camp under cover of the night, and retreated to a position of greater security; they no longer thought of detaining Hannibal from Bruttium, their only hope was to escape out of his reach. Then Hannibal flew once more to the relief of Locri; the terror of the approach of his Numidian cavalry drove the Romans to their ships; all their costly artillery and engines were abandoned; and the siege of Locri, no less disastrous to the Roman

The Roman army retreats: Hannibal raises the siege of Locri.

---

[1] Livy, XXVII. 27.   [2] Plutarch, Marcellus, c. 30.

naval force than to their land army, was effectually A.U.C.546.
A.C. 208.
raised.[1]

During the rest of the season the field was again *He con-tinues mas-ter of the field : the consul Cris-pinus dies of his wounds.* left free to Hannibal, and his destructive ravages were carried on, we may be sure, more widely than even in the preceding year. The army of Marcellus lay within the walls of Venusia ; that of Crispinus retreated to Capua,[2] officers having been sent by the senate to take the command of each provisionally. Crispinus was desired to name a dictator for holding the comitia, and he accordingly nominated the old T. Manlius Torquatus ; soon after which he died of the effect of his wounds ; and the republic, for the first time on record, was deprived of both its consuls, before the expiration of their office, by a violent death.[3]

The public anxiety about the choice of new consuls *The Massi-lians send tidings of Hasdru-bal's being in Gaul.* was quickened in the highest degree by the arrival of an embassy from Massilia. The Massilians, true to their old friendship with Rome, made haste to acquaint their allies with the danger that was threatening them. Hasdrubal, Hannibal's brother, had suddenly appeared in the interior of Gaul ; he had brought a large treasure of money with him, and was raising soldiers busily. Two Romans were sent back to Gaul with the Massilian ambassadors to ascertain the exact state of affairs ; and these officers, on their return to Rome, informed the senate that, through the connections of Massilia with some of the chiefs in the interior, they had made out that Hasdrubal had completed his levies, and was only waiting for the first melting of the snows to cross

---

[1] Livy, XXVII. 28.   [2] Livy, XXVII. 29.
[3] Livy, XXVII. 33.

A.U.C. 546.
A.C. 208.

the Alps.   The senate, therefore, must expect in the next campaign to see two sons of Hamilcar in Italy.[1]

His route out of Spain through Gaul.

Reserving the detail of the war in Spain for another place, I need only relate here as much as is necessary for understanding Hasdrubal's expedition.   Early in the season of 546, while the other Carthaginian generals were in distant parts of the peninsula, Hasdrubal had been obliged with his single army to give battle to Scipio at Bæcula, a place in the south of Spain, in the upper part of the valley of the Bætis ; and having been defeated there, had succeeded, nevertheless, in carrying off his elephants and money, and had retreated first towards the Tagus, and then towards the western Pyrenees, whither Scipio durst not follow him for fear of abandoning the sea-coast to the other Carthaginian generals.[2]   By this movement Hasdrubal masked his projects from the view of the Romans; they did not know whether he had merely retired to recruit his army in order to take the field against Scipio, or whether he was preparing for a march into Italy.[3] But even if Italy were his object, it was supposed that he would follow the usual route, by the eastern Pyrenees along the coast of the Mediterranean ; and Scipio accordingly took the precaution of securing the passes of the mountains in this direction, on the present road between Barcelona and Perpignan ;[4] perhaps also he secured those other passes more inland, leading from the three valleys which meet

<hr>

[1] Livy, XXVII. 36.
[2] Livy, XXVII. 18, 19. Polybius, X. 38. 39.
[3] Polybius, X. 39. Livy, XXVII. 20.   [4] Polybius, X. 40, § 11.

above Lerida into Languedoc, and to the streams which feed the Garonne. But Hasdrubal's real line of march was wholly unsuspected; for, passing over the ground now so famous in our own military annals, near the highest part of the course of the Ebro, he turned the Pyrenees at their western extremity, and entered Gaul by the shores of the ocean, by the Bidassoa and the Adour.[1] Thence striking eastward, and avoiding the neighbourhood of the Mediterranean, he penetrated into the country of the Arverni; and so would cross the Rhone near Lyons, and join Hannibal's route for the first time in the plains of Dauphiné, at the very foot of the Alps. This new and remote line of march concealed him so long, even from the knowledge of the Massilians, and obliged them to seek intelligence of his movements from the chiefs of the interior.[2]

Now, then, the decisive year was come, the point of the great struggle so long delayed, but which the Carthaginians had never lost sight of, when Italy was to be assailed at once from the north and from the south by two Carthaginian armies, led by two sons of Hamilcar. And at this moment Marcellus, so long the hope of Rome, was gone; Fabius and Fulvius were enfeebled by age; Lævinus, whose services in Macedonia and Sicily had been so important, had offended the ruling party in the senate by his opposition to the appointment of Fulvius as dictator two years before, and no important command would as yet be entrusted to him. In

Doubts at Rome about the choice of consuls.

---

[1] Livy, XXVII. 20. Appian. Hispan. 28.
[2] Livy, XXVII. 36, 39.

this state of things the general voice pronounced that the best consul who could be chosen was C. Claudius Nero.[1]

C. Nero.

C. Nero came of a noble lineage, being a patrician of the Claudian house and a great-grandson of the famous censor, Appius the blind. He had served throughout the war, as lieutenant to Marcellus in 540 ; as prætor and proprætor at the siege of Capua, in 542 and 543 ; as proprætor in Spain in 544 ; and lastly as lieutenant of Marcellus in 545.[2] Yet it is strange that the only mention of him personally before his consulship which has reached us, is unfavourable ; he is said to have shown a want of vigour when serving under Marcellus in 540, and a want of ability in his command in Spain.[3] But these stories are perhaps of little authority, and if they are true Nero must have redeemed his faults by many proofs of courage and wisdom ; for his countrymen were not likely to choose the general rashly, who was to command them in the most perilous moment of the whole war, and we know that their choice was amply justified by the event.

M. Livius.

But if Nero were one consul who was to be his colleague ? It must be some one who was not a patrician to comply with the Licinian law, and the now settled practice of the constitution. But there was no Decius living, no Curius, no Fabricius, and the glory of the great house of the Metelli had hitherto, during the second Punic war, been somewhat in eclipse, bearing the shame of that ill-advised

---

[1] Livy, XXVII. 34.
[2] Livy, XXIV. 17 ; XXV. 2, 3. 22 ; XXVI. 17 ; XXVII. 14.
[3] Livy, XXIV. 17 ; XXVI. 17.

Metellus, who dared after the rout of Cannæ to speak of abandoning Italy in despair. The brave and kindly Gracchus, the bold Flaminius, the unwearied and undaunted Marcellus, had all fallen in their country's cause. Varro was living, and had learnt wisdom by experience, and was serving the state well and faithfully, but it would be of evil omen to send him again with the last army of the commonwealth to encounter a son of Hamilcar. At last men remembered a stern and sullen old man, M. Livius who had been consul twelve years before, and had then done good service against the Illyrians, and obtained a triumph, the last which Rome had seen; but whose hard nature had made him generally odious, and who, having been accused before the people of dividing the Illyrian spoil amongst his soldiers unfairly, had been found guilty and fined.[1] The shame and the sense of wrong had so struck him—for, though ungracious and unjust from temper, he was above corruption—that for some years he lived wholly in the country, and though he had since returned to Rome, and the last censors had obliged him to resume his place in the senate, yet he had never spoken there, till this very year, when the attacks made on his kinsman, the governor of Tarentum, had induced him to open his lips in his defence. He was misanthropical to all men, and especially at enmity with C. Nero; yet there were qualities in him well suited to the present need, and the senators suggested to their friends and tribesmen and dependants that no better consuls could be appointed than C. Nero and M. Livius.[2]

A.U.C.547.
A.C. 207.

---

[1] Frontinus, IV. 1. 45.   [2] Livy, XXVII. 34.

The people might agree to choose Livius, but would he consent to be chosen ?   At first he refused altogether : 'If he were fit to be consul, why had they condemned him ? if he had been justly condemned, how could he deserve to be consul ?'   But the senators reproved him for this bitterness, telling him 'that his country's harshness was to be borne like a parent's, and must be softened by patient submission.'   Overpowered, but not melted, he consented to be elected consul.

Then the senators, and especially Q. Fabius, besought him to be reconciled to his colleague.   'To what purpose ?' he replied ; 'we shall both serve the commonwealth the better, if we feel that an enemy's eye is watching for our faults and negligences.'   But here again the senate's authority prevailed, and the consuls were publicly reconciled.[1]   Yet the vindictive temper of Livius still burnt within him so fiercely that, before he took the field, when Q. Fabius was urging him not to be rash in hazarding a battle, until he had well learnt the strength of his enemy, he replied 'that he would fight as soon as ever he came in sight of him ;' and when Fabius asked him why he was so impatient, he answered, ' Because I thirst either for the glory of a victory, or for the pleasure of seeing the defeat of my unjust countrymen.'[2]

It is worth while to remark what gigantic efforts the Romans made for this great campaign.   One consul was to have Cisalpine Gaul for his province, the other Lucania and Bruttium ; each with the usual consular army of two legions, and an equal

---

[1] Livy, XXVII. 35.   Valerius Maximus, IV. 2. 2 ; VII. 2. 6.
[2] Livy, XXVII. 40.   Valerius Maximus, IX. 3. 1.

force of Italian allies. The army of the north was A.U.C. 547. A.C. 207.
supported by two others of equal force; one, commanded by L. Porcius, one of the prætors, was to
co-operate with it in the field; the other, commanded
by C. Varro, was to overawe Etruria, and form a
reserve. In like manner the consul of the army of
the south had two similar armies at his disposal
besides his own; one in Bruttium, of which old Q.
Fulvius once more took the command, and another
in the neighbourhood of Tarentum. Besides these
twelve legions, one legion occupied Capua and two
new home legions were raised for the immediate
defence of Rome. Thus fifteen legions, containing
75,000 Roman citizens, besides an equal number of
Italian allies, were in arms this year for the protection of Italy. In this same year the return of the
whole population of Roman citizens of an age to
bear arms, according to the census, amounted only
to 137,108; and in addition to the forces employed
in Italy, eight legions were serving abroad; two in
Sicily, two in Sardinia, and four in Spain.[1]

Soldiers were raised with a strictness never known Means taken to raise troops.
before; insomuch that even the maritime colonies
were called upon to furnish men for the legions,
although ordinarily exempted from this service, on
the ground that their citizens were responsible for
the defence of the sea-coast in their neighbourhood.
Only Antium and Ostia were allowed to retain their
customary exemption ; and the men within the
military age in both these colonies were obliged to
swear that they would not sleep out of their cities
more than thirty nights, so long as the enemy should

[1] Livy, XXVII. 36.

A.U.C. 547.
A.C. 207.
be in Italy.   The slaves also were again invited to enlist, and two legions were composed out of them ; and after all, so perilous was the aspect of affairs in the north from the known disaffection of Etruria, and even of Umbria, that P. Scipio is said to have draughted 10,000 foot and 1000 horse from the forces of his province, and sent them by sea to reinforce the army of the north ; while the prætor commanding in Sicily sent 4000 archers and slingers for the army of the south.   The lot decided that M. Livius was to be opposed to Hasdrubal, C. Nero to Hannibal.[1]

Hasdrubal crosses the Alps, and advances upon Ariminum.

Meantime Hasdrubal had begun his march from the plains between the Rhone and the Isere, and proceeded to cross the Alps by the route formerly followed by his brother.   It is said that he found the obstacles of all kinds, both those presented by nature, and those offered by the hostility of the inhabitants, far less than had been experienced by Hannibal.   The inhabitants were now aware that the stranger army meant them no ill, that it was merely passing through their valleys on its way to a distant land, to encounter its enemies there.   Nay, it is added that traces of Hannibal's engineering were still in existence ; that the roads which he had built up along the steep mountain sides, and the bridges which he had thrown over the torrents, and the cuttings which he had made through the rocks, after having been exposed for eleven years to the fury of the avalanches, and the chafing of the swollen streams, were even now serviceable to Hasdrubal. At any rate Hasdrubal appeared in Italy sooner than

[1] Livy, XXVII. 38.

either friend or foe had expected him ;[1] and having he descended along its right bank, and sat down before the Latin colony of Placentia. But the colony was one of the faithful eighteen, and did not forget its duty. It closed its gates, and Hasdrubal had no artillery to batter down its walls ; he only lay before it, therefore, long enough for the Cisalpine Gauls and Ligurians to join him, and then pressed forward on his march by the line of the later Æmilian road, towards Ariminum, and the shores of the Adriatic. The prætor L. Porcius retreated before him ; and Hasdrubal sent off four Gaulish horsemen and two Numidians to his brother, to announce his approach, and to propose that they should unite their two armies in Umbria, and from thence advance by the Flaminian road straight upon Rome.[2] Livius had by this time arrived on the scene of action, and had effected his junction with L. Porcius, yet their combined forces were unable to maintain their ground on the frontier of Italy ; Ariminum was abandoned to its fate ; they fell back behind the Metaurus ; and still keeping the coast road,——for the later branch of the Flaminian road, which ascends the valley of the Metaurus, was not yet constructed,——they encamped about fourteen miles farther to the south, under the walls of the maritime colony of Sena.[3]

On the other side of Italy, C. Nero, availing himself of the full powers with which the consuls were invested for this campaign, had incorporated the two legions, which Q. Fulvius was to have commanded

A.U.C. 547.
A.C. 207.

Nero encamps at Venusia.

---

[1] Livy, XXVII. 39. Appian, Hannibal, 52.

[2] Livy, XXVII. 43.   [3] Appian, Hannibal, 52.

 in Bruttium, with his own army, leaving Fulvius at the head of a small army of reserve at Capua. With an army thus amounting to 40,000 foot and 2500 horse Nero fixed his headquarters at Venusia, his object being by all means to occupy Hannibal, and to hinder him from moving northwards to join his brother.[1]

Difficulties in the history of this campaign. At no part of the history of this war do we more feel the want of a good military historian than at the opening of this memorable campaign. What we have in Livy is absolutely worthless; it is so vague, as well as so falsified, that the truth from which it has been corrupted can scarcely be discovered. We are told that Hannibal moved later from his winter quarters than he might have done, because he thought that his brother could not arrive in Cisalpine Gaul so early as he actually did; and we are told that he received information of his having reached Placentia.[2]   Yet, after having heard this, he wastes much time in moving about in the south, first into Lucania, then to Apulia, thence falling back into Bruttium, and finally advancing again into Apulia, and there remaining idle till the fatal blow had been struck in the north. It is added that in the course of these movements he was several times engaged with the Romans, and lost nearly 15,000 men, killed or taken.[3]   Putting aside these absurdities, in which we cannot but recognise the perversions of Valerius Antias or some annalist equally untrustworthy, we must endeavour as far as possible to conjecture the outline of the real story.

[1] Livy, XXVII. 40.   [2] Livy, XXVII. 39.
[3] Livy, XXVII. 41, 42.

With 40,000 men under an active general opposed A.U.C. 547.
to him in the field, and with 20,000 more in his A.C. 207.
rear in the neighbourhood of Tarentum, Hannibal Hannibal's move-
could only act on the offensive by gathering all his ments.
remaining garrisons into one mass, and by raising
additional soldiers, if it were possible, amongst the
allies who yet adhered to him.   This was to be
accomplished in the face of a superior enemy, and,
as Hasdrubal was already arrived on the Po, without
loss of time.   It was for this object apparently that
he entered Lucania, to raise soldiers amongst his
old partisans there; with this view he crossed back
into Apulia, and then moved into Bruttium to join
the new Bruttian levies, which had been collected
by Hanno, the governor of Metapontum.   All this
he effected, baffling the pursuit of Nero, or beating
off his attacks, and having amassed a force sufficient
for his purpose he again turned northwards, re-entered
Apulia, advanced, followed closely by Nero, to his
old quarters near Canusium, and there halted.[1]
Whether he was busy in collecting corn for his farther
advance, or whether he was waiting for more precise
intelligence from his brother, we know not, but we do
not find that he moved his army beyond Canusium.

Admitting, however, that Hannibal was aware of He waits for tidings from his brother.
Hasdrubal's arrival before Placentia, we can under-
stand why his own movements could not but be
suspended, after he had collected all his disposable
force together, till he should receive a fresh communication from his brother.   For from Placentia
Hasdrubal had a choice of roads before him, and it
was impossible for Hannibal to know beforehand

[1] Livy, XXVII. 42.

which he might take.   But on this knowledge his own plans were to depend ; if Hasdrubal crossed the Apennines into Etruria in order to rally the disaffected Etruscans around him, Hannibal might then advance into Samnium and Campania ; if, on the other hand, Hasdrubal were to move eastward towards the Adriatic, thinking it desirable that the two armies should act together, then Hannibal also would keep near the coast, and retracing the line of his own advance after the battle of Thrasymenus would be ready to meet his brother in Picenum or in Umbria.[1]   And it was in order to determine Hannibal's movements that Hasdrubal, when he left Placentia, sent off the six horsemen, as has been already mentioned, to say that he was marching upon Ariminum instead of upon Etruria, and that the two brothers were to effect their junction in Umbria.

Hasdrubal's messengers are taken prisoners, and brought to Nero.

With marvellous skill and good fortune Hasdrubal's horsemen made their way through the whole length of Italy.   But Hannibal's rapid movement into Bruttium disconcerted them ; they attempted to follow him thither, but mistaking their way, and getting too near to Tarentum, they fell in with some foragers of the army of Q. Claudius and were made prisoners.   The prætor instantly sent them under a strong escort to Nero.   They were the bearers of a letter from Hasdrubal to his brother, containing the whole plan of their future operations ; it was written, not in cypher, but in the common Carthaginian

[1] [Another reason for Hannibal's reluctance to move northwards is suggested by Neumann (or rather Faltin), p. 478, in the shape of Hannibal's supposed unwillingness to leave his allies and strong places in Lucania and Bruttium without defence.]

language and character, and the interpreter read its
contents in Latin to the consul.[1]

A.U.C. 547.
A.C. 207.

Nero took his resolution on the instant. He
despatched the letter to the senate, urging the
immediate recall of Fulvius with his army from
Capua to Rome, the calling out every Roman who
could bear arms, and the marching forward the two
home legions to Narnia to defend that narrow gorge
of the Flaminian road against the invader. At the
same time he told the senate what he was going to
do himself. He picked out 7000 men, of whom
1000 were horse, the flower of his whole army; he
ordered them to hold themselves in readiness for a
secret expedition into Lucania to surprise one of
Hannibal's garrisons, and as soon as it was dark he
put himself at their head, leaving his lieutenant, Q.
Catius, in the command of the main army, and
began his march.[2]

Nero leaves
his camp,

His march was not towards Lucania. Already
before he left his camp had he sent forward horsemen on the road leading to Picenum and Umbria,
with the consul's orders that all the provisions of
the country should be brought down to the roadside, that all horses and draught cattle should be
led thither also, and carriages for the transport of
the weaker or wearied soldiers. Life and death
were upon his speed, the life and death of his
country. His march was towards the camp of his
colleague, before Sena; his hope was to crush Hasdrubal with their combined and overwhelming forces,
whilst Hannibal, waiting for that letter which he
would never receive, should remain still in Apulia.

and
marches to
join Livius.

---

[1] Livy, XXVII. 43.   [2] Livy, XXVII. 43.

A.U.C. 547.
A.C. 207.
Nero joins
Livius.

When Nero had reached a sufficient distance from Hannibal, he disclosed the secret of his expedition to his soldiers. They felt the glory of their mission, and shared the spirit of their leader. Nor was it a little thing to witness the universal enthusiasm which everywhere welcomed their march. Men and women, the whole population of the country, crowded to the roadside; meat, drink, clothing, horses, carriages, were pressed upon the soldiers, and happy was the man from whom they would accept them. Every tongue blessed them as deliverers; incense rose on hastily built altars, where the people, kneeling as the army passed, poured forth prayers and vows to the gods for their safe and victorious return. The soldiers would scarcely receive what was offered to them: they would not halt; they ate standing in their ranks; night and day they hastened onwards, scarcely allowing themselves a brief interval of rest.[1] In six or seven days the march was accomplished; Livius had been forewarned of his colleague's approach, and according to his wish Nero entered the camp by night, concealing his arrival from Hasdrubal no less successfully than he had hidden his departure from Hannibal.[2]

They determine to fight without delay.

The new-comers were to be received into the tents of Livius's soldiers, for any enlargement of the camp would have betrayed the secret, and they were more than 7000 men, for their numbers had been swelled on their march; veterans who had retired from war, and youths too young to be enlisted, having pressed Nero to let them share in his enterprise. A council was held the next morning, and

---

[1] Livy, XXVII. 45.   [2] Livy, XXVII. 46.

though Livius and L. Porcius, the prætor, urged Nero to allow his men some rest before he led them to battle, he pleaded so strongly the importance of not losing a single day lest Hannibal should be upon their rear, that it was agreed to fight immediately. The red ensign was hoisted as soon as the council broke up, and the soldiers marched out and formed in order of battle.[1]

The enemy, whose camp, according to the system of ancient warfare, was only half a mile distant from that of the Romans, marched out and formed in line to meet them. But as Hasdrubal rode forward to reconnoitre the Roman army their increased numbers struck him, and other circumstances, it is said, having increased his suspicions, he led back his men into their camp, and sent out some horsemen to collect information. The Romans then returned to their own camp; and Hasdrubal's horsemen rode round it at a distance to see if it were larger than usual or in the hope of picking up some stragglers. One thing alone, it is said, revealed the secret; the trumpet, which gave the signal for the several duties of the day, was heard to sound as usual once in the camp of the prætor, but twice in that of Livius. This, we are told, satisfied Hasdrubal that both the consuls were before him; unable to understand how Nero had escaped from Hannibal, and dreading the worst, he resolved to retire to a greater distance from the enemy, and having put out all his fires, he set his army in motion as soon as night fell, and retreated towards the Metaurus.[2]

Whose narrative Livy has followed here, we can-

A.U.C. 547.
A.C. 207.

Hasdrubal
retreats

along the
banksofthe
Metaurus.

---

[1] Livy, XXVII. 46.　　　　[2] Livy, XXVII. 47.

not tell; it is not that of Polybius, except in part, and some points speak ill for the credibility of its author. According to this account, Hasdrubal marched back fourteen miles to the Metaurus; but his guides deserted him and escaped unobserved in the darkness, so that, when the army reached the Metaurus, they could not find the fords, and began to ascend the right bank of the river, in the hope of passing it easily when daylight came, and they should be arrived at a higher part of its course. But the windings of the river, it is said, delayed him; as he ascended further from the sea, he found the banks steeper and higher, and no ford was to be gained.[1]

Description of the course of the Metaurus.

The Metaurus, in the last twenty miles of its course, flows through a wide valley or plain, the ground rising into heights rather than hills, while the mountains from which it has issued ascend far off in the distance, and bound the low country near the sea with a gigantic wall. But as is frequently the case in northern Italy, the bed of the river is like a valley within a valley, being sunk down between steep cliffs, at a level much below the ordinary surface of the country, which yet would be supposed to be the bottom of the plain by those who looked only at the general landscape, and did not observe the kind of trough in which the river was winding beneath them. Yet this lower valley is of considerable width; and the river winds about in it from one side to the other, at times running just under its high banks, at other times leaving a large interval of plain between it and the boundary.

____

[1] Livy, XXVII. 47. See Note O.

The whole country, both in the lower valley and in the plain above, is now varied with all sorts of cultivation, with scattered houses, and villages, and trees; an open, joyous, and habitable region, as can be found in Italy.   But when Hasdrubal was retreating through it, the dark masses of uncleared wood still no doubt in many parts covered the face of the higher plain, overhanging the very cliffs of the lower valley; and the river below, not to be judged of by its present scanty and loitering stream, ran like the rivers of a half cleared country, with a deep and strong body of waters.

These steep cliffs would no doubt present a serious obstacle to an army wishing to descend to the edge of the river, and if their summits were covered with wood, they would at once intercept the view, and make the march more difficult.   Thus Hasdrubal was overtaken by the Romans and obliged to fight. It is clear from Polybius that he had encamped for the night after his wearisome march; and retreat being fatal to the discipline of barbarians the Gauls became unmanageable, and indulged so freely in drinking that, when morning dawned, many of them were lying drunk in their quarters, utterly unable to move.[1]   And now the Roman army was seen advancing in order of battle; and Hasdrubal, finding it impossible to continue his retreat, marched out of his camp to meet them.[2]

No credible authority tells us what was the amount of his army; that the Roman writers extravagantly magnified it, is certain, and that he was enormously outnumbered by his enemy is no

____

[1] Polybius, XI. 3.   [2] Livy, XXVII. 48.

less so. Polybius [1] says, that he deepened his lines, diminishing their width, and drawing up his whole force in a narrow space, with his ten elephants in front. We hear nothing of his cavalry, the force with which his brother had mainly won his victories, and he had probably brought scarcely any African horse from Spain; what Gaulish horsemen had joined him since he had crossed the Alps we know not. His Gaulish infantry, as many as were fit for action, were stationed on his left, in a position naturally so strong as to be unassailable in front, and its flank would probably be covered by the river. He himself took part with his Spanish infantry, and attacked the left wing of the Roman army, which was commanded by Livius. Nero was on the Roman right, the prætor in the centre. [2]

He is defeated and slain.

Between Hasdrubal and Livius, the battle was long and obstinately disputed, the elephants being, according to Polybius, an equal aid, or rather an equal hindrance, to both parties; [3] for, galled by the missiles of the Romans, they broke sometimes into their own ranks, as well as into those of the enemy. Meanwhile Nero, seeing that he could make no progress on his front, drew off his troops out of the line, and passing round on the rear of the prætor and of Livius, fell upon the right flank and the rear of the enemy. Then the fate of the day was decided; and the Spaniards, outnumbered and surrounded, were cut to pieces in their ranks, resisting to the last. Then, too, when all was lost, Hasdrubal spurred his horse into the midst of a Roman cohort, and there fell sword in hand, fighting,

[1] Polybius, XI. 1.   [2] Livy, XXVII. 48.   [3] XI. 1.

says Livy, with honourable sympathy, as became the son of Hamilcar and brother of Hannibal.[1]

The conquerors immediately stormed the Carthaginian camp, and there slaughtered many of the Gauls, whom they found still lying asleep in the helplessness of brute intoxication.[2] The spoil of the camp was rich, amounting in value to 300 talents; of the elephants, six were killed in the action; the other four were taken alive. All the Carthaginian citizens who had followed Hasdrubal, were either killed or taken; and 3000 Roman prisoners were found in the camp, and restored to liberty. The loss of men on both sides was swelled prodigiously by the Roman writers, ambitious, it seems, of making the victory an exact compensation for the defeat of Cannæ; but Polybius[3] states it at 10,000 men on the side of the vanquished, and 2000 on that of the Romans; a decisive proof that Hasdrubal's army actually engaged cannot have been numerous, for of those in the field few can have escaped. But the amount of slain mattered little; Hasdrubal's army was destroyed, and he himself had perished, and Hannibal was left to fight out the war with his single army, which, however unconquerable, could not conquer Italy.

Polybius[4] praises the heroic spirit of Hasdrubal, saying that he knew when it was time for him to die; that having been careful of his life, so long as there was any hope of accomplishing his great enterprise, when all was lost, he gave his country, what Pericles calls the greatest and noblest gift of a true

Effects of
the victory.

Value of
Hasdru-
bal's life.

---

[1] Livy, XXVII. 49. Polybius, XI. 2.
[2] Polybius. XI. 3.   [3] XI. 3.   [4] XI. 2.

citizen, the sacrifice of his own life.   And doubtless none can blame the spirit of self-devotion to the highest known duty : Hasdrubal was true to his country in his death as in his life.   Yet the life of a son of Hamilcar was to Carthage of a value beyond all estimate : Hasdrubal's death outweighed the loss of many armies ; and had he deigned to survive his defeat, he might again have served his country, not only in peace, as Hannibal did after his defeat at Zama, but as the leader of a fresh army of Gauls and Ligurians, of Etruscans and Umbrians, co-operating with his brother in marching upon Rome.

Hannibal receives intelligence of his brother's death.   With no less haste than he had marched from Apulia, Nero hastened back thither to rejoin his army.   All was quiet there : Hannibal still lay in his camp, waiting for intelligence from Hasdrubal.   He received it too soon, not from Hasdrubal, but from Nero : the Carthaginian prisoners were exhibited exultingly before his camp ; two of them were set at liberty, and sent to tell him the story of their defeat ; and a head was thrown down in scorn before his outposts, if his soldiers might know whose it was.   They took it up, and brought to Hannibal the head of his brother.[1]   He had not dealt so with the remains of the Roman generals ; but of this Nero recked nothing ; as indifferent to justice and humanity in his dealings with an enemy, as his imperial descendants showed themselves towards Rome and all mankind.

Anxiety and joy at Rome.   Meanwhile, from the moment that Nero's march from the south had been heard of at Rome, intense anxiety possessed the whole city.   Every day the

[1] Livy, XXVII. 51.

senate sat from sunrise to sunset; and not a senator A.U.C. 547. was absent: every day the forum was crowded from A.C. 207. morning till evening, as each hour might bring some great tidings; and every man wished to be among the first to hear them. A doubtful rumour arose that a great battle had been fought, and a great victory won only two days before: two horsemen of Narnia had ridden off from the field to carry the news to their home: it had been heard and published in the camp of the reserve army, which was lying at Narnia to cover the approach to Rome. But men dared not lightly believe what they so much wished to be true: and how, they said, could a battle fought in the extremity of Umbria be heard of only two days after at Rome? Soon, however, it was known that a letter had arrived from L. Manlius Acidinus himself, who commanded the army at Narnia: the horsemen had certainly arrived there from the field of battle, and brought tidings of a glorious victory. The letter was read first in the senate, and then in the forum from the rostra; but some still refused to believe: fugitives from a battle-field might carry idle tales of victory to hide their own shame: till the account came directly from the consuls, it was rash to credit it.[1] At last, word was brought that officers of high rank in the consuls' army were on their way to Rome; that they bore a despatch from Livius and Nero. Then the whole city poured out of the walls to meet them, eager to anticipate the moment which was to confirm all their hopes. For two miles, as far as the Milvian bridge over the Tiber, the crowd formed an uninterrupted mass; and when the officers appeared, they

---

[1] Livy, XXVII. 50.

could scarcely make their way to the city, the multitude thronging around them, and overwhelming them and their attendants with eager questions. As each man learnt the joyful answers he made haste to tell them to others: 'the enemy's army is destroyed; their general slain; our own legions and both the consuls are safe.' So the crowd re-entered the city; and the three officers, all men of noble names, L. Veturius Philo, P. Licinius Varus, and Q. Metellus, still followed by the thronging multitude, at last reached the senate-house. The people pressed after them into the senate-house itself: but even at such a moment the senate forgot not its accustomed order; the crowd was forced back; and the consuls' despatch was first read to the senators alone. Immediately afterwards the officers came out into the forum: there L. Veturius again read the despatch; and as its contents were short, and it told only the general result of the battle, he himself related the particulars of what he had seen and done. The interest of his hearers grew more intense with every word; till at last the whole multitude broke out into one universal cheer, and then rushed from the forum in all directions to carry the news to their wives and children at home, or ran to the temples to pour out their gratitude to the gods. The senate ordered a thanksgiving of three days; the prætor announced it in the forum; and for three days every temple was crowded; and the Roman wives and mothers, in their gayest dresses, took their children with them, and poured forth their thanks to all the gods for this great deliverance. It was like the burst of all nature, when a long frost suddenly breaks up, and the snow melts, and the ground resumes its natural colouring, and the streams flow freely. The Roman people seemed at last to breathe and move at liberty: confidence revived; and with it the ordinary business of life regained its activity: he who wanted money found that men were not afraid to lend it; what had been hoarded came out into circulation; land might be bought without the dread that the purchase would be rendered worthless by Hannibal's ravages; and in the joy and confidence of the moment men almost forgot that their great enemy with his unbroken army was still in Italy.[1]

At the end of the year both consuls returned to Rome, and triumphed. Many years had passed since this spectacle had been exhibited in its full solemnity: for Marcellus had only obtained the smaller triumph, or ovation, in which the general passed through the streets on foot. But now the kingly chariot once more carried a Roman consul in the pomp of kingly state up to the temple of the Capitoline Jupiter; and the streets once more resounded with the shouts and rude jests of the victorious soldiers, as they moved in long array after their general. The spoil of Hasdrubal's camp was large; each soldier received a donative of three denarii and a half; and three millions of sesterces in silver, besides eighty thousand pounds of the old Italian copper money, were carried into the treasury. Nero rode on horseback by the side of his colleague's chariot; a distinction made between them, partly because Livius had happened to have the command on the day of the battle, and partly because Nero had come without his army; his province still requiring its usual

A.U.C. 547.
A.C. 207.

The con-
suls' tri-
umph.

---

[1] Livy, XXVII. 51.

 force, as Hannibal was there.   But the favour of the multitude, if we can trust the writers under Augustus, when they speak of his adopted son's ancestor, amply compensated to Nero for this formal inferiority : they said that he was the real conqueror of Hasdrubal, while his name, even in absence, had overawed Hannibal.[1] One thing, however, is remarkable, that Nero was never employed again in a military command : we only hear of him after his consulship as censor.   Fabius and Fulvius and Marcellus had been sent out year after year against Hannibal ; whilst the man whose military genius eclipsed all the Roman generals hitherto engaged in Italy, was never opposed to him again.   Men's eyes were turned in another direction ; and the conqueror of the Metaurus was less regarded than a young man whose career of success had been as brilliant as it was uninterrupted, and who was now almost entitled to the name of conqueror of all Spain.   It is time that we should trace the events of the war in the west, and describe the dawn of the glory of Scipio.

[1] Livy, XXVIII. 9.

CHAPTER V.

THREE generations of Scipios have already been distinguished in Roman history: L. Scipio Barbatus, who was actively engaged in the third Samnite war; L. Scipio, his son, who was consul early in the first Punic war, and obtained a triumph; the Publius and Cnæus Scipio, the sons of L. Scipio, who served their country ably in Spain in the second Punic war, and, as we have seen, were at last cut off there by the enemy, towards the end of the siege of Capua. Publius Scipio, who was killed in Spain, left two sons behind him, Lucius and Publius; of these, Lucius, the elder, became afterwards the conqueror of King Antiochus; Publius, the younger, was the famous Scipio Africanus.

Athens abounded in writers at the time of the Peloponnesian war; but, had not Thucydides been one of them, how hard would it be rightly to estimate the characters of the eminent men of that period! And even Thucydides seems in one instance to have partaken of the common weaknesses of humanity: his personal gratitude and respect for Antiphon has coloured, not indeed his statement of his actions, but his general estimate of his worth; he attributes an over-measure of virtue to the conspirator, who scrupled not to use assassination as a means of overthrowing the liberty and independence of his country. But Polybius, whose knowledge of Rome was that of a foreigner, and for a long time of a prisoner, could not be to Roman history what Thucydides is to that of Greece, even if in natural powers he had approached more nearly to him; and all his accounts of the Scipios are affected by his intimacy with the younger Africanus, and are derived from partial sources, the anecdotes told by the elder Lælius, or the funeral orations and traditions of the family. On the other hand, there was a large party in Rome to whom Scipio was personally and politically obnoxious; and their writers would naturally circulate stories unfavourable to him. Hence, the accounts of his early life and character are varying, and sometimes contradictory; and points apparently the most notorious are stated very differently, so that we know not what to believe. His friend and companion Lælius told Polybius[1] that in his first battle, when only seventeen, he saved his father's life; but Cœlius Antipater said that this was a false pretension, that the consul, P. Scipio, was saved, not by his son, but by the fidelity of a Ligurian slave.[2] By his friends again Scipio is represented as one who, amid all temptations of youth and power, maintained the complete mastery over his passions;[3] while his enemies said that his youth was utterly dissolute, and that the famous story of his noble treatment of the Spanish captive

____

[1] X. 3.   [2] Livy, XXI. 46.
[3] Polybius, X. 18, 19.   Livy, XXVI. 49, 50.

maiden was invented to veil conduct which had really been of the very opposite nature.[1] His common admirers extolled his singular devotion to the gods: he delighted, it was said, to learn their pleasure, and to be guided by their counsel; nor would he ever engage in any important matter, public or private, till he had first gone up to the Capitol, and entered the temple of Jupiter, and there sat for a time alone, as it seemed, in the presence of the god, and doubtless enjoying unwonted communications from his divine wisdom.[2] But Polybius, by temper and by circumstances a rationalist, is at great pains to assure his readers that Scipio owed no part of his greatness to the gods, and that his true oracle was the clear judgment of his own mind.[3] According to him Scipio did but impose upon and laugh at the credulity of the vulgar, speaking of the favour shown him by the gods, while he knew the gods to be nothing. Livy, with a truer feeling, which taught him that a hero cannot be a hypocrite, suggests a doubt, though timidly, as if in fear of the scepticism of his age, whether the great Scipio was not really touched by some feelings of superstition,[4] whether he did not in some degree speak what he himself believed.

A mind like Scipio's, working its way under the peculiar influences of his time and country, cannot but move irregularly, it cannot but be full of contradictions. Two hundred years later the mind of

His religious spirit.

---

[1] Cn. Nævius and Valerius Antias, quoted by A. Gellius, VII. 8.

[2] Livy, XXVI. 19. Polybius, X. 2. 5. 11.

[3] Polybius, X. 2. 5. 7.

[4] XXVI. 19. Sive et ipse capti quadam superstitione animi.

the dictator Cæsar acquiesced contentedly in Epicureanism : he retained no more of enthusiasm than was inseparable from the intensity of his intellectual power, and the fervour of his courage, even amidst his utter moral degradation, But Scipio could not be like Cæsar. His mind rose above the state of things around him ; his spirit was solitary and kingly ; he was cramped by living among those as his equals, whom he felt fitted to guide as from some higher sphere ; and he retired at last to Liternum to breathe freely,[1] to enjoy the simplicity of childhood, since he could not fulfil his natural calling to be a hero king. So far he stood apart from his countrymen, admired, reverenced, but not loved. But he could not shake off all the influences of his time : the virtue, public and private, which still existed at Rome, the reverence paid by the wisest and best men to the religion of their fathers, were elements too congenial to his nature not to retain their hold upon it ; they cherished that nobleness of soul in him, and that faith in the invisible and divine, which two centuries of growing unbelief rendered almost impossible in the days of Cæsar. Yet how strange must the conflict be when faith is combined with the highest intellectual power, and its appointed object is no better than Paganism ! Longing to believe, yet repelled by palpable falsehood, crossed inevitably with snatches of unbelief, in which hypocrisy is ever close at the door, it breaks out desperately, as it may seem, into the region of dreams and visions, and mysterious communings with the invisible, as if longing to find that food in

[1] Livy, XXXVIII. 52, 53. Valerius Maximus. V. 3. 2.

its own creations which no outward objective truth offers to it. The proportions of belief and unbelief in the human mind in such cases, no human judgment can determine: they are the wonders of history; characters inevitably misrepresented by the vulgar, and viewed even by those who in some sense have the key to them as a mystery, not fully to be comprehended, and still less explained to others. The genius which conceived the incomprehensible character of Hamlet would alone be able to describe with intuitive truth the character of Scipio or of Cromwell.[1]

In both these great men the enthusiastic element, which clearly existed in them, did but inspire a resistless energy into their actions, while it in no way interfered with the calmest and keenest judgment in the choice of their means; nor, in the case of Scipio did it suggest any other end of life than such as was appreciated by ordinary human views of good. Where religion contained no revelation of new truth, it naturally left men's estimate of the end of their being exactly what it had been before, and only furnished encouragement to the pursuit of it. It so far bore the character of magic, that it applied superhuman power to the furtherance of human purposes: the gods aided man's work, they did not teach and enable him to do theirs. *Its effect in his life.*

The charge of early dissoluteness brought against Scipio by his enemies is likely to have been exaggerated, like the stories of our Henry V. Yet the sternest and firmest manhood has sometimes followed *Charge against him.*

---

[1] [Ranke, Weltgeschichte II., 249, does not mention Cromwell, but the character he gives of Scipio will inevitably bring Cromwell to the English reader's mind.]

a youth marked with many excesses of passion ; and what was considered an unbecoming interruption to the cares of public business, was held to be in itself nothing blameable. That sanction of inherited custom, which at Rome at this period was the best safeguard of youthful purity, Scipio was not inclined implicitly to regard.

With all his greatness there was a waywardness in him, which seems often to accompany genius : a self-idolatry, natural enough where there is so keen a consciousness of power and of lofty designs : a self-dependence, which feels even the most sacred external relations to be unessential to its own perfection. Such is the Achilles of Homer, the highest conception of the individual hero, relying on himself, and sufficient to himself. But the same poet who conceived the character of Achilles has also drawn that of Hector; of the truly noble, because unselfish hero, who subdues his genius to make it minister to the good of others, who lives for his relations, his friends, and his country. And as Scipio lived in himself and for himself, like Achilles, so the virtue of Hector was worthily represented in the life of his great rival Hannibal, who, from his childhood to his latest hour, in war and in peace, through glory and through obloquy, amid victories and amid disappointments, ever remembered to what purpose his father had devoted him, and withdrew no thought or desire or deed from their pledged service to his country.

Scipio had fought at Cannæ, and after the battle had been forward, it was said, in putting down that dangerous spirit which showed itself among some of high birth and name, when they were purposing to abandon Italy in despair, and seek their fortune in Greece or Egypt or Asia.[1]   His early manhood had attracted the favour of the people; and although the details are variously given, it is certain that he was made curule ædile at an early age, and with strong marks of the general goodwill.[2]   But he had filled no higher office than the ædileship when his father and uncle were killed in Spain, and when C. A.U.C. 543. Nero, after the fall of Capua, was sent out as pro-prætor to command the wreck of their army, and joining it to the force which he brought from Italy, to maintain the almost desperate cause of the Roman arms in the west.

He held his ground, and even ventured, if we War in may believe a story overrun with improbabilities, to Spain after act on the offensive, and to penetrate into the south the Scipios. of Spain, as far as the Bætis.[3]   The faults of the Carthaginian generals were ruining their cause, and vexing the spirit of Hasdrubal, the son of Hamilcar, who alone knew the value of the present opportunity, and was eager to make use of it.   But the other Hasdrubal and Mago thought their work was done, and were only anxious to enrich themselves out of the plunder of Spain.   They disgusted the Spanish chiefs by their insolence and rapacity, while they were jealous of each other, and both, as was natural, hated and dreaded the son of Hamilcar.[4]   Accordingly, all concert between the Carthaginian generals

---

[1] Livy, XXII. 53.   See above, p. 81.
[2] Polybius, X. 4.   Livy, XXV. 2.
[3] Livy, XXVI. 17.   Weissenborn's Note in loc.
[4] Polybius, IX. 11 ; X. 36.

A.U.C. 544.
A.C. 210.

was at an end; they engaged in separate enterprises in different parts of the country; Hasdrubal, the son of Gisco, and Mago, moved off to the extreme west of the peninsula, to subdue and plunder the remoter Spanish tribes; and only Hasdrubal, the son of Hamilcar, remained to oppose the Romans. Nero, therefore, whether he acted on the offensive or no, was certainly unassailed behind the Iberus; and, at the end of the year 544, eighteen months at least after the defeat of the Scipios, the Roman arms had met with no fresh disaster, and the coast of the Mediterranean between the Pyrenees and the Iberus still acknowledged the Roman dominion.

The Romans resolve to prosecute it with more vigour.

It was at this period that the government resolved to increase its efforts in Spain, to employ a larger army there, and to place it under the command of an officer of higher rank than Nero, who was only propraetor. It is probable that Hasdrubal's expedition to Italy was now seriously meditated, and that the Romans, being aware of this, were anxious to detain him in Spain; but, even without this special object, the importance of the Spanish war was evident, and it was not wise to leave the Roman cause in Spain in its present precarious state, in which it was preserved only by the divisions and want of ability of the enemy's generals. Accordingly, the tribes were to meet to appoint a proconsul, who should carry out reinforcements to Spain, and, with a propraetor acting under him, take the supreme command of the Roman forces in that country.

Scipio is elected proconsul for the Spanish war,

To the surprise of the whole people P. Scipio, then only in his twenty-seventh year, and who had filled no higher office than that of curule aedile,

came forward as a candidate.[1]   It is said that he A.U.C. 545.
had no competitors, all men being deterred from A.C. 209.
undertaking a service which seemed so unpromising ;
whereas Scipio himself had formed a truer judgment
of the state of affairs in Spain, and felt that they
might be restored, and that he himself was capable
of restoring them.   He expressed this confidence
strongly in all his addresses to the people ; and
there was that in him which distinguished his boldness from a young man's idle boastings, and communicated his hope to his hearers.[2]   At the same
age, and nearly under the same circumstances, in
which Napoleon was appointed in 1796 to take
the command of the French army of Italy, was P.
Scipio chosen by the unanimous voice of the
Roman people to take the command of their army
in Spain.   And great as were the consequences of
the appointment of Napoleon, those which followed
the appointment of Scipio were greater and far
more lasting.

At the same time a new proprætor was to be and goes
sent out in the room of C. Nero, whose year of with large
command was come to an end.   His successor was reinforce-
M. Junius Silanus,[3] who had been prætor two years ments to
before, and since that time had been employed in Spain.
overawing the party disaffected to Rome in Etruria.
The two new generals were to take with them large
reinforcements, amounting to 10,000 foot, 1000
horse, and a fleet of thirty quinqueremes.   The
troops were embarked at the mouth of the Tiber ;
and the fleet proceeded along the coasts of Etruria,

---

[1] Livy, XXVI. 18.   Polybius, X. 6.
[2] Livy, XXVI. 19.   Polybius, X. 6.   [3] Livy, XXVI. 19.

Liguria, and Gaul, till it arrived safely at Emporiæ, a Massaliot colony, lying immediately on the Spanish side of the Pyrenees. Here the soldiers were disembarked, and proceeded by land to Tarraco; the fleet followed, and the headquarters of the proconsul were established at Tarraco for the winter, as it was too late in the season to admit of any active operations immediately.[1]

View of Spain.

And now that Spain had received that general and that army, by whom her fate was fixed through all after-time—for the expulsion of the Carthaginians from the peninsula decided its subjection to the Romans, and though the work of conquest was slow, and often interrupted, it was not the less sure—let us for a moment survey the earliest known state of this great country; what Spain was, and who were the earliest Spaniards, before Romans, Goths, and Moors, had filled the land with stranger races, and almost extirpated the race and language of its original people.

Description of the Spanish peninsula.

The Spanish peninsula, joined to the main body of Europe by the isthmus of the Pyrenees, may be likened to one of the round bastion towers which stand out from the walls of an old fortified town, lofty at once and massy. Spain rises from the Atlantic on one side, and the Mediterranean on the other, not into one or two thin lines of mountains divided by vast tracts of valleys or low plains, but into a huge tower, as I have called it, of table-land, from which the mountains themselves rise again like the battlements on the summit. The plains of Castile are mountain plains, raised nearly 2000 feet above the level of the sea; and the elevation of the city

____
[1] Livy, XXVI. 19. 20.

MARE CANTABRICUM.
GALLIA
Pyrenaei
Volcae
Salluvii
Massilia
Rhodanus
Narbo Martius
S. Gallicus
Ruscino
M.
Illiberis
Emporiae
Vascones
Atanagria
Ilergetes
Ausetani
Nerda
Lacetani
Iberus F.
Indigetes
Tarraco
Laeetani
Barcino
Ceretani
Iberus F.
Onusa?
MARE BALEARICUM
Sicoris
Numantia
Iberus F.
Vaccaei
Arbocala
Celtiberi
Balcares
Iae
Minor
Duris
Astures
Major
HISPANIA
Carpetani
Etovisga
Saguntum
Ebusus
Tagus F.
Toletum
Vettones
Oretani
Olcades
Sucro F.
Bigerra
LUSITANIA
Tagus F.
Mituryi
Castulo
Longiotica?
Carthago nova
Baetis F.
Tader F.
MARE IBERICUM
Turdetani
Illiberri
Conii
Munda
Baetis F.
Gades
Burin.
Fretum Gaditanum MARE IBERICUM
SPAIN
to illustrate
the campaigns of Hannibal
and the two Scipios.
1:10.000.000
0 30 100 130 300 210
Milia passuum Romanorum.
Longitude of 0 Greenwich

of Madrid is nearly double that of the top of Arthur's Seat, the hill or mountain which overhangs Edinburgh. Accordingly the centre of Spain, notwithstanding its genial latitude, only partially enjoys the temperature of a southern climate; while some of the valleys of Andalusia, which lie near the sea, present the vegetation of the tropics, the palm tree, the banana, and the sugar cane. Thus the southern coast seemed to invite an early civilisation; while the interior, with its bleak and arid plains, was fitted to remain for centuries the stronghold of barbarism.

Accordingly the first visits of the Phœnicians to Spain are placed at a very remote period. Some stories ascribed the foundation of Gades to Archaleus, the son of Phœnix—Phœnix and Cadmus being the supposed founders of Tyre and Sidon, and belonging to the earliest period of Greek tradition;[1] while other accounts of a more historical character made the origin of Gades contemporary with the reign of the Athenian Codrus, that is, about a thousand years before the Christian era.[2] Three hundred years later the prophet Isaiah[3] describes the downfall of Tyre as likely to give deliverance to the land of Tarshish; that is, to the south of Spain, where the Phœnicians had established their dominion. In the time of Ezekiel, the Tyrian trade with Spain was most flourishing; and the produce of the Spanish mines, silver, iron, tin, and lead, are especially mentioned as the articles which came from Tarshish to

Early Phœnician settlements in Spain. The Basques, a remnant of the aboriginal inhabitants.

---

[1] [See Etym. Magnum, s. v. Γάδειρα. Preller, Griechische Mythologie, II. 208, note 2. Mullenhoff, Deutsche Alterthumskunde, I. 69. Mövers, Die Phönizier, I. 431. Delgados, Medallas Autonomas de Espana, II. 43. Archaleus no doubt= Hercules.]   [2] Velleius, I. 2.   [3] XXIII. 10.

the Phœnician ports.[1]   Nor did the Phœnicians confine themselves to a few points on the sea coast: they were spread over the whole south of Spain; and the greatest number of the towns of Turditania were still inhabited in Strabo's time by people of Phœnician origin.[2]   They communicated many of the arts of life to the natives, and among the rest the early use of letters; for the characters which the Iberians used in their writing before the time of the Romans[3] can scarcely have been any other than Phœnician.   The Phœnicians visited Spain at a very remote period; but they found it already peopled.   Who the aboriginal inhabitants were, and from whence they came, it is impossible to determine. The Greeks called them Iberians, and said that, although they were divided into many tribes, and spoke many various dialects, they yet all belonged to the same race.[4]   It cannot be doubted that their race and language still exist; that the Basques, who inhabit the Spanish provinces of Guipuscoa, Biscay, Alava, and Navarre, and who in France occupy the country between the Adour and the Bidassoa, are the genuine descendants of the ancient Iberians.   Their language bears marks of extreme antiquity; and its unlikeness to the other languages of Europe is very striking, even when compared with Welsh, or with Sclavonic.   The affinities of the Welsh numerals with those of the Teutonic languages, and the Greek and Latin, are obvious at

---

[1] Ezekiel, XXVII. 12.   [2] III. 2, Cas., p. 149.

[3] Strabo, III. 1, Cas., p. 139.

[4] Herodotus in Constantine Porphyrogenitus, De Administrando Imperio, 23.   Τὸ Ἰβηρικὸν γένος—διώρισται ὀνόμασιν ἓν γένος ἐὸν κατὰ φῦλα.

the first glance; and the same may be said of most
of the Sclavonic numerals : but the Basque are so
peculiar that it is difficult to identify any one
of them, except 'sei,' 'six,' with those of other
languages.[1]　　And an evidence of its great antiquity
seems furnished by the fact that the inflexions of
the nouns and verbs are manifestly so many distinct
words, inasmuch as they exist in a separate form as
such.　We suspect this reasonably of the terminations
of the nouns and verbs of Greek and Latin; but in the
Basque language it can be proved beyond question.[2]

We have seen that the Phœnicians were settled
amongst the Iberians in the south ; and Keltic tribes
were said to be mixed up with them in parts of the
north and centre, forming a people whom the Greeks
called Keltiberians.　　How far strangers of other

Various
traditions
of early
settle-
ments.

[1] I give the Welsh from Pughe's Welsh Grammar, Denbigh,
1832 ; the Sclavonic (Bohemian), from Dobrowsky, Lehrgebäude
der Böhmischen Sprache, Prag, 1819: the Basque from Larramendi,
Arte de la Lingua Bascongada, Salamanca, 1729.

Numerals from 1 to 10.

	WELSH.	SCLAVONIC.	BASQUE.
One	Un	Geden	Bat
Two	Dau	Dwa	Bi
Three	Tri	Tri	Hirú
Four	Pedwar	Etyn	Lau
Five	Pump	Pēt	Bost
Six	Chwech	Ssest	Sei
Seven	Saith	Sedm	Zazpi
Eight	Wyth	Osm	Zortzi
Nine	Naw	Dewēt	Bederatzi
Ten	Deg	Deset	Amár. *Author's Note.*

[2] See W. Humboldt's Dissertation on the Basque Language in
Adelung's Mithridates, vol. iv. pp. 314–332. [See also J. W. J.
Van Eys "Grammaire Comparée des Dialectes Basques" (Paris,
1879), "Outlines of Basque Grammar" (London, 1883), and Han-
nemann's "Prolegomena zur Baskischen Sprache" (Leipsic, 1884).]

races were to be found in Iberia it is difficult to decide. One or two Greek colonies from Massilia, such as Rhoda and Emporiæ, were undoubtedly planted on the shore of the Mediterranean, just within the limits of Iberia, immediately to the south of the Pyrenees.[1] These belong to the times of certain history; but stories are told of invasions of Spain, and of colonies founded on its territory, on which in their present form we can place no reliance. Carthaginian writers spoke of a great expedition of the Tyrian Hercules into Spain, at the head of an army of Medes, Persians, Armenians, and other nations of the east.[2] Megasthenes,[3] the Greek traveller and historian of India, said that Tearco, king of Æthiopia, and Nabuchodonosor, king of the Chaldæans, had both carried their arms as far as Spain. Amongst the innumerable countries which were made the scene of the adventures of the Greek chiefs on their return from Troy, after they had been scattered by the famous storm, the coasts of Iberia, and even its coasts upon the ocean, are not forgotten.[4] Other stories, as we have seen, claimed a Greek origin for Saguntum; while others, again, called it a Rutulian colony, from the Tyrrheno-Pelasgian city of Ardea.[5] The settlements of the Greek chiefs on their way home from Troy are mere romances, as

---

[1] Strabo, III. 4, Cas., pp. 159. 160. [2] Sallust, Jugurth. c. XVIII.

[3] Quoted by Strabo, XV. 1. § 6, Cas., p. 687, and by Josephus, Antiq. X. 11. § 1. and contr. Apion. I. 20. Strabo's character of Megasthenes is not favourable: διαφερόντως ἀπιστεῖν ἄξιον Δηϊμάχῳ τε καὶ Μεγασθένει. II. 1, Cas., p. 70.

[4] Strabo, III. 2, Cas., pp. 149,150.

[5] Livy, XXI. 7. See Niebuhr, vol. i., p. 43, note 127. I. 38 of Isler's German edition of 1873. Mommsen, I. 153.

unreal as the famous siege of Paris by the Saracens in the days of Charlemagne, or as the various adventures and settlements of Trojan exiles, which were invented in the middle ages. Whether any real events are disguised in the stories of the expeditions of Hercules, of Tearco, and of Nabuchodonosor, is a question more difficult to answer: for the early migrations from the east to the west are buried in impenetrable obscurity. But the Persians and Æthiopians may have made their way into Spain before historical memory, as the Vandals and Arabs invaded it in later times; the fact itself is not incredible, if it rested on any credible authority.

Not knowing, then, what strange nations may at one time or other have invaded or settled in Spain, we cannot judge how much the Iberian character and manners were affected by foreign influence. *State of agriculture in Spain.* Agriculture was practised from a period beyond memory; but the vine and olive, and perhaps the flax, were first introduced into the south of Spain by the Phœnicians, and only spread northwards gradually, the vine and fig advancing first, and the olive, as becomes its greater tenderness, following them more slowly and cautiously. Even in Strabo's time the vine had scarcely reached the northern coast of Spain; and the olive, when Polybius wrote, appears not to have been cultivated north of the Sierra Morena.[1] Butter supplied the place of oil to the inhabitants of the northern coast, and beer that of wine.[2]

In the character of the people some traits may be recognised, which even to this day mark the Spaniard. *Character of the Iberians.*

---

[1] III. 4, Cas., p. 164.
[2] Strabo, III. 3, Cas., p. 155. Polybius in Athenæus, I. 28.

The grave dress,[1] the temperance and sobriety, the unyielding spirit, the extreme indolence, the perseverance in guerilla warfare, and the remarkable absence of the highest military qualities, ascribed by the Greek and Roman writers to the ancient Iberians, are all more or less characteristic of the Spaniards of modern times. The courtesy and gallantry of the Spaniard to women has also come down to him from his Iberian ancestors: in the eyes of the Greeks it was an argument of an imperfect civilisation that among the Iberians the bridegroom gave, instead of receiving, a dowry; that daughters sometimes inherited to the exclusion of sons, and, thus becoming the heads of the family, gave portions to their brothers, that they might be provided with suitable wives.[2] In another point the great difference between the people of the south of Europe and those of the Teutonic stock, was remarked also in Iberia: the Iberians were ignorant, but not simple-hearted; on the contrary, they were cunning and mischievous, with habits of robbery almost indomitable, fond of brigandage, though incapable of the great combinations of war.[3] These, in some degree, are qualities common to almost all barbarians; but they offer a strong contrast to the character of the Germans, whose words spoke what was in their hearts, and of whose most powerful tribe it is recorded that their ascendency was maintained by no other arms than those of justice.[4]

Importance of Spain to the Carthaginians.

Spanish soldiers had for more than two centuries

[1] Strabo, III. 3, Cas., p. 155. μελανείμονες ἅπαντες.
[2] Strabo, III. 4, Cas., p. 165.   [3] Strabo, III. 3, Cas., p. 154.
[4] Tacitus, German. 22. 35.

formed one of the most efficient parts of the Carthaginian armies,[1] and on this account the Carthaginian
government set a high value on its dominion in
Spain. But this dominion furnished Carthage with
money, no less than with men. The Spanish mines
had been worked for some centuries, first by the Phœnicians of Asia, and latterly by their Carthaginian descendants, yet they still yielded abundantly. And some
of them have been worked for two thousand years
since the Carthaginians were driven out of the country,
and to this hour their treasures are unexhausted.[2]

These mines existed for the most part in the Spanish
mountains which divide the streams running to the mines.
Guadiana from those which feed the Guadalquiver.[3]
This is the chain so well known by the name of the
Sierra Morena: but the several arms which it pushes
out towards the sea eastward and southward, were
also rich in precious metals; and some mines were
worked in the valley of the Guadalquiver itself, as
low down as Seville. The streams, moreover, which
flowed from these mountains, brought down gold
mingled with their sand and gravel;[4] and this was
probably collected long before the working of the
regular mines began. But in the time of the second
Punic war the mines were worked actively; and, a
hundred years earlier, the cinnabar, or sulphuret of
quicksilver, of the famous mines of Almaden, was
well known in the markets of Greece.[5] The Carthaginians honoured as a hero or demi-god the man
who first discovered the most productive silver mines;

[1] Herodotus, VII. 165.   [2] Strabo, III. 2, Cas., 146–148. See Note P.
[3] Strabo, III. 2, Cas., p. 142.   [4] Strabo, III. 2, Cas., p. 146.
[5] Strabo, III. 2, Cas,, p. 147.

and one of these was in the immediate neighbourhood of New Carthage itself.[1] Others were nearer the Guadalquiver, at Castulo and Ilipa ; or on the feeders of the Guadiana, as at Sisapo,[2] the ancient name of the place near to which the great quicksilver mines were worked, now known as the mines of Almaden. One large and most productive silver mine, yielding 300 pounds daily, is said to have been opened by Hannibal himself,[3] who, while he was in Spain, had married the daughter of one of the chiefs of Castulo,[4] and perhaps had acquired some possessions through her in the mining district, as Thucydides had through his wife in Thrace.

Scipio's first measures in Spain.

The immense resources which the Carthaginians derived from their Spanish dominion seemed now more than ever secured to them by the destruction of the Roman army under the two Scipios, and the consequent retreat of the Romans behind the Iberus. But the divisions between their generals, and the arrogance with which their officers now treated the Spaniards, as if it was no longer worth while to conciliate them, had made a fatal opening, exposing their power to the most deadly blow which it had yet sustained. Scipio, with intuitive sagacity, observed this opening, and with decision no less admirable struck his blow to the heart of his enemy. He formed his plans at Tarraco during the winter, as soon as the season allowed his fleet to co-operate with him, he put it and his army in motion ; and while the three Carthaginian generals were in places

---

[1] Polybius, X. 10, § 11.   Strabo, III. 2, Cas., p. 148.
[2] Polybius, X. 38, § 7.   Strabo, III. 2, Cas., p. 142.
[3] Pliny, XXXIII. 6 (31).   [4] Livy, XXIV. 41.

equally remote from one another, and from the point A.U.C. 545.
threatened by the enemy, Scipio crossed the Iberus, and A.C. 209.
led his land and sea forces to besiege New Carthage.[1]

His early and most intimate friend, C. Lælius, He marches
commanded the fleet; the proprætor, M. Silanus, against
was left behind the Iberus with 3000 foot and 500 New Car-
horse, to protect the country of the allies of Rome, thage.
while Scipio himself led 25,000 foot and 2500
horse on his expedition.   Polybius declares that the
march from the Iberus to New Carthage was performed in seven days; but as, according to his own
reckoning, the distance was not less than 325
Roman miles, the accuracy of one or both of his
statements may well be questioned.[2]   Three degrees
of latitude divide Carthagena from the Ebro; and
the ordinary windings and difficulties of a road in
such a distance must make it all but an impossibility
that an army with its baggage should have marched
over it in a single week.   However the march was
undoubtedly rapid, and the Roman army established
itself under the walls of New Carthage, while all
succour was far distant, and when the actual garrison of a place so important did not exceed 1000
men.   To the protection of a force so small was
committed the capital of the Carthaginian dominion
in Spain, the base of their military operations, their
point of communication with Africa, their treasures
and magazines, and the hostages taken from the different Spanish tribes to secure their doubted fidelity.[3]

The present town of Carthagena stands at the Position of
head of its famous harbour, built partly on some New Carthage.

---

[1] Polybius, X. 6–9. Livy, XXVI. 42.
[2] Polybius, X. 9. 7 ; III. 39. 5.   [3] Polybius, X. 8.

 hills of tolerable height, and partly on the low ground beneath them, with a large extent of marshy ground behind it, which is flooded after rains, and its inner port surrounded by the buildings of the arsenal, running deeply into the land on its western side.   But in the times of the second Punic war the marshy ground behind was all a lagoon, and its waters communicated artificially with those of the port of the arsenal; so that the town was on a peninsula, and was joined to the mainland only by a narrow isthmus, which had itself been cut through in one place to allow the lagoon water to find an outlet.[1]   Scipio then encamped at the head of this isthmus, and having fortified himself on the rear, with the lagoon covering his flank, he left his front open that nothing might obstruct the free advance of his soldiers to storm the city.[2]

Scipio attacks it,   Accordingly, without delay, he was preparing to lead on his men to the assault when he was himself assailed by Mago, who with his scanty garrison made a desperate sally along the isthmus against the Roman camp.   After an obstinate struggle the besieged were beaten back into the town with loss, and the Romans, following them, fixed their ladders to the walls and began to mount.   But the height of the walls was so great that the long ladders necessary to reach their summit broke in some instances under the weight of the soldiers who crowded on them; and the enemy made their defence so good that towards afternoon Scipio found it expedient to recall his men from the assault.[3]

---

[1] Polybius, X. 10.   Livy, XXVI. 42.   See Note Q.
[2] Polybius, X. 11.   [3] Polybius, X. 12, 13.   Livy, XXVI. 45.

He had told his men before the assault began that
the god Neptune had appeared to him in his sleep,
and had promised to give him aid in the hour of
need, so manifest, that all the army should acknowledge his interposition.[1]   For the lagoon, it seems,
was so shallow that even the slight fall of the tide
in the Mediterranean was sufficient to leave much
of it uncovered, as is the case at this day in parts
of the harbour of Venice.   This would take place in
the afternoon, and Scipio ordered 500 men to be
ready with ladders to march across the lagoon as
soon as the ebb began.   Then he renewed his assault
by the isthmus, and whilst this in itself discouraged
the enemy, who had hoped that their work for the
day was over, and whilst the soldiers again swarmed
up the ladders, and the missiles of the besieged were
beginning to fail, the 500 men who were in readiness boldly rushed across the lagoon, and, having
guides to show them the hardest parts of it, reached
the foot of the walls in safety, applied the ladders
where there were no defenders, and mounted without
opposition.[2]

No sooner had they won the walls than they
hastened to the main gate of the city, towards the
isthmus, and when they had burst it open their
comrades from without rushed in like a torrent.   At
the same moment the scaling parties on each side of
the main gate overbore the defenders, and were now
overflowing the ramparts.   Mago reached the citadel
in safety, but Scipio in person pushed thither with
1000 picked men, and the governor, seeing the

A.U.C. 545.
A.C. 209.
and carries
the walls.

The town is
taken and
plundered.

---

[1] Polybius, X. 11.   Livy, XXVI. 45.
[2] Polybius, X. 14.   Livy, XXVI. 46.

city lost, surrendered.   The other heights in the town were stormed with little difficulty, and the soldiers, according to the Roman practice, commenced a deliberate massacre of every living creature they could find, whether man or beast, till, after the citadel had surrendered, a signal from their general called them off from slaughter, and turned them loose upon the houses of the town to plunder.   Yet it marks the Roman discipline that even before night fell order was restored.   Some of the soldiers marched back to the camp, from whence the light troops were summoned to occupy one of the principal heights of the town; Scipio himself, with 1000 men, occupied the citadel, and the tribunes got the soldiers out of the houses, and made them bring all their plunder into one heap in the market-place, and pass the night there quietly, waiting for the regular division of the spoil, which was to take place on the following morning.[1]

Scipio's conduct to the prisoners.   When the morning came, whilst the usual distribution of the money arising from the sale of the plunder was made by the tribunes, Scipio proceeded to inspect his prisoners.   All were brought before him together, to the number of nearly 10,000.   He first caused them to be divided into three classes. One consisted of all the citizens of New Carthage, with their wives and families; all these Scipio set at liberty, and dismissed them to their homes unhurt. The second class contained the workmen of handicraft trades, who were either slaves, or, if free, only sojourners in the city, enjoying no political rights. These men were told that they were now the slaves

[1] Polybius, X. 15.   Livy, XXVI. 46.

of the Roman people, but that, if they worked well and zealously in their several callings, they should have their liberty at the end of the war.   Meantime they were all to enter their names with the quæstor, and a Roman citizen was set over every thirty of them as an overseer.   These workmen were in all about 2000.   The third class contained all the rest of the prisoners, domestic slaves, seamen, fishermen, and the mixed populace of the city; and from these Scipio picked out the most able-bodied, and employed them in manning his fleet, for he found eighteen ships of the enemy at New Carthage, and these he was enabled to add to his own naval force immediately, by putting some of his own seamen into them, and filling up their places with some of the captives, taking care, however, that the number of these should never exceed a third of the whole crew.   The seamen thus employed were promised their liberty at the end of the war, like the workmen, if they did their duty faithfully.[1]

The Carthaginian prisoners and the Spanish hostages were still to be attended to.   The former were committed to the care of Lælius, to be taken forthwith to Rome; and there were amongst them fifteen members of the great or ordinary council of Carthage, and two members of the council of elders. The Spanish hostages were more than 300, and amongst them were many young boys.   To show kindness to these was an obvious policy; accordingly Scipio made presents to them all, and desired them to write home to their friends, and assure them that they were well and honourably treated, and that

A.U.C.545.
A.C. 209.

His kind treatment of the Spanish hostages.

[1] Polybius, X. 16, 17. Livy, XXVI. 47.

they would all be sent back safely to their several countries, if their countrymen were willing to embrace the Roman alliance. Particular attention was shown to the wife of a Spanish chief of high rank, who had been recently seized as a hostage by Hasdrubal, son of Gisco, because her husband had refused to comply with his demands for money. Her treatment had been rude and insolent, if not worse ; but Scipio assured her that he would take as delicate care of her and of the other Spanish women as he would of his own sisters or daughters. This honourable bearing of the young conqueror, for Scipio was not more than twenty-seven years of age, produced a deep impression all over Spain.[1]

Magazines taken in the city.

After this important conquest Scipio remained for a time at New Carthage, and busied himself in exercising his soldiers and seamen, and in setting his workmen to labour in manufacturing arms.[2] He had taken a considerable artillery in the place, a large sum of money, abundant magazines of corn, and about sixty-three merchant ships in the harbour with their cargoes ; so that, according to Livy, the least valuable part of the conquest of New Carthage was New Carthage itself.[3]

Lælius carries the news of this conquest to Rome.

Lælius with his prisoners arrived at Rome after a voyage of thirty-four days, and brought the welcome news of this great restoration of the Roman affairs in Spain.[4] Amidst the confusions of the chronology of the Spanish war it is not easy to ascertain the exact time at which Lælius reached Rome. But it is probable that he arrived there early in the year

---

[1] Polybius, IX. 11, X. 18, 35. Livy, XXVI. 47. 49.   [2] Polybius, X. 20.
[3] XXVI. 47.   Polybius, X. 19.   [4] Livy, XXVII. 7.

545, perhaps at that critical moment when the dis- A.U.C. 545.
A.C. 209.
obedience of the twelve colonies excited such great
alarm, and when the destruction of the army of
Cn. Fulvius at Herdonea was still fresh in men's
memories. Scipio's victory was therefore doubly
welcome, and his requests for supplies were favour-
ably listened to ; for his army, although victorious,
was still in want of many things, the old soldiers
especially, who had been ill-clothed and worse paid
during several years. Accordingly we find that a
sum of fourteen hundred pounds' weight of gold was
brought out from the treasure reserved for the most
extraordinary occasions, and expended in purchasing
clothing for the army in Spain.[1]

Scipio himself returned from New Carthage to The rest of
Tarraco, taking his Spanish hostages with him.[2]   It the year
was early in the season ; but we hear of no other passes in inaction.
military action during the remainder of the year.
This on Scipio's part is easily intelligible : his army
was too weak to hold the field against the combined
forces of the enemy ; and it was his object to
strengthen himself by alliances with the natives,
and to draw them off from the service of Carthage,
if he could not induce them to enter that of Rome.
He had struck one great blow with vigour, surprising
the enemy by his rapidity : but what had been won
by vigour might be lost by rashness ; and, after so
great an action as the conquest of New Carthage, he
could well afford to lie quiet for the rest of the year,
waiting for his supplies of clothing from Rome, and
strengthening his interest amongst the chiefs of
Spain. The inactivity of the Carthaginian generals

[1] Livy, XXVII. 10.   [2] Livy, XXVII. 17. Polybius, X. 34.

A.U.C. 545.
A.C. 209.

would be more surprising, if we did not make allowance for the paralysing effect of their mutual jealousies.   No efficient co-operation could be contrived between them; and Hasdrubal, Hannibal's brother, was too weak to act alone, and, disgusted with the conduct of his colleagues, was probably anxious to husband his own army carefully, looking forward now more than ever to the execution of his long-projected march upon Italy.   Thus there was a pause from all active operations in Spain for several months; whilst in Italy Fabius had recovered Tarentum, and he and Fulvius were on the point of being succeeded in the consulship by Marcellus and Crispinus.

Decline of the Carthaginian influence in Spain.

The loss of Tarentum made it more important than ever that Hasdrubal should join his brother in Italy ; while the growing disposition of the Spaniards to revolt to Rome rendered the prospect of success in Spain less encouraging.   But with no Carthaginian accounts remaining, and amidst the confusions, omissions, and contradictions, of the Roman historians, it is almost impossible to give a satisfactory explanation of the events of the ensuing year, 546, in Spain. Masinissa, then a very young man, the son of a Numidian king, named Gala,[1] was sent over from Africa with a large body of Numidian cavalry to reinforce Hasdrubal, the son of Hamilcar, principally, it is said, in order to his march into Italy.[2]   Still Hasdrubal made no forward movement, but remained in a very strong position near a place called variously Bæcula or Bebula, situated in the upper valley of the Guadalquiver, near the mining district ; and

<hr>

[1] Livy, XXIV. 49. XXV. 34. See Macaulay's note to Livy, XXIV. 49.
[2] Appian, Hispan. 25. Livy, XXVII. 5, § 11.

there he seemed rather disposed to await Scipio's A.U.C. 546. attack than to assume the offensive.[1] He saw that A.C. 208. the fidelity of the Spaniards to Carthage was deeply shaken, not only by the loss of their hostages, but by the encouraging treatment which the hostages themselves had received from the Romans. This feeling had been working ever since the fall of New Carthage, and now its fruits were daily becoming more manifest; insomuch that, when the time at which Scipio was expected to take the field drew near, Mandonius and Indibilis, two of the most influential of the Spanish chiefs, retired with all their followers from Hasdrubal's camp, and established themselves in a strong position, from which they might join the Romans, as soon as their army should appear in the south.[2] On the other hand, Scipio's Roman force was strengthened by his having laid up his fleet and draughted the best of his seamen into the legions, to increase the number of his soldiers. And although a combined effort of the three Carthaginian generals might yet have recovered New Carthage, or at any rate kept Scipio behind the Iberus, nothing of this sort was attempted; and Hasdrubal Gisco, jealous, it seems, both personally and politically of Hannibal's brother, left him unaided to sustain the first assault of the enemy.

Hasdrubal, the son of Hamilcar, therefore, under these circumstances, was doubtless anxious to carry into effect his expedition into Italy. Yet, not wishing it to be said that he had abandoned his colleagues, he resolved first to try his strength with

Hasdrubal leaves Spain.

---

[1] Polybius, X. 38. Livy, XXVII. 18. Appian, Hispan. 24.
[2] Polybius, X. 35. Livy, XXVII. 17.

A.U.C. 546.
A.C. 208.

Scipio to see what Spanish tribes would actually join him, and whether by offering battle in a favourable position he could repulse the enemy, and thus break that spell of Scipio's fortune which was working so powerfully. But in this hope he was disappointed. Scipio advanced from the Iberus to the valley of the Bætis, or Guadalquiver, before Hasdrubal saw anything of the armies of his colleagues hastening to his aid ; many Spanish tribes joined the Roman army at the Iberus, Mandonius and Indibilis hastened to it as soon as it approached the place where they were posted, and Hasdrubal, unable to maintain his strong position, and, if we believe Scipio's statement, seeing it in the act of being carried by the enemy at the close of a successful assault, retreated accordingly, not towards the southern sea, nor towards the western ocean, but northwards towards the Tagus,[1] and from thence, as we have seen, towards the western Pyrenees, there recruiting his army from those tribes which had not yet come under the influence of Rome, and preparing for that great expedition to Italy of which we have already related the progress and the event.

Increase of
Scipio's in-
fluence.

Before Hasdrubal finally retreated he had lost many prisoners. All those who were Spaniards were sent home free without ransom by the politic conqueror, and he liberally rewarded those Spanish chiefs who had already come over to his side. They on their part saluted him with the title of king. The first Hasdrubal, the founder of New Carthage, had lived in kingly state amongst the Spaniards, and they probably thought that Scipio meant to do

---

[1] Polybius, X. 38, 39. Livy, XXVII. 17, 18. Appian, Hispan. 25–28.

the same, and would pass the rest of his life in their A.U.C. 546.
country. But the name of king, although perhaps A.C. 208.
not ungrateful to Scipio's ears, was intolerable to
those of his countrymen, nor would he have been
contented to reign in Spain over barbarians; his
mind was already turned towards Africa, and anticipated the glory of conquering Carthage. So he
repressed the homage of the Spanish chiefs, and
desired them to call him, not king, but general. He
then took possession of the strong position which
Hasdrubal had evacuated, and there he remained
during the rest of the season, watching, so it is said,
the movements of Hasdrubal Gisco and Mago, who
were now come upon the scene of action. On the
approach of winter he again returned to Tarraco.[1]

Such is the account given by Polybius of the Difficulties
events of the war in Spain during the summer of in the account of the
the year 546 ; and such, no doubt, was the state- campaign.
ment given by Scipio himself, and obtained by
Polybius from Scipio's old friend and companion, C.
Lælius. What Silenus said of these same events
we know not; and it is possible that Hasdrubal's
account of them was never known, owing to his
subsequent fate, so that Silenus may have had no
peculiar information about them, and may have
passed them over slightly. It is evident that
Scipio's pretended victory at Bæcula was of little
importance. Hasdrubal carried off all his elephants,
all his treasure, and a large proportion of his infantry :
he was not pursued; he retreated in the direction
which best suited his future movements; and these
movements he effected without the slightest inter-

[1] Polybius, X, 38, 40. Livy, XXVII. 19.

A.U.C. 546.
A.C. 208.

ruption from the enemy. Scipio did not follow him, says Polybius,[1] because he dreaded the arrival of the other Hasdrubal and Mago; he remained in the south, therefore, to keep them in check, and to prevent them from attacking New Carthage; and not doubting that Hasdrubal would follow his brother's route, and attempt to enter Gaul by the eastern Pyrenees, he detached some troops from his army to secure the passes of the mountains, and other defensible positions between the Iberus and the frontiers of Gaul.[2] It is probable that his notions of the geography of the western parts of Spain and Gaul were so vague that he had no conception of the possibility of Hasdrubal's marching towards the Alps, without coming near the Mediterranean. The line which he actually took from the western Pyrenees, to the upper part of the course of the Rhone, through the interior of Gaul, was one of which Scipio in all probability did not even suspect the existence.

Reasons for Hasdrubal's delay.

It may be asked why Hasdrubal, whose great object was to reach Italy, did not commence his march at the beginning of the year without waiting so long at Bæcula, especially after the desertion of Mandonius and Indibilis had taught him that the Spaniards were no longer to be relied on. But he had himself on a former occasion won over the Celtiberians from the army of Scipio's father, and any reverse sustained by the Romans might tempt the Spanish chiefs to return to their old alliance. It is possible also that he waited so long at Bæcula for another reason, because he wished to carry with him as large a sum of money as possible; and he was

---

[1] X. 39.   [2] Polybius, X. 40.

daily drawing a supply from the abundant silver A.U.C. 546.
mines in the neighbourhood. The success of his A.C. 208.
expedition depended on his being able to raise
soldiers amongst the Cisalpine Gauls, as well as
amongst the tribes of north-western Spain; and for
both these purposes ready money was most desirable.

A more inexplicable point in the story of these Jealousies of the Car-
transactions is the alleged discord between Hasdrubal thaginian
and the other Carthaginian generals, when one of generals.
them, Mago, was his own brother, and was not only
a soldier of tried ability, but is expressly said to
have conducted the war in Spain in accordance with
Hannibal's directions, after Hasdrubal had marched
into Italy.[1] Whether Mago was placed under
Hasdrubal Gisco's orders, and could not act inde-
pendently, or whether jealousy, or any other cause,
really made him careless of his brother's success and
safety, we cannot pretend to determine: the interior
of a Carthaginian camp, and still more the real
characters and feelings of the Carthaginian generals,
are entirely unknown to us.

The one great advantage possessed by Scipio, far Ascend-
more important than his pretended victory at Bæcula, ency of
was the remarkable ascendency which he had ob- Scipio over the minds
tained over the minds of the Spaniards. Every- of the
thing in him was at once attractive and imposing; Spaniards.
his youth, and the mingled beauty and majesty of
his aspect; his humanity and courtesy to the Spanish
hostages and to their friends; his energy and ability
at the head of his army. Above all, there was
manifest in him that consciousness of greatness, and
that spirit, at once ardent, lofty, and profound, which

[1] Polybius, IX. 22.

naturally bows the hearts and minds of ordinary men, not to obedience only and respect, but to admiration, and almost to worship. The Carthaginian generals felt, it is said, that no Spanish troops could be trusted, if brought within the sphere of his influence; Mago must go over to the Balearian islands and raise soldiers there, who might be strangers to the name of Scipio, while Masinissa should follow the course pursued by Mutines in Sicily, and scour the whole country with his Numidian cavalry, relieving the allies of Carthage, and harassing the states which had revolted.[1] But Masinissa himself was not secure from Scipio's ascendency; his nephew had been made prisoner at Bæcula, and had been sent back to him without ransom;[2] some conciliatory messages were probably addressed to him at the same time, and Scipio never lost sight of him, till two years afterwards he gratified the Numidian's earnest wish for a personal interview, and then attached him for ever to the interests of Rome.[3]

Hasdrubal evades Scipio, and marches into Italy.

Meanwhile that memorable year was come, when the fortune of Rome was exposed to its severest trial, and rose in the issue signally triumphant. Vainly did Scipio's guards keep vigilant watch in the passes of the eastern Pyrenees, looking out for the first signs of Hasdrubal's approach, and hoping to win the glory of driving him back defeated, and of marring his long-planned expedition to Italy. They sat on their mountain posts, looking earnestly southwards, while he for whom they waited was passing far on their rear northwards, winning his way

---

[1] Livy, XXVII. 20.   [2] Livy, XXVII. 19.
[3] Livy, XXVIII. 35.

through the deep valleys of the chain of Cebenna, A.U.C. 547. or the high and bleak plains of the Arverni, till he A.C. 207. should descend upon the Rhone, where it was as yet unknown to the Massaliot traders, flowing far inland in the heart of Gaul. Hasdrubal had accomplished his purpose ; his Spanish soldiers were removed out of the reach of Scipio's ascendency ; the accumulated treasures of his Spanish mines had purchased the aid of a numerous band of Gauls ; and the Alps had seemed to smooth their rugged fastnesses to give him an easy passage. All the strength which Rome could gather was needed for the coming struggle ; and Scipio, as we have seen, sent a large detachment from his own army, both of Roman soldiers and of Spaniards, to be conveyed by sea from Tarraco to Etruria, and to assist in conquering the enemy in Italy, whose march he had been unable to stop in Spain.

Thus, with Hasdrubal's army taken away from the Carthaginian force in Spain, and with the Roman army weakened by its contributions to the defence of Italy, the Spanish war was carried on but feebly during the summer of the year 547. A new general of the name of Hanno had been sent over to take Hasdrubal's place, and he and Mago proceeded to raise soldiers amongst the Celtiberians in the interior,[1] while Hasdrubal Gisco was holding Bætica, and while Scipio was still in his winter quarters at Tarraco. But some Celtiberian deserters informed Scipio of the danger, and he sent M. Silanus with a division of his army to put it down. A march of extreme rapidity enabled him to surprise the enemy;

The campaign of 547 not marked by any decisive events.

<hr>

[1] Livy, XXVIII. 1.

 the best of Hanno's new levies were cut to pieces, the rest dispersed. Hanno himself was made prisoner, but Mago carried off his cavalry and his old infantry without loss, and joined Hasdrubal Gisco safely in Bætica.[1] The formation of a Carthaginian army in the centre of Spain was thus effectually prevented, and Scipio, encouraged by this success, ventured to resume the offensive, and to advance in pursuit of Hasdrubal Gisco into the south. Hasdrubal, instead of risking a general action, broke up his army into small detachments, with which he garrisoned the more important towns. Scipio shrank from the tedious and difficult service of a series of sieges in a country at a distance from his resources, and where Mago and Masinissa with their cavalry would be sure to obstruct, if not destroy, all his communications. But to avoid the discredit of retreating without having done anything, he singled out one of the wealthiest and strongest of the towns thus garrisoned against him, by name Oringis, and sent his brother, L. Scipio, with a large division of his army to attack it. It was stormed after an obstinate resistance, and the conqueror, true to his brother's policy, after carrying off his Carthaginian prisoners in the garrison, restored the town unplundered to its Spanish inhabitants.[2] Thus much having been achieved for the honour of the Roman arms, Scipio carried back his whole army behind the Iberus, sent off L. Scipio to Rome with Hanno and his other prisoners of distinction, and himself went into winter quarters as usual at Tarraco.[3]

[1] Livy, XXVIII, 1. Appian, Hispan. 31.
[2] Livy, XXVIII. 3.   [3] Livy, XXVIII. 4.

But before the end of the season he must have received intelligence of the battle of the Metaurus. The troops which he had sent to Italy were probably, in part at least, sent back to him, and every motive combined to make him desirous of marking the next campaign by some decisive action.   Nero, whom he had succeeded in Spain, had won the greatest glory by his victory over Hasdrubal; it became Scipio to show that he too could serve his country no less effectively.

The Carthaginian general, whether he had been reinforced from Africa, or whether he had used extraordinary vigour in his levies of soldiers in western Spain, took the field early in the spring of the year 548, with an army greatly superior to that of his enemy.   If Polybius, or rather Scipio, may be trusted, he had 70,000 foot, 4000 horse, and thirty-two elephants; while the Roman army, with all the aids which Scipio could gather from the Spanish chiefs in the Roman alliance, did not exceed 45,000 foot, and 3000 horse.[1]   Hasdrubal took up a position in the midst of the mining district, near a town, which is variously called Elinga and Silpia,[2] but neither its real name nor its exact situation can be determined.   His camp lay on the last hills of the mountain country, with a wide extent of open plain in front of it.   He wished to fight, and if possible on this ground, favourable at once to his superior numbers and to his elephants.

---

[1] Polybius, XI. 20.   Livy, XXVIII. 12.

[2] Elinga in the MSS. and old text of Polybius has been altered into Ilipa, on the authority of Strabo; in the text of Livy the name stands Silpia.

Scipio, no less anxious to bring on a general battle, marched straight towards the enemy. But when he saw their numbers, he was uneasy lest the faith of his Spanish allies should fail, as it had towards his father: he dared not lay much stress on them; yet without them his numbers were too weak for him to risk a battle. His object therefore was to use his Spaniards for show, to impose upon the enemy, while he won the battle with his Romans. And thus, when the day came, on which he proposed to fight, he suddenly changed his dispositions. For some days previously, both armies had been drawn up in order of battle before their camps; and their cavalry and light troops had skirmished in the interval between. All this time the Roman troops had formed the centre of Scipio's line, opposite to Hasdrubal's Africans, while the Spanish auxiliaries in both armies were on the wings. But on the day of the decisive battle, the Spaniards formed the centre of Scipio's army, while his Roman and Italian soldiers were on the right and left. The men had eaten their breakfast before day; and the cavalry and light troops pushed forward close under the camp of the enemy, as if challenging him to come out and meet them. Behind this cloud of skirmishers the infantry were fast forming, and advancing to the middle of the plain; and when the sun rose, it shone upon the Roman line with its order completed; the Spaniards in the centre, the Romans and Italians on the right and left; the left commanded by M. Silanus and L. Marcius, Scipio in person leading his right.[1]

The assault of the Roman cavalry and light troops

----

[1] Polybius, XI. 22. Livy, XXVIII. 14.

called out Hasdrubal's army; the Carthaginians poured forth from their camp without waiting to eat, just as the Romans had done at the Trebia; their cavalry and light troops engaged the enemy; while their infantry formed in its usual order, with the Spanish auxiliaries on the wings, and the Africans in the centre. In this state the infantry on both sides remained for a time motionless; but when the day was advanced, Scipio called off his skirmishers, sent them to the rear, through the intervals of his maniples, and formed them behind his infantry on both wings; the light infantry immediately behind the regular infantry, and the cavalry covering all.

For a few moments the Roman line seemed advancing evenly to meet the line of the enemy. But suddenly the troops on the right wing began to wheel round to the left, and those on the left wing wheeled to the right, changing their lines into columns; while the cavalry moved round from the rear, and took up its position on the outside of the columns; and both infantry and cavalry now advanced with the utmost fury against the enemy. Thus the centre of the Roman army was held back by the rapid advance of its wings; and the Africans in Hasdrubal's centre were standing idle, doing nothing, whilst the battle was raging on their right and left, and yet not venturing to move from their position to support their wings, because of the enemy in their front, who threatened every moment to attack, yet still advanced as slowly as possible, to give time for the attacks on the two wings to complete their work. And this work was not long:

Roman and Italians veterans were opposed to newly-raised Spaniards; men well fed to men exhausted by their long fast; men perfect in all their movements, and handled by their general with masterly skill, to barbarians confused by evolutions which neither they nor their officers could deal with. As usual, the elephants did as much mischief to friends as to foes; and the Carthaginian wings, broken and slaughtered, began to fly. Then the Africans in the centre commenced their retreat also; slowly at first, as men who had not themselves been beaten; but the flight of their allies infected them; and the Romans pressed them so hardly, that they too rushed towards their camp with more haste than order.[1] The battle was won; and Scipio said that the camp would have been won also, had not a violent storm suddenly burst on the field of battle, and the rain fallen in such a deluge that the Romans could not stand against it, but were obliged to seek the shelter of their own camp. Their work, however, was done; not least probably by the effect which the battle would have on the minds of the Spaniards. In the Carthaginian army their countrymen had been exposed to defeat and slaughter, while the Africans had looked on tamely, and moved neither hand nor foot to aid them; on the other hand, the Spaniards in Scipio's army had obtained a victory, with no loss to themselves: it had been purchased altogether by the blood of the Romans.

Destruction of the Carthaginian dominion in Spain.

Accordingly the Carthaginian generals found that the contest in Spain was virtually ended. The Spanish soldiers in their army went over in large

[1] Polybius, XI. 23, 24. Livy, XXVIII. 15, 16. See Note R.

bodies to the enemy; the Spanish towns opened their gates to the Romans, and put the Carthaginian garrisons into their hands. Hasdrubal and Mago, closely followed by the enemy, retreated by the right bank of the Bætis to the shores of the ocean, and effected their escape by sea to Gades. Masinissa left them, and went home to Africa, not, it is said, without having a secret interview with M. Silanus, and settling the conditions and manner of his defection. Scipio himself returned by slow marches to Tarraco, inquiring by the way into the merits or demerits of the various native chiefs, who came crowding round him to plead their services, and to propitiate the favour of the new conqueror of Spain. Silanus, whom he had left behind in the south to witness the final dispersion of the army of Hasdrubal, soon after rejoined him at Tarraco, and reported to him that the war was over, that no enemy was to be found in the field, from the Pyrenees to the Pillars of Hercules.[1] Scipio therefore sent off his brother to Rome, to announce the completion of his work.

His own mind was already turned to another field of action: the expulsion of the Carthaginians from Spain seemed to him only to be valued as it might enable him the easier to carry the war into Africa. He had already won the support of Masinissa: but he desired to secure a more powerful ally; and accordingly he sent Lælius over to Africa, to sound the dispositions of the Masæsylian king, Syphax, the most powerful of all the African princes, and who, although at present in alliance with the Carthaginians, had been, not many years since, their enemy.

A.U.C. 548.
A.C. 206.

Scipio crosses to Africa, and negotiates with Syphax.

---

[1] Livy, XXVIII. 16.

Syphax told Lælius that he would negotiate only with the Roman general in person; and Scipio, relying on his own personal ascendency, and affecting in all things what was extraordinary, did not hesitate to leave his province, and to cross over from New Carthage to Africa, with only two quinqueremes, in order to visit the Masæsylian king. No less fortunate than Napoleon, when returning from Egypt to France in his solitary frigate, Scipio crossed the sea without accident, and entered the king's port in safety, with the wind so brisk and fair as to carry him into the harbour in a straight course, in a very short time after his ships had first been seen from the shore.[1] In the harbour, by the strangest of chances, were seven ships of the Carthaginians, which had just brought Hasdrubal from Spain with the very same object as Scipio, to secure the alliance of King Syphax; it having been known, probably, that a Roman officer had lately visited his court, with purposes which could not be doubtful. Hasdrubal and Scipio met under the roof of Syphax; and by his special request, they were present at the same entertainment.[2] Lælius, who had accompanied his friend to Africa, magnified the charms of his address and conversation, according to his usual practice, and told Polybius many years afterwards, that Hasdrubal had expressed to Syphax his great admiration of Scipio's genius, which, he said, appeared to him more dangerous in peace than in war.[3] Lælius further declared that Syphax was so overcome by Scipio's influence as to conclude a

<hr>

[1] Livy, XXVIII. 17.   [2] Livy, XXVIII. 18.
[3] Polybius, XI. 24A, § 4.   Livy, XXVIII. 18.

treaty of alliance with him,[1] which treaty, however, A.U.C. 548.
A.C. 206.
we may be very sure, was not one of those which
Polybius found preserved in the Capitol.   It is
very possible that Syphax amused Scipio with fair
promises; but in reality Hasdrubal negotiated more
successfully than his Roman rival; and the beauty
of his daughter, Sophonisba, was more powerful over
the mind of Syphax than all the fascinations of
Scipio's eloquence and manners.[2]   Scipio, however,
was satisfied with the success of his mission, and
returned again to New Carthage.

It is manifest that, when Scipio and Silanus re- Insurrec-
tion of the
Spaniards.
turned from the south of Spain to Tarraco, after the
dispersion of the Carthaginian army, they imagined
that their work was done; and they cannot have
expected to be called out again to active operations
in the same year.   But, after Scipio's return from
his voyage to Africa, we find him again taking the
field in the south; we find a general revolt of the
Spanish chiefs, who had so lately joined him, and,
what is most startling, we find his own Roman
army breaking out into an alarming mutiny.   Livy's
explanation is simply that the present appeared
a favourable opportunity to punish those Spanish
towns which had made themselves most obnoxious
to Rome in the course of the war, and on which it
would not have been expedient to take vengeance
earlier.[3]   But surely, if any such intention had been
entertained a few weeks sooner, the Roman army
would never have been marched back behind the
Iberus, but would have proceeded at once to attack

---

[1] Livy, XXVIII. 18.   [2] Livy, XXIX. 23.
[3] Livy, XXVIII. 19.

 the obnoxious towns, as soon as Hasdrubal and Mago had retired to Gades, and the Carthaginian army was broken up. Either the Spaniards must have given some new provocation, which called Scipio again into the field, or some new motive must have influenced him, which hitherto he had not felt, and, outweighing all other considerations, forced him to retrace his steps to the south.

Probable
causes of it. Either of these causes is sufficiently probable. Mago had by this time received instructions from Hannibal, and acting under such direction, he was not likely to abandon Spain to the Romans without another struggle. We read of a Carthaginian garrison in Castulo, which is said to have fled thither after the dispersion of Hasdrubal's army,[1] but it may also have been sent thither by Mago from Gades, to assist in organising a new rising against the Romans. The mines were still in his hands, and he probably employed their treasures liberally. Nor were causes wanting to rouse the Spaniards, without any foreign instigation. If they had admired Scipio, they had since found that his virtues did not restrain the license of his army: the Roman soldiers had fleshed themselves with the plunder of Spain, and were likely to return after a moment's respite and fall again upon their prey. On the other hand, the Roman army, like the Spaniards afterwards in America, may have been so eager to prosecute their conquest, and to win more of the wealth of Spain, that their general found it impossible not to gratify them, or they may have shown symptoms of license and turbulence which made it desirable to keep them

----

[1] Livy, XXVIII. 20.

actively employed, that they might not have leisure to contrive mischief; whatever was the cause, the Roman army again marched into the south of Spain. L. Marcius was ordered to attack Castulo, Scipio himself laid siege to Illiturgi.

Illiturgi stood on the north or right bank of the Bætis, near to the site of the present town of Andujar, and not far therefore from Baylen, and from the scene of the almost solitary triumph of the Spanish arms in the war with Napoleon. Its people had been allies of the Carthaginians, and had revolted to Rome, when the two Scipios first advanced into the south of Spain;[1] but after their defeat and death Illiturgi had gone back to the alliance of Carthage, and the Roman fugitives from the rout of the two Scipios, who escaped to Illiturgi, were either cut off by the inhabitants or given up by them to the Carthaginians. Such was the Roman account of the matter, and Castulo was charged with a similar defection after the defeat of the Scipios, a defection, however, not aggravated, as at Illiturgi, by any particular acts of hostility.[2]

Vengeance was now to be taken for this alleged treason. Without any terms of peace offered or solicited on either side, the Romans prepared to attack Illiturgi, and the Spaniards with all their national obstinacy to defend it. They fought so stoutly that the Romans were more than once repulsed, and Scipio was at last obliged to offer to lead the assault in person, and was preparing to mount the first ladder, when a general shout of his soldiers called upon him to forbear: with an overwhelming

A.U.C. 548.
A.C. 206.

Situation and state of Illiturgi.

Its capture and destruction.

---

[1] Livy, XXIII. 49. [2] Livy, XXVIII. 19.

rush of numbers they crowded up the ladders, in many places at once, and drove the defenders by main force from the ramparts. At the same moment Lælius scaled the walls on the opposite side of the city, and some African deserters who were now in the Roman service, men trained to all feats of daring activity, climbed up the almost precipitous cliff on which the citadel was built, and surprised it without resistance.[1] Then followed a horrible massacre, in which neither age nor sex was spared, and when the sword had done its work upon the people fire was let loose upon the buildings of the city, and Illiturgi was totally destroyed.

Capture of Castulo ;

Scipio then marched to Castulo to support L. Marcius, who had been able, it seems, to make no impression with the force under his separate command. But Scipio's arrival, fresh from the storming of Illiturgi, struck terror into the besieged, and the Spaniards hoped to make their peace by surrendering not their town only but a Carthaginian garrison, which was engaged jointly with them in its defence. The Romans treated Castulo, says Livy, more mildly than they had treated Illiturgi, which seems to imply that even at Castulo blood was shed after the town was taken, though it did not amount to an indiscriminate massacre.[2]

of Astapa : self-devotion of its inhabitants.

After this second conquest Scipio left it to L. Marcius to complete the work, whether of vengeance or of ambition, by the subjugation of the other towns of Bætica, while he himself returned to New Carthage.[3] Marcius crossed the Bætis, and received

---

[1] Livy, XXVIII. 19, 20.   [2] Livy, XXVIII. 20.
[3] Livy, XXVIII. 21.

the submission of some of the towns on the left A.U.C. 548.
A.C. 206.
bank; but the inhabitants of one place, Astapa,
which had rendered itself obnoxious by carrying on
an active guerilla warfare against the Roman detached
parties and communications, exhibited one of those
shocking instances of desperation which testify so
painfully to the miserable lot of the vanquished in
ancient warfare.　They erected a great pile in the
middle of their city, on which they threw all their
ornaments and most valuable property, and then
bade their wives and children ascend it, and sit
down quietly on the top.　Fifty chosen men were
left to keep watch beside the pile, while the rest of
the citizens sallied out against the Romans, determined to fight till they were cut to pieces.　They
fell to a man, selling their lives dearly; in the
meanwhile the fifty men left by the pile performed
their dreadful task; they set it on fire; they
butchered the women and children who were placed
on it, and then threw themselves into the flames.
The Roman soldiers lost their plunder, and exclaimed
against the desperate ferocity of the people of
Astapa.[1]

After this tragedy the neighbouring towns sub- Offer to
mitted, and Marcius returned to his general at New surrender Gades.
Carthage.　But he was not allowed to rest; for a
secret deputation came to Scipio from Gades, offering
to surrender the city to him, along with the Carthaginian fleet and garrison employed in maintaining
it, and Mago their general, Hannibal's brother.
Again therefore Marcius took the field with a light
division of the army, and Lælius accompanied him

[1] Livy, XXVIII. 22, 23.　Appian, Hispan. 33.

A.U.C. 548.
A.C. 206.

by sea with a small squadron, to ascertain whether the offer could really be executed.[1]

Scipio's illness: mutiny in the Roman army.

It was now late in the summer; and the season, combined with the fatigue and excitement which he had undergone, brought on a serious illness upon Scipio, which rumour magnified, spreading the tidings over Spain that the great Roman general could not live. At once, it is said, the fidelity of the Spanish chiefs was shaken: Mandonius and Indibilis, who had regarded Scipio with such extreme veneration, cared nothing for the Roman people, and prepared to assert their country's independence by driving out the Roman army.[2] But a worse mischief was threatening: a division of 8000 Roman or Italian soldiers, who were quartered in a stationary camp on the Sucro, at once as a reserve for the army engaged in the field, and as a covering force to keep the more northern parts of Spain quiet, broke out into open mutiny; and having driven their tribunes from the camp, they conferred the command on two private soldiers, the one C. Atrius, of the allied people of the Umbrians, and the other C. Albius, of the Latin colony of Cales. It is probable that this division of Scipio's army consisted almost entirely of Latins and Italian allies; and the generals chosen accordingly represented both of these, and assumed the full state of Roman generals, causing the lictors to go before them, and to bear the rods and axes, which were the symbol of the consul's imperium, his absolute power of life and death.[3]

Its causes: Scipio's recovery.

The alleged grievance of the mutinous soldiers

[1] Livy, XXVIII. 23.　　　　[2] Livy, XXVIII. 24.
[3] Livy, XXVIII. 24.

was, that their pay was greatly in arrears. This A.U.C. 548.
indeed was likely to be the case, the treasury of A.C. 206.
Rome being ill able to meet the numerous demands
for the public service; and as the Spanish army
had avowedly been left to its own resources as to
money, it is probable that the soldiers were allowed
to plunder the more freely, in order to reconcile
them to their not being paid in the regular manner.
Scipio himself was charged with injuring the discipline of his army by his indulgence; here, as in
other things, it was in his character to rely on his
own personal ascendency; and he thought that he
might dispense with the constant strictness necessary
to ordinary men, as he was sure that his soldiers
would never be disobedient to him. But, however
lax his discipline was, troops at a distance from the
seat of war, and quartered amongst a friendly or
submissive people, must be somewhat restrained in
their license of plunder; and accordingly, even
before Scipio's illness, the soldiers on the Sucro
complained that they were neither paid regularly as
in peace, nor allowed to provide for themselves as
in war. And when they heard that Scipio was at
the point of death, and that the Spaniards in the
north were revolting from Rome, they hoped to draw
their own profit out of these troubled waters, and,
following the example of the Campanians at Rhegium,
to secure a city for themselves, and to live in luxury
upon the plunder and the tributes of the surrounding people.[1]   It is said that Mago from Gades sent
them money, to prevail on them to enter into the
service of Carthage, and that they took the money,

---

[1] Livy, XXVIII. 24.

but did no more than appoint their own generals, take oaths of fidelity to one another, and remain in a state of open revolt from Rome.[1] They probably thought that they might establish themselves in Spain without serving any government at all; and that their own swords were more to be relied on than Mago's promises. While this was the state of affairs on the Sucro, tidings came, not of Scipio's death, but of his convalescence; and presently seven military tribunes arrived in the camp, sent by Scipio to prevent the soldiers from breaking out into any worse outrage. The tribunes affected to rejoice that matters had not been carried to any greater extremity; they acknowledged the former services of the troops, and said that Scipio was not a man to forget or leave them unrewarded; meanwhile the general would endeavour to raise money from the subject tribes of Spain, to make good their arrears of pay. Accordingly soon afterwards a proclamation appeared, inviting the soldiers to come to New Carthage to receive it.[2]

The mutineers come to New Carthage. Scipio's recovery was felt from one end of Spain to the other; the revolted Spaniards gave up their hostile purposes, and returned quietly to their homes; and the soldiers on the Sucro, moved at once by the fear of resisting one whom the gods seemed to favour in all things, and by the hope of receiving, not only pardon for their faults, but the very pay which they demanded, resolved to march in a body to New Carthage. As they drew near to that city the seven tribunes, who had visited their camp on the Sucro, came to meet them, gave them

<hr>

[1] Appian, Hispan. 34.　　　　[2] Livy, XXVIII. 25.

fair words, and mentioned, as if incidentally, that ^{a.u.c. 548.} M. Silanus, with the troops at New Carthage, was ^{a.c. 206.} to march the next morning to put down the revolt of Mandonius and Indibilis.   Delighted to find that Scipio would thus be left without any force at his disposal, they entered New Carthage in high spirits : there they saw the troops all busy in preparations for their departure; and they were told that the general was rejoiced at their seasonable arrival, to supply the place of the soldiers who were going to leave him.   In perfect confidence they dispersed to their quarters for the night.[1]

Thus the prey had run blindly into the snare. They are surrounded. The seven tribunes, who met the soldiers on their march, had each been furnished with the names of five of the principal ringleaders, whom they were to secure in the course of the evening without disturbance.   Accordingly they invited them to supper in their quarters, seized them all, and kept them in close custody till the next morning.   But all else was quiet ; the baggage of the army which was to take the field against the Spaniards began to move before daybreak ; about dawn the columns of the troops formed in the streets, and marched out of the town.   But they halted at the gates, and parties were sent round to every other gate to secure them all, and to take care that no one should leave the city.   In the meantime the troops from the Sucro were summoned to the forum to meet their general ; and they crowded impatiently to the place, without their arms, as was the custom of the Greek soldiers on similar occasions.   No sooner were they all

[1] Livy, XXVIII. 26.

 assembled, than the columns from the gates marched into the town, and occupied all the streets leading to the market-place. Then Scipio presented himself on his tribunal, and sat awhile in silence. But as soon as he heard that the prisoners, who had been secured on the preceding evening, were brought up, the crier with his loud clear voice commanded silence, and Scipio arose to speak.[1]

The mutiny is quelled by the punishment of the ring-leaders. The scene had been prepared with consummate art, and its effect was overwhelming. The mutinous soldiers saw themselves completely in their general's power; they listened in breathless anxiety to his address, and with joy beyond all hope heard his concluding sentence, that he freely pardoned the multitude, and that justice would be satisfied with the punishment of those who had misled them. The instant he ceased speaking the troops posted in the adjoining streets clashed their swords on their shields, as if they were going to attack the mutineers, and the crier's voice was again heard calling the names of the thirty-five ringleaders, one after another, to receive the punishment to which they had been condemned. They were brought forth already stripped and bound, each was fastened to his stake, and all underwent their sentence, being first scourged, and then beheaded. When all was finished the bodies were dragged away to be thrown out of the city; the place of execution was cleansed from the blood; and the soldiers from the Sucro heard the general and the other officers swear to grant them a free pardon with an entire amnesty for the past. They were then summoned by the crier, one by one,

[1] Livy, XXVIII. 26.

to appear before the general to take the usual A.U.C. 548.
military oath of obedience, after which each man A.C. 206.
received his full arrears of pay.[1]   Never was mutiny
quelled with more consummate ability ; and Scipio's
ascendency over his soldiers after this memorable
scene was doubtless more complete than ever.

The punishment of the mutineers, however, we The re-
are told, rendered the revolted Spaniards desperate. volted
Thinking that they had already done enough to draw Spaniards
down Scipio's vengeance, they resolved to try the dued.
chances of war, and again took the field, and began
to attack the allies of the Romans on the north of
the Iberus.   Scipio lost not a moment in marching
in pursuit of them ; he was not sorry to employ his
soldiers against the enemy, as the surest means of
effacing the recollection of their recent disorders ;
and he spoke of the Spaniards with bitter contempt,
as barbarians equally powerless and faithless, on
whom he was resolved to take signal vengeance.   In
ten days he marched from New Carthage to the
Iberus ; and on the fourth day after crossing the river
he came in sight of the enemy.   He engaged and
totally defeated them, not, however, without a loss
of more than 4000 men killed and wounded, and
immediately after the battle the chiefs threw themselves on his mercy.   He required nothing more
than the immediate payment of a sum of money,
which was to make good the money lately advanced
or borrowed to pay the soldiers after the mutiny ;
and then, leaving Silanus at Tarraco, he returned to
New Carthage.[2]

---

[1] Polybius, XI. 30.   Livy, XXVIII. 29.   Appian, Hispan. 36.
[2] Polybius, XI. 31-33.   Livy, XXVIII. 31-34.

A.U.C. 548.
A.C. 206.
Scipio's
interview
with Masi-
nissa.

Even yet he would not allow himself to rest. Leaving the mass of his army at New Carthage he joined L. Marcius, his lieutenant, in the neighbourhood of Gades, for the sole purpose, it is said, of gratifying Masinissa's earnest desire of a personal interview. Masinissa had returned from Africa to Gades, and was professedly consulting with Mago how one more attempt might be made to restore the Carthaginian dominion in Spain. But his mind was already made up to join the Romans; and he took the opportunity of a pretended plundering excursion with his Numidian cavalry to arrange and effect a meeting with Scipio. He too, it is said, like all other men, was overawed at once and delighted by Scipio's personal appearance, manner, and conversation; he promised the most zealous aid to the Romans, and urged Scipio to cross over as soon as possible into Africa, where he might be able to serve him most effectually.[1] Scipio's keen discernment of character taught him the value of Masinissa's friendship; and his journey from New Carthage to Gades, in order to secure it, was abundantly rewarded afterwards; for, had Masinissa fought in Hannibal's army, Scipio in all probability would never have won the day at Zama.

Mago evacu-
ates Spain,
and makes
prepara-
tions in
Minorca for
invading
Italy.

Mago heard of the termination of the mutiny in the Roman army, and of the defeat of the revolted Spaniards in the north; and he found that the Roman army was again returned to New Carthage, and that all hopes of making head against Rome in Spain were for the present at an end. Hannibal summoned him to Italy; and the Carthaginian

[1] Livy, XXVIII. 35.

government, acting, as it seems, cordially upon A.U.C. 548. Hannibal's views, ordered him to obey his brother's A.C. 206. call. It was not the least bold enterprise of this great war, to plan the invasion of Italy from Gades, at a time when the whole of Spain, from the Pillars of Hercules to the Pyrenees, was possessed by the enemy. But Scipio, to strengthen his land forces, had laid up the greater part of his fleet; and the exertions of the Carthaginian government, or his own, had provided Mago with a naval force, small probably in point of numbers, but consisting of excellent ships manned by skilful seamen, and capable, if ably used, of rendering effectual service. He was supplied with money from Carthage; and he levied large contributions, it is said, on the people of Gades, and even emptied their treasury, and stripped their temples.[1] He then put to sea so late in the season that Scipio was gone back to Tarraco, and was preparing to return to Rome; and the Roman army being gone into its winter quarters behind the Iberus, New Carthage was left to the protection of its own garrison. This encouraged Mago to attempt to surprise the place, but in this he failed; he then crossed over to the island of Pityusa (Iviza), which was held by the Carthaginians, and having there received supplies of provisions and of men, he proceeded to attack the two Balearian islands, now called Majorca and Minorca. He was repulsed from the larger island, but made himself master of the smaller; there he landed his men, and drew up his ships, and purposed to pass the winter, the season securing him from any attack by sea,

---

[1] Livy, XXVIII. 36.

A.U.C. 548.
A.C. 206.

perhaps even hiding his movements altogether from the knowledge of the Romans; while he lay in readiness to catch the first return of spring, and to run over to Italy and establish himself on the coast of Liguria, in the midst of a warlike population, furnishing the materials of a future army.[1]

Treaty with Gades. Scipio returns to Rome.

Spain was thus abandoned by the Carthaginians, and Gades, left to itself, went over to the Roman alliance, and concluded a treaty with L. Marcius, which for two centuries formed the basis of its relations with Rome.[2] He had probably been left in command at New Carthage when Scipio returned to Tarraco. Scipio himself was known to be desirous of leaving Spain and offering himself as a candidate for the consulship; and accordingly L. Lentulus and L. Manlius Acidinus were appointed proconsuls, to succeed him and M. Silanus in the command of the Roman army and province. Scipio meanwhile, accompanied by C. Lælius, returned to Rome; he could not have a triumph, because he had been neither consul nor prætor, but he entered the city with some display, with an immense treasure of silver, in money and in ingots, which he deposited in the treasury, and his name was so popular that he was elected consul immediately, with an almost unanimous feeling in his favour. His colleague was P. Licinius Crassus, who at that time held the dignity of Pontifex Maximus.[3]

Prospects of the war in Italy.

Thus the war, being altogether extinguished in Spain, was reduced as it were to Italy only; and

---

[1] Livy, XXVIII. 37.

[2] Livy, XXVIII. 37. Appian. Hispan. 37. See Cicero pro Cornelio Balbo, c. XVII.   [3] Livy, XXVIII. 38.

there it smouldered rather than blazed, for Hannibal A.U.C. 548.
with his single army could do no more than main- A.C. 206.
tain his ground in Bruttium. Was it possible that
Mago might kindle a fierce flame in Liguria ? might
blow up the half-extinguished ashes in Etruria, and,
reviving the fire in the south, spread the conflagration
around the walls of Rome ? This was not beyond
possibility, but Scipio, impatient of defensive warfare, and himself the conqueror of a vast country,
was eager to stop the torrent at its source, rather
than raise barriers against it, when it was sweeping
down the valley; he was bent on combating Hannibal,
not in Italy, but in Africa.[1]

[1] See Note S.

NOTES.

Note A, p. 20, l. 32.

THE question, in what direction this famous march was taken, has been agitated for more than eighteen hundred years; and who can undertake to decide it? The difficulty to modern inquirers has arisen chiefly from the total absence of geographical talent in Polybius. That this historian indeed should ever have gained the reputation of a good geographer, only proves how few there are who have any notion what a geographical instinct is. Polybius indeed laboured with praiseworthy diligence to become a geographer; but he laboured against nature; and the unpoetical character of his mind has in his writings actually lessened the accuracy, as it has totally destroyed the beauty of history. To any man who comprehended the whole character of a mountain country, and the nature of its passes, nothing could have been easier than to have conveyed at once a clear idea of Hannibal's route, by naming the valley by which he had ascended to the main chain, and afterwards that which he followed in descending from it. Or, admitting that the names of barbarian rivers would have conveyed little information to Greek readers, still the several Alpine valleys have each their peculiar character, and an observer with the least power of description could have given such lively touches of the varying scenery of the march, that future travellers must at once have recognised his description. Whereas the account of Polybius is at once so unscientific and so deficient in truth and liveliness of painting, that persons who have gone over the several Alpine passes for the very purpose of identifying his descriptions, can still reasonably doubt whether they were meant to apply to Mont Genevre, or Mont Cenis, or to the Little St. Bernard.

On the whole, it appears to me most probable, that the pass by which Hannibal entered Italy was that which was known to the Romans by the name of the Graian Alps, and to us as the Little St. Bernard. Nor was this so circuitous a line as we may at first imagine. For Hannibal's object was not simply to get into Italy, but to arrive in the country of those Cisalpine Gauls with whom he had been corresponding, and who had long been engaged in wars with the Romans. Now these were the Boii and Insubrians; and as the Insubrians, who were the more westerly of the two, lived between the Adda and the Ticinus, the pass of the Little St. Bernard led more directly into the country of his expected allies, than the shorter passage into Italy by the Cottian Alps, or Mont Genevre.—*Author's Note.*

[The opinion of Polybius expressed in the above note is so important—half the debated points of this war turning upon the comparative authority of Polybius and Livy—and was at the time it was set down (1841) so novel, that I have thought it well to put together a number of the different judgments which have been passed on this historian.

Dr. Arnold's unfavourable view was strongly held, and grew with his increased familiarity with Polybius's narrative. Thus on Sept. 21, 1835, he wrote to Bunsen:—"I have been and am working at two main things, the Roman History and the nature and interpretation of Prophecy. For the first I have been working at Hannibal's passage of the Alps. How bad a geographer is Polybius, and how strange that he should be thought a good one! Compare him with any man who is really a geographer, with Herodotus, with Napoleon, —whose sketches of Italy, Egypt, and Syria, in his Memoirs, are to me unrivalled,—or with Niebuhr, and how striking is the difference. The dulness of Polybius's fancy made it impossible for him to conceive or to paint scenery clearly, and how can a man be a geographer without lively images of the formation and features of the country which he describes? How different are the several Alpine valleys, and how would a few simple touches of the scenery which he seems actually to have visited, yet could neither understand nor feel it, have decided for ever the question of the route! *Now* the account suits no valley well, and therefore it may be applied to many; but I believe the real line was by the Little St. Bernard, although I cannot trace those particular spots which De Luc and Cramer fancy they could recognise. I thought so on the spot (*i.e.* that the spots could not be traced) when I crossed the Little St. Bernard in 1825, with Polybius in my hand, and I think so still." On January 28, 1841, he wrote again to Bunsen :—"The text of Polybius appears to me to be in a very unsatisfactory state, and the reading of the names of places in Italy worth next to nothing. I am sorry to say that my sense of his merit as an historian becomes less and less continually ; he is not only 'einseitig,' but in his very own way he seems to me to have been greatly over-valued, as a military historian most especially. I should like to know what Niebuhr thought of him." In some unpublished notes on the 'Roman Legion, etc.' Dr. Arnold goes so far as to say, " The description of the Roman camp is not clearly given, because Polybius is so very bad a writer."

This adverse opinion was at that time almost peculiar to Dr. Arnold. The view of Gronovius was that of most scholars : " Postquam civilibus Romanorum legibus cognoscendis paululum incubuissem, accedit ut ad *Polybii* curam vocarer ; quo incomparabili scriptore quanto plus utebar, eo acriorem quotidie mihi infudit sui amorem, sic ut non destiterim ex illo tempore semper eum habere sub manum et aliquid observare."[1] The great historian, to whom Dr. Arnold looked up with an almost filial respect, wrote of Polybius with special reference to the Second Punic War : " As far as we possess his work, we cannot look for anything further or better ; his third book is a master-work, and there is nothing in it that leaves the mind of the reader unsatisfied."[2] Niebuhr fully accepts Polybius's account of the passage of the Alps as against Livy's, and says : " In the account of Polybius there is not one feature which is not perfectly correct, and founded upon accurate observation."[3] The only important exception to the general chorus of praise I find in a letter of Lobeck to Brandstätter in 1844. Lobeck simply says: "Of Polybius I have never had a great opinion."[4] During the last forty years the reputation of Polybius has

---

[1] Quoted by Creuzer, *Historische Kunst der Griechen*, p. 44, note 2.   [2] Niebuhr, IV. 156.
[3] IV. 173.   [4] *Philologus* for 1849, p. 764.

rather advanced than gone back, but there has been a strong
counter-movement also, and an increasingly large number of
influential voices have been raised in disparagement of his
pretensions as a geographer. The popular view is thus
forcibly expressed by Mr. Freeman : " Polybius is like a
writer of our own times ; with far less of inborn genius, he
possessed a mass of acquired knowledge of which Thucydides
could never have dreamed. He had, like a modern historian,
read many books and seen many lands ; one language at
least beside his own must have been perfectly familiar to
him ; he had conversed with men of various nations, living
in various states of society and under various forms of government. He had himself personally a wider political experience than fell to the lot of any historian before or after
him. . . . A man must have lived through a millennium in
any other portion of the world's history to have gained with
his own eyes and his own ears such a mass of varied political
knowledge as the historian of the decline and fall of Ancient
Greece acquired in the limits of an ordinary life."[1] Mommsen's view is also favourable, but adds some strong critical
touches to the portrait. " Never, perhaps," he says,[2] " has
any historian united within himself all the advantages of
an author drawing from original sources so completely as
Polybius. The legend, the anecdote, the mass of worthless
chronicle-notices are thrown aside ; the description of countries and peoples, the representation of political and mer-
cantile relations,—all the facts of such infinite importance
which escape the annalist because they do not admit of being
nailed to a particular year,—are put into possession of their
long suspended rights. In the procuring of historic materials
Polybius shows a caution and perseverance such as are not,
perhaps, paralleled in antiquity ; he avails himself of documents, gives comprehensive attention to the literature of
different nations, makes the most extensive use of his
favourable position for collecting the accounts of actors and
eye-witnesses, and, in fine, methodically travels over the
whole domain of the Mediterranean states and part of the
coast of the Atlantic Ocean." After alluding to the shallow

[1] *Federal Government*, I. 226. Compare the same writer's *Rede
Lecture on the Unity of History*, p. 22 foll.
[2] **English Translation, IV. 466.**

rationalism and excessive turn for generalisation which are
to be counted against these merits, Mommsen goes on : "His
conception of relations is everywhere dreadfully jejune and
destitute of imagination ; his contemptuous and pert mode
of treating religious matters is altogether offensive. The
narrative, preserving throughout an intentional contrast to
the usual Greek historiography with its artistic style, is
correct and clear, but flat and languid, digressing with
undue frequency into polemical discussions or into bio-
graphical, not seldom very self-sufficient, description of his
own experiences. . . . Polybius is not an attractive author ;
but as truth and truthfulness are of more value than all
ornament and elegance, no other author of antiquity perhaps
can be named to whom we are indebted for so much real
instruction." Nissen, lastly, the first volume of whose
Italische Landeskunde was published in 1883, is alone, or
almost alone,[1] in venturing a thorough-going defence of
Polybius as geographer. After explaining the immense
opportunities offered to a geographer by the throwing open
of the western world to the Greek mind at the beginning of
the second century, Nissen goes on : " To have formed an
adequate conception of this new time, and to have risen to
its demands on the geographical, as well as on the historical,
side, is the merit of Polybius of Megalopolis. An eventful
life had carried him from the Alps to Cape Verde, and from
the coasts of the Atlantic far into the depths of Asia. He
was, perhaps, one of the greatest travellers that antiquity
produced, and can be said without exaggeration to have
seen double and treble as much of the world as the roving
and yarn-spinning Father of history. He is a born critic
from the crown of his head to the sole of his feet. . . . It
was Polybius who brought the basin of the western Mediterranean, Italy, Gaul, Spain, and northern Africa, into the
domain of Greek literature. To his hand is due the oldest
description of Italy as an independent member of the inhabited world, as a connected whole from the Alps to the
Straits of Messina. The author employed an exile of seventeen years' duration to make himself acquainted with that
country from end to end. His strength does not lie in the

---

[1] Compare also Prof. F. Voigt's lecture on the Battle of Thrasymene
in *Philologische Wochenschrift*, III. 1580 foll., esp. p. 1590.

advancement of the problems of universal geography, but in the treatment of historical topography. The topographical sketches which he has embodied in his history may be regarded as real models; they are clear, definite, and to the point, as well as inspired by a large conception. From the accumulation of barbaric names he refrains even more than we quite like; he makes use of familiar analogies for the purpose of awakening clear ideas, and chooses simple forms to incorporate his thought. The section on the Po basin may serve for an example; it would be difficult to render the relation of the basin to the Alps on the one side, and to the Apennine peninsula on the other, so clearly with a less expenditure of means. How blessed is personal observation the example of this writer very plainly shows. It is true that when in his old age he set to work upon his book his memory often deceived him, and his authorities led him astray. His mastery of Greek topography is far more assured than that of Italy, Spain, and other such lands never before subjected to scientific investigation. Here are to be found numerous errors in detail, which our maps expose at once; nevertheless, even so, the general merit of his topography remains unimpeachable, if one measures it by the standard of his time."[1]

The above extracts fairly represent the favourable modern view of Polybius. It will be seen that, as a rule, the question of his geographical capacity has been put somewhat into the background. It has commonly been taken for granted that, because Polybius is a master of political speculation, and because his authority on a point of constitutional history is great, that therefore his opinion on a geographical point is invariably to be accepted without demur, and that when he and Livy absolutely disagree on such points, the mere authority of the older writer is enough to settle the question. But it is, or should be, clear that a man may possess many of the gifts of the historian, but not that peculiar faculty for vividly and accurately conceiving a large mass of country as a whole, which distinguishes in our own day Ernst Curtius and the late John Richard Green, but which does not distinguish either Grote or Mommsen. The geographical statements of Polybius must be taken on their merits and not

<hr>

[1] *Italische Landeskunde*, I. 12-14.

allowed to pass muster without even a decent pretence of inquiry, simply because Polybius has won for himself a deserved authority in quite other matters. So far as this has been done, the general tendency of modern criticism is undoubtedly towards Dr. Arnold's unfavourable view, which was a revolutionary heresy at the time when it was expressed, but is now on its way to become a commonplace.

In the following very instructive and interesting passage Ihne [1] admits, while palliating and explaining Polybius's weakness as a geographer: "It is even to the present day an unsolved question by which road Hannibal marched to and across the Alps, although Polybius describes it at full length, and was well qualified to do so, having, only fifty years after Hannibal, travelled over the same ground, with a view of giving a description of it in his great historical work. But the descriptions which the ancient writers give of localities are, for the most part, exceedingly defective and obscure. Even from Cæsar's own narrative we cannot make out with certainty where he crossed the Rhine and the Thames, and where he landed on the coast of Britain. The imperfect geographical knowledge possessed by the ancients, their erroneous notions of the form and extent of countries, of the direction of rivers and mountain ranges with regard to the four cardinal points, [2] in some measure account for these inaccuracies. Not being accustomed, from their youth upwards, to have accurate maps before their eyes, they grew up with indistinct conceptions, and were almost accustomed to a loose and incorrect mode of expression when speaking of such matters. [3] But it seems that, apart from this imperfect knowledge of geography, they lacked the keen observation of nature which distinguishes the moderns. As they seem all but insensible to the beauties of landscape, they

---

[1] III. 171 (English edition, 1871). Compare Bosworth Smith's *Carthage and the Carthaginians*, p. 198.

[2] Thus (III. 47, § 2) Polybius fancies the source of the Rhone to be due north of the Adriatic, and its course from east to west.—*Ihne's Note.*

[3] What can be more vague than such expressions as δυσχωρίαι and εὔκαιροι τόποι, which Polybius uses (III. 50, § 3)? Again, when he describes a locality as situated μεταξὺ τοῦ Πάδου καὶ τοῦ Τρεβία ποταμοῦ, he leaves it undecided whether it is on the right or the left bank of the Trebia, and thus he has given rise to the controversy about the situation of the battle-field in question.—*Ihne's Note.*

were careless in the examination and study of nature; and
their descriptions of scenery are seldom such that we can
draw an accurate map or picture after them, or identify the
localities at the present time. Moreover, the permanent
features of landscape—the mountains, rivers, glens, lakes,
and plains—had seldom names universally known and
generally current, as is the case at present; nor were there
accurate measurements of distances, heights of mountains,
width of passes, and the like. Where, in addition to these
defects, there were even wanting human habitations, towns
or villages with well-known and recognisable names, it
became impossible to describe a route like that of Hannibal
across the Alps with an accuracy that excludes all doubts."

H. Droysen, who has had occasion to examine one or two
of Polybius's geographical statements in detail, is more un-
compromising. "Polybius," he says,[1] "passes for an entirely
trustworthy author in all his statements; he himself frequently and emphatically asserts the complete trustworthiness
of the information he communicates, and criticises, often in a
drastic, not unfrequently in a petty fashion, the inaccuracies
or, in his own phrase, falsehoods of other authors. It is
therefore not without interest to examine whether the statements of Polybius always correspond to the demands which
he makes on others. Two parts of the narrative of the
Spanish War of Scipio Africanus, the description of the
position of New Carthage, and the account of Scipio's march
on that place, afford the opportunity for such an examination." Droysen proceeds to point out, as Dr. Arnold (*Life*,
II. 268) had pointed out before him, that Polybius's description of New Carthage will by no means square with the
modern maps. As regards the town and its environs, the
"north" of Polybius is really east, and his account only
becomes intelligible on that assumption. But on this
assumption Polybius's description of the entrance of the
harbour, and of the island (which can only be Escombrera)
covering it, is all wrong. As regards the harbour, the points
of the compass are pretty accurate in Polybius; so it appears
that he had one 'Orientirung' as regards the town, and quite
another as regards the harbour. The island is described by
Polybius as a kind of breakwater in front of the harbour,

---

[1] *Rheinisches Museum*, XXX. 62-67 (1875).

leaving a narrow entrance on each side,—which is quite erroneous. Droysen holds that, as regards the description of New Carthage, we cannot acquit Polybius of negligence. As regards the account of Scipio's march on New Carthage, he charges Polybius with deliberate falsification. The historian says that Scipio marched with 25,000 infantry and 2500 cavalry from the Ebro to New Carthage in seven days. Polybius knew (III. 39) that the distance was over 300 miles, and, as an old soldier, must have known that such a march for such an army in a country without roads or bridges was out of the question. In another essay in the same volume of the *Rheinisches Museum* on Polybius's description of the battle of Baecula, Droysen (p. 284) comes to the conclusion that, if the fragments of the eleventh book fairly represent the matter, " we are enabled to make more accurate acquaintance with Polybius, who is commonly admired as a competent military authority, on the military side; this test, at all events, puts in a far from favourable light his capacity to understand and explain military operations." In his *History of Ancient Geography* Mr. Bunbury has a section on Polybius purely as geographer.[1] Here are some of his judgments : " Notwithstanding the valuable information acquired by Polybius concerning the Alps, and its great superiority to that of his predecessors, we must not assume that he had anything like a clear geographical acquaintance with the course and configuration of that great chain." " His mode of estimating their heights (of the Alps) was singularly rude and imperfect." " His description of the Rhone as having its source ' in the most northerly parts of the Alps, above the inmost recess of the Adriatic,' and flowing from thence towards the S.W., sufficiently indicates how vague, or rather how utterly erroneous, was his conception of the general configuration of the Alpine chain." In the same strain Ranke[2] writes : " Polybius has a fundamentally false picture in his mind of the triangle of Italy, the triangle of the Alps, and the course of the Rhone ; what he says of the course of the Po betrays also an erroneous geographical conception ; and if he tells us that he had been himself on the spot, it remains very dubious how far he carried such personal investigation, and of what nature were his inquiries." Mr. Douglas Freshfield (to whose view, as that

[1] II. 16 foll.　　[2] *Weltgeschichte*, III. part 2, p. 187.

of a man who is a first-rate geographer himself, and who approaches Polybius solely on the geographical side, I attach exceptional importance in this discussion) has so convinced himself of "Polybius's carelessness as a topographer,"[1] that, addressing an audience which really knows the Alps, he does not think it worth while to go about to prove it. Two recent German writers, who have given special attention to the Battle of Thrasymene,[2] both absolutely throw over Polybius's account of the ground and of the engagement, and it is to be observed that Nissen himself, whose thorough-going defence of Polybius I have already quoted, in that epoch-making essay on the Battle of Thrasymene,[3] which is the starting-point of all recent competent discussion of the subject, practically accepts Livy's account in preference to that of Polybius, and only brings Polybius into accord with Livy by a desperate perversion of the former's meaning, in which he has found no followers. Lastly, Carl Neumann, whose posthumous *Zeitalter der Punischen Kriege* (1883), admirably edited and supplemented by his pupil Gustav Faltin, is the most recent, full, and competent discussion of the whole period that has appeared in Germany, raises his conviction of Polybius's incapacity and untrustworthiness as a geographer almost to the level of an axiom. "Even granted," he writes,[4] "that Polybius might have gained from his journey a general idea of the higher Alps, yet he was by no means the man to supply a geographical description of them which should supply his readers with a clue to find their way amid that labyrinth. The fact that he plumes himself with great self-complacency on his superiority and better knowledge in geographical matters does not affect the truth. He was unable to find his way about in the plain, much less in the maze of mountain-valleys. It is only necessary to read his general description of the shape of Italy to convince one's self of his incapacity in this connection. As regards our special region (the Alps), he supplies us with the plainest proofs that even

---

[1] See his essay on the Pass of Hannibal in the *Alpine Journal* for 1883, p. 292.

[2] H. Stürenburg, *De Romanorum cladibus Trasumenna et Cannensi;* and Faltin, in *Rheinisches Museum*, XXXIX. 268, 273, and *Berliner Philologische Wochenschrift*, IV. 1017.

[3] *Rheinisches Museum*, XXII. 565 foll.   [4] p. 283.

his points of the compass are all wrong. In his view, for instance, the Rhone rises above the inmost recess of the Adriatic, and then flows always westwards, and always at the north edge of the North Alps, till it reaches the Sardinian Sea. That he applies this blunder to the lower course of the Rhone as well as to the upper is shown by his making Hannibal march *eastwards* up the stream immediately after he had crossed the river. How, in view of such a cardinal error in the fundamental conceptions of the historian, it can nevertheless be assumed as something beyond doubt that he cannot but have furnished the most serviceable and intelligible account of the march of Hannibal is inconceivable." Elsewhere, in a passage which looks very much like a reminiscence of Dr. Arnold, Neumann [1] says : "Polybius has absolutely no talent for the conception of geographical relations," and in his account of the Battles of Trebia and Lake Thrasymene,[2] he unhesitatingly prefers Livy to Polybius. So strong and so numerous have the critics of Polybius as geographer, in fact, become, that a champion of the orthodox view complains [3] that "it seems to be becoming quite the fashion to speak disparagingly of Polybius." The fashion may easily be carried too far, and I merely quote the words to show that Dr. Arnold's view—which, so far as it was unfavourable, was directed to two points—Polybius's incapacity as geographer, and his imperfect power of literary presentation—has found plenty of champions. It is to be hoped that English editors and historians of this period will not be content to go on repeating, without any serious attempt to weigh the statements of Polybius, that on geographical points, "where Livy differs from Polybius, his authority is worthless." [4]]

---

[1] p. 286. [2] p. 317, 334. Compare also p. 357, note 1.

[3] Prof. F. Voigt of Berlin in the *Philologische Wochenschrift*, III. 1590.

[4] The general result of recent inquiry is to confirm the judgment passed by Nissen (*Rheinisches Museum*, XXII. 566), himself a thorough-going believer in Polybius, on these particular books of Livy. Nissen says : "Die annalistische Ueberlieferung in der dritten Dekade zeugt grossentheils von einer Güte, welche späteren Partien durchaus fehlt, und liefert unter schonender und sorgfältiger Behandlung eine Menge unverächtlicher Daten zur Schilderung des denkwürdigsten Krieges, der je auf Italischem Boden geführt wird."

Note B, p. 27, l. 13.

Such is the story of the earliest recorded passage of the Alps by civilised men, the earliest and the most memorable. Accustomed as we are, since the completion of the great Alpine roads in the present century, to regard the crossing of the Alps as an easy summer excursion, we can even less than our fathers conceive the difficulties of Hannibal's march, and the enormous sacrifices by which it was accomplished. He himself declared that he had lost above thirty thousand men since he had crossed the Pyrenees, and that the remnant of his army, when he reached the plains of Italy, amounted to no more than twenty thousand foot and six thousand horsemen ; nor does Polybius seem to suspect any exaggeration in the statement.   Yet eleven years afterwards Hasdrubal crossed the Alps in his brother's track without sustaining any loss deserving of notice; and 'a few accidents '[1] are all that occurred in the most memorable passage of modern times, that of Napoleon over the Great St. Bernard.   It is evident that Hannibal could have found nothing deserving the name of a road, no bridges over the rivers, torrents, and gorges, nothing but mere mountain-paths, liable to be destroyed by the first avalanche or landslip, and which the barbarians neither could nor cared to repair, but on the destruction of which they looked out for another line, such as for their purposes of communication it was not difficult to find.   It is clear also, either that Hannibal passed by some much higher point than the present roads over the Little St. Bernard, or Mont Cenis ; or else, as is highly probable,[2] that the limit of perpetual snow reached

---

[1] "On n'eut que peu d'accidens."—*Napoleon's Memoirs*, vol. I., p. 261.

[2] Even as late as the year 1646, Evelyn's description of the passage of the Simplon in September can scarcely be recognised by those who know only its present state.   He speaks of the house in which he lodged at Sempione, as "half covered with snow," and says that "there is not a tree or bush growing within many miles ; " whereas now the pines are so luxuriant about the village that the road seems to run through an ornamental park.   And, again, above Sempione, Evelyn was told by the country people "that the way had been covered with snow since the creation ; no man remembered it to be without."   And he speaks of the descent towards Brieg by the old

to a much lower level in the Alps than it does at present. For the passage of the main chain is described as wholly within this limit; and the 'old snow' which Polybius speaks of was no accidental patch, such as will linger through the summer at a very low level in crevices or sunless ravines; but it was the general covering of the pass which forbade all vegetation, and remained alike in summer as in winter. How great a contrast to the blue lake, the green turf, the sheep and cattle freely feeding on every side tended by their shepherds, and the bright hues of the thousand flowers, which now delight the summer traveller on the Col of the Little St. Bernard!

I have little doubt as to Hannibal's march up the Tarentaise; but the Val d'Aosta puzzles me. According to any ordinary rate of marching, an army could never get in three days from the Little St. Bernard to the plains of Ivrea; not to mention that the Salassians of that valley were such untamable robbers, that they once even plundered Cæsar's baggage, and Augustus at last extirpated them by wholesale.[1] And yet Hannibal on the Italian side of the main chain sustains little or no annoyance. I have often wished to

road as being made for some way "through an ocean of snow."—*Memoirs*, vol. I., pp. 220, 221.

[In the *Alpine Journal* for 1883, p. 279, note, Mr. Douglas Freshfield writes:—"King (*Italian Valleys of the Pennine Alps*) and Arnold fall into a groundless conclusion as to a change in the Alpine climate by failing to make allowance for the variations in individual seasons. In one year the carriage passes are open (for wheels) in April, in another not till mid-June. I speak from personal experience. As to the time of Evelyn's passage Arnold was naturally deceived by the words 'in September,' interpolated—in brackets—by some transcriber. The context shows plainly that Evelyn crossed the Simplon before May 20 (old style), for he drew a bill on England at Venice on April 23, 1646, and he paid a bill for six weeks' medical attendance at Geneva in the first week of July of the same year." This appears to be correct; compare pp. 176, 187, 194 of the edition of Evelyn's Diary in the *Chandos Classics*.]

[[1] "In the assumption that the plain of Aosta was, for Hannibal and his historians, the end of the Alps, and the failure adequately to recognise the facts that the lower Val d'Aosta is a prolonged defile, dangerous to armies, and that the distance to the plain by this route is consequently double, roughly speaking, what it is by the more southern passes, Mr. Bosworth Smith follows all other upholders of the Little St. Bernard. Here is the fatal flaw in their argument." Freshfield in *Alpine Journal*, XI. 287, note.]

examine the pass which goes by the actual head of the
Isère, by Mont Iseran, and descends by Usseglio, not exactly
on Turin, but nearly at Chivasso, where the Po, from running
N. and S., turns to run E. and W.[1]   In some respects, also,
I think Mont Cenis suits the description of the march better
than any other pass.   I lay no stress on the Roche blanche;
it did not strike me when I saw it as at all conspicuous;
nor does the λευκόπετρον mean any remarkably white cliff,
but simply one of those bare limestone cliffs, which are so
common both in the Alps and Apennines.—*Author's Note.*

[On the line of Hannibal's march from the Rhone to the
basin of the Po certainty is not attainable; but the general
result of recent inquiry has been to throw the gravest
doubts upon the pass (the Little St. Bernard), upheld till
quite recently by the majority of modern writers on the
subject.   The chief votes are as follows :—for the Little St.
Bernard—General Melville, Wickham and Cramer, Niebuhr,
Arnold, Law, Mommsen, Ihne, Capes, and Bosworth Smith;
for the Mont Cenis—Ukert, Ellis, Ball, Maissiat, and
Nissen; for the Mont Genèvre — Hennebert, Desjardins,
Dübi,[2] and Neumann; for the Col du Clapier—Perrin; and
for the Col d'Argentière—Douglas Freshfield.   Any one
who will take the trouble to read, along with Livy and
Polybius, Neumann, 274-305; Capes (Livy, Books XXI. and
XXII.), pp. 307-315; Freshfield (*Alpine Journal* for 1883),
267-300; and Hermann Schiller's review of the present
position of the whole question in the *Berliner Philologische
Wochenschrift*, IV. 705, 737, 769, will be supplied with all
the existing materials for a judgment.

The first thing to be done is to state the geographical
problem in its simplest form.   A commander approaching
the Alps from the S.W., with the intention of passing into
Italy otherwise than by the coast route, has a maze of

[1 Dr. Arnold appears to have intended to make a personal examination of this pass in his summer tour in 1842.   On the 3d May
1842 he wrote to Bunsen (*Life and Correspondence*, II. 268) :—"I
hope to finish vol. III. of *Rome* before the end of the holidays; and then,
in the last month of them, my wife and I are going, I believe, to have
a run abroad.   I do not know where we shall go exactly, but I think
very likely to Grenoble and the Val d'Isère."   The fulfilment of this
scheme was prevented by Dr. Arnold's death on the 12th June following.]

2 In the *Jahrbuch des Schweizer Alpenclubs* for 1884.

mountains before him, to which three clues are supplied by three rivers cutting deeply into it and leading to the foot of the main mountain-wall, on the other side of which lies Italy. These are the Rhone, the Isère, and the Durance. The first-named, which will take him to the Great St. Bernard, is out of the question, as being too far north, and leading to a pass both more difficult and higher than can be found within a much more manageable distance. There remain the Isère, which will take him to the foot of the Little St. Bernard, and the Durance, which will take him to the foot of the Mont Genèvre. Accordingly, Ranke [1] states the question as simply a choice between the Little St. Bernard and the Mont Genèvre. But both the Isère and the Durance have tributaries, also leading to the foot of passes, high up on their course. The Isère has the Arc, which leads to Mont Cenis, while the Durance has the Ubaye, which leads to the Col d'Argentière; and, therefore, though we may be confident that Hannibal's line of march was up the Durance, or, as the case may be, up the Isère, we still have to choose between the two possible passes on each route. On the whole, then, there are two possible routes, and four possible passes; the latter being, in order from north to south, the Little St. Bernard, the Mont Cenis, the Mont Genèvre, and the Col d'Argentière. Their heights (in feet) are—Little St. Bernard, 7076; Mont Cenis, 6859; Mont Genèvre, 6101; and Col d'Argentière, 6538. From this point of view—and it is a very important one, as Hannibal crossed the Alps late in the season [2]—the two southern passes, in particular the Mont Genèvre, have a considerable advantage. This consideration alone suffices to dismiss the Col du Clapier (8125 feet), which is a mere variant of the Mont Cenis route, and for which, so far as I can discover, the only serious argument is that it commands an exceptionally good view of Italy.[3] This point of the view of Italy is one of those on which it is not ad-

[1] *Weltgeschichte*, II. part I., 213.

[2] The setting of the Pleiades (Livy, XXI. 35) in B.C. 218 is put by a German astronomer (Neumann, 299) as late as November 7. A French astronomer (*Berlin Phil. Woch.* IV. 772) assigns it to October 28. In any case the season was dangerously far advanced.

[3] See the analysis of Perrin's argument for the Col du Clapier in *Berlin Phil. Woch.*, IV. 769 foll.

visable to lay stress. Any pass which supplies a look down-
ward on a sunnier region will do all that is required. The
point is only of importance in so far as it can be pressed
against the Little St. Bernard; where there is no such view
at all, but where the descending path, in Neumann's words,[1]
"seems to lead straight upon the most awful icy summits,
the masses of Mont Blanc." Nor do I attach the slightest
importance to Polybius's 'white rock,' which can be found
without difficulty on any conceivable pass that may be suggested. I agree also with Mr. Freshfield in thinking that
such statements of distances as are supplied by Polybius cannot safely be used as a criterion, and are indeed practically
worthless. As for the requirement that the top of the pass
should supply a space large enough for an army to encamp,
it is fulfilled by all four passes; but it is to be observed
that such an encampment on a high and woodless pass like
the Little St. Bernard at the end of October or beginning of
November is more improbable than would be a similar
encampment on, say, the Mont Genèvre.[2] Lastly, I hold
strongly that nothing can be gained from demonstrations—
or, to speak more accurately, assertions—that this or that
pass was not used in antiquity. Mr. Freshfield[3] has successfully proved against Desjardins[4] that the Mont Cenis
was so used; and no one at all familiar with a mountain
country and the life of its inhabitants can doubt that all
practicable passes were used from the first beginnings of
human habitation in the upper valleys. We happen to
know of one tribe that they lived about the sources of the
Druentia and Duria, and must therefore have had perpetual
intercommunication among themselves across the watershed,[5]
that is to say, in this particular case, across the Mont
Genèvre. The Romans were the first to make regular roads
across the lower passes, but armies had forced a passage
over more than one of them long before Hannibal;[6] and

---

[1] p. 301.   [2] Neumann, 300.   [3] *Alpine Journal*, XI. 292 foll.
[4] *Géographie de la Gaule Romaine*, II. 93.
[5] Strabo, IV. 6, § 5, Cas. 203.
[6] Polybius, III. 48, σύμβαινει τοὺς Κελτοὺς τοὺς παρὰ τὸν Ῥοδανὸν
ποταμὸν οἰκοῦντας οὐχ ἅπαξ, οὐδὲ δὶς πρὸ τῆς Ἀννίβου παρουσίας, οὐδὲ
μὴν πάλαι, προσφάτως δέ, μεγάλοις στρατοπέδοις ὑπερβάντας τὰς Ἄλπεις
παρατετάχθαι μὲν Ῥωμαίοις, συνηγωνίσθαι δὲ Κελτοῖς τοῖς τὰ περὶ τὸν
Πάδον πεδία κατοικοῦσι.

the Gallic mercenaries who were summoned from the Rhone valley to Cisalpine Gaul must have crossed in large bodies by the Great St. Bernard—a pass greatly more difficult than the Mont Genèvre or the Col d'Argentière.[1]

A consideration of the comparative heights of the passes, as well as of the fact that Hannibal crossed the Rhine somewhere about Avignon,[2] leads naturally to the conclusion that, in accordance with the information which his assiduous preliminary inquiries had procured him,[3] his intention was to cross from Gaul to Italy at the upper end of the valley of the Durance. But the encounter of his Numidians with the Roman cavalry, and the knowledge that to follow the Durance from its junction with the Rhone would take him in a south-easterly direction, within dangerous proximity of Marseilles and of that Roman army which we are expressly told he did not want to fight,[4] changed his plans. He shook off the Romans by moving up the left bank of the Rhone to the neighbourhood of Valence and the junction of the Isère. So far both our authorities agree. The question now is whether, having accomplished the object of this march—for Scipio, despairing of overtaking him, had promptly gone back to the coast and taken ship for Italy,—Hannibal still adhered to his original plan, and struck across country to the upper waters of the Durance, or whether, finding himself on the Isère, he changed his plans entirely, and followed up that river with the idea of crossing into Italy either by the Little St. Bernard or the Mont Cenis. There is some doubt as to what Polybius supposed him to have done ; but there can be no question at all that Livy describes him as having taken the former course. From the Rhone, Livy says,[5] "Hannibal marched towards the Alps, not, however, pursuing a direct course, but turning leftwards to the country of the Tricastini, from which again he passed to that of the Tricorii, along the extreme frontier of the Vocontii, a route at no point embarrassing until he reached the river Druentia." The Tricastini dwelt in the western highlands between the Drôme and the Isère, their capital in later times being

<hr>

[1] Polybius, II. 22, 23.   Plutarch, *Marcellus*, 3, 6.
[2] Polybius, III. 42, 45, 49.   Livy, XXI. 32.   Neumann, 276.
[3] Polybius, III. 34, 48.   [4] Livy, XXI. 31.
[5] XXI. 31.   Church and Brodribb's translation.

Augusta Tricastinorum, now Aoust on the Drôme. The statement that Hannibal did not take the direct road to Italy, but turned leftwards, is thus explained by Mr. Douglas Freshfield [1]:—" Hannibal turned to the left from the confluence of the Rhone and Isère, leaving the direct road to Italy on his right. One direct road from this point is quite clear on the map. It leads up the valley of the Drôme. This was in Livy's time a well-known Roman highroad. By following the Isère Hannibal, as he faced the Alps, or, as Polybius says, eastwards, turned away from it to the left." In fine, according to Livy, Hannibal marched up the Isère to the neighbourhood of Grenoble, then took to the valley of the Drac, and crossed from the upper waters of that river, by the Col Bayard, to the upper waters of the Durance. Whether Livy took him into Italy by way of the Mont Genèvre or the Col d'Argentière may be disputed, but that he took him out of the upper valley of the Durance is certain.

Unfortunately, Polybius is not so definite. He gives no geographical names of any kind [2] between Hannibal's departure from the Isère and his descent into Italy, and it is possible to doubt whether his pass was—(1) the Little St. Bernard; (2) the Mont Cenis; or (3) that of Livy, by way of the upper valley of the Durance. The starting-point with him, as with Livy, is the confluence of the Rhone and the Isère. " Quitting" he says,[3] " the island [4] at the junction of the

[1] *Alpine Journal*, XI. 272. This is also the explanation of Weissenbom (see his edition of Livy, note to XXI. 31) and Neumann, 292. The 'direct course' would have taken Hannibal over the Col de Cabre.

[2] This was in accordance with an unfortunate theory which Polybius explains and justifies, III. 36. In regard to Livy's names it is of course *possible* that he did not find them in any of his authorities, but took the trouble to supply them from the geographical knowledge of his time. This is Nissen's view. (*Italische Landeskunde*, I. 155.) In that case the names would be worth little or nothing as evidence.

[3] III. 50. Polybius's account of Hannibal's route will be found in an accurate and elegant translation by Messrs. Church and Brodribb as an appendix to their translation of Livy, Books XXI.–XXV., p. 325.

[4] The 'island' (cf. Polybius, III. 49; Livy, XXI. 31) was the great triangle formed by the confluence of the Rhone and Isère. " Isola," says Mr. Freshfield (*Alpine Journal*, XI. 270, note), " is now a common name in the Italian Alps for villages situated between two streams above their junction." It has not, so far as I know, been pointed out that the true parallel to this 'island'—and a very exact one—is the

Rhone and the Isère, Hannibal marched about eighty miles along the river and then began his ascent of the lower slopes of the Alps." This 'along the river'—παρὰ τὸν ποταμόν —is a formidable difficulty in the way of those who would make Polybius and Livy tell the same story. "I cannot bring myself to believe," says Mr. Freshfield [1] candidly enough, "that Polybius meant by 'the river' anything but the Rhone. But I think he used the expression 'along the river-bank' to cover the general direction of the march up to the Alps through the Rhone country." Neumann, who also seeks to reconcile Livy and Polybius, has a different explanation. [2] "By 'the river' Polybius naturally could only mean the Rhone, which according to his notion has a continuous course from east to west at the northern side of the Alps. Modern historians have regarded as an attested fact what is only the necessary consequence of a fundamentally erroneous general conception." Neither of these explanations is very comforting, but they are the only ones, for the suggestion that Polybius meant to say that Hannibal *retraced his steps along the river-bank* till he reached the neighbourhood of Avignon, and then, presumably, took the Durance valley at this lower point, may be dismissed. It does an excessive violence to Polybius's text without any compensating advantage in the shape of reconciling his account with that of Livy. It must be admitted that the ordinary interpretation of Polybius, which makes him take Hannibal another eighty miles 'up stream' from the junction of the Isère to the neighbourhood of Vienne, is not easily rejected. Another difficulty for the reconcilers is Polybius's account of Hannibal's conflicts with the Allobroges, who inhabited the country north of the Isère from Vienne to the lake of Geneva, including the mountains of Savoy, and with whom therefore Hannibal, if he had kept south of the Isère, would apparently have had nothing to do. Mr. Freshfield's answer is that these race-names were loosely used "to include a whole confederacy of more or less independent tribes," and that we are told that the chieftains of the Allobroges had been fol-

'Island of Meroe,' formed by the junction of the rivers Nile and Atbara.   Pliny, N. H., II. 73 ; V. 9 ; VI. 29.   Strabo, I. 2, § 25 ; XVII. 1, § 2 ; XVII. 2, § 2.

[1] *Alpine Journal*, XI. 275.   [2] p. 293.

lowing Hannibal for days (therefore possibly out of their own proper territory) before they fell upon him.[1] Neumann[2] is more summary. Polybius, he says, "certainly did not find the name of the Allobroges in his original authority, but worked it in to suit his own erroneous notions." It will be seen that, as regards these two points, Livy and Polybius can only be brought into harmony by assumptions with which a sound criticism can have nothing to do.

On the other hand, I lay no stress on the supposed irreconcilable difference between Livy and Polybius as to the point at which Hannibal descended into Italy. Livy undoubtedly brings Hannibal out among the Taurini, whose capital was Turin; it is commonly said that Polybius brings him out among the Insubres, whose capital was Milan.[3] If this were really so, it would be necessary to suppose that Polybius took Hannibal across the Alps by way of the Little St. Bernard; but I agree with Nissen (p. 156) that Neumann has adduced strong arguments for the view that Polybius also made Turin the terminus of the march. Neumann points out[4] in the first place that, according to Livy, it was agreed by *all* writers (inter omnes constet) that Hannibal came out upon Turin. It is impossible to suppose that Livy ignored so important a writer as Polybius, and one to whom he was himself so much indebted, and it follows, therefore, that he believed Polybius to have espoused this view. Neumann's second argument is to lay stress upon the word τολμηρῶς in the statement of Polybius (III. 56) that Hannibal κατῆρε τολμηρῶς εἰς τὰ περὶ τὸν Πάδον πεδία, καὶ τὸ τῶν Ἰσόμβρων ἔθνος. There was no need of "audacity" in descending among the Insubres, who were his best friends, and Neumann's view is that the word conceals the fact that on his way to the Insubres Hannibal had to fight his way through the unfriendly tribe of the Taurini. In any case it must be admitted that if we suppose Hannibal to have crossed by the Little St. Bernard, and to have arrived, say, at Ivrea, it was a very extraordinary proceeding on his part to go out of his way to attack the Taurini on the S.W., when Scipio was at Placentia on the

------

[1] *Alpine Journal*, XI. 275.   [2] p. 297
[3] Polybius, II. 34; Strabo, V. 1, § 6.   [4] p. 288.

S.E.   The probabilities certainly are that he only attacked
the Taurini because he had to pass through their territory
on his way to the Insubres, with whom they (the Taurini)
were at feud.   A third argument and a very strong one, to
which Neumann does not refer, is that in a passage on the
Alps, which is apparently only one long quotation from
Polybius, Strabo[1] mentions the pass through the country
of the Taurini as that taken by Hannibal.   This testimony
can only be invalidated by supposing, as Mommsen[2] supposes,
that Strabo is here not quoting from Polybius, but merely
giving his own personal opinion.   I agree, however, with
Bunbury[3] and Ranke[4] in thinking that the words are
simply a quotation from Polybius.   In that case there may
be a doubt whether Polybius took Hannibal across the Alps
by the Mont Cenis, the Mont Genèvre, or the Col d'Argentière, but there can be no doubt that he did *not* take him
by the Little St. Bernard.

I think, then, it may very well be maintained that
Polybius referred to the Insubres as Hannibal's ultimate
objective,[5] not as the race on whom he descended immediately from the Alps; but, even so, it should be clearly
realised that this does not necessarily effect the reconciliation
of Polybius with Livy.   The pass of Mont Cenis also would
have brought Hannibal out upon Turin, and that is the pass
which Nissen[6]—who accepts the authority of Polybius, but
who agrees with Neumann's interpretation of the passages I
have just quoted from Polybius and Livy—believes him to
have taken.

The conclusion of the whole matter seems to be that
Livy, who tells a clear and consistent story, whose description of Alpine scenery is remarkably accurate and just,[7] and

[1] IV. 6, § 12—εἶτα τὴν διὰ Ταυρίνων ἣν Ἀννίβας διῆλθεν.

[2] *C. I. L.*, V. 2, p. 809.

[3] *History of Ancient Geography*, II. 37.   See also Freshfield in
Alpine Journal, XI. 276, 280.

[4] *Weltgeschichte*, III. part 2, p. 191.

[5] This is also Desjardins's view.—*Geographie de la Gaule Romaine*,
II. 93.

[6] *Italische Landeskunde*, I. 156.

[7] See in particular the description of the Durance (XXI. 31), and
the remark on the greater steepness of the Italian slope of the Alps
(XXI. 35).

who appears to have faithfully copied out a good authority, takes Hannibal to Italy from the head of the Durance valley ; while Polybius, whose vague and colourless account deserves all that Dr. Arnold has said of it, can only be reconciled with Livy by one or two dubious expedients, and, on the whole, if he had anything definite in mind at all, appears to have had in mind the Mont Cenis.

It remains to state briefly the case as between the Mont Genèvre and the Col d'Argentière. To some of Mr. Freshfield's arguments—particularly those relating to the supposed difficulty about the Insubrians, which I think Neumann has successfully shown to be no difficulty at all—I attach but slight importance. But the personal impressions of a man with Mr. Freshfield's knowledge of the Alps have their weight, and Mr. Freshfield says :—"So far as I can judge, after having made a personal inspection of the routes, the natural features of this pass (Col d'Argentière) and its approaches agree better than those of any other with the account given of Hannibal's march by Polybius and Livy."[1] His great argument, however, and a really strong one, is the passage which he quotes from Varro.[2] "Alpes quinque viis Varro dicit transiri posse : una quæ est juxta mare per Liguras ; altera qua Hannibal transiit ; tertia qua Pompeius ad Hispaniense bellum profectus est ; quarta qua Hasdrubal de Gallia in Italiam venit ;[3] quinta quæ quondam a Græcis possessa est, quæ exinde Alpes Graiæ appellantur." Now this list certainly appears to give the passes in their geographical order from south to north, and if this is so, it is not easy to find a flaw in the interpretation of Mr. Freshfield, who reads them off as follows :—(a) Cornice ; (b) Argentière ; (c) Genèvre ; (d) Cenis ; (e) Little St. Bernard. In other words, an early and careful author like Varro expressly tells us that Hannibal crossed by the Col d'Argentière.

---

[1] *Alpine Journal*, XI. 290.

[2] Preserved by Servius on Virg. *Æn.*, X. 13.

[3] Hasdrubal seems to have made his way further north into Gaul than his brother, to judge from Livy, XXVII. 39—"non enim receperunt modo *Arverni* eum," etc.—and would therefore naturally cross by one of the northerly passes. It is perhaps worth mentioning that Appian, whose authority, however, on any geographical point is null, says, in contradiction to Varro, that Hasdrubal took the *same* pass as Hannibal.—Appian, *Hannibal*, 52.

A letter of Pompey, preserved by Sallust,[1] also says that he (Pompey) took a different route from that of Hannibal, and one more convenient to the Romans (nobis opportunius). Hermann Schiller[2] recognises the force of Freshfield's argument, but objects that the first of the passes mentioned by Varro may have been the Col di Tenda. This, however, would make no difference. The second pass to the northward would still be the Col d'Argentière. Nor will it do to make the Col di Tenda the second pass, as it is altogether out of the question that it should have been the pass used by Hannibal. On the whole, we must admit with Schiller[3] that "the chances of the Mont Genèvre and the Col d'Argentière have decidedly improved." I should be disposed to go even further, and to say that Mr. Freshfield, who has the advantage of being the last man to review the whole question in the light of his predecessors' labours and of his own personal experience—for I do not regard Colonel Perrin, with his Col du Clapier, as a serious rival—at present holds possession of the field.]

Note C, p. 35, l. 5.

There is a passage in the third volume of Niebuhr's Life, in a letter to the Count de Serre, in which he says that Hannibal at the Trebia acted like Napoleon at Marengo, throwing himself between the Romans and the line of their retreat, by Placentia and Ariminum. I believe that this is right, and that Hannibal was on the right bank of the Trebia between the Romans and Placentia, so that the expression in Livy is correct. The Romans had several emporia on the right bank of the Po, above Placentia, Clastidium, Victumviæ, etc. From these their army, I suppose, was fed; and the taking of Clastidium thus helped to force them to a battle. Polybius's words are equally clear with Livy's. The front of the Roman centre, he says, despaired of retreating to their own camp, κωλυόμενοι διὰ τὸν ποταμὸν καὶ τὴν ἐπιφορὰν καὶ συστροφὴν τοῦ κατὰ κεφαλὴν ὄμβρου· (the

---

[1] Sallust, *Fragm.* 4, quoted by Nissen, *Italische Landeskunde*, I. 156, note 3.

[2] In *Berliner Philologische Wochenschrift*, IV. 772.   [3] *Ibid.*

rain having made the river deeper than it had been in the morning) : τηροῦντες δὲ τὰς τάξεις ἀθρόοι μετ᾽ ἀσφαλείας ἀπεχώρησαν εἰς Πλακεντίαν. It is still a difficulty how Sempronius could have been allowed to effect his junction with Scipio while Hannibal was actually lying between them ; but I suppose that he must have turned off to the hills before he approached Placentia, and so have left Hannibal in the plain on his right.—*Author's Note.*

[The difficulty as regards this battle is whether the Roman camp was pitched on the right or left bank of the Trebia. The view of Niebuhr and Dr. Arnold is represented among recent writers by Ihne. The current view, which puts the Roman camp on the right bank, is thus stated by Mommsen (Engl. Trans. II. 117, note) : " Polybius's account of the battle on the Trebia is quite clear. If Placentia lay on the right bank of the Trebia where it falls into the Po, and if the battle was fought on the left bank while the Roman encampment was pitched upon the right (both of which points have been disputed, but are nevertheless indisputable), the Roman soldiers must certainly have passed the Trebia in order to gain Placentia, as well as to gain the camp. But those who crossed to the camp must have made their way through the disorganised portions of their own army and through the corps of the enemy that had gone round to their rear, and must then have crossed the river almost in hand to hand combat with the enemy. On the other hand, the passage near Placentia was accomplished after the pursuit had slackened ; the corps was several miles distant from the field of battle, and had arrived within reach of a Roman fortress ; it may even have been the case, although it cannot be proved, that a bridge led over the Trebia at that point,[1] and that the *tête de pont* on the other bank was occupied by the garrison of Placentia. It is evident that the first passage was just as difficult as the second was easy, and therefore with good reason Polybius, military judge as he was, merely says of the corps of

---

[1] Neumann, I think, disposes of this suggestion. The bed of the stream is excessively wide in its lower course, and the bridge would have been a colossal affair for that early period of the Roman settlement in Cisalpine Gaul. The present bridge consists of twenty-two arches and is nearly 500 yards long. See Neumann, 309, note 3.

10,000, that in close columns it cut its way to Placentia
(III. 74, 6), without mentioning the passage of the river
which in this case was unattended with difficulty. The
erroneousness of the view of Livy, which transfers the
Phenician camp to the right, the Roman to the left bank of
the Trebia, has lately been repeatedly pointed out." In
reality the question is by no means a simple one. After
the engagement of the Ticinus, Scipio crossed that river and
retired upon Placentia. Hannibal, on the other hand,
marched westwards along the Po till he came to a suitable
place, and there built a bridge of boats. He then marched
down the right bank. Two days brought him into the
neighbourhood of Scipio. On the third day he drew out in
line of battle in view of the Romans. They showed no
sign, and he accordingly pitched his camp above five miles
off. While he was thus stationary he received envoys from
the Boii, dwelling presumably about Parma and Mutina, to
the south-east of Placentia and the Trebia, on the way to
Ariminum. The next move came from Scipio, who marched
towards the Trebia, and the hilly ground adjoining it—
ὡς ἐπὶ τὸν Τρεβίαν ποταμὸν, καὶ τοὺς τούτῳ συνάπτοντας
γεωλόφους—with the idea of finding ground less suitable
than the neighbourhood of Placentia to Hannibal's formidable
cavalry. The Numidians attacked and burnt the empty
camp, thus giving the Romans time to cross the Trebia and
pitch their camp on the other side of it. Having accomplished this, Scipio waited for Sempronius, while Hannibal
stayed quietly in (apparently) a new camp which he had
pitched at the same distance of five miles from Scipio.
While the armies were in these positions Sempronius appears
to have joined Scipio with his army, marching from Ariminum, and Hannibal took by treachery the Roman stronghold of Clastidium, lying some twenty or thirty miles to the
westward from Placentia, higher up the valley of the Po.
Hannibal also attacked the Gauls dwelling 'between the
Trebia and the Po' (whatever that may mean), and devastated
their territory. They asked Sempronius for help, and he
crossed the Trebia to give it them. The Romans got the
best of it in the cavalry skirmish which ensued, and Hannibal, not being yet ready, declined a general engagement.
A day or two afterwards he not only accepted, but provoked

it. The Romans crossed the Trebia to fight him. The stream had been greatly swollen by rains in the mountains on the previous night, and ran breast-high, so that it could only with difficulty be forded. The rain continued all day (διὰ τὴν συνεχείαν τῆς νοτίδος, Polyb. III. 73, § 3), and even became fiercer (τὴν ἐπίφοραν καὶ σύστροφὴν τοῦ κατὰ κεφαλὴν ὄμβρου, Polyb. III. 74, § 5), finally changing into or being accompanied by snow (Polyb. III. 74, § 11). The battle turning against the Romans, 10,000 of them made their way safely to Placentia (Polyb. III. 74, § 6, μετ᾽ ἀσφαλείας ἀπεχώρησαν εἰς Πλακεντίαν).

The above is Polybius's account, and it will be seen that he omits the essential point. He tells us that Scipio crossed the Trebia twice—the first time to pitch his camp, the second time to fight the battle. But we are left to study the map and to weigh all the circumstances of the case before we can come to a probable conclusion as to the point which Polybius could have settled by a single word. Did Scipio cross from the right bank of the Trebia to the left to pitch his camp, and then recross it to fight the battle? or did he cross from left to right in the first place, and then from right to left? As has been seen, Dr. Arnold takes the former view, Mommsen the latter. Livy's account in the main agrees with that of Polybius, but he adds the very important detail (XXI. 56) that those survivors of the Roman army who had saved themselves by crossing the river and taking refuge in the Roman camp recrossed it again at night on rafts, and so got safely to Placentia. If, therefore, Livy knew the position of Placentia, he must have supposed that the Roman camp was on the left or west bank of the river, and that the battle took place on the right bank. Polybius in no way contradicts this; he simply leaves the point unsettled. The question therefore is, whether Livy's story will fit the geography, and is consistent with other features of the narrative. If the Roman camp was on the left bank of the river, the Carthaginian camp was on the right. In other words, Hannibal was between Scipio and his line of retreat. He was also between Scipio and Sempronius. He was just in the place to receive a legation from the Boii, who could not so easily have reached him if he had lain on the western bank of the Trebia, and if a Roman army had been posted between him

and their territory. But he was by no means in the place to
attack Clastidium, still less to use it as his granary while
he was encamped on the Trebia (Livy XXI. 48 : id horreum
fuit Pœnis sedentibus ad Trebiam). The junction of Sempronius with Scipio is also difficult to explain, as Dr. Arnold
has pointed out, if we suppose Hannibal to have been east
of the Trebia. Apparently nothing could in that case have
been easier than for Hannibal to prevent it. These are very
serious difficulties, but the other theory has its difficulties
also. The note which I have quoted from Mommsen's
Roman History is an attempt to explain away the most
obvious of these. If the battle took place upon the left
bank, then the 10,000 who fought their way through and
got safely to Placentia must have crossed the Trebia that
afternoon, in its lower course, in order to reach that stronghold. But by that time the mountain stream, swollen by
the rains of a night and day, must have been a truly formidable obstacle. An Apennine stream may be a mere thread
of water in a waste of stones in a dry summer season ; but
no streams fill with more tremendous rapidity even in summer, and it was then December. To this Neumann's answer
is : [1] "It is true that after rains, or in the winter season, the
Trebia pours a furious torrent from its mountain gorge, but
in the plain the mass of water expands over the ample space
of its wide-banked bed, so that even in flood the lower course
of the stream does not attain any considerable depth." It
is for those who have the requisite local knowledge to say
whether the answer is adequate ; I am content with pointing out that, if Mommsen's note is to hold good, it must be
supplemented by some such explanation. Another difficulty
is this. If Scipio's first camp was immediately under the
walls of Placentia, which is over two miles to the east of
the Trebia, he was on the right bank of that river. His
second camp, therefore, pitched after the river had been
crossed, was on the left bank. The battle accordingly took
place on the right bank, and the view of Niebuhr and Dr.
Arnold is correct. In order to get over this difficulty Neumann [2] says boldly that Scipio's first camp was on the left
bank of the Trebia. Yet the phrase of Polybius (III. 66)
is στρατοπεδεύσας περὶ πόλιν Πλακεντίαν, and the statement

----

[1] p. 308.   [2] p. 309.

that Scipio supposed himself to have brought his troops into a safe place—τὰς δυνάμεις εἰς ἀσφαλὲς ἀπηρεῖσθαι νομίζων— seems to refer to the immediate proximity of the fortress. Livy also (XXI. 47) says of the Roman troops, ‘Placentiam pervenere,’ and of the Carthaginian advanced guard, ‘Placentiam ad hostes contendunt.’   In face of these phrases Neumann sees the difficulty of supposing that the Roman camp was, in fact, on the other side of the Trebia, over two miles off, and he accordingly suggests [1] that both Livy and Polybius were ignorant of the true position of Placentia, and supposed it to have lain on the left bank of that river.   And yet, if either Polybius or Livy knew anything at all of the geography of this region, they surely must have known the position of the ancient and famous colony of Placentia.

It will be seen that there are difficulties in either theory, and that phrases like Mommsen’s ‘indisputable’ are out of place.]

Note D, p. 39, l. 24.

[It is agreed that Hannibal, starting from the northern side of the Apennines somewhere between Placentia and Bologna, crossed that range and the marshes of the Arno, and, marching by Flaminius, who was posted at Arretium, got between him and Servilius, who was marching from Ariminum towards Rome.   But there is a controversy as to the passage of the Apennines, and still more as to the passage of the marshes, different views being upheld by Nissen (*Rheinishes Museum*, XXII. 565-577), Faltin (*Hermes*, XX. 71-90, and *Berliner Philologische Wochenschrift*, IV. 1017 foll.), Voigt (*Philologische Wochenschrift*, III. 1580 foll.), and Neumann (pp. 330-333).   The general character of this part of the Apennines is thus indicated by Dr. Arnold (unpublished journal of his tour in Italy in 1827 ; extract dated Bologna, April 20, 1827) : “In the Alps the mountains are so high that it is out of the question to go right over them, and the road therefore threads the valleys till it can find some low point in the main ridge over which it can be carried. But in the Apennines you go straight across the whole width of the chain, and as they have a great number of projecting

---

[1] p. 318.

arms which wind about so as not to run at right angles with the main ridge, but often parallel to it, so the road in crossing these has several deep valleys to descend into, and then to mount again ; and from the top of the central ridge these great arms, with their intersecting valleys, form a magnificent variety of outline." The marsh district is thus described by Nissen (*Italische Landeskunde*, I. 232) : "The Arno is to the Apennines as the moat to the rampart. The district between the two falls into three wide basins, separated by parallel ridges. The Pisan hills (3001 feet) separate the coast from the Pescia valley, the Monte Albano (1886 feet) separates the Pescia valley from that of the Ombrone, and the mountains of Mugello, with their summit of Monte Giovi (3211 feet), separate the valley of the Ombrone from that of the Sieve." "The Serchio and Arno," says Neumann (p. 331), "have here formed a broad flood-belt, which, if it had not been tamed by cultivation, would have sunk into a wild and hideous morass. With the decline of Pisa in the Middle Ages that did actually once more come about, for the great marshes of Cascine di S. Bossone to the west of Pisa, and those of Viareggio north of the Serchio, have been transformed from swamp into corn-land only within this century. The many lakes and marshes which even now alternate in this region with cultivable land remind one that not so long ago land and water here struggled for the mastery. But in antiquity the marsh-land must have extended from the mouth of the Arno till past Empoli, a tract 32 miles long and about 13 miles broad, into which the Pisan hills pushed themselves forward, peninsula fashion, from the north, and from which the Cerbaia and a few smaller rocky knolls, like that one on which Pisa lay, rose like islands. Remnants of this vast morass are the Bientina lake, which even now is about 26 feet above the sea-level, and the Fucecchio marsh, through which the Maestro Canal conducts the waters of the Pescia to the Arno. The mass of detritus which the Arno carries with it has made the stream a clayey yellow. Its inundations and the consequent deposit gradually contributed to raise the level of the ground, till man's industry drained the soil and transformed the rich alluvium into the most smiling corn-land. But in antiquity, before the river had been embanked, the whole district must have been under water in the spring, whenever the flood-waters of the Arno poured from the gorge between Signa and Monte-lupo.   Even the higher level between Florence and Pistoia must have been then in great part flooded, since it was impossible for that narrow gorge to carry off the whole mass of waters fast enough."

A commander on the northern side of the Apennines, whose objective is the valley of the Lower Arno, has a choice of passes.   He can either take the easiest and most familiar pass of all, from Parma by way of La Cisa to Pontremoli and the river Magra, and so by Luna (between Lerici and Massa) and Lucca to Pisa; or he can take the more direct, but higher and more difficult, route from Regium Lepidum (Reggio) to Luna; or from Mutina (Modena) to Lucca by the valleys of the Secchia and Serchio; or from Bologna to Pistoia by the valley of the Reno, the route now followed by the railway; or from Faenza or from Forli direct upon Florence. The two last routes may be dismissed; they would have brought Hannibal too near to the Roman army at Ariminum. The Reggio route is unlikely; it seems to offer no advantages which are not offered by the Parma or Modena routes, and it is certainly more difficult.   But it is not so easy to decide whether Hannibal started from Parma or from Modena or from Bologna.   The question to a certain extent turns upon the interpretation of a passage in Livy (XXII. 2).   The passage runs : " Dum consul placandis Romæ dis habendoque dilectui dat operam, Hannibal profectus ex hibernis, quia jam Flaminium consulem Arretium pervenisse fama erat, cum aliud longius ceterum commodius ostenderetur iter, propiorem viam per paludes petit, qua fluvius Arnus per eos dies solito magis inundaverat."   If, in making this contrast between the 'shorter way' and the 'longer but easier' one, Livy was thinking of the passage of the Apennines, we must suppose him to have settled the matter against the route from Parma to Lucca by way of Pontremoli.   As compared with the Modena or Bologna route, this route would certainly have been *longius ceterum commodius*.   Accordingly Dr. Arnold (p. 39) says that Hannibal "crossed the Apennines, not by the ordinary road to Lucca, descending the valley of the Macra " (*i.e.* the road from Parma by way of Pontremoli), " but, as it appears, by a straighter line down the valley of the Auser or Serchio." In both cases the terminus was Lucca, but in the latter case the starting-point was Modena. But what if Livy was not thinking of the Apennines at all? I confess I see much plausibility in the view that both Livy and Polybius take the passage of the Apennines for granted, as having been accomplished without serious difficulty of any kind, and that Livy conceives Hannibal to have been at the *south* side of the Apennines at the time when he had to make his choice between the 'longer but more convenient route' and 'the nearer way through the marshes.' The Modena route was shorter, no doubt, but it is not easy to suppose that Livy could have described it as the 'nearer way through the marshes.' It led to, not through the marshes, just as much but no more than did the Parma route. On the whole, I think it probable that the choice of routes was intended by Livy to refer, not to the Apennines, but to the Arno valley. In that case we are left without any positive criterion to enable us to decide the respective claims of the three routes across the mountains. But, if Livy's language cannot be pleaded in favour of the Modena route, it must be admitted that the chances of that route are thereby lessened. If there is no positive evidence to be quoted in its favour, it can hardly maintain its own against the easier, though slightly longer pass from Parma. Remembering his experience on his first attempt to cross the Apennines,[1] Hannibal was likely to prefer the lower and easier pass, even if it was a little longer. Livy and Polybius tell us so little that certainty is by no means attainable, but the probabilities seem to me to point to either the Parma or the Bologna route. The latter is preferred by Nissen, the former by Neumann, Voigt, and Faltin. The final choice must depend on the view taken of Hannibal's route through the marsh-land, and of the line of march followed by him, after he had extricated himself from it, with the object of throwing himself between Flaminius and that general's line of retreat. I will state briefly the opposing views.

Nissen takes Hannibal across the Apennines from Bologna to Pistoia, and thence through the wide valley of the

---

[1] See p. 36. The reality of this attempt has been doubted, but without sufficient ground. See Faltin, "Der Einbruch Hannibals in Etrurien," in *Hermes*, XX. 73, 74.

Ombrone to Fæsulæ. The pivot of his argument is the importance which he attributes to the position of Pisa. Pisa on the west coast corresponded to Ariminum on the east ; the one guarded the Apennines, the other the Po, and each was the terminus of a great Roman road, with advanced posts pushed still further forward. The advanced posts of Ariminum were Cremona and Placentia ; of Pisa, Luna and Lucca. Moreover, Pisa was not less important as a port—and a port intended primarily for warlike purposes—than as the key of the Apennines. It follows with something like certainty that the place was strongly garrisoned and fortified.[1] In Nissen's view Pisa and Lucca, being connected by a difficult river, make up a single defensive position, as regards the Apennines, between them. Lucca itself commanded the passage of the Serchio and the Apennine road from Modena, while the outpost of Luna commanded (a) the coast road, (b) the road from Parma by Pontremoli, (c) the short but difficult route from Reggio. Now, with the Romans strongly posted at Pisa (Lucca, Luna) and at Arretium, Hannibal's game obviously was to strike in between those two positions. He could not waste his time and weary his Gauls by besieging and reducing Lucca and Pisa. We must therefore look for a route which should bring him to the Arno at a point to the east of that strong position. At Pistoia two roads debouch from the hills, one coming from Bologna, the other from Modena. The latter is difficult and easily blocked, and the probabilities lie with the former, the feasibility of which is confirmed by the fact that it is the present railway route. It is not much over twenty miles from Pistoia to Fæsulæ, but if those miles were all swamp, Hannibal might well have spent four days and three nights over them. All this region was an unsettled border district, exposed to the incursions of the Ligurians, and may well have fallen back into swamp, even though there may be ground for thinking that under Etrurian rule it had long previously been reclaimed and civilised. From Fæsulæ Hannibal moved southward along the valley of the Arno.

The writers who have discussed the subject since the appearance of Nissen's famous essay, agree in taking Hanni-

---

[1] For the military importance of Pisa consult the references given by Nissen, *Rhein. Mus.*, XXII. 566.

bal across the Apennines from Parma to Lucca, and discard the Bologna-Pistoia route, mainly from the conviction that the distance (from Pistoia to Fæsulæ) is too small for Hannibal to have spent four days and three nights on the march before finding firm ground near Fæsulæ. But having brought him to Lucca, they differ as to his future route. Neumann (pp. 332, 333) takes him from Lucca in a south-easterly direction to Monte Albano, thence to the neighbourhood of Florence, and thence by San Casciano, Greve, and Monte San Savino to the Val Chiana. Voigt takes him from Lucca to Florence by way of Pescia and Pistoia. Faltin's view is that the Ombrone basin was too near to Flaminius at Arretium and too important for it to have been possible for Flaminius to neglect it. He thinks that Pisa was garrisoned, and that the neighbourhood of Fæsulæ, if not held in force, was at least carefully watched. It is therefore, he holds, necessary to bring Hannibal from the north to the south side of the Arno valley on a line some-where between Pisa and Fæsulæ, and at a safe distance from both. Faltin accordingly takes him from Lucca to Empoli. When Hannibal was at Lucca he had the choice between the two routes, the 'longer but more convenient one' by Pescia, Pistoia, Prato, to Florence, and the 'nearer way through the marshes.' The former would have enabled him to cling to the feet of the hills, and to secure firm camping-ground at night. The latter involved terrible sufferings, but it was shorter, and it had the prime merit of enabling Hannibal to elude Roman observation altogether. He might well have taken as much as four days and three nights to reach Empoli from Lucca across the marshes. Once at Empoli he took the Elsa valley and marched by Siena to Fojano. The rich lands which he devastated were in the Val Chiana, not in the narrow valley of the upper Arno, and he did not begin the work of destruction till he had reached a point south of Flaminius, and had cut off his line of retreat to Rome. The 'Fæsulas petens' of Livy (XXII. 3) is against this theory, but in reality the passage is quite inexplicable on the sup-position that Livy meant the Fæsulæ near Florence, and Faltin assumes the existence of another Fæsulæ in the neighbourhood of Cortona.[1]

[1] The Fæsulæ of the Gallic War, B.C. 225 (Polybius, II. 25), can-not be the Fæsulæ near Florence. In a note on this battle Dr. Arnold

The chief difficulty in the way of Faltin's view is that it presupposes that Lucca was left open, while Pisa was garrisoned. This is not impossible, but it is unlikely, and I regard the difficulty as serious. If Lucca was strongly held, it surely could have blocked all the western passes, and we are then driven to suppose either that Hannibal took the Bologna route, or that he diverged from one of the western passes and came down by a circuitous route upon Pescia. It will be seen that all the recent writers think it necessary to bring Hannibal to the south of Flaminius by another route than that of the Arno valley. Neumann takes him by Greve and San Savino, Faltin by the valley of the Elsa and Siena, while Höfler lets him march up the Arno as far as Montevarchi, but thence takes him up the Ambra valley to Siena, and so into the Val Chiana. It is indeed hardly conceivable that Hannibal could have simply marched past Flaminius at Arretium without being forced to accept battle, not, as at Thrasymenus, in a position chosen by himself, but in one chosen by the Roman general, and it is almost necessary to suppose that Hannibal left the Arno valley either below Florence or shortly above it. In that case he would leave the Romans on his left—'lævâ relicto hoste,' says Livy (XXII. 3)—and come down unperceived and unexpected upon their rear.]

Note E, p. 41, l. 24.

Niebuhr, in the letter quoted in note C, speaks of the following view of Thrasymenus as absolutely certain. Flaminius with Servilius was originally at Ariminum, expecting Hannibal by that road. But when he heard that Hannibal had entered Etruria by the marshes of the Lower Arno, he hastened over the Apennines to Arezzo, eager to cover the road to Rome. He moved then by Cortona upon Perugia ; but Hannibal turned to the right and followed the western side of the lake towards Chiusi ; then, turning short

(III. 474) says : "The text of Polybius (II. 25) places this battle at *Fæsulæ ;* this should clearly be corrected into *Rusellæ.* The Italian names of places in our manuscripts of Polybius are continually corrupt." The 'Fæsulanus ager' of Sallust, *Cat.,* 43 (see Dietsch's note, and Mannert, *Geographie der Griechen und Römer,* I. 396) also points to another Fæsulæ.

round, occupied the defile of Passignano, and spreading out his right upon the hills, forced the long Roman column by a flank attack into the lake, while he engaged the head of it in the defile. Polybius and Livy differ decidedly as to the scene of the main battle: the latter represents it as taking place in the defile of Passignano, where the Romans had their right flank to the lake. But Polybius says that only the rear was caught there; most of the army had cleared the defile and turned to the left into a valley running down at right angles to the lake, so that the lake was exactly on their rear. And the modern road does so turn from the lake to ascend the hills towards Perugia: the only difficulty is (I have been twice on the ground) that there is nothing that can be called a valley; for the road ascends almost from the edge of the lake: still it is true that the hills do form a small combe, so that an army ascending from the lake might have an enemy on both its flanks on the hillsides above it.—*Author's Note*.

["Thrasymenus is a noble lake in point of size, and some of the hills round it are well wooded. Its sides, however, are reedy, and the air on the banks is unwholesome. The scene of the battle is either where the road leaves the lake to go up the hill to Magione, or else at some further point beyond the point at which the modern road leaves it: Sanguinetto is clearly *not* the place."[1] "At Thrasymenus I thought as before of the scene of the battle, except that it struck me that the road between Passignano and the head of the lake runs for some way so completely hemmed in between the cliff and the water that it seems impossible to fancy that any general could have passed blindfold through a spot so perilous. The whole question turns on the line of the ancient road, which nothing but very careful investigation on the spot can ascertain; if it followed the present line certainly the battle was fought at the foot of the hill by which you now ascend to Magione; if, on the other hand, it left the lake at an earlier point, without passing through Passignano, then Sanguinetto may have been the scene."[2]

---

[1] Dr. Arnold's unpublished journal of tour in Italy in 1825; extract dated Perugia, July 19, 1825.

[2] Dr. Arnold's unpublished journal of tour in Italy in 1827; extract dated May 11, 1827.

The modern discussion of this subject was started by the publication of Nissen's essay, 'Die Schlacht am Trasimenus,' in 1867 (*Rheinisches Museum*, XXII. 565-586), and has been continued by H. Peter (*Historicorum Romanorum Relliquiæ*, I. ccxxvi.), Neumann (pp. 332-336), Höfler (*Sitzungsberichte der K. Akademie der Wissenschaften*, p. 13 foll. Vienna, 1870), Voigt (*Philologische Wochenschrift* for 1883, III. 1580-1598), Stürenburg (*De Romanorum cladibus Trasumenna et Cannensi*, Leipsic, 1883), and Faltin (*Rheinisches Museum*, XXXIX. 260-273, and *Berliner Philologische Wochenschrift*, IV. 1017, foll.) The general result has been to weaken the authority of Polybius and to raise that of Livy. It would seem that Polybius's account obliges us to lay the scene of the battle between Torricella and Magione, but it is to be observed that Höfler, who shares with Dr. Arnold the advantage of having been more than once upon the ground, positively declares that the valley as described by Polybius exists only upon paper. Dr. Arnold's remarks are more cautious, but, as will be seen by a reference to p. 41, they come to much the same thing. As to Livy's account, it is now almost universally agreed that that writer put the battle on the north shore, in the neighbourhood of Tuoro. As the modern discussion of the whole question is scattered mainly in periodicals and dissertations, and is not easy of access to many students, I proceed to summarise it.

According to Nissen, Flaminius did quite rightly in breaking up his camp at Arretium and moving south in order to join Servilius, who meanwhile had left Ariminum, somewhere about Perugia, so that combined they might crush Hannibal. He could not let Hannibal make himself master of the Flaminian road without a struggle. It is true he underrated Hannibal, but that, at the time, was pardonable. The natural route from Arretium to the Flaminian road lay by way of Lake Thrasymenus, and this Flaminius followed. On the north-western corner of the lake the spurs of Gualandro come down almost to the water, while on the north-east the heights of Passignano descend even more directly to the water's edge. Between Gualandro and Passignano the ground is of the shape of an antique bow, the hill on which Tuoro stands projecting far enough into the comparatively level ground to form two basins of about equal size. Hannibal took up his position on the Tuoro hill, placed his Balearic slingers and other light-armed troops at Passignano, the Gauls and all the cavalry on Gualandro. The attack began after Flaminius had passed to the east of the southernmost spurs of Gualandro, and while the greater part of his army was in the first basin, between Gualandro and Tuoro. The Roman advanced guard forced it way through the enemy past Passignano, while the Roman rear was driven into the defile by the charge of Hannibal's cavalry. This is all in accordance with Livy, who distinctly represents the Romans as having the lake on their flank. But Polybius describes the scene of the battle as a narrow valley, with the lake at the entrance of it, closed at its further extremity by a hill, and commanded by high ridges on either side. According to him the Romans fought with their backs to the lake and their faces to a hill on which Hannibal was posted. Nissen admits that this is Polybius's conception of the battle, but attempts to reconcile the two stories by the supposition that Polybius's authority was a Roman present at the battle, and that that Roman described the battle from the point of view of a participator in it. That is to say, when the Romans, advancing from west to east along the northern shore of the lake, were first attacked, they turned to the left so as to face the bulk of their enemy at Tuoro, while their backs were towards the lake.

Stürenburg in the main follows Nissen, but he holds that Polybius must be thrown over, and rejects Nissen's attempt to reconcile him with Livy by the expedient I have just explained. Polybius, who takes the main Roman army quite away from the lake, imagines a long, narrow valley with heights on both sides, closed in front by the hill on which Hannibal was posted, and with the lake behind. But there is nothing like that on the ground. Stürenburg holds that Polybius either misunderstood his authorities, or arbitrarily invented the whole scene in order to suit preconceptions of his own, and P. Meyer, who reviews his essay in the *Philologische Wochenschrift*, III. 680-683, agrees with him. Stürenburg's other point of difference from Nissen is that he puts the Gauls and cavalry on the *east* side only of Gualandro. Faltin (*Rheinisches Museum*, XXIX. 260-273) throws over Polybius and follows Livy. The only mistake he finds in Livy is in XXII. 4, § 7—'in frontem *lateraque* pugnari cœptum.' It was only on one flank that there was fighting, not on both, as the Roman right flank was covered by the lake. Faltin posts Hannibal in the recess or basin, east of Tuoro, the Baleares on the Tuoro hill, the Gauls on the east side only of Gualandro. and leaves Passignano unguarded. He further cuts the words παρὰ τὴν λίμνην out of Polybius's text (III. 83, § 2) as inconsistent with the rest of his account.

Voigt, whose lecture on the battle is published in the *Philologische Wochenschrift*, III. 1580 foll., defends Polybius, and maintains Torricella-Magione as the scene of the battle. He urges that Polybius knew Etruria exceptionally well, and that his account of that country is copied by Strabo. He lays stress on Livy's 'lateraque,' which he says is not explicable on Livy's own theory of the battle, but is on that of Polybius. He is convinced that the accounts of Livy and Polybius are irreconcilable. Of course Polybius's account will not fit the northern shore of the lake, but it will fit the road from Torricella to Magione, running between the steep heights of Monte del Lago and Colognola. This position also explains Livy's 'ex saltu evasere' (XXII. 6, § 8); the 'paulo latior campus' of Livy (XXII. 4, § 2) is at the opening of the valley on the lake at Torricella.

Faltin finally (*Berliner Philologische Wochenschrift*, IV. 1017 foll.) reviews and criticises Voigt. He makes the point that *Torricella is too far off.* Polybius does not give the Roman army time to get through (*a*) the defile of Gualandro; (*b*) the open northern shore; (*c*) a second defile 2½ to 4 miles long, before it reached the scene of battle. Polybius seems to know nothing of the open northern shore. It may be admitted that the Torricella valley has steep heights on either side, and so far answers to the description of Polybius. But how about the αὐλὼν ἐπίπεδος (Polyb. III. 83, § 1), and 'paulo latior campus' (Livy, XXII. 4, § 2)? The small opening of the Torricella valley could hardly have been thus described; and the idea of cavalry on the steep hillside above the Passignano defile is ridiculous. If Polybius had Torricella in view, he has shown himself a very incompetent topographer, for the essential feature—the open space at the end of the defile, and at the beginning of

the valley—is wanting.   Most of Voigt's objections to Livy
are only objections to Nissen's interpretation of him.   There
is nothing wrong about Livy's 'e saltu evasere.'   The
'saltus' is the 'paulo latior campus.'   (This last statement
is highly questionable.)

It only remains to draw attention, with Peter (I. ccxxvii.),
to Livy's description of the place of ambush as 'ubi maxime
montes Cortonenses Trasumennus subit.'   Unless Livy had
an altogether erroneous map in his head, this phrase makes
it certain that, for him, the scene of the battle was the
northern shore.   I purposely avoid pronouncing between
the different views I have summarised, as I am strongly of
opinion that the question is now in a state at which it can
only be advanced by some scholar with the opportunity and
inclination to make a thorough and leisurely personal examination of the ground, texts in hand.   I subjoin the latter.

Livy, XXII. 4-6 :—"Hannibal, quod agri est inter Cortonam
urbem Trasumennumque lacum, omni clade belli pervastat, quo
magis iram hosti ad vindicandas sociorum iniurias acuat; et iam
pervenerant ad loca nata insidiis, ubi maxime montes Cortonenses
Trasumennus subit.   Via tantum interest perangusta, velut ad
id ipsum de industria relicto spatio; deinde paulo latior patescit
campus; inde colles insurgunt.   Ibi castra in aperto locat, ubi
ipse cum Afris modo Hispanisque consideret; Baliares ceteramque
levem armaturam post montes circumducit; equites ad ipsas fauces
saltus, tumulis apte tegentibus, locat, ut, ubi intrassent Romani,
obiecto equitatu clausa omnia lacu ac montibus essent.

"Flaminius quum pridie solis occasu ad lacum pervenisset, in ex-
plorato postero die vixdum satis certa luce angustiis superatis,
postquam in patentiorem campum pandi agmen coepit, id tantum
hostium, quod ex adverso erat, conspexit; ab tergo ac super caput
deceptæ[1] insidiæ.   Pœnus ubi, id quod petierat, clausum lacu ac
montibus et circumfusum suis copiis habuit hostem, signum
omnibus dat simul invadendi.   Qui ubi, qua cuique proximum
fuit, decucurrerunt, eo magis Romanis subita atque improvisa res
fuit, quod orta ex lacu nebula campo quam montibus densior
sederat, agminaque hostium ex pluribus collibus ipsa inter se satis
conspecta eoque magis pariter decucurrerant.   Romanus clamore
prius undique orto, quam satis cerneret, se circumventum esse
sensit, et ante in frontem lateraque pugnari coeptum est, quam

---

[1] *Decepere*, Lipsius; *haud dispectæ*, Zingerle.

satis instrueretur acies aut expediri arma stringique gladii possent.
Consul, perculsis omnibus, ipse satis, ut in *re* trepida, impavidus
turbatos ordines, vertente se quoque ad dissonos clamores, instruit,
ut tempus locusque patitur, et quacunque adire audirique potest,
adhortatur ac stare ac pugnare iubet : nec enim inde votis aut
imploratione deum, sed vi ac virtute evadendum esse ; per medias
acies ferro viam fieri et, quo timoris minus sit, eo minus ferme
periculi esse.   Ceterum præ strepitu ac tumultu nec consilium nec
imperium accipi poterat, tantumque aberat, ut sua signa atque
ordines et locum noscerent, ut vix ad arma capienda aptandaque
pugnæ competeret animus, opprimerenturque quidam onerati magis
iis quam tecti.   Et erat in tanta caligine maior usus aurium quam
oculorum.   Ad gemitus vulneratorum ictusque corporum aut
armorum et mixtos strepentium paventiumque clamores circum-
ferebant ora oculosque.   Alii fugientes pugnantium globo illati
hærebant ; alios redeuntes in pugnam avertebat fugientium agmen.
Deinde, ubi in omnes partes nequicquam impetus capti, et ab
lateribus montes ac lacus, a fronte et ab tergo hostium acies
claudebat, apparuitque, nullam nisi in dextera ferroque salutis
spem esse, tum sibi quisque dux adhortatorque factus ad rem
gerendam et nova de integro exorta pugna est, non illa ordinata
per principes hastatosque ac triarios, nec ut pro signis antesignani,
post signa alia pugnaret acies, nec ut in sua legione miles aut
cohorte aut manipulo esset ; fors conglobabat et animus suus cuique
ante aut post pugnandi ordinem dabat, tantusque fuit ardor ani-
morum, adeo intentus pugnæ [animus], ut eum motum terræ, qui
multarum urbium Italiæ magnas partes prostravit avertitque cursu
rapidos amnes, mare flumiuibus invexit, montes lapsu ingenti
proruit, nemo pugnantium senserit.

"Tres ferme horas pugnatum est et ubique atrociter ; circa
consulem tamen acrior infestiorque pugna est.   Eum et robora
virorum sequebantur, et ipse, quacunque in parte premi ac laborare
senserat suos, impigre ferebat opem, insignemque armis et hostes
summa vi petebant et tuebantur cives, donec Insuber eques (Ducario
nomen erat) facie quoque noscitans consulem, "*En*" inquit "hic
est" popularibus suis, "qui legiones nostras cecidit agrosque et
urbem est depopulatus ; iam ego hanc victimam manibus per-
emptorum fœde civium dabo."   Subditisque calcaribus equo per
confertissimam hostium turbam impetum facit, obtruncatoque prius
armigero, qui se infesto venienti obviam obiecerat, consulem lancea
transfixit ; spoliare cupientem triarii obiectis scutis arcuere.   Mag-
næ partis fuga inde primum cœpit ; et iam nec lacus nec montes
pavori obstabant ; per omnia arta præruptaque velut cæci evadunt.

armaque et viri super alium alii præcipitantur. Pars magna, ubi locus fugæ deest, per prima vada paludis in aquam progressi, quoad capitibus humerisque exstare possunt, sese immergunt; fuere, quos inconsultus pavor nando etiam capessere fugam impulerit; quæ ubi immensa ac sine spe erat, aut deficientibus animis hauriebantur gurgitibus aut nequicquam fessi vada retro ægerrime repetebant, atque ibi ab ingressis aquam hostium equitibus passim trucidabantur. Sex millia ferme primi agminis, per adversos hostes eruptione impigre facta, ignari omnium, quæ post se agerentur, ex saltu evasere, et quum in tumulo quodam constitissent, clamorem modo ac sonum armorum audientes, quæ fortuna pugnæ essent, neque scire nec perspicere præ caligine poterant. Inclinata denique re, quum incalescente sole dispulsa nebula aperuisset diem, tum liquida iam luce montes campique perditas res stratamque ostendere fœde Romanam aciem. Itaque ne in conspectos procul immitteretur eques, sublatis raptim signis, quam citatissimo poterant agmine, sese abripuerunt. Postero die, quum super cetera extrema fames etiam instaret, fidem dante Maharbale, qui cum omnibus equestribus copiis nocte consecutus erat, si arma tradidissent, abire cum singulis vestimentis passurum, sese dediderunt; quæ Punica religione servata fides ab Hannibale est, atque in vincula omnes coniecti."

Polybius III. 82 § 9-84.—ὅ γε μὴν ᾿Αννίβας ἅμα μὲν εἰς τοὔμπροσθεν ὡς πρὸς τὴν ῾Ρώμην προῄει διὰ τῆς Τυρρηνίας, εὐώνυμον μὲν πόλιν ἔχων τὴν προσαγορευομένην Κυρτώνιον καὶ τὰ ταύτης ὄρη, δεξιὰν δὲ τὴν Ταρσιμέννην καλουμένην λίμνην· ἅμα δὲ προάγων ἐπυρπόλει καὶ κατέφθειρε τὴν χώραν, βουλόμενος ἐκκαλέσασθαι τὸν θυμὸν τῶν ὑπεναντίων. ἐπεὶ δὲ τὸν Φλαμίνιον ἤδη συνάπτοντα καθεώρα, τόπους δ' εὐφυεῖς συνεθεώρησε πρὸς τὴν χρείαν, ἐγίνετο πρὸς τὸ διακινδυνεύειν. ὄντος δὲ κατὰ τὴν δίοδον αὐλῶνος ἐπιπέδου, τούτου δὲ παρὰ μὲν τὰς εἰς μῆκος πλευρὰς ἑκατέρας βουνοὺς ἔχοντος ὑψηλοὺς καὶ συνεχεῖς, παρὰ δὲ τὰς εἰς πλάτος κατὰ μὲν τὴν ἀντικρὺ λόφον ἐπικείμενον ἐρυμνὸν καὶ δύσβατον, κατὰ δὲ τὴν ἀπ' οὐρᾶς λίμνην τελείως στενὴν ἀπολείπουσαν πάροδον ὡς εἰς τὸν αὐλῶνα παρὰ τὴν παρώρειαν, διελθὼν τὸν αὐλῶνα παρὰ τὴν λίμνην,[1] τὸν μὲν κατὰ πρόσωπον τῆς πορείας λόφον αὐτὸς κατελάβετο, καὶ τοὺς ῎Ιβηρας καὶ τοὺς Λίβυας ἔχων ἐπ' αὐτοῦ κατεστρατοπέδευσε, τοὺς δὲ Βαλιαρεῖς καὶ λογχοφόρους κατὰ τὴν πρωτοπορείαν ἐκπεριάγων ὑπὸ τοὺς ἐν δεξιᾷ βουνοὺς τῶν παρὰ τὸν αὐλῶνα κειμένων, ἐπὶ πολὺ παρατείνας ὑπέστειλε, τοὺς δ' ἱππεῖς καὶ τοὺς Κελτοὺς ὁμοίως τῶν εὐωνύμων βουνῶν κύκλῳ περιαγαγὼν παρεξέτεινε συνεχεῖς, ὥστε τοὺς ἐσχάτους εἶναι κατ' αὐτὴν τὴν εἴσοδον τὴν παρά τε τὴν λίμνην καὶ τὰς παρωρείας φέρουσαν εἰς τὸν προειρημένον τόπον.

---

[1] See p. 388.

'ο μὲν οὖν 'Αννίβας, ταῦτα προκατασκευασάμενος τῆς νυκτὸς καὶ περιειληφὼς τὸν αὐλῶνα ταῖς ἐνέδραις, τὴν ἡσυχίαν εἶχεν. ὁ δὲ Φλαμίνιος εἵπετο κατόπιν, σπεύδων συνάψαι [τῶν πολεμίων]· κατεστρατοπεδευκὼς δὲ τῇ προτεραίᾳ πρὸς αὐτῇ τῇ λίμνῃ τελέως ὀψὲ τῆς ὥρας, μετὰ ταῦτα τῆς ἡμέρας ἐπιγενομένης, εὐθέως ὑπὸ τὴν ἑωθινὴν ἦγε τὴν πρωτοπορείαν παρὰ τὴν λίμνην εἰς τὸν ὑποκείμενον αὐλῶνα, βουλόμενος ἐξάπτεσθαι τῶν πολεμίων. οὔσης δὲ τῆς ἡμέρας ὁμιχλώδους διαφερόντως, 'Αννίβας ἅμα τῷ τὸ πλεῖστον μέρος τῆς πορείας εἰς τὸν αὐλῶνα προσδέξασθαι καὶ συνάπτειν πρὸς αὐτὸν ἤδη τὴν τῶν ἐναντίων πρωτοπορείαν, ἀποδοὺς τὰ συνθήματα καὶ διαπεμψάμενος πρὸς τοὺς ἐν ταῖ ἐνέδραις, συνεπεχείρει πανταχόθεν ἅμα τοῖς πολεμίοις. οἱ δὲ περὶ τὸν Φλαμίνιον παραδόξου γενομένης αὐτοῖς τῆς ἐπιφανείας, ἔτι δὲ δυσσυνόπτου τῆς κατὰ τὸν ἀέρα περιστάσεως ὑπαρχούσης, καὶ τῶν πολεμίων κατὰ πολλοὺς τόπους ἐξ ὑπερδεξίου καταφερομένων καὶ προσπιπτόντων, οὐχ οἷον παραβοηθεῖν ἐδύναντο πρός τι τῶν δεομένων οἱ ταξίαρχοι καὶ χιλίαρχοι τῶν 'Ρωμαίων, ἀλλ' οὐδὲ συννοῆσαι τὸ γινόμενον. ἅμα γὰρ οἱ μὲν κατὰ πρόσωπον, οἱ δ' ἀπ' οὐρᾶς, οἱ δ' ἐκ τῶν πλαγίων αὐτοῖς προσέπιπτον, διὸ καὶ συνέβη τοὺς πλείστους ἐν αὐτῷ τῷ τῆς πορείας σχήματι κατακοπῆναι, μὴ δυναμένους αὐτοῖς βοηθεῖν, ἀλλ' ὡς ἂν εἰ προδεδομένους ὑπὸ τῆς τοῦ προεστῶτος ἀκρισίας. ἔτι γὰρ διαβουλευόμενοι τί δεῖ πράττειν ἀπώλλυντο παραδόξως. ἐν ᾧ καιρῷ καὶ τὸν Φλαμίνιον αὐτὸν δυσχρηστούμενον καὶ περικακοῦντα τοῖς ὅλοις προσπεσόντες τινὲς τῶν Κελτῶν ἀπέκτειναν. ἔπεσον οὖν τῶν 'Ρωμαίων κατὰ τὸν αὐλῶνα σχεδὸν εἰς μυρίους καὶ πεντακισχιλίους, οὔτ' εἴκειν τοῖς παροῦσιν οὔτε πράττειν οὐδὲν δυνάμενοι, τοῦτο δ' ἐκ τῶν ἐθισμῶν αὐτὸ περὶ πλείστου ποιούμενοι, τὸ μὴ φεύγειν μηδὲ λείπειν τὰς τάξεις. οἱ δὲ κατὰ πορείαν μεταξὺ τῆς λίμνης καὶ τῆς παρωρείας ἐν τοῖς στενοῖς συγκλεισθέντες αἰσχρῶς, ἔτι δὲ μᾶλλον ταλαιπώρως διεφθείροντο. συνωθούμενοι [μὲν] γὰρ εἰς τὴν λίμνην οἱ μὲν διὰ τὴν παράστασιν τῆς διανοίας ὁρμῶντες ἐπὶ τὸ νήχεσθαι σὺν τοῖς ὅπλοις ἀπεπνίγοντο, τὸ δὲ πολὺ πλῆθος μέχρι μὲν τοῦ δυνατοῦ προβαῖνον εἰς τὴν λίμνην ἔμενε τὰς κεφαλὰς αὐτὰς ὑπὲρ τὸ ὑγρὸν ὑπερίσχον· ἐπιγενομένων δὲ τῶν ἱππέων, καὶ προδήλου γενομένης ἀπωλείας, ἐξαίροντες τὰς χεῖρας καὶ δεόμενοι ζωγρεῖν καὶ πᾶσαν προϊέμενοι φωνὴν τὸ τελευταῖον οἱ μὲν ὑπὸ τῶν πολεμίων, τινὲς δὲ παρακαλέσαντες αὐτοὺς διεφθάρησαν. ἑξακισχίλιοι δ' ἴσως τῶν κατὰ τὸν αὐλῶνα τοὺς κατὰ πρόσωπον νικήσαντες παραβοηθεῖν μὲν τοῖς ἰδίοις καὶ περιίστασθαι τοὺς ὑπεναντίους ἠδυνάτουν, διὰ τὸ μηδὲν συνορᾶν τῶν γινομένων, καίπερ μεγάλην δυνάμενοι πρὸς τὰ ὅλα παρέχεσθαι χρείαν· ἀεὶ δὲ τοῦ πρόσθεν ὀρεγόμενοι, προῆγον πεπεισμένοι συμπεσεῖσθαί τισιν, ἕως ἔλαθον ἐκπεσόντες πρὸς τοὺς ὑπερδεξίους τόπους. γενόμενοι δ' ἐπὶ τῶν ἄκρων, καὶ τῆς ὁμίχλης ἤδη πεπτωκυίας, συνέντες τὸ γεγονὸς ἀτύχημα, καὶ ποιεῖν οὐδὲν ὄντες ἔτι δυνατοὶ διὰ τὸ τοῖς ὅλοις ἐπικρατεῖν καὶ πάντα προκατέχειν ἤδη τοὺς πολεμίους, συσ-

τραφέντες ἀπεχώρησαν εἴς τινα κώμην Τυρρηνίδα. μετὰ δὲ τὴν μάχην
ἀποσταλέντος ὑπὸ τοῦ στρατηγοῦ μετὰ τῶν Ἰβήρων καὶ λογχοφόρων
Μαάρβα καὶ περιστρατοπεδεύσαντος τὴν κώμην, ποικίλης αὐτοῖς ἀπορίας
περιεστώσης, ἀποθέμενοι τὰ ὅπλα παρέδοσαν αὐτοὺς ὑποσπόνδους, ὡς
τευξόμενοι τῆς σωτηρίας.]

Note F, p. 55, l. 20.

[An attempt has been made by Professor F. Voigt
(*Berliner Philologische Wochenschrift*, IV. 1561 foll.) to
work out this part of the campaign in detail. Professor
Voigt, who follows Polybius all through, and who maintains
his narrative of these events to be a much better one than
that of Livy, gives the following account of what took place
between Hannibal's leaving Apulia for Campania and his
escape from the trap laid for him by Fabius :—Hannibal,
starting from Arpi, went through the country of the Hirpini,
past Beneventum, to Telesia. The direct road by Æquum
Tuticum and Forum Novum was no doubt barred by Fabius,
who lay encamped at Æcae. Hannibal, therefore, made
a wide circuit by way of Aquilonia. The reason for bringing
him into the Ager Falernus from Telesia is that Polybius
tells us he came by way of the Mons Eribianus, which can
be plausibly identified with the *massif* north of Telesia, one
of whose summits is still called Monte Erbano. We finally
find Hannibal in the Ager Falernus, north of the river Vulturnus, with his camp pitched near Casilinum. Fabius
followed, and Hannibal found himself in a trap, with a deep
river on the south—he would certainly have crossed the
Vulturnus unless either (*a*) it was unfordable, or (*b*) the
attempt was too dangerous to be made in the neighbourhood
of a hostile army—the sea on the west, and hills on the
north and east. The possible exits were—1. The road on
the north bank of the Vulturnus, by which Hannibal had
come. 2. The Via Appia on the coast. 3. The road over
the Mons Massicus by Suessa. 4. The road by Teanum,
between Massicus and the eastern ridge which continues the
Mons Tifata across the stream, and of which the highest
part is now known as Monte Maggiore. Fabius posted himself on the eastern side of Massicus, and sent Minucius to
close the Appian road and Suessa pass. He himself was in

the neighbourhood of Teanum, and therefore guarded the easiest and most obvious exit of all. He also strengthened the garrison of Casilinum and occupied the hill Callicula with 4000 men. This last must mean the hill abutting on the north bank of the Vulturnus, east of Casilinum, and commanding the river road. Hannibal sent the oxen over the depression by Bellona—a depression marked enough to account for this hill (Callicula) having a special name of its own—where there is a footpath, and thus drew off the attention of the strong Roman guard, while he himself quietly followed the river road. Fabius, with the bulk of his army, could not have been very near, or he would have done more, particularly against the Spaniards on the following morning. But he had to guard the wide exit by Teanum, and probably did not venture nearer to the Vulturnus than Cales.]

Note G, p. 71, last line.

[In this passage and on p. 73, where the Romans are spoken of as 'badly armed, without cuirasses, with light and brittle spears, and with shields made only of ox-hide,' several points of interest are raised as to the Roman armament. The first difficulty is contained in the description of the helmets 'now uncovered for battle.' It would appear that Roman soldiers on the march were accustomed to carry their helmets in a leather covering hanging from their chests. See Rheinhard's note to his edition (Stuttgart, 1881) of Cæsar, B. G., II. 21. The use of shield-cases—*involucrum* —is more familiar, and supported by a greater number of authorities ; but helmet-cases seem to have been used as well. A passage in Plutarch—*Vita Luculli*, XXVII. § 6, p. 510—states this positively. Tigranes, watching the movements of the Roman army, thinks that they are preparing to take flight ; Taxiles warns him that their equipment is not that of the march but of the battle-field :
καὶ ὁ Ταξίλης, βουλοίμην ἄν, εἶπεν, ὦ βασιλεῦ, γένεσθαι τι τῷ σῷ δαίμονι τῶν παραλόγων, ἀλλ' οὔτ' ἐσθῆτα λαμπρὰν οἱ ἄνδρες λαμβάνουσιν ὁδοιποροῦντες οὔτε θυρεοῖς ἐκκε- θαρμένοις χρῶνται καὶ κράνεσι γυμνοῖς, ὥσπερ νῦν τὰ σκύτινα τῶν ὅπλων σκεπάσματα περισπάσαντες, ἀλλὰ

μαχομένων ἐστὶν ἡ λαμπρότης αὕτη καὶ βαδιζόντων ἤδη
πρὸς τοῖς πολεμίοις. The same practice may possibly be
referred to by Frontinus, *Strat.* IV. 1, § 43 : "quattuor
legiones eduxit armatas, et consistere ordinibus, detectis
armis velut in acie, jussit."

Dr. Arnold's description of the Roman sword is perhaps
mistakenly transferred from the description of the Spanish
sword by Polybius (III. 114) and Livy (XXII. 46). It is
true that the Spanish sword was adopted for the Roman army,
but only *after* the Second Punic War. Suidas (s.v. μάχαιρα,
II. 731, Bernhardy) says : Οἱ Κελτίβηρες τῇ κατασκευῇ
τῶν μαχαιρῶν πολὺ διαφέρουσι τῶν ἄλλων· καὶ γὰρ κέντημα
πρακτικὸν καὶ καταφορὰν ἔχει δυναμένην ἐξ ἀμφοῖν τοῖν
χεροῖν. ᾗ καὶ Ῥωμαῖοι τὰς πατρίους ἀποθέμενοι μαχαίρας,
ἐκ τῶν κατ’ Ἀννίβαν, μετέβαλον τὰς τῶν Ἰβήρων. In the
same way Polybius (VI. 23) says of the Roman sword of
his day : Ἅμα δὲ τῷ θυρεῷ μάχαιρα· ταύτην δὲ περὶ τὸν
δεξιὸν φέρει μηρὸν, καλοῦσι δ’ αὐτὴν Ἰβηρικήν. Ἔχει δ’
αὕτη κέντημα διάφορον, καὶ καταφορὰν ἐξ ἀμφοῖν τοῖν μεροῖν
βίαιον, διὰ τὸ τὸν ὀβελίσκον αὐτῆς ἰσχυρὸν καὶ μόνιμον
εἶναι. The later Roman sword was a short, stabbing sword,
imitated from the Spanish weapon. The best account of its
use is given by Vegetius (I. 12) : 'Præterea non cæsim, sed
punctim ferire discebant. Nam cæsim pugnantes non solum
facile vicere, sed etiam derisere Romani. Cæsa enim, quovis
impetu veniat, non frequenter interficit, cum et armis vitalia
defendantur et ossibus. At contra puncta, duas uncias
adacta, mortalis est.' A suggestion of Fröhlich,[1] to the
effect that the adoption of the Spanish sword was due to
Scipio, who employed the artificers captured at Carthagena
mainly in making swords, and thus entirely re-armed his
troops, is worth considering. It is not easy to determine
what the old Roman sword, used before and during—at least
the greater part of—the Second Punic War, was like. The
passages I have quoted would make it probable that there
was a marked difference between the early Roman and the
Spanish sword, and that therefore the former was rather a
cutting than a stabbing weapon. But Polybius's description[2]

---

[1] Die Bedeutung des zweiten Punischen Krieges für die Entwickelung des Römischen Heerwesens, p. 46 (Leipsic, Teubner, 1884).

[2] II. 33, § 5-6.

of the Battle of Telamon, 225 B.C., is not easily reconcilable with this view. When they came to close quarters, the Romans, he says, τοὺς μὲν Κελτοὺς ἀπράκτους ἐποίησαν. ἀφελόμενοι τὴν ἐκ διαρσέως αὐτῶν μάχην, ὅπερ ἴδιον ἐστι Γαλατικῆς χρείας, διὰ τὸ μηδαμῶς κέντημα τὸ ξίφος ἔχειν· αὐτοὶ δ' οὐκ ἐκ καταφορᾶς, ἀλλ' ἐκ διαληψέως ὀρθαῖς χρώμενοι ταῖς μαχαίραις, πρακτικοῦ τοῦ κεντήματος περὶ αὐτὰς ὑπάρχοντος, τύπτοντες εἰς τὰ στέρνα καὶ τὰ πρόσωπα, καὶ πληγὴν ἐπὶ πληγῇ φέροντες, διέφθειραν τοὺς πλείστους τῶν παραταξαμένων. It appears from this passage that the ancient Roman weapon was not a mere broadsword, but could be used for stabbing with formidable effect. In this case the Spanish sword was not an entire innovation, but rather a development and improvement on the existing Roman weapon. But the whole subject is involved in great obscurity. A beautiful and instructive reproduction of the later (Spanish) sword of the Roman legionary is to be seen in the wonderful Gallo-Roman museum at St. Germain.

The passage on the inferiority of the Roman armament on p. 73 is at first sight scarcely intelligible in view of the fact that Hannibal armed his picked African troops with the spoils of the Roman dead, after the Battle of Thrasymene. But a careful reading of Dr. Arnold's text makes it clear that he is referring to the Roman cavalry *only*, and that consequently Hannibal's recognition of the superior equipment of the Roman *infantry* has nothing to do with the matter. Dr. Arnold was alluding to the passage in which Polybius (VI. 25) states that in his own day the Roman cavalry were equipped after the Greek fashion, but that of old—τὸ παλαιόν—their armament was decidedly inferior. It is, however, a question what period Polybius had in mind. Köchly and Rustow (*Griechische Kriegschriftsteller*, Part II. Introduction, p. 53) suggest that the Romans introduced the Greek equipment for their cavalry in the time of Pyrrhus. In that case the Roman cavalry was no longer 'badly armed' by the time of the Second Punic War.]

<h3 style="text-align:center">Note H, p. 75, l. 15.</h3>

[The attempt to fix the scene of the Battle of Cannæ encounters exactly the same difficulty as the similar attempt to determine the scene of the Battle of the Trebia. Did the battle take place upon the left or upon the right bank of the river Aufidus? Dr. Arnold decides for the latter; of recent years Hesselbarth has taken the same view. But Mommsen, Ihne, Schillbach, Stürenburg, Neumann, put the battle on the left bank, and it must be allowed that at present that view is almost universal. Ihne's remarks (*History of Rome*, II. 232) are worth quoting :—

"It looks almost as if Polybius had intentionally avoided the decisive words *right* and *left.*. His words leave the position of the two camps, and consequently the locality of the battle, quite undetermined. We must therefore try to fix it from other data. As we see from Livy (XXII. 43), Hannibal was encamped near Cannæ, *i.e.* on the right bank of the Aufidus. Nothing is said of his moving to the other side of the river [1] until he crossed on the day of battle (Livy, XXII. 46; Polybius, III. 113, § 6). This alone proves conclusively that the field of battle was on the left bank. Moreover, Polybius states that the Romans had their right wing on the river, and the Carthaginians the left. If, with this position, the two armies had been drawn up on the right bank, it would follow that the Romans had actually marched past the Carthaginian army and were now standing between it and the sea. Nothing is reported of such an extraordinary and dangerous manœuvre. Nevertheless, Arnold (see above, p. 68) assumes it as certain, as he is obliged to do, because he places the battle on the right bank. Now there appears to be no inducement for the selection of this bank as the field of battle beyond the statement of Polybius and Livy that the Roman army, leaning with their right wing on the river, had their faces turned to the south. But, though the general course of the Aufidus is from south-west to north-east, there is near Cannæ a decided bend in the river to the south or south-east, so that even on the left bank of the river the Romans could front towards the south, and yet rest on the river with their right wing."

Hesselbarth, who professes to tell the story exclusively from Polybius, puts the battle on the *right* bank. The Romans, he says, coming from Geronium, reached the

---

[1] But Hesselbarth, as we shall see, explains Polybius, III. 111, § 11, as a statement to this effect.

Aufidus at a point where it runs in a northerly direction, but nothing is said of their crossing it. Hannibal, who had previously taken Cannæ, and was presumably encamped on the right bank of the stream, in the neighbourhood of that place which was his granary, now pitched his camp on the same bank as the Romans (Polybius, III. 111, § 11), *i.e. he crossed the stream.* The Romans put a second smaller camp on the right bank, but kept their larger one on the left. Varro crossed the stream from the larger camp to give battle, and drew out his army on the right bank. Hannibal crossed, or, strictly speaking, recrossed, also, and the battle was fought on the right bank.

Stürenburg maintains the left bank. His arguments are :—1. The hilly ground on the right bank does not leave room for such great armies, whereas the left bank is an endless plain—'vast expanse of unvariegated plains' is the phrase of Swinburne (*Travels in the Two Sicilies*, I. 169). 2. Livy (XXII. 44, § 2) says that the bank on which the smaller Roman camp was situated—and it is at all events certain that the battlefield and this smaller camp were on one and the same bank—'was not held by any hostile force.' But the Carthaginians held Cannæ, and Cannæ was on the right bank; therefore the battle was on the left bank. 3. Both Polybius and Livy expressly state that the Romans had their right flank resting on the river. But if the battlefield was on the right bank, then the Romans could only have had their right flank on the river by having their backs to the sea, with no sure line of retreat, and the flight of the fugitives to Canusium and Venusia would be unintelligible.

Neumann (366 foll.) also puts the battle on the left bank, and adds the conjecture that the object of the Roman generals in accepting battle on that bank was to compel Hannibal to still further weaken his numerically inferior force by leaving detachments in his camp and in Cannæ. He agrees with Hesselbarth in admitting that the statement of both Polybius and Livy that the Carthaginians in line of battle looked north, while the Romans looked south, cannot well be reconciled with the left bank. Hesselbarth, however, boldly says that the statement is 'a serious geographical blunder.' Neumann also believes it to be worthless, and adds—'Es ist uberdies bekannt wie schlecht die meisten alten Schriftsteller sich nach den Himmelsgegenden orientieren, und wie ungenau sie in solchen Ausdrücken sind.' In view of these admissions from advocates of the rival theory—admissions which the nature of the ground almost compels—the contention in the final sentence of the passage I have quoted from Ihne must be given up.

The certain points appear to be the following :—1. Hannibal was in occupation of Cannæ, which was on the right bank of the Aufidus. 2. There were two Roman camps on different sides of the river ; the smaller one was lower down the river, and more towards the east. 3. The battle was on the same side as the smaller camp. 4. The Romans had their right flank on the river. The two plans of Cannæ in this volume show how either theory can be worked out, so as to fulfil these four necessary conditions. In a general way it is to be said for the left bank that it is more suitable for the deployment of vast masses of men, and above all for cavalry ; but on the other hand it may be urged that the Romans would have avoided it, and have transferred the fight to the right bank, if they could, for that very reason. The retreat upon Canusium and Venusia is more easily explained if the battle took place upon the left bank than if it took place upon the right, for in the latter case the Romans—with their right flank upon the river—must have had the Carthaginian army more or less between themselves and those places. Believers in the right bank, on the other hand, are justified in laying stress on the positive statement of both Polybius and Livy as to the direction in which the two armies looked, and in pointing to the fact that the advocates of the rival theory have practically no alternative but to make the rather bold assumption that both Polybius and Livy were altogether mistaken. It remains for a military specialist to go carefully over the ground, texts in hand. Such a man would, for instance, be able to say at once whether it was possible to manœuvre 80,000 or 90,000 men in one army on the right bank.]

Note I, p. 90, l. 11.

It seems to me that the Latin colonies and Hannibal's want of artillery were the main causes of his failure. The

Romans had in these colonies, not one of which he ever took, fortresses in the heart of the countries which revolted to him. Thus Apulia revolted; but the Romans still held Luceria, Venusia, and Brundisium; Samnium revolted; but the Romans held Æsernia and Beneventum; and so on. Casilinum cost him a siege of several weeks; but the Romans recovered it in a much shorter time. If he had engaged Archimedes as his engineer in chief, and got Philip to send him artillery, he would have done far better; for the Macedonian princes seem to have carried their artillery to great perfection. As it was, his only very strong arm was his cavalry; for his infantry, veterans as they were, could never beat the Roman raw levies behind works. It appears to me that the sieges are the great defect of Hannibal's operations in Italy; and thus, as soon as his army moved from any place, the inhabitants who had joined him were at the mercy of the Roman garrisons. And their colonies were very strong garrisons; Venusia was originally settled with 20,000 colonists.—*Author's Note.*

[Writing to Bunsen on Jan. 28, 1841, Dr. Arnold (*Life and Correspondence*, II. 214) repeats and illustrates this opinion. "I think," he writes, "that the Latin colonies and Hannibal's want of artillery and engineers saved Rome. Samnium would not rise effectually while its strongest fortresses, Beneventum, Æsernia, etc., were in the hands of the enemy. If the French artillery had been no better than Hannibal's, and they had had no other arm to depend on than their cavalry, I believe that the Spaniards by themselves would have beaten them; for every town would then have been impregnable, and the Guerillas would have starved the army out." Mommsen also is worth quoting. Hannibal, he says,[1] "knew Rome better than the simpletons who in ancient and modern times have fancied that he might have terminated the struggle by a march on the enemy's capital. Modern warfare, it is true, decides a war on the field of battle; but in ancient times, when the system of attacking fortresses was far less developed than the system of defence, the most complete success in the field was on numberless occasions neutralised by the resistance of the walls of the capitals." The superiority of the defence is illustrated by the siege of

[1] English translation, II. 141.

Syracuse. No important place in Italy was taken by regular siege during the war, either by Hannibal or by the Romans. Most often treachery, as at Tarentum, Arpi, and Casilinum, sometimes famine, as at Capua, did the work. In Spain Carthago Nova was taken by a brilliant *coup de main*. And yet there is something surprising in Hannibal's weakness on this side. He besieged and took Saguntum in due form (Livy, XXI. 7-8, 11-12, 14), and one cannot help asking why he did not do the same in Italy. If he took elephants across the Alps, he could surely take a siege train. Moreover, an ancient army was not obliged, like a modern army, to take its artillery with it wherever it went. It could make its artillery when it reached the scene of action. Cæsar's account of his campaigns furnishes a most singular contrast to Hannibal's great effort against Rome. Cæsar conquered Gaul just because he was a master of the art of siege, and no strong place could hold out against his inventive genius and unlimited resource. Hannibal failed in Italy largely because he could not do what Cæsar did. The art of attack had no doubt greatly advanced by Cæsar's time. It may also be suggested that, as the commander of a small army in a hostile country, Hannibal could not afford to fritter away his strength in sieges. The moral effect of constant victories was necessary, if he was to hold his ground, and necessary above all to secure the fidelity of his Gauls, who would simply have left him if he had wearied them with laborious sieges, while they were bent on the more exciting and attractive business of fighting and plundering.

It should be borne in mind that Hannibal was not backed by the whole strength of Carthage as he should have been, and that his numbers were constantly inferior to those of the Romans. Polybius (II. 24) gives a picture of the disproportion of force at the disposal of the combatants which suggests the question, not, how was it that Hannibal failed? but, how was it that he ever had a chance of winning?]

Note J, p. 101, l. 20.

[The Western nations seem to have first learnt the use of the elephant in war from Alexander's Indian campaigns.

When Alexander left India he took 200 elephants with him down the Indus, and a certain proportion of these reached Europe.[1] We find them used in the wars of the Diadochi, and Pyrrhus took them with him to Italy. Xanthippus appears to have taught the Carthaginians how to use their own African elephants for this purpose. Similarly, the famous inscription found by Cosmas Indicopleustes at Adulis (Zoula) mentions the elephants used by Ptolemy Euergetes in his Asiatic campaigns, and obtained by that Ptolemy himself and his father as the result of hunting expeditions in Ethiopia. These facts are of considerable interest in view of the current theory that the African elephant is untamable. The English army employed elephants to carry the guns to Magdala—but they were Indian elephants; Gordon also imported a few Indian elephants to Khartoum. The African elephant has disappeared from its old haunts in Algeria and Tunis. It was probably exterminated, like other wild beasts, by the advance of Roman settlement in those regions, coupled with the great demand for wild beasts at the games, and for ivory.[2] There is, however, no reason to think that the present African elephant is a different species; and it has recently been suggested that what was done in antiquity could be done now, and that, instead of the costly absurdity of importing Indian elephants into Africa—and thus bringing coals to Newcastle—the African elephant could be trained for all the usual purposes of peace for which the Indian elephant is now used. Josef Menges, the well-known German agent for African wild beasts at Berbera, has suggested, in two interesting letters to the *Cologne Gazette*,[3] that the taming of African elephants for such purposes would have two excellent results —it would avert the extermination of the noble beast, and it would provide for Central Africa an unequalled beast of burden. At present there is no beast of burden in tropical Africa. The camel cannot live there, and the work of transport is very inefficiently done by native bearers. The only

[1] Arrian, VI. 2, 15-17, 28; VII. 3.

[2] See my *Roman Provincial Administration*, p. 76, note 8. Any one interested in the point will find further references in Jung, *Romanische Landschaften*, p. 172, and Friedländer, *Sittengeschichte Roms.*, II. 145 (French translation).

[3] Printed in that journal in the early part of June, or end of May, 1885.

question is, therefore, whether there is any hope of taming
the African elephant and making an efficient beast of burden
of him.   Herr Menges does not deny that the Indian
elephant is more tractable than the African one; but he
maintains from long personal experience that the African
elephant is quite tamable.   About 150 of them have actually
been sent to Europe, and are not found unmanageable in
zoological gardens and menageries.   Now comes an interesting point, for the sake of which I have gone more fully into
this subject than I should otherwise have done.   Herr
Menges allows that Indian elephants and a certain number
of Hindoo tamers must be imported into Africa in the first
place, so as to carry out the capture and taming of African
elephants on a great scale.   Side by side with this statement
I feel disposed to put the passages in which Polybius and
Appian speak of Hannibal's elephant-drivers as 'Indians.'
Thus Polybius III. 46 : τῶν δὲ θηρίων εἰθισμένων τοῖς
'Ινδοῖς ; I. 40 : θήρια δὲ σὺν αὐτοῖς τοῖς 'Ινδοῖς ἔλαβε δέκα ;
XI. 1 : τῶν δὲ θηρίων τὰ μὲν ἕξ ἅμα τοῖς ἄνδρασιν ἔπεσε,
τὰ δὲ τέτταρα διωσάμενα τὰς τάξεις ὕστερον ἑάλω μεμονω-
μένα καὶ ψιλὰ τῶν 'Ινδῶν ; Appian, *Hannibal*, 42 : τοῖς δ'
ἐλέφασι τοὺς 'Ινδοὺς ἐπέβησε.   It would appear therefore
that the Western nations could not dispense with Indian
mahouts for the management of the strange and formidable
beasts, and that among the motley host which Hannibal led
across the Alps we must find room for a hundred or so of
dark-skinned Hindoos.]

Note K, p. 111, l. 28.

[Compare Nissen in *Rheinisches Museum*, XXII. 570 :
" Der fundamentale Unterschied zwischen dem antiken und
modernen Italien beruht nämlich darin, dass dieses ein ent-
waldetes wasserarmes, jenes ein wald und wasserreiches Land
war." See also the chapter on the climate of Italy in Nissen's
Italische Landeskunde, I. 374 foll.]

Note L, p. 168, l. 11.

According to Livy, Hannibal collects all the boats which
are to be found on the Vulturnus, orders his men to provide

themselves with provisions for ten days, and *crosses in the night.* (XXVI. 7.) He *remains on the right bank the next day and night,* then moves by Cales in agrum Sidi-cinum, and there *remains one day plundering.* He advances by the Latin road, per Suessanum, Allifanumque et Casi-natem agrum. He then *remains for two days under Casinum,* plundering the country in all directions. He goes on by Interamna and Aquinum to Fregellæ, where he finds the bridges over the Liris broken down; he ravages the ager Fregellanus with peculiar spite for that reason; and then advances by Frusino, Ferentinum, and Anagnia, in agrum Lavicanum. From thence he goes over Algidus to Tusculum, descends to Gabii, thence marches down in Pupiniam, and pitches his camp eight miles from Rome. He moves his camp ad Anienem, three miles from Rome, and there estab-lishes stativa; he himself advancing along under the walls from the Colline gate to the temple of Hercules, to look about him. On the next day he crosses the Anio, and offers battle to the enemy; a storm breaks off the action. Next day he offers battle again, and there comes a second storm. He falls back ad Tutiam fluvium, six miles from Rome. He plunders the temple of Feronia, and marches to Eretum : from thence he goes to Reate, Cutiliæ, and Amiternum. From thence through the Marsian and Marrucinian territory by Sulmo, through the Pelignian territory into Samnium, and from Samnium into Campania. From Campania into Lucania, thence into Bruttium, and thence to Rhegium.

Here are traces of two accounts jumbled together. The march from the Vulturnus, as far as the camp in Pupinia, eight miles from Rome, is all highly consistent and probable, and comes, I suspect, either from Fabius or Cincius. But the advance to the Anio, the crossing it to offer battle, and then the retreat ad Tutiam, belong to a different story, that namely which made Hannibal advance upon Rome from Reate. For in advancing by the Latin road, or the Via Gabina, he had nothing to do with the Anio; and if he crossed the Anio to offer battle, he must have been between Rome and the Roman army, and the Roman army would have been between him and the Tutia. This, then, is all absurd and inconsistent.

Again, according to Livy, Fulvius had heard beforehand

of Hannibal's design, and had warned the senate of it; he receives an answer from Rome, selects 15,000 foot and 1000 horse, crosses the Vulturnus on rafts, after a long delay, because Hannibal had burnt all the boats, advances to Rome by the Appian way, and arrives by the Porta Capena just as Hannibal had reached Pupinia. Now, according to Polybius, Hannibal set out for Rome only five days after his arrival before Capua: there was no time therefore for Fulvius to send to Rome and get an answer before Hannibal set out. Again, Casilinum being in the power of the Romans, the passage of the Vulturnus was in their own hands, and the story about the rafts is an absurdity.

Appian says that Hannibal marched with urgent haste through many and hostile nations, some of whom could not and some did not try to stop him; and thus he arrived on the Anio, and encamped at 32 stadia from Rome. The Romans break down the bridge over the Anio; and two thousand men from Alba Marsorum come valiantly to the aid of Rome. This all agrees with Cœlius, and supposes evidently that Hannibal advanced through Samnium and by Reate. The 'many and hostile nations' are the Pelignians, Marsians, Marrucinians, and Sabines.[1] Thus, too, he arrives naturally on the Anio; and the Albensians, seeing him pass through their country, set off at once by the Valerian road to Rome, to be ready to meet him. Had he advanced by the Latin road, they would have known nothing about his march, and he would have been between them and Rome.

Fulvius then, according to Appian, hastens to Rome, and meets Hannibal on the Anio, with the river between them. Hannibal ascends the right bank of the river to turn it by its source. Fulvius ascends the left bank watching him. Hannibal leaves some Numidians behind, who cross the river when Fulvius was gone, plunder all the country round the walls, and then rejoin Hannibal. Hannibal goes round by the sources of the river; and, as it was only a little way to Rome, he steals out by night with three squires to have a look at it, and then takes fright and returns to Capua. Fulvius follows him; and Hannibal, in attempting to surprise his camp on the road, is sadly foiled. He then marches off to *winter in Lucania;* and Fulvius rejoins Appius before

---

[1] See p. 409.

Capua. This is beneath criticism; but I observe that the story of Fulvius being too cunning for Hannibal is given by Livy at the assault of the Roman lines before Capua, and is probably as true of one as of the other. Again, the line of retreat here indicated is by the Latin road; the ascending the Anio shows this, and is inconsistent with the retreat by Reate.

Cœlius Antipater had expressly given Hannibal's advance upon Rome thus :—

From Campania into Samnium, and thence to the Pelignians, that is, by the present great road up the Vulturnus to Venafro; thence by Isernia and Castel di Sangro to the Five Mile plain; then passing by Sulmo to the Marrucinians; thence by Alba to the Marsians; thence to Amiternum and Foruli: from Amiternum, by Cutiliæ, Reate, and Eretum, upon the Anio.

What a confusion! which neither Nauta nor Prinsterer meddle with. The road from Sulmo to Amiternum is simple enough; descending along the Gizio to the Aterno or Pescara at Popoli, thence ascending to the high upland plain by Navelli and Civita Retenga, and so by Aquila to Amiternum (S. Vittorino). But conceive a man—to say nothing of an army in a hurry—going down from Popoli to Chieti, then turning back to Sulmona, and going over by the Forchetta to Celano, and thence by Rocca di Mezzo into the valley of Aquila. All this folly arises from the untimely correction 'in Marrucinos,' where the MSS. give corruptly 'Martinos,' 'Martianos,' 'Maceranos,' etc. Cœlius supposed that Hannibal, instead of descending from Sulmo towards Popoli, turned to his left,[1] and crossed the mountains by the Forchetta to Celano, and thence either by Rocca di Mezzo over the mountains to Aquila, or else by the Cicolano, and down the valley of Tornimparte. Instead of 'Marrucinos,' the better correction would be 'Marrubios,' or 'Marruvios'—the people of Marruvium, a Pelignian town on the east or south-east shore of the lake Fucinus.

---

[1] At Raiano. This is still a carriageable road. Keppel Craven calls the pass Furca Caruso. [No map on a scale consistent with the size of this volume would enable the reader to fully understand the points raised by Dr. Arnold in this discussion. But Kiepert's great map of Central Italy (4 sheets, Reimer, Berlin, 1881) makes everything clear, and that map ought to be in every good school library.]

According to Polybius, Hannibal, five days after his arrival before Capua, left his fires burning at night, and set off after supper. He marched by *vigorous and uninterrupted marches through Samnium*, always exploring and preoccupying the ground near the road with his advanced guard : and, whilst all at Rome were thinking only of Capua, he suddenly crossed the Anio, and encamped at a distance of not more than four miles from Rome. He intended the next day to assault the city; but the consuls, with their two newly-raised legions, encamped before the walls. He then gives up the assault, and sets about plundering the country and burning the houses in all directions. After this (how long after is not said, nor why, but we must suppose after Fulvius had arrived from Capua) the consuls advance boldly, and encamp within ten stadii of Hannibal. Then Hannibal, having filled his army with plunder, and thinking that his diversion must now have taken effect at Capua, commenced his retreat. But the bridges over the Anio had been broken down ; and in fording the river he was attacked, and sustained some loss ; his cavalry, however, served him so well that the Romans returned to their camp, ἄπρακτοι. He continued his march hastily, which the enemy thought was through fear ; so they followed him close, but keeping to the higher grounds. He was moving in haste upon Capua ; but *on the fifth day of his retreat*, learning that the Romans there were still in their lines, he halted to wait for his pursuers, and, turning upon them, attacked their camp by night and stormed it. The Romans rallied by daybreak on a steep hill which he could not force ; so he would not wait to besiege them, but marched through Apulia and Bruttium, and nearly succeeded in surprising Rhegium.

Again what a narrative ! with no details of time or place, jumping at once from a five days' march from Rome into Apulia, and merely implying that Hannibal's retreat was on the right bank of the Anio. But this mention of the Anio, connected with the expression 'marching through Samnium,' seems to show that Polybius, like Cœlius, made Hannibal advance by a circuitous route upon Rome, and not by the Latin road.

The season of the year must have been early according to the Roman calendar—not later than April, whatever that was by true time ; because the levy of the two city legions was only half finished. But unless the Roman calendar was at least two months behind true time, how could Hannibal have passed such defiles as that of Rocca-Valloscura (between Castel di Sangro and Sulmo) ; or such passes as those between Isernia and Castel di Sangro? Would not the snow have covered the ground at such a season?—*Author's Note.*

[On this subject Dr. Arnold wrote to Mr. Justice Coleridge (*Life and Correspondence*, II. 239) on the 1st September 1841 : " My historical perplexity has caused me many hours of work, and I cannot yet see land. It shows me how the most notorious facts may be corrupted, even very soon after the occurrence, when they are subjected to no careful and judicious inquiry. Hannibal's march from Capua upon Rome, to effect a diversion for the besieged town, is of course one of the most striking parts of the whole war. I want to give it in detail, and with all the painting possible. But it is wholly uncertain by what road he advanced upon Rome, whether by the Latin road direct from Capua, or by an enormous circuit through Samnium—just the road which we took last summer from Capua to Reate—and so from Reate on Rome. Cœlius Antipater, Polybius, and Appian all either assert or imply the latter. Livy says the former, and gives an account of the march, from Fabius, I think, or Cincius, which is circumstantial and highly probable ; but he is such a simpleton that, after having written a page from Cincius or Fabius, he then copies from some other writer who had made him take the other road ; and, after bringing Hannibal by the Latin road, he makes him cross the Anio to approach Rome, and tells divers anecdotes, which all imply that he came by the Valerian or Salarian road ; for of course the Latin road has no more to do with the Anio than with the Arno. The evidences and the probabilities are so balanced, and all the narratives are so unsatisfactory, that I cannot tell what to do about it. And the same sort of thing occurs often, with such constant uncertainty as to the text—in Livy—the common editions being restored conjecturally in almost every page where the MSS. are utterly corrupt, that the Punic War is almost as hard in the writing as in the fighting." The fullest modern discussion of the subject is contained in an essay by H. Haupt in the *Mélanges Graux* (Paris, Thorin, 1884). As this essay is not easily accessible to most English students I subjoin a pretty ample summary of it.

Haupt begins by stating that on almost every point the contradiction between Polybius and Livy is formal. But, putting Polybius aside for the present, he devotes the bulk of his essay to an inquiry into the source and character of the other stories which we find in Livy and Appian. It has been maintained, he remarks, that Cœlius Antipater is the unique authority of Livy. What is true is that, as regards the part of the war in question, *Cœlius Antipater is the unique authority of Appian.* Haupt defends this view by the following arguments :—(1) Appian says that, in marching on Rome, Hannibal traversed the territory of many hostile nations, of whom some vainly resisted, others did not venture. It is hardly probable, therefore, that Appian should have conceived of Hannibal as marching direct on Rome by the Latin road.[1] Livy takes him by this road 'through Campania and Latium,' but knows nothing of any such combats. (2) Appian says that 2000 men came from Alba Fucentia almost at the same time as Hannibal, and were incorporated in the Roman army. Now, how did these Albans get to Rome? If Hannibal followed the Latin road, is it likely that (*a*), a little Æquian town 60 miles from Rome should have heard of his march in time to get to Rome before him? or that (*b*) they should not have been deterred from such a march by the dread of falling into the hands of Hannibal's Numidians on the way? They were, in fact, fugitives—Appian, *Hann.* 39, says that they got arms from the consuls—driven upon Rome by the enemy who threatened their own town. This idea is confirmed by Cœlius Antipater, who says, according to Livy (XXVI. 11), that Hannibal passed from the Marrucini to the Marsi by way of Alba. Appian (*Hann.* 39) says that a number of fugitives hastened to Rome from the open country. (3) Appian says that Hannibal, on nearing Rome, found the bridge over the Anio cut, and therefore marched up the stream, while the Numidian cavalry crossed it by swimming, and devastated the environs of Rome. Fulvius, arriving from Capua, at first devotes himself to watching Hannibal's movements from the opposite

[1] See p. 405.

bank, but is diverted from that task by the Numidians, and, while he is thus occupied, Hannibal manages to cross with the bulk of his army. Now all that is unintelligible if we suppose Hannibal to be approaching Rome *from the south ;* but if we suppose that Appian, like Cœlius (Livy, XXVI. 11), made Hannibal approach from the north, probably along the Via Salaria, it is all right.

As for Dio, his authority is Livy. There is not the smallest contradiction in point of fact between Dio's story (in *Zonaras*) of the march and of the taking of Capua, and Livy's; moreover, the general arrangement, the form of the story, sometimes the phraseology, coincide in both. Dio, in this part of the story, differs much from Appian.

What were the authorities of Livy? Anyhow not Cœlius. (Livy, XXVI. 11.) Livy's account is a jumble. He begins by describing Hannibal's march by the Latin road :—" puis sans qu'on puisse voir où il aurait quitté une source pour puiser dans une autre, il poursuit le cours des événements jusqu'à la retraite d'Hannibal, lequel franchit l'Anio." At this point Livy mentions Cœlius, and says that on the march and on the retreat of Hannibal he and Cœlius are in contradiction. His source, therefore, was not Cœlius. The same conclusion follows from Livy's account (XXVI. 5, 6) of Hannibal's last fights before Capua, where Livy accepts a certain story, and mentions a certain other which he does not accept. Now the latter is apparently the story given— though transferred to another part of the campaign—in Appian (*Hann.*, 41). Therefore (on the assumption that Appian's reliance on Cœlius has been proved) the latter story is Cœlius's. Haupt conjectures that the source of Livy was Valerias Antias. His reasons are :—(1) The authority for the story of the fight before Capua (see above) is not mentioned by Livy, but Livy seems to regard him as an exaggerator. Now this is the way in which Livy always speaks of Valerius Antias (Livy, XXVI. 49; XXXIII. 10; III. 5; XXX. 19; XXXVI. 19, 38; XXXVIII. 23; XLV. 43. Unger in *Philologus*, Supplementband III., Abth. 2, 1878). (2) Livy (XXVI. 8) contains, *apropos* of Hannibal's menace, an improbable proposal attributed to one P. Valerius. " Plus l'ensemble du recit parait invraisemblable, plus est important le detail qui fait decouvrir la vraie voie du salut par un

Valerius. Nous ne croyons pas nous égarer en voyant là
une invention nouvelle de la vanité de Valerius Antias."
(3) In Books XXV.-XXX. Livy only cites four Roman
sources—Cœlius, Piso, Clodius Licinus, and Valerius Antias.
He cites Cœlius six times, Piso and Clodius each once,
Valerius seven times. He therefore uses Valerius a good
deal. In Book XXVI. he refers only to Cœlius and Valerius.

Taking, therefore, Valerius Antias to be the source of
Livy, there are three different stories, those of—(1) Polybius;
(2) Cœlius Antipater; (3) Valerius Antias. According to
(2) and (3) Fulvius marched from Capua to the succour of
Rome. Polybius says that troops which happened to be at
Rome were organised for the defence of Rome by the two
consuls, Cn. Fulvius Centumalus and P. Sulpicius Galba.
But one reason, and one only, could have withdrawn Fulvius
from the siege of Capua, and that was the knowledge that
there were no troops in Rome. Now the exact contrary of
this is to be inferred from both Polybius—who describes one
legion as already formed, another as forming—and Livy.
If there were no troops at Rome, how could Fabius have
opposed the summoning of Fulvius, and how could troops
have been sent from Rome to Spain, even before Hannibal's
withdrawal? And even if troops were wanted, there was
an army nearer Rome than that of Capua—that, namely,
under the command of M. Junius Silanus in Etruria. The
following general objections may be urged against the story
told by Appian and Livy—the Roman annalistic story. It
obliges us to believe that (1) Hannibal kept his secret so
badly, that, before he even started, a messenger was on the
way to Rome to announce his coming; (2) that he marched
by a very roundabout route, and with inconceivable slowness; (3) that having succeeded in drawing off Fulvius, he
never took advantage of his success, and instead of attacking
the weakened army of Capua, turned off to Bruttium. This,
though the whole object of the march presumably was to
draw off the Capuan army, or enough of it to enable him to
crush what was left. The story of Fulvius is a mere legend.
It comes from a confusion between Fulvius Centumalus and
the old Fulvius, the proconsul. It was necessary to give
Fulvius the time to enable him to get to Rome as soon as
Hannibal. Therefore Cœlius sends him on the long round

through Samnium, the Marrucini, etc. As to Valerius Antias (*i.e.* Livy), it is true that he makes Hannibal go by the Latin road, and so far he is not so much astray as Cœlius. But even he takes care that Hannibal does not hurry. There is a day's rest at Teanum, two at Casinum. At Fregellæ the bridge is broken down, and the army occupies itself with ravaging the country. "Ce n'etait donc point la peine qui Hannibal prît un chemin plus court : il n'avait pas le droit de devancer à Rome les legions de Fulvius."

Haupt therefore fully accepts the story of Polybius. On the other hand, Neumann (p. 439, note) urges that the "story which Polybius follows is the invention of Roman vanity. The Romans liked to pretend that the besieging army never let itself for a moment be disturbed by the move of Hannibal ; but the reports of the terror felt at Rome hardly square with that imperturbable confidence." Neumann thinks that part of the Capuan army—about a third of its total strength—was actually detached for the relief of Rome. He believes that Polybius points rather to the circuit through Samnium than to the Latin road, and refuses to accept the fragment of Polybius—which does not mention Fulvius as before Capua at all, but only Appius Claudius—as against the more detailed story in which Appian and Livy in the main agree. Voigt, finally, points out (*Berliner Philologische Wochenschrift*, IV., 1628, note 95) that Livy takes Hannibal to Rome by way of Cales, Teanum (Ager Sidicinus), Suessa, Allifæ, Casinum, Interamna, Aquinum, etc., and that, as a glance at the map will show, 'Suessa, Allifæ, and Interamna, have no business here.']

Note M, p. 184, l. 13.

[A similar opinion of the Spanish War has been expressed by other historians of Rome. Peter (*Geschichte Roms.* I. 398) says : " Die Ereignisse in Spanien lassen sich bei der Unzulänglichkeit unserer Kenntnisse der alten Geographie nur sehr unvollkommen erkennen." Mommsen (II. 155, English translation) takes much the same view : " It is impossible with the very imperfect and, in point of chronology especially, very confused accounts which have come down to us, to give a satisfactory view of a war so conducted." Ihne, finally, remarks (*Römische Geschichte*, II. 223): "Unsere Unkenntniss der Geographie des alten Spanien macht die Kriegerischen Begebenheiten in diesem Lande zum Theil unverständlich und die Erzählung derselben langweilig und fruchtlos." Nevertheless several meritorious efforts have been made of late years to unravel this peculiarly tangled skein. I may refer the reader to Keller's essay, 'Zu den Quellen des Hannibalischen Krieges,' in the *Rheinisches Museum* for 1874 (XXIX. 88-96), and the same writer's 'Zweite Punische Krieg und seine Quellen' (Marburg, 1875). Keller's view is that much faith can be put in Appian's account of this war, and that Appian's authority was King Juba. The dissertation by Hermann Genzken, 'De Rebus a P. et Cn. Corneliis Scipionibus in Hispania gestis' (Gottingen, 1879), is a most praiseworthy attempt to disentangle the chronology of the first portion of the war; but that portion only. He starts from the assumption that Livy's story cannot be accepted as it stands. For instance, Livy (XXIII. 26-29) has crammed into five months of the year B.C. 216 a crowd of events which could not possibly have all taken place within so limited a time. Livy also repeats, sometimes contradicts, himself. Genzken's theory is that Livy had two authorities before him. The first gave a continuous narrative of the doings of the Scipios in Spain. Livy used this faithfully; but he had to weave it in to his own more general narrative, which included Italy and Sicily as well as Spain, and he has not always woven it in well. He has sometimes allotted to one year events which really belonged to another. The second authority which Livy is supposed to have used gave a quite different account of some points; but Livy has worked it into his story, side by side with the material derived from the first authority, without noticing the contradictions in which he was thereby sometimes involved. Genzken proceeds to work out these positions in detail. He also gives a chronological narrative of the war from B.C. 218 to B.C. 211, allotting a separate section to each year, and not always distributing the events as Livy has distributed them. Johann Frantz has worked over the ground since Genzken, in an essay entitled 'Die Kriege der Scipionen in Spanien' (Munich, Ackermann, 1883). He is not content with surveying a part of the field, as Genzken was, but carries his discussion down to B.C. 206. Frantz thinks that for this war Appian—whose authority he agrees with Keller in believing to have been Juba—and Dio, whose authority was Cœlius Antipater, are more important than is commonly supposed. His main object is to point out the falsifications introduced into Livy's narrative—though not, probably, in the first place by Livy—for the purpose of magnifying the achievements of the Scipios. He goes through the history of the war in detail, year by year, with this object, and at the same time works out his own account of what actually took place. It may be noted that he puts the defeat and death of the two Scipios in the year B.C. 212 —Genzken puts it in 213; he puts the capture of New Carthage in 209, and the Battle of Bæcula in the same year. Faltin, who is, as always, jealous for the good name of Livy, states his views partly in his note to Neumann, p. 322, partly in his review of Frantz's essay in the *Philologische Wochenschrift* for 1883, III. 1618.]

Note N, p. 263, l. 22.

[Dr. Arnold writes to Bunsen on January 28, 1841 (*Life and Correspondence*, II. 213): "I think that both Flaminius and Varro have been maligned, and that the family papers of the Scipios, and the 'Laudatio M. Marcelli a filio habita,' have falsified the history grievously." In a published extract from his journal (*Life and Correspondence*, II. 370) he writes, under date July 20, 1840: "Spoleto is still beautifully visible at the end of the plain behind us. I can conceive Hannibal's Numidians trying to carry it αὐτοβοεὶ after they had carried all this delicious plain; and if the colony shut its gates against them, and was not panic-struck by the terror of Thrasymenus, it did well, and deserved honour, as did Nola in like case, although Marcellus's son lied about his father's life no less valiantly than he did about his death." The extremely uncritical attitude towards Marcellus, which I find in Neumann (pp. 449, 461, etc.), is surprising in the case of a writer generally so open-eyed.]

Note O, p. 286, l. 14.

[The following is a published extract from Dr. Arnold's journal (*Life and Correspondence*, II. 373), dated 'Banks of the Metaurus, July 21, 1840': "Livy says, 'the farther Hannibal got from the sea, the steeper became the banks of the river.' We noticed some steep banks, but probably they were much higher twenty-one centuries ago ; for all rivers have a tendency to raise themselves, from accumulations of gravel, etc. ; the windings of the stream, also, would be much more as Livy describes them, in the natural state of the river. The present aspect of this tract of country is the result of 2000 years of civilisation, and would be very different in those times. There would be much of natural forest remaining ; the only cultivation being the square patches of the Roman messores, and these only on the best land. The whole plain would look wild, like a new and half-settled country. One of the greatest physical changes on the earth is produced by the extermination of carnivorous animals ; for then the graminivorous become so numerous as to eat up all the young trees, so that the forests rapidly diminish, except those trees which they do not eat, as pines and firs." I know no recent discussion of this battle except that which is devoted to its purely tactical aspects by Chauvelays (*L'Art Militaire chez les Romains*, pp. 217-222). A brief article by François Lenormant (*Revue Archeologique* for 1882, XLIV. 31) gives all the particulars known about a silver patera found in a tomb on the battlefield, and bearing an inscription in Iberian characters. Lenormant believes it to have been the property of one of Hasdrubal's Spanish officers.]

Note P, p. 311, l. 11.

[Consul Joel of Cadiz in his last Report (*Reports from Her Majesty's Consuls of the Manufactures, Commerce, etc., of their Consular Districts*, Part VI., July 1885, p. 916 foll.), after a brief reference to Phenician mining operations in the province of Huelva, proceeds :—

"Certain it is that the first miners, who left behind them unmistakable traces of their nationality, were the Romans, and one stands in wonder at the magnitude of their operations, and the knowledge and pertinacity they display. There is barely a single deposit they did not either work or investigate, abandoning it, after a trial of the ore, if it proved poor, and the best recommendation nowaday in favour of a new mine is that it bears traces of Roman working. The extraction of minerals was effected through number-less shafts, which literally riddle the ground. These were always sunk in pairs about six feet apart, having frequent communication with each other for ventilation ; and sets of these coupled shafts are found in such close proximity that they can only be accounted for on the supposition that the extraction of minerals was given over to a number of small contractors, each of whom might have a certain surface or claim allotted to him, on which he sunk his own shafts. The ore, when brought to the surface, was taken to the nearest valley and smelted in furnaces, the triturated ironstone of the Creston being probably used as flux, and the fuel from the then abundant oak, cork, and arbutus trees of the neighbourhood. Enormous deposits of slag are found near all the mines, estimated to contain, in all the province, about 20,000,000 tons, representing a total amount of about 26,000,000 tons of raw ore smelted ; truly an imposing figure. Samples of slag, taken from parts of the heaps not exposed to atmospheric action, contain as much as 1·46 per cent of copper, and show that the smelting could not have been very perfect. This well-organised industry was, however, suddenly broken up on the alarm of the Gothic invasion, and all the mines were abandoned with their workings still rich in ore. During the Moorish dominion some mines were worked—coins of Saracenic origin having been found in the province of Cordoba—but the mines of the province of Huelva were unworked until reopened in modern times. The first attempts at modern workings seem to have been made under Philip II., and between the years 1560 and 1640 a number of mines were explored, but it is only in 1725 that Wolter, Tiquet, and Sanz obtained practical results in Rio Tinto. In 1840 a new activity was imparted to the mining industry ; over 300 mines being denounced in the following years, owing probably to the introduction of the wet process of cementation by Prieto. Among the mines worked at this time may be mentioned Castillo de los Guardias, Pena de Hierro, Concepcion, Tinto, Chaparrita, Coronada, and San Miguel. In the beginning of 1853 M. Ernest Deligny, a French Engineer, came to the province, and, guided chiefly by the deposits of Roman slag, he discovered and claimed successively Cueva de la Mora, Poyatos, Herrerias, San Telmo, Tharsis, Zarza, and Santo Domingo, in several of which he started operations. After numerous vicissitudes a French company, formed by the Duke of Glucksburg and M. Duclerc, obtained at last tangible results at Tharsis, in 1858. Since then the development of these mines advanced with rapid strides; in 1866 the Tharsis Sulphur and Copper Company was formed; in 1873 the Rio Tinto Company was started, and the result of these companies' extensive operations is too well known to require further remark. In order, however, to give an idea of what has been accomplished by these companies, it must be remembered that the difficulty of transport in a hilly country, utterly devoid of any sort of road (so much so that all carriage had to be effected on mule back, along rough bridle tracks), and the want of native enterprise in the construction of independent railways, soon rendered it imperative on them to construct railways of their own for the full development of their mines. The Buitron Company first constructed a three-feet six-inch gauge line, 57 kilomètres long, to San Juan, on the river Tinto, whence their produce is taken to the Odiel in barges for transhipment; then the Tharsis Company established a line 46 kilomètres long, with a four-feet gauge, to a pier on the river Odiel, where their produce is shipped; and finally the Rio Tinto Company built a three-feet six-inch gauge line, 83 kilomètres long, to the Odiel, where it is served by a magnificent pier. The Huelva and Seville Railway was next built, and the Huelva and Zaffra line is nearly completed, both undertaken by independent railway companies. The great export traffic on these lines, and the imports of pig iron, coal, and other materials, together with the traffic in the mining establishments, where large quantities of ore are turned over thrice for local treatment, necessarily implies a large amount of rolling stock and locomotives, and consequently the establishment of extensive workshops, with English foremen and workmen. The mines, also lying generally at some distance from the villages, required houses to be put up for the staff and workmen, thus forming little English colonies, around which an enormous mining population soon gathered, so that these mines gradually developed into small towns, with all their requirements—schools, churches, etc. As an example of this, it may be stated that the Rio Tinto Company is said to employ 10,000 workmen, with a total population of 30,000 souls; and the Tharsis Company 4000 workmen, with a total population of 7000 souls."

So far as regards the Rio Tinto copper mines, I am able to supplement the above information with the following very interesting details contained in a letter from my friend Mr.

George Carrow, who is at present employed in an official capacity in those mines. Mr. Carrow writes :—

"The Rio Tinto copper mines, situated in the Sierra Morena, 36 miles from the sea, chiefly consist of an immense deposit of cupriferous iron pyrites. They were superficially worked by the Phœnicians and then largely opened out by the Romans, who, judging by the extent of their galleries, must have held these mines many years. During the last ten years the mines have been thoroughly opened out by an English company, and, in the course of tunnelling and extending, hundreds of old Roman galleries have been discovered. Especially in the Open Cast, a large basin-shaped quarry, a large quantity of these old galleries have been cut through, the side of the quarry being in some places completely honey-combed with them. The skill shown in mining is astonishing. The galleries are made as small as possible with a flat, not arched, top, and just sufficient space for two men to work. The miners seem to have followed almost by instinct the richest and softest veins of copper ore, and, taking into consideration the fact that their only means of extraction were the pick, chisel, and hammer, the distance and depth to which they carried their galleries and shafts is astonishing. At the present time one of the great dangers in wet weather in almost all parts of the mine is the chance of cutting through an old Roman gallery or shaft, and so tapping the water of which they are often full. In many places where a large mass of rich soft ore occurred, the Romans have worked out large spaces, carefully supporting the roof and walls with timber of the evergreen oak, some of which are still sound enough to make a walking-stick out of the heart. The great difficulty must have been ventilation, as even slave labourers must have had air to breathe, and the mine, even with our present good ventilation, is still very hot in some parts. I have been in a recently found Roman working in which it was impossible to remain even for a moment on account of the sulphurous gas given off by the decomposing mineral, the latter being so hot that you could not bear the hand upon it. In this atmosphere labour, even though compulsory, must have been impossible without mechanical ventilation. Yet, as the marks of the chisel are clearly to be seen on the rock at the end of the driving, it is certain that men did work there, and as wooden water-wheels and cogwheels are often found in the galleries, it seems almost certain that the Romans, so skilled in other branches of mining, were not ignorant of mechanical ventilation. The ore after extraction was treated on the spot with charcoal made from the forests which once surrounded the mines; remains of old rudely constructed furnaces have been found, and large heaps of slag. The latter, containing as it does only ·05 to ·2 per cent of copper, puts to shame our modern smelting, and shows what a complete knowledge of the art was possessed by the Romans, who produced such clean slag with rude materials. Very few copper works of the present day can keep their slag as low as ·3 per cent of copper."

The above evidence is illustrated in the most curious and interesting way by the following passage from Diodorus Siculus (V. 36-38):—

Ὕστερον δὲ πολλοῖς χρόνοις οἱ μὲν Ἴβηρες, μαθόντες τὰ περὶ τὸν ἄργυρον ἰδιώματα, κατεσκεύασαν ἀξιόλογα μέταλλα· διόπερ ἄργυρον κάλλιστον καὶ σχεδόν τι πλεῖστον κατασκευάζοντες, μεγάλας ἐλάμβανον προσόδους. Ὁ δὲ τρόπος τῆς μεταλλείας καὶ τῶν ἔργων τοιοῦτός τις ἐστι παρὰ τοῖς Ἴβηρσιν· Ὄντων χαλκοῦ καὶ χρυσοῦ καὶ ἀργύρου μετάλλων θαυμαστῶν, οἱ μὲν ἐργαζόμενοι τὰ χαλκουργεῖα τὸ τέταρτον μέρος χαλκοῦ καθαροῦ ἐκ τῆς ὀρυττομένης γῆς λαμβάνουσι. τῶν δὲ ἀργυρευόντων τινὲς ἰδιωτῶν ἐν τρισὶν ἡμέραις Εὐβοϊκὸν ἐξαίρουσι τάλαντον. πᾶσα γὰρ ἡ βῶλος ἐστὶ ψήγματος συμπεπηγότος καὶ ἀπολάμποντος μεστή. Διὸ καὶ θαυμάσαι τὶς ἂν τήν τε τῆς χώρας φύσιν, καὶ τὴν φιλοπονίαν τῶν ἐργαζομένων αὐτὴν ἀνθρώπων. Τὸ μὲν οὖν πρῶτον οἱ τυχόντες τῶν ἰδιωτῶν προσεκαρτέρουν τοῖς μετάλλοις, καὶ μεγάλους ἀπεφέροντο πλούτους διὰ τὴν ἑτοιμότητα καὶ δαψίλειαν τῆς ἀργυρίτιδος γῆς· ὕστερον δὲ τῶν Ῥωμαίων κρατησάντων τῆς Ἰβηρίας, πλῆθος Ἰταλικὸν ἐπεπόλασε τοῖς μετάλλοις, καὶ μεγάλους ἀπεφέροντο πλούτους διὰ τὴν φιλοκερδίαν. Ὠνούμενοι γὰρ πλῆθος ἀνδραπόδων, παραδιδόασι τοῖς ἐφεστηκόσι ταῖς μεταλλικαῖς ἐργασίαις. Οὗτοι δὲ κατὰ πλείονας τόπους ἀνοίξαντες στόμια, καὶ κατὰ βάθους ὀρύττοντες τὴν γῆν, ἐρευνῶσι τὰς πολυαργύρους καὶ πολυχρύσους πλάκας τῆς γῆς· καταβαίνοντές τε, οὐ μόνον εἰς μῆκος ἀλλὰ καὶ ἐπὶ τὸ βάθος παρεκτείνοντες ἐπὶ πολλοὺς σταδίους τὰ ὀρύγματα, καὶ πλαγίους καὶ σκολιὰς διαδύσεις ποικίλως μεταλλουργοῦντες, ἀνάγουσιν ἐκ βυθῶν τὴν τὸ κέρδος αὐτοῖς παρεχομένην βῶλον. . . . Οἱ δὲ κατὰ τὴν Ἰσπανίαν μεταλλουργοὶ ταῖς ἐλπίσι μεγάλους σωρεύουσι πλούτους ἐκ τούτων τῶν ἐργασιῶν. Τῶν γὰρ πρώτων ἔργων ἐπιτυγχανομένων διὰ τὴν τῆς γῆς εἰς τοῦτο τὸ γένος ἀρετήν, ἀεὶ μᾶλλον εὑρίσκουσι λαμπροτέρας φλέβας, γεμούσας ἀργύρου τε καὶ χρυσοῦ. Πᾶσα γὰρ ἡ σύνεγγυς διαπέπλεκται πολυμερῶς τοῖς ἑλιγμοῖς τῶν ῥάβδων. Ἐνίοτε δὲ καὶ κατὰ βάθους ἐμπίπτουσι ποταμοῖς ῥέουσιν ὑπὸ τὴν γῆν, ὧν τῆς βίας περιγίνονται, διακόπτοντες τὰς ῥύσεις αὐτῶν τὰς ἐμπιπτούσας τοῖς ὀρύγμασι πλαγίοις· Ταῖς γὰρ ἀδιαψεύστοις τοῦ κέρδους προσδοκίαις πιεζόμενοι, πρὸς τὸ τέλος ἄγουσι τὰς ἰδίας ἐπι-

420 NOTES.

βολάς · καὶ τὸ πάντων παραδοξότατον · ἀπαρύττουσι γὰρ τὰς ῥύσεις
τῶν ὑδάτων τοῖς Αἰγυπτιακοῖς λεγομένοις κοχλίαις, οὓς Ἀρχιμήδης ὁ
Συρακούσιος εὗρεν, ὅτε παρέβαλεν εἰς Αἴγυπτον· διὰ δὲ τούτων συνεχῶς
ἐκ διαδοχῆς παραδιδόντες μέχρι τοῦ στομίου τὸν τῶν μετάλλων τόπον
ἀναξηραίνουσι, καὶ κατασκευάζουσιν εὔθετον τὴν πρὸς τὰς ἐργασίας
πραγματείαν. Φιλοτέχνου δ' ὄντος τοῦ ὀργάνου καθ' ὑπερβολὴν, διὰ
τῆς τυχούσης ἐργασίας ἄπλετον ὕδωρ ἀναρριπτεῖται παραδόξως, καὶ πᾶν
τὸ ποτάμιον ῥεῦμα, ῥᾳδίως ἐκ βυθοῦ πρὸς τὴν ἐπιφάνειαν ἐκχεῖται.[1] ...
Οἱ δ' οὖν ταῖς ἐργασίαις τῶν μετάλλων ἐνδιατρίβοντες, τοῖς μὲν κυρίοις
ἀπίστους τοῖς πλήθεσι προσόδους περιποιοῦσιν · αὐτοὶ δὲ κατὰ γῆς ἐν
τοῖς ὀρύγμασι καὶ καθ' ἡμέραν καὶ νύκτα καταξαινόμενοι τὰ σώματα,
πολλοὶ μὲν ἀποθνήσκουσι διὰ τὴν ὑπερβολὴν τῆς κακοπαθείας · (ἄνεσις
γὰρ ἢ παῦλα τῶν ἔργων οὐκ ἔστιν αὐτοῖς, ἀλλὰ ταῖς τῶν ἐπιστατῶν
πληγαῖς, ἀναγκαζόντων ὑπομένειν τὴν δεινότητα τῶν κακῶν, ἀτυχῶς
προΐενται τὸ ζῆν) τινὲς δὲ ταῖς δυνάμεσι τῶν σωμάτων, καὶ ταῖς τῶν
ψυχῶν καρτερίαις ὑπομένοντες, πολὺν χρόνον ἔχουσι τὴν ταλαιπωρίαν.
αἱρετώτερος γὰρ αὐτοῖς ὁ θάνατός ἐστι τοῦ ζῆν, διὰ τὸ μέγεθος τῆς
ταλαιπωρίας. Πολλῶν δὲ ὄντων περὶ τὰς εἰρημένας μεταλλείας παρα-
δόξων, οὐχ ἥκιστ' ἄν τις θαυμάσειε, διότι τῶν μεταλλουργείων οὐδὲν
πρόσφατον ἔχει τὴν ἀρχὴν, πάντα δὲ ὑπὸ τῆς Καρχηδονίων φιλαργυ-
ρίας ἀνεῴχθη, καθ' ὃν καιρὸν τῆς Ἰβηρίας ἐπεκράτουν. Ἐκ τούτων
γὰρ ἔσχον τὴν ἐπὶ πλεῖον αὔξησιν, μισθούμενοι τοὺς κρατίστους
στρατιώτας, καὶ διὰ τούτων πολλοὺς καὶ μεγάλους πολέμους δια-
πολεμήσαντες.]

Note Q, p. 314, l. 17.

[On May 3, 1842, Dr. Arnold wrote to Bunsen about
his plans for that year's continental tour :—"If I can get to
Carthagena, it would be a great satisfaction to me; for
Polybius's account is so at variance with Captain Smyth's
survey of the present town and port, that it is utterly per-
plexing." I have already (see note A, p. 358) summarised
Droysen's discussion of Polybius's account of Carthagena.
It is needless to say that Droysen fully concurs with Dr.
Arnold's view. The best modern map of the harbour of
Carthagena is that 'published at the Admiralty, 4th Oct.
1884,' and described as 'from a Spanish Govt. Survey,
1881.']

[1] See *Archæologia Æliana*, VII. 280.

Note R, p. 332, l. 14.

[This battle of Elinga has been a good deal discussed of late from the tactical point of view. Chauvelays, in particular, in his excellent *L'art Militaire chez les Romains* (Paris, Plon, 1884), devotes a large amount of space to it (pp. 223-272). Chauvelays' account of the battle is briefly summarised and criticised by Rudolf Schneider in the *Berliner Philologische Wochenschrift*, IV. 928, 929.]

Note S, p. 349, l. 14.

[The history thus ends abruptly. 'Rugby, May 5th' is written in Dr. Arnold's handwriting on the back of the last page of his manuscript but one, and on the 12th June Dr. Arnold died. The heading only of the chapter which would have followed was written. It is as follows :—

CHAPTER XLVIII.

Last Years of the War in Italy—Consulship of P. Scipio— Scipio in Sicily—Siege of Locri—Scipio in Africa— His Victories over Hasdrubal Gisco and Syphax—The Carthaginians recall Hannibal and Mago from Italy.— A.U.C. 548 to A.U.C. 551.

A final chapter, or perhaps a couple more, would have carried the story to the Battle of Zama, and the end of the war. As Dr. Arnold did not live to do this, I have no idea of attempting to supplement his work—which is after all a unity, the subject being the duel between Hannibal and Rome in Italy—in my own words. But, in pursuance of my plan of at least indicating the more important works in which the discussion of this war has been continued since Dr. Arnold's death, I may refer the reader to the closing chapters (really contributed by Prof. Faltin) of Neumann's

Zeitalter der Punischen Kriege, and above all to Zielinski's essay on 'Die Letzten Jahre des zweiten Punischen Krieges' (Leipsic, Teubner, 1880). Mommsen has contributed an important note on the position of Zama to Hermes for 1885, XX. 144-156.]

INDEX.

THE END.

Printed by R. & R. CLARK, *Edinburgh*.

The Roman System of Provincial Administration to the Accession of Constantine the Great,

Being the Arnold Prize Essay for 1879,

By W. T. ARNOLD, B.A.,

Formerly Scholar of University College, Oxford.

Crown 8vo.   6s.

Mr. Arnold's Essay last year obtained the prize founded in honour of Dr. Arnold, his grandfather. It is an admirable specimen of careful and thorough work; and in addition to its intrinsic merits, it stands quite alone as a brief and simple sketch of the Roman provincial administration.—*Academy.*

As a whole, indeed, the book is the best English summary of the subject, and if in this review undue space may seem to be given to its defects, it is because we hope that Mr. Arnold may in time supersede it by a more complete work, and may not be unwilling to learn what are the faults he has specially to be careful in avoiding.—*Athenæum.*

We sincerely trust that Mr. Arnold's success will stimulate him to remove by further studies the necessary imperfections of the present volume, arising partly from lack of fuller acquaintance with the sources of information, and partly from his being compelled to adapt his materials to the dimensions of an essay. It is absolutely impossible to compress the history of Roman provincial administration, extending over seven hundred years, within such narrow limits. With wider reading, more systematic arrangement of topics, and a clearer separation between the technical and historical, the author might produce a work of inestimable value to the students of this period of Roman history. In its present form we strongly recommend it to the notice, not of the historian alone, but also of the English politician, for there are many striking analogies between the Roman and British colonial dependencies. The history of that ancient colossal system, with the causes of its prosperity and ultimate decay, is full of lessons for those who have a share in guiding the destinies of its modern counterpart.—*British Quarterly Review.*

A volume not unworthy of the illustrious name of its author, by its comprehensive and masterly clearness of exposition, and the fulness of its inquiry. It may be confidently recommended to students as a text-book for which they will learn to be grateful.—*Daily News.*

Prize essays are not generally worth reproduction, but that of Mr. W. T. Arnold, late scholar of University College, Oxford, which gained the Arnold Prize in 1879, is an exception to this rule. His essay on the *Roman System of Provincial Administration* is an exhaustive and accurate summary of the chief results of modern inquiry into the principles upon which Imperial Rome contrived to keep in hand her vast and heterogeneous empire ; one of the most important of those principles, as Mr. Arnold is properly careful to show, being the share of duties and responsibilities everywhere left to the local magistrates of the innumerable provincial towns. The *municipium* was, in fact, the basis of the Roman provincial administration ; and the gradual transfer of responsibilities from the municipal magistrates to the imperial governor marks the gradual decline of the brightest feature in that administration and foreshadows its collapse. Mr. Arnold's book ought to prove a valuable handbook to the student of Roman history, and it is satisfactory to note that a grandson of Dr. Arnold, in whose memory the Arnold Prize was founded, has inherited an aptitude for historical studies.—*Guardian.*

All parts of the book are well written and scholarly, but the last half, covering less familiar ground, appears to us to have on the whole the most merit. It is not only comparatively new but very important ground, inasmuch as it is in the period of the later Empire, and especially in its financial and municipal systems, that the most important points of connection between ancient and modern institutions may be traced.—*New York Nation.*

Mr. Arnold's interesting book is of a class by no means common in England, and we unhesitatingly recommend it to both scholars and students.—*Notes and Queries.*

Those who wish, not merely to know the details of the Roman Provincial system, but to measure the results of the system both for good and for evil, may learn much from Mr. Arnold's pages.—*Saturday Review.*

We may congratulate Mr. Arnold on having produced an essay worthy of being associated with the memory of the great historian and scholar whose name he bears.—*Spectator.*

A work on a learned subject by a young writer is apt to be very full indeed of learning ; and Mr. Arnold's Essay absolutely bristles with names, and cases, and references. This is, however, a very good fault, and we think he may be fairly congratulated on having produced a work which will be of great utility to historical students of much longer standing than himself. He has made a beginning worthy of the great historian whose name he inherits.—*Westminster Review.*

MACMILLAN AND CO., LONDON.